TEMPUS

Lore of Tellus
Book Three

E A Purle

Lore of Tellus,
Book Three

WHEN THE SANDS OF TIME SHIFT, I WILL BE YOUR PORTAL

The World of Tellus

Books in the Lore of Tellus series so far

Firestone – Book One
Orbis – Book Two
Tempus – Book Three

Previously in

ORBIS

Hugh Geber has found himself at a dead end. Robert J Smithson is hot on their heels, and the Elf King is on the move once more. The book he and Barrington are desperate to find is missing, with a mysterious note in its place. Left with no other choice, they have to head home to Portis-Montis empty handed, knowing they are not the only ones seeking the book.

Hugh wants to bury his problems, but when he opens a letter from his presumed-deceased father, his decision to ignore his troubles comes back to bite him. A meeting with Balinas Collins in the university library adds to his woes, causing Hugh and Barrington to follow the path being laid in front of them.

Now they must continue searching for the missing book, but also try to carry out a task Balinas has set them, all whilst trying to evade the long arm of the law. Will they find the book first? Or will Smithson beat them to it? Will the Elf King regain his seat, and the power he so desperately yearns for? Only time will tell, but that time is running out. Fast!

Editorial Review of Tempus

This third novel in E A Purle's fantasy series, Lore of Tellus, sees Hugh Geber and his friends on the hunt for another book of lore, this time, taking them to parts of their world as yet unexplored. As the story develops, so does Purle's imagination and witty take on the New and Old Worlds, adding comedy and new elements to the adventure as the characters look danger in the face once more in their quest for the books that mean so much to their past and future.

Lynn Godson, The Digital Wordsmith

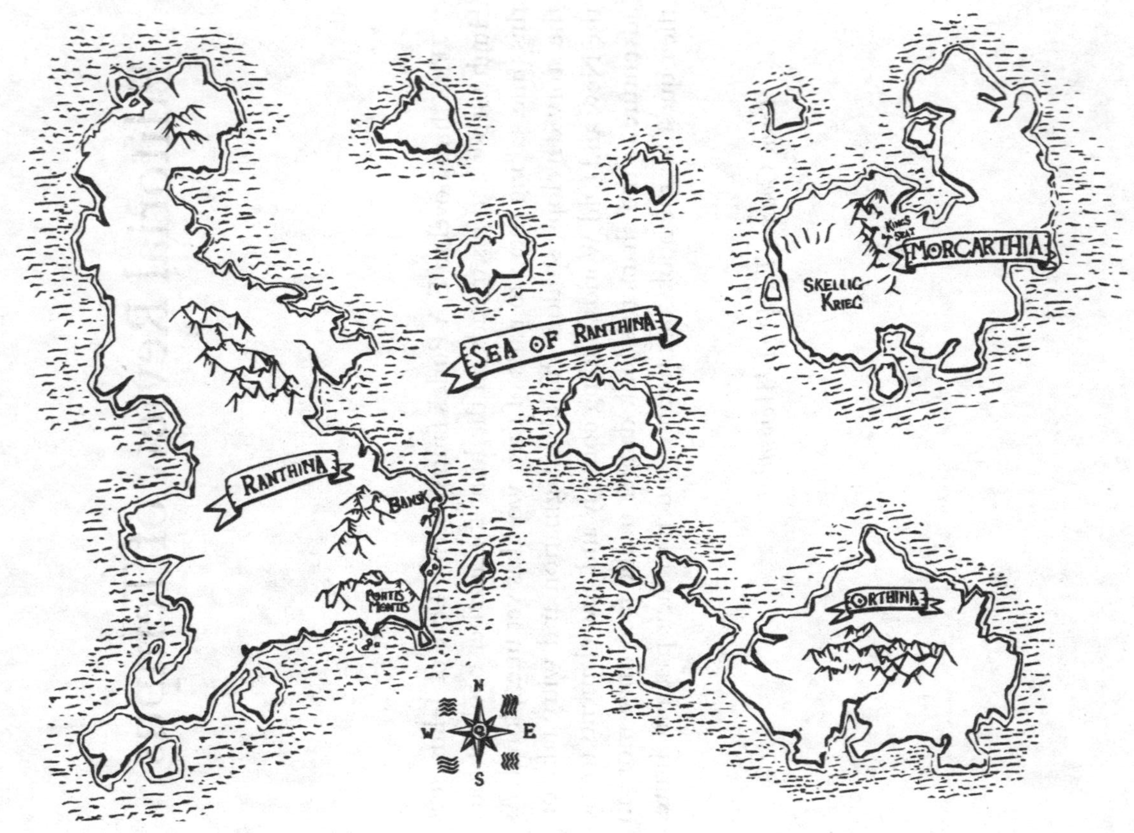
SEA OF RANTHINA
MORCARTHIA
SKELLIG-
KRIEG
KING'S SEAT
RANTHINA
BANSK
PONTIS MONTIS
ORTHINA
N
E
S
W

ISLE OF FEY
SYRENI BAY
KILLINSFOLK
FOREST OF FEY
MEADOW DOWN
ANDROSSAN

First Edition Published July 2023

Paperback: 978-1-7398965-3-9

Hardback: 978-1-7398965-4-6

eBook: 978-1-7398965-5-3

For my children Seb & Josie
With all my love
Dad x

Chapter 1

Hugh rolled back over onto his side of the bed as she lay next to him, breathless. He was clammy from the exertion. Since they had reunited back in the Chamber of Prophccy, Hugh had never thought it would be like this.

"Wow," he said between breaths. "Just … wow!"

"You can say that again," she said.

The door to their room opened, bathing them in bright light. It was Emily. She gasped, paused for a beat, taking in the scene in front of her, before slamming the door shut. He looked down to Adelia, then back to the doorway.

"Emily, wait!" said Hugh in her wake.

But it was too late. The damage was done.

Hugh, Barrington and Emily had been hiding safely in the living quarters of the Collins family for two months since their return from Skellig-Krieg. The trio had agreed that it would be best to sit the winter out with the Collins family. They were receiving regular reports on the movements of Smithson and his minions, who had also returned home to Portis-Montis for the duration of the winter. The New World authorities thought they had all died a grisly death at the tentacles of the kraken, which left them no choice but to stay within the confines and safety of the library and the attached living space.

The head librarian, Balinas Collins, informed the trio that the Collins home was carved from old lava tubes. They bored deep into the mountain, giving the family a helping hand when setting up home for themselves all those years ago. Hugh thought it would be cold, damp and dark living within the complex of tunnels, but to his surprise, it was quite the opposite.

When the group returned from their last trip, Balinas had lined up a surprise for their return in the form of Adelia. She was Hugh's ex-sister-in-law, who had run from a broken marriage some years previously. Unbeknown to Hugh, she and Balinas were still in contact. She was living alongside the rest of the temporary guests, and her presence was an unwelcome one amongst some members of the group; but it gave Barrington immense joy to watch his friend juggle the relationships he had with both Adelia and Emily.

With time on their hands, Hugh and the others spent their days working on independent activities. Balinas worked with Hugh on his skills used within the sight – the plane of the unseen, where the magic of the world flows through. Hugh had nearly come a cropper in Skellig-Krieg, when part of his rune armour hadn't been up to scratch, causing the malevolent beings within the sight to wear away at his life-force each time he entered. It was tiring trying to keep up with the rigorous training schedule Balinas had set up for him, and Hugh had hidden away in recent weeks, immersing himself in his father's notebook to avoid the workload. The book was practically welded to him these days, and he carried it everywhere he went.

Hugh awoke to the sound of the first daily call of the runners' horn, his mind taking him back to the events of the previous night. He moaned, and shielded his face. A chink of morning light cut through the dark bedroom, streaming through a hole in the wall, illuminating Hugh's face. From the angle of light and the sound of the runners' horn, he deduced it to be eight in the morning. One of the good things about the runners – the parcel delivery system set up for the tight streets of Portis-Montis – was that you could set your clocks by them. He rolled over in the bed, finding the space next to him vacant. He sat up, looked around, and saw he was alone in the vast room. His mind scanned back through the previous night's events, and he slapped a hand to his forehead, cursing to himself. He pulled himself out of bed, the sounds of his movements echoing around the cavernous room. Why anyone needed a bedroom this big was beyond him, but he couldn't complain at the free accommodation.

Now dreading what Emily was going to say to him, Hugh made his way down to the dining hall, following the regular route through the maze of tunnels hewn from the mountain. As he entered the cavernous space, its gilt carvings gave the room a warm glow. He was greeted by Emily and Barrington.

"Ah, Hugh, my dear friend. You have finally joined us in the world of the living, have you?" said Barrington, gesturing to a space next to Emily.

"Erm, yes," he said awkwardly, avoiding Emily's gaze.

"It's alright, I won't bite," she said as he sat down, and she embraced him. "What's wrong? Don't worry about last night. All is forgiven."

"It is?"

"Yes, silly. You were talking in your sleep again. Don't ask me what about though. It was all mumbling, and then you became …"

"What?"

"Well, if you must know, you were rather amorous. Again." She looked down, going coy.

"Oh, I see," said Hugh, who felt his cheeks burning up. "So, you were with me for the whole night then?"

"Of course, what would make you say that?"

"Oh, it's nothing really, it must have been a dream." He looked awkwardly across at Barrington.

"I can go, if you two want to be alone," said Barrington and made moves to leave the room.

"No, stay, please," said Hugh, who didn't want to be questioned any further. "How are things progressing with your ... clock?"

"It's all coming together well, thank you. It's lucky I found the books on watchmaking. I feel that this will make real difference to maritime industry ... ah, what fortuitous timing. Good morning, Adelia."

Everyone turned to see the new arrival walking towards them. She stopped dead, looking at Emily, who glared back. Barrington looked from Emily to Hugh and waited for the battle to begin. Hugh gulped.

"Well ... erm ..." he said.

"No need to worry, I was leaving anyway," said Emily curtly. She stood and left the room, without looking back.

"She's in a good mood," said Adelia.

"Can you at least try to get on?" said Hugh, shaking his head.

"What? It's not me, it's her!" she said, sitting in Emily's space, giving Hugh a hug and a peck on the cheek. Barrington sat with raised eyebrows.

"What now?" said Hugh.

"Oh, nothing," he said, a smug look on his face.

"I wish you would stop doing that; it's really not helping."

"I merely observe the events that are taking place around me. It's not my fault if you disapprove of my reaction."

Hugh let out a sigh.

"I need a walk to clear my head."

"But what about breakfast?" said Adelia.

"I'm not hungry," he said, getting up from the table.

He marched towards the staircase leading to the library, stomping as he went.

Barrington looked to Adelia, and she nodded towards the silence left in Hugh's wake. Barrington nodded in agreement, then headed after his friend. He had to walk quickly to catch up with him, listening for the tell-tale sound of footsteps, until he eventually caught up with him near the top of the stairs.

"Hugh, old bean. I'm sorry, I didn't mean to offend you."

Hugh turned on his friend.

"Well, you are doing a poor job of it!"

Barrington took a step backwards.

"I'm sorry," said Hugh, in a gentler tone. "It's hard enough living in confinement here, without the added stress of juggling Emily and Adelia. I've already said, numerous times, there is nothing happening between myself and Adelia, and there never has been."

Barrington looked at Hugh with raised eyebrows once more.

"Really? I've seen the looks you give each other. I dare say Emily has too."

"Really, there is nothing going on. I've spoken to Emily about this numerous times."

"And Adelia?" Barrington's words hung in the air, making the silence more awkward, Hugh paying great attention to the floor. "If you truly want to be with Emily, you'll need to tell her. By keeping silent, you are being unfair to everyone involved, including yourself."

"It's difficult, alright, I just need time to sort it all out. Listen, can we drop this for now? I'm tired of repeating myself."

"Well, my friend, may I leave you with a little piece of advice? Whatever you decide to do, you must act soon, otherwise you risk losing both of them. I'm always here if you need to chat, and I promise to do my best not to wind you up, however difficult that may be." He gave Hugh a wry smile.

"Fine, now please can me move onto something different?"

"Alright, let's talk about finding the next book."

"*Really?*"

"Yes, *really*. It's been weeks since you spent any time in the library. These books won't find themselves, and we can't hide in here forever."

"But Smithson hasn't left Portis-Montis in months. Plus, I don't want to be seen out in the library by Collins."

Barrington let out a sigh.

"Hugh, they cannot touch you here, not whilst you are under the protection of the library. Balinas has explained this more than once. Speaking of Balinas, how are your lessons coming along?"

Hugh shrugged, unable to think up a good excuse.

"I only ask," said Barrington, "as the last time I spoke to Balinas, he thought you were avoiding his classes."

Hugh went to walk on, but Barrington stopped him.

"Hugh, you cannot walk away from this one. It's important to keep up with the lessons, we can't afford to lose you."

"Alright, I'm sorry. I'm just finding the lessons tough at the moment."

"Are you sure you're not being distracted?"

"I thought we agreed to move on from this subject."

"I'm not talking about the ladies. I'm talking about your father's book," he said, looking down at the notebook Hugh held in his hand.

Hugh tried to hide it in his jacket but failed.

"I need to figure out what my father was writing in here so we can re-trace his steps. There has to be something important that he wrote down, otherwise why would he have sent it back to me?"

"Listen, Hugh, I don't mean to nag, but you need to focus on what matters right now. I understand the book is important, but I feel as though you are missing the bigger picture. Balinas is only trying to help. He'll only take so much rebuffing, before he gives you up as a lost cause. He has a library to run, you know. Come on, let's head there now. Maybe we can catch the old fellow before he gets too busy."

He didn't give Hugh the chance to argue as he grabbed him by the arm and practically dragged him towards the direction of the Great Library.

The Great Library normally had its doors wide open for all to enter as they wished. However, the winds of change were blowing strongly, forcing the Collins family to take drastic action, and the magnificent room found itself sealed off once more. Only the Collins family members could enter and leave the space. A small access door allowed provisions to be brought in from Portis-Montis. Each time it opened, Hugh's stomach dropped, but it only ever revealed a different Collins family member to the one he feared. He lived in constant worry, despite many reassurances from Balinas, that Elgrid Collins would enter the room at any moment. As the head of the Collins family, Elgrid was the Collins assigned to the university chancellor Robert Smithson, the one person Hugh was trying to avoid.

The smell of parchment and leather-bound books reached Hugh's nose before he and Barrington had even reached the magnificent space. His breath was taken away every time he stepped into the amazing room. The amount of knowledge it held would impress the most disinterested person. Balinas had once told Hugh that the books contained knowledge and power, and today the power was certainly flowing. Balinas greeted them at the door.

"Gentleman, what a lovely surprise. Hugh, you've made it to the library at last."

Hugh felt uneasy, and he looked away. He could sense Balinas probing him, looking for a response. This was quickly followed by the usual tingling sensation he had all over his body whenever he was near any amount of magical power. He didn't want to face it today.

"Don't look so ashamed, Hugh. All of us have to face our fears."

"It's not a fear ..."

Balinas looked at Hugh with eyebrows raised.

"Not you as well!"

Hugh pushed past Balinas, if only to avoid being questioned further. He walked a few steps into the great palace of knowledge before stopping dead. Hugh already knew that the room changed size according to the current user's requirements. The larger the question, the more knowledge required, the larger the library became. Today, the space was enormous. Hugh squinted to see the doors, any empty void between them being filled with books of all imaginable description. Since the start of the latest escalation of violence involving the Elf King and his enemies, Balinas had put out a call for all literature belonging to the library to be returned for safekeeping. Books were stacking up on every available surface whilst they awaited being assigned to their new homes. The Collins family appeared unable to keep up with the workload.

"Ah, I see you have noticed our little problem," said Balinas from over Hugh's shoulder.

"Where did all these books come from?" asked Hugh.

"Since we recalled all the literature belonging to the library, we've discovered how much the old room holds. Anyone wishing to get hold of information may now only do so by request. It's a huge undertaking, but one that has to be done in these uncertain times. We cannot afford for any of our precious books to be lost or destroyed," Balinas told him.

Hugh watched the Collins family members as they walked up and down the numerous aisles between the bookshelves. Some of them were carrying books, whilst others held pieces of paper with information requests on them from the outside world.

"I've never seen the room this big," said Hugh.

"This number of books requires many shelves. When you include the amount of knowledge being accessed daily, you can understand why the room is expanding so quickly. If it keeps growing like this, we'll have to invest in some trolley bikes. Your friend here has certainly been putting the room to good use," said Balinas.

"What do you mean?" asked Hugh, looking to Barrington.

"No need to ask, my dearest Hugh, I can show you."

Barrington walked down the steps with excitement and practically skipped through the space. Hugh found it hard to keep up with him, tripping over numerous books. At one point he had to stop a pile of books toppling over, which Barrington knocked in his haste to show Hugh what he was working on, before giving way to members of the Collins family, who were all on official business of sorts.

Hugh was perspiring by the time he caught up with Barrington. He wondered if it was worth the effort. The space in front of them opened up, and Hugh's breath was taken away. Stacks of books surrounded a large, brass construction which seemed to tick away to itself. Barrington stood next to the strange machine, looking very proud of himself.

"Ta da!"

"Erm? What's this?" said Hugh.

"Well, surely it's obvious?"

Hugh looked on confused, giving Barrington no choice but to explain.

"This, my dear friend, is based on the ancient Morcarthian donkeybird clock. I found some books on them, and it gave me an idea. One problem, when at sea, is knowing what time zone you are in when travelling east or west. This clock is incredibly accurate, meaning we can keep it on Portis-Montis time and make our calculations from there."

Hugh looked at the clock, then at his friend. It stood a good two feet taller than Barrington. Balinas appeared next to Hugh.

"It's good, isn't it," he said encouragingly.

"Erm, yes," said Hugh. "It's a tad … large, don't you think?"

"What on earth do you mean?" asked Barrington, looking offended.

"What I mean to say is … it's a magnificent machine. It must have taken you many hours to source the parts. And build such a … but it's not very … well, you know …"

"*What*?"

"Well, it's not easily transportable, is it?"

Barrington scoffed.

"Utter tripe, dear boy. I can always rely on you to spoil the mood."

Hugh frowned but said nothing.

"Now, now, Barrington," said Balinas. "There's no need to be rude. I'm sure that's not what Hugh meant, was it, Hugh?"

Hugh stammered, being put on the spot.

"Erm, not at all."

"Yes, well, you'll not find anything built to this quality anywhere," said Barrington. "I can assure you of that."

He tapped the side of the clock. A spring *boinged* out from within the mechanism, quickly followed by a cog flying in the opposite direction. It narrowly missed a Collins carrying a pile of books, who ducked just in time. He walked away, shaking his head.

"I didn't need those bits anyway," said Barrington, attempting to cover up the mistake with gusto. "I mean, look at *this*."

He guided Hugh and Balinas around to the front. Numerous cogs of all shapes and sizes moved in synchronicity, working to move the extravagant hands. Hugh took in the clock face. It appeared to have been carved by an angry butcher, wielding a blunt breadknife.

"Ah, I see you are admiring my fabulous decorations. They're good, aren't they? Carved by yours truly." He took a bow.

Hugh looked to Balinas, who nodded encouragingly.

"Yes!" he said, a little overenthusiastically. "They wouldn't look out of place amongst the fine decorations of the ceiling."

He smiled back to Balinas, who had one eyebrow raised and mouth slightly open. They craned their necks to the ceiling, its fresco depicting scenes from the past, plus what was yet to come. Barrington moved the conversation forward.

"The precise craftsmanship of the clock makes it the most accurate in the world."

"Erm, no, it's not, I'm afraid," said Balinas, looking at a pocket watch. "What?"

"The time, it's not correct. By my reckoning, it's almost half an hour out."

"Eh? You must be confused," said Barrington, "or reading the face wrong, my dear fellow, because—"

A loud whirring noise commenced just above his head. A fly wheel had kicked into action, followed by a series of fast-moving cogs and chains. Hugh watched as a miniature set of counterweights dropped. Two doors opened up, and miniature figures appeared through them. They looked like the Collins family, in miniature version, hard at work, spinning around and bending. They watched, as the little figurines waltzed around the clock face, cleaning as they moved. This also came as a surprise to Barrington, as he, too, stood open-mouthed.

The show continued, with a musical rendition playing out. This added to the drama of the figures, who had given up their fixed positions and began scaling their way up the mechanical menagerie. They stopped at a point above the face, where two wooden doors were carved. Together they worked as a team to open them, and Hugh saw the doors were, in fact, replicas of the great library doors. The mini-Collins family pulled the doors open to a fanfare, causing Hugh to look around to see if there was a live orchestra hidden somewhere.

The music drew to a great crescendo, leaving the awaiting audience, which now included numerous Collinses who had stopped work to watch the unfolding show, with bated breath as they waited for act two to begin from within the clock.

"Well, it's never done that before," said Barrington.

He was about to continue when he was cut off by another whirring noise. Numerous clunks emanated from deep within the clock, and the cogs began spinning around at high speed, with some ricocheting out of the clock itself, embedding themselves into the balcony above. Something was moving within the machine, and the crowd took a collective step backwards. A multi-coloured bird, wearing a massive grin, soared in and out of the clock. On each arrival into the room, it let out an "Eee-Ore" causing everyone to cover their ears to keep out the awful, ear-splitting noise.

Nine ear-splitting calls later, the donkeybird disappeared, and the Collins family miniatures headed back to their assigned places and were whisked off into the clock once more. The audience stood in stunned silence, unsure if that was the end.

"See, it's exactly half an hour early," said Balinas, pointing to his pocket watch. "It's eight thirty."

Barrington stood, breathing heavily. Hugh looked at him.

"Are you sure you built this clock without any help?"

The colour rose in Barrington's face until Hugh thought he might explode.

"*I said NO MUSIC!* And what the bloody hell were those Collinses doing on *my clock*?"

He marched off, leaving the rest of the room to go about its business. Balinas and Hugh watched Barrington head off into the crowd of the Collins family. He thought he saw a smirk on some of the Collinses' faces.

"They do like to have their fun," said Balinas, chuckling to himself and shaking his head. He turned to Hugh. "I think we ought to leave our friend to his troubles. Follow me, I wish to show you something."

He took Hugh to a door he hadn't seen before then pulled out a large set of keys of various shapes and sizes – an unwieldy selection – but he found the correct key right away. He slipped it into the lock and twisted. Hugh could hear many mechanisms clicking into place, followed by a large clunk, and the door swung open, revealing an ominous, unlit room. Balinas stepped through the door and was instantly swallowed by darkness. Hugh debated whether he should follow when Balinas' voice called out to him.

"Well, come along, we can't wait all day."

Hugh tentatively stepped into the dark abyss, turning in time to see the door close behind him, trapping him in the infinite darkness.

Chapter 2

Hugh was now breathing rapidly, arms out in front of him, attempting to feel for anything tangible. His finger poked into something damp and soft, and he let out a yelp of surprise.

"Ow! Do you mind?" said Balinas.

A lamp flickered into life, to reveal Balinas clutching his left eye. He glared at Hugh with his right eye, and Hugh dropped his arms and attempted to calm his breathing.

"Sorry, I may have panicked there for a moment."

"Really? I couldn't have guessed. At least the lessons are paying off."

Hugh looked at him in confusion.

"You appear," said Balinas, "to have stayed within the realm of the living. Normally, at the first whiff of panic, you disappear into the sight. It's a shame you have been avoiding me, we were really getting somewhere." He looked at Hugh, still glaring at him in an awkward silence.

Hugh moved uneasily on the spot and cleared his throat.

"So, what is this place, then?" he said, looking around.

They were standing at the bottom of the shaft. Hugh looked up into the darkness, following a set of chains that ran down the back wall to ground level. They disappeared below the wooden floor. Balinas was standing next to a lever connected to something below their feet.

He grasped the handle and pulled it hard towards himself, and the floorboards juddered as the chains rattled into life. The walls began moving downwards, and the door disappeared out of sight.

"What's going on? Where has the door gone? Why are the walls moving?"

"It is not the walls and door that are moving, dear Hugh. The floor we are on is moving upwards. We're on a levitating internal floating trestle."

"That's a bit of a mouthful. Couldn't you think of a shorter word for it?"

"You would think, but we haven't found a suitable word that fits yet." Balinas wiped a stray tear from his left eye.

The floor seemed to move at a snail's pace; Hugh stood in silence whilst Balinas hummed pleasantly to himself. An eerie rumbling noise reverberated around the shaft, as a large set of counterweights passed by. They were set into a channel in the wall opposite the chains.

"Ah, good, that means we are past the halfway point."

"Halfway point to where?" asked Hugh. "Where are you taking me?"

"Patience, dear Hugh, patience. If you had chosen to keep up with your lessons, you would already know. However, time is not on our side, so you must see this now."

"What do you mean, 'time is not on our side'?"

"Winter won't last forever, and if our spies' reports are correct, our dear friend Smithson is about to be on the move once more. We are also getting reports that the Elf King is back onto the trail of the books. Together, it doesn't paint a pleasant picture."

"I can't see how I'm supposed to help with all of this. I have no funds to compete with Smithson's wealth, nor do I have the skills of the Elf King."

"Nonsense. You can use the sight, which is one more skill Smithson doesn't have. I dare say you are coming up fast on the Elf King's abilities. As for money, the Collins family has its own reserves, certainly enough to fund your trips."

"If what you're saying is true, about Smithson and the Elf King, then we have little time to plan for trips, let alone get ahead of them."

"Did you think I would wait for you to catch up with world events? I have already been planning ahead, which reminds me, do you have a watch?"

Hugh looked to Balinas, then pulled out an old pocket watch that had belonged to his father.

"Ah, old mementoes from the past?"

"Yes," said Hugh. "He always carried this with him, but alas, it's not the timepiece it once was. I believe that too much sea water made its way into the mechanism, rendering it useless."

"Here," said Balinas, reaching back into his own pocket. "I always carry a spare with me. I think your need will be greater than mine. It's an Ever-Right, so it should never let you down. It's an old family heirloom, but I have no need for two watches."

He passed it to Hugh. It was heavy in his hand and still warm from its previous owner's pocket, and it also seemed to pulse gently with every tick. It was made of silver and had several bezels to operate the different parts. It looked very complicated.

"Oh, Balinas, I really can't take this from you."

"No, really, I insist. Take it as a gift from me. I fear if you use Barrington's clock, it could lead you into all sorts of trouble."

"Yes, well, I doubt we'll have use for any watches or sea clocks yet."

The floor slowed as another door appeared. As it levelled with the floor, everything stopped with a jolt, which jarred Hugh's back.

"Welcome, Hugh, to the room of time."

Balinas opened the door, and light filled the platform. Hugh had to shield his face from the sunlight streaming in. With his eyes adjusting to the light, he took in the surrounding room.

He stood, looking out across the city, with its many streets filling the vista in front of him. Seven wooden pipes with wax mouthpieces came out of the wall, and each of them was polished to a shine. The smell of wax and polish gave the space a homely feel. As Hugh walked further into the room, the mahogany floor creaked underfoot. At the end of the row of pipes, a pair of wing-backed chairs guarded a fireplace, its embers glowing gently in the morning light. All around them, filling every inch of wall space, were watches, sand timers and steam clocks – all hissing and ticking and whirring away gently to themselves.

"What is this place? And what are those pipes for?"

"This is the room of time, the place where world time is measured and kept. You could say this is where time starts and ends. Those pipes are for the runners' horns. They run down through the hill to pipes across the city, though only the first two are used for the runners themselves. Together they make up part of the old defence system which used to protect Altum Castle that stood on this site before the university. Let us hope that we never have to use them in anger again."

"What happens if you have to use them?"

"They will obliterate most objects in the path of the sound waves, when blown in the correct formation. It would certainly cut pathways through the city; I can assure you."

A shiver went down Hugh's spine. He looked down at the watch, which was still beating away in his hand.

"Are you sure you wish me to have this? And why is it pulsing?"

"Certainly! That is no ordinary watch, Hugh. There are many sister watches, including the one that sits on the wall over there. It can sense that she is close to a sister watch, so that is why she's vibrating." He pointed to a case in the wall where the watch was locked. "Since her very creation, that one has been used to keep time up here. Your watch links up to these sister watches and can be used as a *portal*, for want of better words. You have to be within range of one of the other watches to use it. This model has most of its functions disabled, apart from the timekeeping aspects. We keep her locked away just in case, but I can reactivate her when needed."

Hugh turned the watch over in his hands. It had an intricate pattern engraved into it. A patterned line, with no beginning or end, woven around the outside. In the centre was a symbol made up of an upside-down triangle, overlapped with a circle. Within that was a small circle in the centre. Words filled the space between the symbol and the pattern:

WHEN THE SANDS OF TIME SHIFT, I WILL BE YOUR PORTAL

"It goes by the name of Tempus and forms part of the Tempus collection. They have helped me out over the years. There used to be maps to go with each watch, but alas, they have all disappeared. Seeing as I'm trapped here by my job, I see no reason to keep hold of it. This was the first one they ever made, and it has more features than the average timepiece. Look after it, and it will look after you."

"I certainly will."

"Well, I see no reason to linger around up here for longer than is needed. It was important that you saw this space today, Hugh; you never know when it might come in handy."

"Balinas, I really don't understand why you've shown me all of this, or why I need to know."

"Sometimes, dear Hugh, it's better to have received knowledge and not have use for it, than have need for knowledge with no way of getting hold of it." He turned on his heel and headed towards the door before Hugh could question him further.

Hugh studied the watch with intent as they returned to the library. If there were any special features, he was flummoxed if he could work them. The platform bumped to a stop, and Balinas headed out of the door with Hugh hot on his heels.

They were now wandering slowly through the library whilst everyone else worked around them. Hugh moved his attention to the other matters of the day – Emily and Adelia. Balinas looked back to Hugh as he walked.

"What is it that bothers you, Hugh?"

Hugh felt his insides churn, but he said nothing. He knew Balinas would search inside of his head, looking for the answers. He let him see.

"Ah, troubles of the heart are always a difficult thing to conquer, but I feel as though you are using this an excuse to avoid the bigger picture, no?"

"I don't know what you are talking about."

"I'm sure you don't," said Balinas. "You've been avoiding this room, and me, for many weeks now. We began the extra training for the sight, and although you know the runes of protection, it takes time and practice to really gain full use of their cover. Listen, Hugh, I know that this whole experience has been thrust upon you, and you are more than justified in asking why. For instance, why did the fates choose you and not some other poor soul?"

Hugh walked along, staring at his feet. Balinas came to a halt.

"The truth is, Hugh, that your destiny lies along this path, whether you like it or not. The weavers were working hard long before you were born. As I have said to you before, our futures are already written for us. It's the journey we take there that is the important part. We can either go kicking and screaming, fighting it all the way, or we can accept our fate and make the most of the journey."

"It just seems too overwhelming," said Hugh, finally letting go and opening up. "I sometimes fear that maybe the fates have it wrong, that they have the wrong person for the job."

"I understand this is no easy task, but you have come so far already. In order to complete the task ahead of you, you must accept the fact you have to do it, grab it with both hands, and make it your own. You must not only think you can do it but *tell* the universe that you can do it, for that's the only way to succeed. If you believe you can't do it, then you will fail at the task. It's as simple as that. The end destination is coming, even if you don't want it to."

Balinas stopped talking, distracted by a scuffle occurring over by the come-and-go door. He looked over, attempting to see what was happening, before turning back to Hugh.

"It looks as though our exultant leader is attempting to get into the library. I advise you to think on what we have talked about, Hugh. In the meantime, I will arrange a meeting for us all to have a catch up later. If I were you, I'd scarper from here. If Smithson sees you, he will go berserk."

Hugh's head was full of questions that would have to wait. The fear of being seen by Smithson chilled him to the core. He nodded, before turning back into the room. The Collins family seemed to sense he wanted to disappear, and they filled the space behind him as he moved. He could hear Smithson in the background, still battling to get into the library.

"What do you mean I cannot come in? … Yes, I understand the current situation … Yes, well, I'm the chancellor of the university and demand to be – how dare you talk to me like that! Collins, I want this man reprimanded … what do you mean he's only doing his job? What are you hiding in there?"

Hugh didn't wait to hear the rest of the argument. He scurried to get out of the room as fast as he could. The man sounded irate enough without him seeing Hugh. He chanced a quick glance over his shoulder, which made his worst fear a reality, as he looked directly into the eyes of Smithson. It was as if the space between them disappeared. The voice filled the space and rang in Hugh's ears.

"GEBER!"

He ran as fast as his legs could take him from the room.

Chapter 3

Hugh battled through the chaos of the library, trying to reach the room of prophecy, a chamber hidden deep under the library. It was only accessible to those who knew of it. Smithson was already breaking through the defence at the library door. The sounds of many books dropping to the floor told him that the Collins family were running to defend the library and its occupants. Hugh climbed the stairs at speed, not daring to look behind him.

"GET BACK HERE! Somebody stop him. Get out of the ruddy way!" Smithson bellowed across the library.

He was like a rabid animal, clawing his way through the room. Nobody could stop him. Eventually, Hugh reached the top of the luxurious, red-carpeted staircase, its thick pile plush underfoot. He used the polished handrail to pull himself around the corner, making it to the correct aisle, and scrabbled for the book he so desperately needed. He struggled to find the correct spine, so numerous were the books to choose from. His hands were shaking as the noise within the library intensified. He had lost all control of his fingers as they slipped over the numerous spines. At last, he fumbled upon the right book and, hearing footsteps heading his way, gave it a sharp tug. Something within the bookcase clicked, and the concealed entrance opened.

Hugh descended into the depths, leaving the secret entrance to close behind him. The sound of someone preventing it from closing reached his ears, causing the adrenalin to boost his legs into a higher gear. He began panicking, regretting not closing the door properly, as he heard someone beginning to descend behind him. He picked up his pace and nearly lost his footing more than once. He detested spiral staircases, as they always made him feel dizzy. He burst into the room of prophecy, running headlong into Emily.

"Ow! Hugh? What's going on?"

Hugh didn't answer her question straight away, grabbing the first book he could get his hands on – an opened copy of *Magical Water Creatures and Where to Find Them*. He turned and shoved it into Emily's hands. "Hey! I was reading that!"

"I don't care, just get ready, and smack Smithson with that when he runs through the door," said Hugh, still out of breath, dripping with sweat. He grabbed another large tome from the bookcase.

"Smithson? Hugh! Tell me what is going on this instant!"

"Smithson, coming now…" he said, gasping for air.

The sound of the footsteps coming down the stairs was getting louder. Emily's eyes widened with fear.

"What, here…now?"

"*Yes,*" said Hugh in exasperation. "Just hit him as hard as you can."

The footsteps were nearly at the bottom.

"Ready?"

Emily nodded, the book gripped tightly in her hands.

"NOW!"

They swung the books around with such force that Smithson didn't stand a chance. Both books came together over his face, and he collapsed to the floor like a sack of potatoes. Hugh and Emily dropped their books to the floor, looking into each other's eyes, panting. The mound on the floor between them groaned.

Emily looked down, then back to Hugh.

"But you said…"

"Oh, dear."

"You have to understand me when I say, we really thought you were Smithson," said Hugh.

"We?" said Emily. "You were the one who ran in here flustered and told me he was coming. How was I *supposed* to react?"

"Alright, well maybe I jumped the gun a bit."

"*You think?*" said Barrington.

He was propping himself up, rubbing his head. It took Emily a while to revive him, as the force they hit him with knocked him out cold.

"What made you think Smithy was behind you, anyway?" he asked. "The room is hidden to all those unaware of it."

"I panicked," said Hugh. "I heard the shouting, then footsteps chasing me. I thought he was behind me."

"As you can see, it was I who ran in behind you. You were careless, leaving the door open like that. It could have been Smithson following you. Or for all you knew, the Elf King could have infiltrated the Collins family. Then where would we have been, hrmmm? In a lot of trouble, that's where."

"I think Hugh's got the message now, Barrington." Balinas had appeared at the bottom of the staircase, looking unimpressed.

Adelia followed behind him, locking eyes with Emily before stepping further into the room.

"Hugh," said Balinas, "I commend you in your thinking to get the books, but Barrington is right. If you had checked the door before descending, you could have saved him running into your trap."

"Why is everyone laying into Hugh?" said Adelia, placing a hand on his forearm.

At her touch, Hugh tingled all over.

"It's not his fault he's hyped up," she said. "With all this talk of the Elf King and constant worry about being caught by Smithson, I'm not surprised he panicked and ran."

"And who made you the expert?" said Emily, nostrils flared.

"I think you'll find I was here for Hugh, a lot more than you over the years," said Adelia, folding her arms.

"I beg your pardon?"

Hugh stood awkwardly between the two women, looking from one to the other.

"You heard what I said. I was here more than you. I grew up with him."

"So did I!"

"You *ran off* one night! It took him months to get over the fact you just disappeared. We were there for each other." She planted a soft kiss on his cheek. "Isn't that right, Hugh?"

"Oh, was he now?" said Emily, now turning to Hugh, head tilted.

He sensed her beginning to loom over him and leaned in towards Adelia, to where her head was nearly resting on his shoulder.

"Not like that, Emily," he said, trying to diffuse the situation.

"Oh, really?" Adelia dug her nails into his arm.

Hugh winced.

"Ladies, please, control yourselves," said Balinas, irritably. "This is not the time for a falling out. We must remain calm and collected if we're to get through this in one piece."

"Oh, I was just enjoying that," said Barrington, so quietly that Hugh almost missed it.

"Well, it appears the attack on your friend hasn't caused permanent damage," he said looking at Hugh. "There's no need to look surprised. We heard your conversation whilst we *calmly* walked down the stairs."

Hugh looked to the floor again, unwilling to meet his eye. The room was left in an uneasy silence.

"If nobody has any objections," said Barrington, rubbing his head, "I would like to get up off the floor."

"Of course, how rude of us leaving you down there," said Balinas, encouraging the rest the group to help him up.

Barrington stood unsteadily, closing his eyes with the pain. Balinas ran to a chest of drawers, pulling out numerous items, before finding what he was after.

"Take this, it should make you feel much better."

Barrington took the bottle from him and popped the cork out.

"Now before you take it…" Balinas began, but Barrington necked the lot in one go. He smacked his lips together and looked back at the elf, passing him back the bottle.

"You were saying?"

Balinas was busy studying the bottle, then he sniffed it.

"Erm? Well, that's unusual?"

"What?"

"Well, usually, if one were to drink the bottle in one go then…" He stopped talking.

Barrington looked like a startled pigeon that had just flown headlong into a window. Everyone watched as he went rigid and then fell backwards like a plank of wood.

"… yes, well, I would expect him to do that."

They gathered around Barrington, who was now emitting a sort of high-pitched squeak, eyes wide open and face contorted. Hugh tapped him with his foot.

"Is this normal?"

"Everything up to the squeak is, yes."

"So, what is that?"

"Well, that's a new one to me. Mind you, he drank the entire thing." Balinas studied the bottle, then clucked to himself. "Of course… silly me."

Everyone looked at him, waiting for an explanation as he sat in his seat and shook his head. But none seemed to be forthcoming.

"Of course, *what*?" said Emily.

"Eh?"

"You said, of course, then missed off the crucial information."

"Ah, yes, well, this particular panacea is a tad out of date."

"How much out of date?"

"Oh, only by eighty, perhaps ninety years."

"*What?*" Hugh and Emily said in unison.

"Errrm, what's happening now?" said Adelia, looking at Barrington, for he was now making a gurgling noise.

"He's gonna blow!" said Hugh.

He and Emily jumped out of the way. Adelia wasn't quick enough. Barrington sat bolt upright and projected his full load onto Adelia, who took the full brunt of the wave. He sat wiping his chin off, looking confused, the sound of vomit dripping to the floor.

"What just happened?" he said, looking around the room whilst rubbing his head. He looked across to Adelia. "Dear me, what happened to you? And why am I on the floor?"

"Did you know that would happen?" asked Hugh, looking to Balinas.

"Naturally, that's why I moved over here."

"And you didn't think it prudent to warn us?"

"I suppose the gurgling was a big giveaway," said Emily, hiding a smirk.

"Not to me, it wasn't," said Adelia.

"Please accept my most sincere apology," said Balinas. "There's a screen over there, with spare clothes. We're about the same size, so they should fit. Emily, fetch the mop and bucket, please."

"What?"

"You heard me, please don't make me repeat myself. Laughing at someone else's misfortune is not something I take lightly. We are a team now, and it's time we all acted like one."

Emily huffed before setting to her duties, scowling at Adelia as she was being helped by Hugh to the screen. It was good fortune that

Barrington came out unscathed from the incident. Balinas helped him off the floor and sat him in his chair to recover, giving him water to rinse his mouth out along with a bucket just in case there was a follow-up emission. It wasn't long before they were sitting around the table, discussing the unfolding situation.

"So, now that Smithson has realised you're alive and confirmed your location, it won't take him long to make a play to get you arrested again," said Balinas. "We'll need to formulate a plan to get you out of here. We can keep you safe for a short time, but even the library has its limits."

Hugh looked stunned.

"But you said the library was safe. Are you now saying that we are not safe here?"

"Well, it is … *was* safe. I can assure you Smithson will stop at nothing to flush you out of here. We will bolster the security arrangements to prevent any further breaches in the security."

"If he can't get into the library, we have to stay here, surely."

"Smithson can't get in, but a Collins family member can. The head of the family serves him. I expect he'll be here regularly now, spying on Smithson's orders. We can only hope that he upholds the family code."

They sat in an uneasy silence, leaving the words Balinas said to echo around the chamber.

"Well, I, for one, refuse to sit here like a sitting duck," said Barrington. He got to his feet, swayed, then sank back into the chair.

"We cannot go out onto the streets," said Emily. "You can guarantee they'll be looking out for us and will station half the city guard outside the university, that's if they haven't done so already."

"What about the sally port?" asked Adelia. "You could sneak out. Maybe Augustus could help."

"That's a no on both counts," said Balinas. "He's grounded for the foreseeable future whilst they look into the incident outside the tunnel, which brings me to my next point - the sally port being watched around the clock since you were seen entering it."

"Then we're stuck here?" asked Hugh.

Balinas shook his head.

"Not quite. I saw this situation unfolding long before it happened." He tapped the side of his nose knowingly. "I employed a team of tunnellers to dig a secret route out of the university."

"How on earth did you get them in unseen?"

"The restoration work being done on the burnt-out alchemy lab gave us a good cover story."

Hugh's stomach turned over.

"Don't remind me about it."

"There's no need to worry about *that*," he said, "it's all in the past. They've been tunnelling non-stop for the past few months. They had a stroke of luck finding more of the old lava tubes, the only issue being they couldn't get too close to the sea."

"How come?" asked Emily.

"They said the ground near to the docks was unsuitable for tunnels, and the existing lava tunnels were all flooded. It's alright, they surfaced only one street away from the port. It's in a lovely little tea parlour, and the owner was quite amenable to helping. The tunnellers said the service was good and promised to be frequent customers when in town."

"Oh, how quaint. Maybe we could get a cream bun on the way out. Or afternoon tea. I'm sure we'll have lots of time. Ooo, we could get a postcard for Hamish and Heather, let them know how we're getting on."

Hugh sighed.

"Come on, Em. It's not like Balinas had much choice in the matter. What's the name of this tea parlour if you don't mind me asking? Is it trustworthy?"

"Oh, I can assure you that this person is the pillar of their community. We can trust her. It's the Mme Domina Noctis Tea Parlour."

Barrington choked on the water he was drinking, sending a fine mist into the air. Balinas looked at him.

"Are you alright, dear fellow?"

"Is that the parlour *directly* opposite the docks?"

"Why, yes, do you know it?" He raised is eyebrows and gave a wry smile.

"I … well, yes, I've heard of it."

"Then you'll know it's the perfect place from which to reach the boats. All that's left to do now is arrange transport. I know just the person to help. Your friend Wanda should be able to sort us out with transport, should she not?"

"I think she'd be able to arrange an airship, but how do we meet with her to arrange it?"

"Never you mind about that," said Balinas. "Leave it to me. It'll have to be by sea, I'm afraid. The airdock will be too risky, especially as everyone's looking for you."

"What about Heather? Can we not call on her and the rune wing?"

"I'm afraid not. She said they had to strip it down, something to do with a dent in the wing. But that doesn't mean she's not available."

Barrington flushed with colour and went quiet.

"That reminds me," said Balinas, "we'll need to get a guide sorted. I think this is the start of a plan coming together. Yes, Hugh, I see you have some questions."

Hugh was sitting quietly, mulling over the thought of setting foot outside the library when Balinas caught him up short.

"Yes, I do … do I?"

"Don't keep it all in your head, dear boy; share it with the room."

Before Hugh could process the thoughts running through his mind, Emily was already there. She too possessed the skill to see inside people's heads.

"I think Hugh is quite comfy here and would rather leave the task until a later date." She sat smiling at him.

'*You know I hate it when you do that,*' said Hugh into Emily's head.

'*I can read you like a book, Hugh Geber,*' Emily replied without speaking a word.

'*She's got you there,*' said Balinas, joining in with the silent conversation.

"Fine!" said Hugh out loud, making everyone jump. "I don't think we're anywhere ready for this trip. We don't know where we're going or what we're looking for."

"And whose fault is that?" asked Barrington.

Hugh shot him a look, but Barrington wasn't backing down.

"What? You've kept yourself hidden away when you could have been working towards the next stage. Emily's been working hard getting up to scratch with her book of lore, and even Adelia has got stuck into daily life, helping me with the clock. That reminds me, I'll need some helpers to get that to the dock."

"You aren't seriously suggesting bringing that thing with you, are you?" said Hugh.

"Why, of course. It'll help keep me distracted on our voyage of discovery. You know I hate going by water. Balinas, can your chaps help move it for me?"

"I don't see why not. They can reassemble some of it for you, just to get you going, that is."

"Seems like a good idea to me. It would be a shame to lose any parts overboard."

Adelia looked excitable.

"Maybe I can come, you know, give you a hand to tinker with it?" She looked from Barrington to Hugh.

"Well, I suppose you could," said Hugh. "It would be good to have an extra pair of hands."

Emily scoffed.

"No, she can't come. She'll only hinder us. Besides, she doesn't have a clue about what we're doing."

"Yes, I do!" said Adelia. "Hugh has filled me in on some details, and I'm sure I can learn the rest along the way."

"Oh, has he really? Well, that's nice? Has he filled you in on the finer details of the story so far? I mean, why not shout it from the rooftops for all to hear?"

"Sorry, am I missing some part of the conversation here?" snapped Adelia. "I didn't realise the information was his to keep. I believe it involves the Geber family, and I am a Geber, after all."

"Barely."

"What?"

"Oh, come on … you deserted the family at the first opportunity! You ran from your *husband,* remember him?"

"You're a fine one to talk. Leaving in the middle of the night, no message, no goodbye. At least I said my farewell properly to Hugh."

Emily rounded on Hugh.

"You said she left without saying goodbye!"

Hugh rubbed the back of his neck.

"I … but … it really wasn't like that. I mean, alright, so we may have said our farewells…like we always did. I didn't know she was planning on leaving. It wasn't on the night she left anyway, maybe a day or two before? But it was nothing."

"That's not what you said on the night?" said Adelia, a wry smile on her face.

"Adelia, please, you're not helping. It was nothing out of the usual, Em."

"Nothing out of the usual? What the bloody hell is the usual?" said Emily.

The ground was starting to shake.

"Will you all stop fighting!" Balinas' voice boomed around the chamber.

Everything fell silent.

"I will not stand for this anymore. This is a room of great power, and with you two bickering, you risk destroying my life's work. The raw power of the universe flows directly through this room and is extremely reactive to emotion."

Emily looked away but said nothing.

"Now then," said Balinas, composing himself. "I think it would be best if you stayed here, Adelia. We'll need all the help we can get."

Adelia stood open-mouthed, unable to take in the words she was hearing. She turned to Hugh.

"Well? Are you at least going to try to fight for me?" She looked to Hugh, eyes welling up, as he stood mute. "*Fine!* I can see where I'm not needed!" She let out a scream of rage and stormed up the stairs.

Hugh turned to Emily, but she rejected him.

"Don't … just, don't." She walked off and, not wanting to follow Adelia's route, headed to behind the screen, leaving only the sound of sobbing in her wake.

"That went *swimmingly* well," said Barrington.

Hugh stared open-mouthed at the lack of support from his friend then turned to leave.

"Hugh, wait," said Balinas, "what about planning the next stage?"

"Not now," he said and turned to head after Adelia.

Chapter 4

Smithson was sitting in his room at the B&B. It was an establishment well-suited to his needs and expectations. The wood-panelled walls were polished to a high sheen, allowing light to bounce around the dark room. A gramophone was playing in the reception area, but it was so loud as to be a distraction while he studied the box on his desk. He had happened upon it in his room back in Dallum, finding it under a loose floorboard. He recognised it as a relic from the Old World, and just having it nearby made him feel dirty, as though he were cheating on the New World life he had forged for himself. Yet, something kept drawing him back to the object. His fingers fell across the runes as they shimmered and shone in an almost tactile way. He knew these symbols to be Old World text, but what they represented, he couldn't recall.

He turned his attention to the book which had been retrieved from his office at his request several months previously. Collins also desired the book, but Smithson could not fathom why. It only logged trips that his father, Robert Smithson, and and Hugh's father, Frederick Geber had been on, with a few handy maps drawn in. He desperately needed more information, which was increasingly scarce. He had tried and failed to gain full access to the library to see if he could find more information, but his entry had been denied by the meddling librarians. To make things worse, his servant's reports were confirmed – Geber was indeed being hidden within the room. Smithson also overheard Collins letting slip of more books of power whilst talking to his apprentice. Even though it meant more work, getting ahead of the game was crucial. He'd be damned if Geber was going to beat him.

They needed to remove Geber from the picture. If that meant using force, then so be it. Questions would be raised about the reappearance of the wretched group of outlaws, and Smithson was feeling the pressure to put an end to their little game. He had not long returned from the city guard office to arrange the final details of his plan. By the end of play that day, they would all be in custody. A knock at the door interrupted his thoughts.

"Enter. Ah, Collins," he said, sliding the book into the pile of papers on the desk, "and of course, your little apprentice, as loyal as a lapdog."

The apprentice glared at Smithson through narrowed eyes.

"Don't look at me like that," snapped the chancellor. "If I had any choice in the matter, I would've left you in the mess we found you in. What do you want, Collins?"

His servant was balancing on his heels, waiting for the attention to come his way.

"For a start, more respect for my apprentice. His name is Maso."

"Yes, yes, whatever. Have you found some information, or are you here to brag about your toy?"

"Now that's not the way to address your most loyal servant, *is it?*" Smithson huffed.

"Fine. Please tell me what news you have."

"That's better. This arrived for you. It has the king's stamp on it."

Collins passed a sealed letter to Smithson, who snatched it eagerly. He ripped it open, and his eyes scanned quickly from left to right. Then he turned the short letter over, expecting to find more, but it was blank.

"Anything wrong, sir?"

"What? No, everything's fine," he said not sounding too certain.

"Why would you think otherwise?"

"Oh, nothing really. It's just that you appear to have expected more from the letter. Was it important?"

"The content of this letter doesn't concern you, Collins."

"Suit yourself, but if I could give you a little advice. It does not pay to keep one's master waiting, not if they are expecting you to come up with something *meaningful*."

Smithson locked eyes with his servant – neither wishing to yield. Eventually he broke the stalemate.

"Whatever communications I receive, be it from the Old World or the New, I assure you I am a servant to nobody."

"Oh, is that how you see it? Suit yourself. Even the simpletons in the room can see you're torn between the powers who pay you, and the new master who wishes to reward you with treats. It doesn't matter if the deal is paid or a reward for your hard efforts, the simple fact remains. There will always be a master, and there will always be … a servant."

Smithson sat tight-lipped, refusing to retort to Collins.

"The trick," said Collins, "is knowing on which side of the line you stand. I know which side of the line I stand. The question is, do you have any idea where you are currently placed?"

Smithson sat back in his seat, pondering that.

"Very clever, Collins. But I'm sure where I stand with things. For starters, my job doesn't have the title of 'servant' in its name."

"You may have me there, sir, but what is in a name? I prefer to not judge a man by the title on his desk. Unless you hold the ultimate keys of power, then I'm afraid you will never be the true master." He stood, smiling smugly back at Smithson, who was now chewing the inside of his mouth. "If that's all Sir requires, I have urgent jobs to do."

Collins turned to leave the room, but Smithson spoke, stopping him in his tracks.

"I need to retrieve some information from the library."

"But Sir isn't allowed into the library. I thought we covered that one earlier."

"Yes, thank you, Collins. I'm fully aware that I'm not allowed within ten feet of the place. You, however, have full access."

Collins stood, looking Smithson in the eye. The quiet sound of music seemed to fill the space. Eventually, Collins sighed.

"Fine, what do you wish me to do?"

Chapter 5

Three days had passed since the meeting in the Chamber of Prophecy. Hugh was working hard on trying to win Emily back round whilst trying to focus his efforts on the next stages of the plan. She had made it clear to him how she felt, and it was now down to Hugh to make up his mind. Though the conversation between the pair was polite whenever they were in the same room, she had given him clear signals that the situation had to be sorted. She had taken to sleeping in a different chamber and studied the lore book of magic by day, attempting to give him the time and space to think.

Hugh was now spending more time in the library, scanning the shelves, looking for anything to point him in the right direction in terms of finding the remaining two books. There was very little information, and his thoughts often wandered to the book of alchemy and its whereabouts. He spent hours playing with the Orbis, attempting to get a bearing on it only to have the needles swing around wildly and inconclusively, leaving him downhearted.

With luck not on his side, he returned to his father's notebook, reading its many pages, some of which were in code. Balinas tried to help him decipher what was written, but to no avail. It needed more time than they had. Whatever it was, his father meant it to be hidden. Then there was the map of an island. It looked unlike any landmass

Hugh had seen before, yet his father had drawn symbols all over it. There were flowers, oxen and strange sea creatures.

He returned to scanning the shelves of the great room for answers, but his search did not bear fruit. So many books were being deposited in the room daily that the shelves appeared faster than he could look at them. No sooner had he reached the end of a section than more cases were added, causing him to start the search all over again.

It seemed there weren't any books in the Chamber of Prophecy that could help, and any time he entered the room, he sensed Emily's thoughts aimed in his direction. Even though she had her nose buried deep into *One Thousand Poisonous Plants and How to Spot Them*, he could feel her attention flashing over to him. Since they had shared their energies in the sight, part of Emily's energy resided in Hugh and vice versa. He knew he was running out of time with Emily and the task to find the books. His mind was brought back into the room, as he had to duck due to a flash of light which hit the wall behind him, leaving a sizeable dent in its wake. He looked across at Emily, who had a staff in one hand and a finger on the text in the open book, mid spell cast.

"Jeez, Em, careful!"

"Sorry, didn't realise *that* was going to happen."

Truth be told, he was fed up with searching the windowless rooms bereft of daylight save for what came through the tiny ventilation shafts carved into the mountainside. He couldn't even talk to his best friend about the situation.

Barrington was still deep into working on his clock. The room was full of springs, cogs and other clock paraphernalia. Balinas was getting somewhat tetchy now that it was taking up so much precious space on the library floor. Barrington refused to let the Collins family dismantle the clock, saying he had "almost got it accurate". The final straw came when the hour chimed, and the face dropped off. Cogs and springs flew out across the room, sending people diving for cover as errant bits of metal embedded themselves into the bookshelves and nearly took out Balinas. He finally put his foot down and called another meeting. The group reconvened in the Chamber of Prophecy. Sitting around the table, nobody wanted to speak or meet each other's gaze. The room had an uneasy tension as the usually calm Balinas surveyed them with annoyance.

"Well? Does anybody wish to get the ball rolling? No…? Then, I guess it's down to me." He let out a long, controlled sigh. "Have you completely forgotten yourselves? Did you ignore what I said? The situation is critical. We have neither the time nor resources to be fighting amongst ourselves. The longer you spend dragging your heels here, the more time you are giving the Elf King and his troops to gather more support. We haven't time to be procrastinating."

"Well, actually I've been busy with my project," said Barrington.

"Nor do we have time to be tinkering with our clocks." He glared at Barrington, who sank back into his chair. "You have caused enough trouble as it is with this *hobby* of yours. I was willing to let you use the space in the beginning, but it's turning into a nightmare. Damn cogs and springs flying all over the place like missiles. It's only a matter of time before someone is seriously injured."

Hugh chuckled to himself.

"See, I told you so."

"Don't you sit there all smug, Hugh Geber," said Balinas, and Hugh felt himself go hot. "You've been skulking around for weeks. It took a good kick up the arse from me to get you moving. Now you are stuck trying to figure out coded messages which could hold the answers to all of our questions. I would've thought you'd have made more effort, given the urgency of the situation."

Emily nodded, which took the attention away from Hugh.

"You can stop nodding as well. You want to explore the spells in the book of magic and read some of the other fantastic books within this room, I understand. But, you should be helping Hugh, not hiding away in the corner. You nearly destroyed this entire room with that staff the other day, and I won't stand for it."

He stamped his foot on the floor.

"That was an accident."

"Yes, well that *accident* nearly cost Hugh his life."

When Adelia rolled her eyes, Balinas swung around to look at her. She gulped.

"You may well be sitting there, keeping your head down, young lady, but I assure you, you're equally to blame for this situation. Your return to Portis-Montis has not been without its difficulties. I understand your need to be back in your home town, but the timing could have been a little better." He stood there, breathing heavily, his nostrils flared. "Well? Do you all want to at least say sorry?"
One by one, they looked at one another. Slowly, they mumbled an apology. Balinas sucked in his cheeks, tilted his head and cupped his ear.

"Sorry, Balinas," they all chimed in unison.

"That's better. I've never talked to adults like this before. It's a disgrace. From this point forward, I want all differences set aside and you to work together as a team."

They all nodded but said nothing.

"I'll take your silence as assent. Right, let's move the situation forward. There's another reason I called this meeting, and it's to do with events happening in the outside world. The situation is critical."

"I think we've got the message, loud and clear," said Barrington. "We must work together to find the books."

"That's not it. You've been so cooped up in here, stuck in your own little bubbles, that life's overtaken you." He took in a deep breath, standing with a grave look on his face.

"What is it, Balinas?" asked Emily, reaching out to touch his hand.

"It's Skellig-Krieg. The Elf King's forces are camped one mile away from the city gates, and they are digging in for the battle."

The silence swelled to fill the room.

"The New World forces will stop the man, surely?" said Barrington.

"I'm afraid not. The city's troops have only recently been training for battle, and their numbers are small. Reinforcements are being sent across from Bansk, but it will barely boost the numbers needed. This is one of the biggest tests of the New World powers since the Great War, and they are ill equipped to fight this new threat. We have been at peace for so long that nobody can remember the skills needed for a real battle. You saw first-hand how fast they are working to catch up by reinstating the city wall.

"Most of the people expelled from the city were upset about being turfed from their homes, all because they either had links to the Old World or couldn't prove their New World status. I'm pretty certain that most of them were annoyed enough to want to take revenge and so have joined the Elf King's forces."

"But my parents," said Barrington, "they're in grave danger."

"That is true, but trust me, we have people working to evacuate those unable to leave the city freely. Some people have the wrong papers. Others, including your parents, have connections with the Old World and could find themselves on trial. We have no choice but to smuggle them into the Old World. We have our people arranging train tickets to Dallum, and suitable accommodation will be found upon their arrival. I only hope we can get them all out before it all kicks off."

Hugh was feeling numb. He couldn't believe it was actually happening.

"What about Alfred?" he asked, clearing his throat, his concern for his uncle drying his mouth.

"He'll be fine. He has escape plans if things don't go our way."

Hugh swallowed and nodded, as the words sunk in. Emily was already getting up from the table.

"I'm going to fight."

"Me too," said Barrington, joining her.

"You can't go there," said Balinas. "To do so would endanger those you care about further."

"Balinas, my life and my job are over there. I will be needed to help defend the greenhouses, and *nobody* is going to stop me."

"And I wish to get my parents to safety myself," said Barrington.

"And what do you think will happen if you are seen or, worse, captured? Will the people and places that you care about be safe then? Or will they become targets? I'm telling you both now, you're not going, and that's my final word on the issue. Now *sit down!*" His voice dominated the space, and the pair begrudgingly re-took their seats. "I understand your concerns, but you will have to take my word on this one."

The two of them scowled back at Balinas, and Hugh could hear the words that Emily was thinking. Balinas looked at her.

"This isn't a game we're playing here. One wrong move can cause more damage than I can describe. This is now a life critical situation. Let those on the ground in Skellig-Krieg do their jobs without the added stress of having to watch over a pair of wanted people. The greenhouses will be fine without you, Emily. Your duty now is to help retrieve the books of lore."

"Oh yes, how could we forget?" said Barrington. "As long as the books are safe, who cares about everyone's families?"

"I assure you, it gives me no pleasure holding you back from your loved ones, but the truth of the matter is we are all in grave danger if we choose not to go after the books."

"It's alright for you, sitting here in your stone palace. You have no family, so why should it bother you?"

"I beg your pardon?"

"You heard me. Maybe if you had a family of your own, then you might see this in a different light! Damn you!" he smacked his fist on the table in front of him.

Hugh had never seen his friend looked so angry.

"Barrington, take it easy."

"It's alright, Hugh," said Balinas turning to Barrington. "So, you think it's *easy* for me? You think that I sit in my stone palace with no cares in the world? Maybe you think I take joy in watching the world I spent so many years building and nurturing destroy itself? It may appear that I'm too old to have any relatives, but that's not the case. You're sceptical, but I assure you I've a family of my own, some of whom are in harm's way. Maybe I haven't seen them for a long time, maybe I have, but you would never know. The truth would be far too complicated for one such as yourself to comprehend.

"I've witnessed many horrors in my lifetime, Barrington Delphin, horrors that only haunt you in your nightmares. Do you never question what happened to the great Altum Castle that once stood on this very site? Or wonder what it's like to watch my own children head into battle, not knowing if they would return alive or in a box? Do you not think that it pained me to see the castle being destroyed by powers so evil that it not only robbed me of my ancestral home but my wife as well? I tell you, I had to stand up, fight the pain, to where it nearly took my life-force away. Such a thing can kill an elf, but I fought to stay just to save the last remnants of a life that once was. I couldn't let her death be in vain. So, I stayed and fought, and we won the battle, pushing the forces of evil back.

"Do you not think that I consider all of you family? I lost many good friends the first-time round; I don't wish to relive that again. You think I relish the thought of sending you all into danger, facing up to an unseen enemy? I don't wish to see history repeat itself, and if the situation were different, I would be by your sides. But we have to do what has to be done if we're to save Tellus. Our world. Because that's what it boils down to. It's not about you, your parents, your job, your uncle, or the man you yearn to be with. This is so much bigger than that. I've been there, I've seen it all and lost more than you could ever imagine.

"So, don't you dare question me, Barrington Delphin!" said the aged elf, a tear rolling down his cheek. "Don't you bloody dare."

Barrington looked like a man beaten, Balinas' words cutting deeply into him.

"Right ... well ... I suppose ..." He cleared his throat, turned on his heel and left the room.

Emily looked to Hugh to do something. He stood there, limp as a wilted summer lettuce.

"For goodness' sake!" She turned and left the room.

Balinas dropped himself into his chair, deflated. Hugh looked to him, then across to Adelia.

"I think I need to talk to Barrington."

Adelia nodded, and Hugh ran after his friends.

Hugh was back up in the library. When he enquired about the situation outside the university, he was informed that there were numerous members of the city guard stationed at the main doors to the building. The newer restrictions and powers put in place to hold them back meant they were currently barred from entering the library, as it was closed to all but essential staff. With the university in upheaval, the students had been sent home until further notice. It had come as a shock to the powers of the New World to learn of the untimely resurrection of the three fugitives. They were currently making plans for their eventual arrest. How long that would be, Hugh could not say, but time was running out. The Collins family had already gone beyond the call of duty to help protect him and the others.

Hugh sought to find his friends, to see if he could resolve the current stalemate. He eventually found them in a side room off the main floor. Like the rest of the library, this room was stacked floor to ceiling with books. Barrington and Emily were squeezed around a small table. It was safe to say, Barrington was not overjoyed to see him.

"Oh, it's you. Has he sent you to drag us back?"

"Don't be like that," said Hugh.

"Like what? My parents are old and infirm. They can barely look after themselves, let alone try to escape from a city on the brink of annihilation. How can I be expected to turn a blind eye to their plight. I cannot leave them Hugh, I just can't. I have to know they are safe."

"I understand, I really do."

"Do you though, really? You have no-one in danger over there."

"Excuse me? I hardly think that's a fair comment to make, is it? What about Alfred, or have you forgotten he lives there too?"

"No, Hugh, we haven't forgotten," said Emily. "Alfred's more than capable of looking after himself. I'm with Barrington on this one. I think we need to go to Skellig-Krieg first, help with the fight. Once everyone is safe, we can search for the next book of lore."

"Alfred is still in danger," Hugh said. "You can't say his safety is guaranteed, just because he's younger. He's not that far behind your parents, Barrington."

"I will not fight you on this one, Hugh. You've to do what you think is morally right. As must we."

"What? So, this is it, is it? Think about what Balinas said. This is way above our personal troubles. We have to decide whether to pick up the quest and find the books. That is what is morally right. The fate of the world is in our hands, and you want to make a mercy mission? Now is not the time for us to split and go our separate ways. We're supposed to be a team; or have you forgotten that?"

"You don't seriously believe him, do you?"

"I do, Barrington. I believe, deep within my soul, that we need to do this." He looked to Emily. "Come on, you must understand what's at stake. Heck, even Smithson understands the power of these books, and he hates the Old World. If he or the Elf King get their hands on the books of lore, they'll gain more power than we can imagine. Then it won't matter if the greenhouses are there, or if Barrington's parents are alive. Where do you think he will go if he cannot reach us? He'll go for what hurts us the most."

"Which is why I wish to get my parents to safety, and why Emily needs to protect all she's ever worked for. I'm sorry Hugh, but if this is how it's got to be, then so be it."

Hugh stood, staring as the pair, hoping for either of them to see the reality of what they were facing and to reconsider their choices.

"So, that's it then. We part company here?"

Barrington puffed his cheeks out, letting the air pass through his lips.

"Em? Are you standing by this decision?" She went to move as if she were going to stand and join Hugh, but Barrington placed a hand on her forearm.

"Sorry, Hugh, but we've made our choice."

"Sod the both of you!"

"Hugh wait!" said Emily.

But it was too late. Hugh turned on his heel and marched from the room. As Emily stood, a tear rolled down her cheek.

"No luck then?"

Balinas was sitting at the table, his eyes red and puffy, drinking tea with Adelia. Hugh pulled up a chair next to him.

"Not to worry, young Hugh, not to worry." He patted Hugh gently on the hand. "I couldn't imagine that it would ever end up like this."

"So, what happens now?" said Hugh.

"Well, we have to plan for the worst-case scenario."

"Really, is there no other way?"

"Hugh, you cannot do this on your own, and I cannot leave my post here."

"Maybe I could step in?" said Adelia.

Hugh and Balinas to look at her, eyebrows raised.

"It's just a suggestion," she said.

"That *might* work. What do you think?" said Hugh.

"Well, it may get us to a suitable number. You'll need to be brought up to speed, of course, and we have little time to prepare."

"It would be an honour to help the family cause," she said.

"We won't be needing any extra help or any more hangers on." Emily had just entered the room. "We have enough people going in harm's way without adding more to the mix."

"Em? What's going on?" said Hugh, getting up from the table.

Her eyes were red and puffy.

"I can't do it, Hugh. I can't leave you behind again."

"Oh, Em. I'm so sorry for everything."

"This wasn't an easy decision, Hugh, but we have to do what is right, no matter what our hearts want us to do."

"Oh … right. So, has Barrington left then?"

"No, he's right here," said Barrington, rounding the bottom of the spiral staircase.

Hugh was taken aback to see his friend entering the room.

"Barrington? What about your parents? I thought you wanted to rescue them, and you had to do your thing whilst I did mine?"

"Well, it's still the case that I wish to rescue my parents, but Emily convinced me it would be wrong for us to leave you in your time of need."

Hugh thought there was something in his friends' words that made them sound as though they were spoken begrudgingly.

"If we're to move forwards together, then I need to know there's no lingering doubt. We can't do this if we're not all fully dedicated."

"Like I've already said, I would be wrong to desert you at this crucial time. I intend on keeping my word, no matter how much it irks me."

"Well, if we're all agreed, then I think we ought not waste any more time," said Balinas, before anyone changed their minds.

He walked off to retrieve a heavy book, one which Hugh recognised to be the *Book of Prophecy*. He dropped it heavily onto the table, causing it to land with a thud, sending a plume of dust into the air. He turned the pages quickly, scanning the text whilst muttering to himself. The group gathered around to see what he was searching for.

Adelia stood in awe and watched as words seemingly appeared in front of their very eyes.

"What's that? And how do the words appear like that?"

Hugh attempted to explain it to her.

"The book was created many centuries ago by the elders, and it had foretold everything up to now. It also shows events which are to happen, but it only reveals the destination and events, not the path we are to choose or how to arrive there. We are in charge of that."

"Well remembered, Hugh," said Balinas. "I'm pleased some things I talk about are retained for future reference."

Balinas was still tracing a finger across the page as he spoke, and he resumed his search for the information he was looking for. It seemed to take a while, but just as Hugh retook his seat, Balinas found what he needed.

"Ah-ha! Here we are. I knew I would find it eventually."

Hugh stood again and looked over his shoulder at the strange symbols on the page. A moment before, they had appeared out of nowhere, and now they were static. Hugh knew this could mean only one thing. The book had revealed information on the task that lay ahead of them. The only issue was that they had to decipher what it was saying.

"So, what's it saying this time, old chap," said Barrington. He had brightened up with the thought of getting outside the university. "Are we off back to our usual stomping grounds in Skellig-Krieg? We could cover a few tasks at once. I could move my parents to safety, and Hugh could pop in and see Alfred. He has some explaining to do after nearly getting us killed in Skellig-Krieg."

Hugh's mind was briefly pulled back to the explosion near to the large EGF symbol before Balinas spoke once more.

"No," said Balinas, his voice shaky. He cleared his throat. "No. You aren't going to Skellig-Krieg."

"Then maybe Bansk?" said Hugh.

Balinas slowly shook his head.

"No, this won't be the usual scenario that you are familiar with. I think you are to be sent in a different direction. It speaks of a book that's deep within the sea, held in the bay where the merfolk live. You must go visit the people that live beneath the waves, who share a family link to one of the three book finders."

"Share a family link to one of the three book finders," said Hugh. "What's that supposed to mean?"

"I haven't the faintest idea," said Barrington.

Emily shook her head.

"Seriously?"

"What?" said Barrington.

"Nothing."

Hugh watched the pair, looking confused, but Balinas was already scanning the writing further.

"Oh my, that's not good."

"What?" said Hugh.

He attempted to read the strange writing as if the words might have become legible since last he looked.

"Oh, it's nothing, really," said Balinas, attempting to wave his last comment away.

Hugh attempted to look into Balinas but found his way blocked.

"Hugh, you cannot just force your way into someone's head. It's bad manners," said Balinas. "They have to agree to let you in."

Hugh chewed the inside of his cheek.

"You do it to me all the time."

"That's because you let me in willingly. If you didn't want me to find something, I guarantee, you could block me out. Another lesson you missed out on."

"So, what are *you* hiding, then?"

Balinas nodded then let out another sigh.

"It speaks of the journey this time."

"But, I thought you said it would only speak of what is to come?"

"Yes, that's true, but even I am not infallible, Hugh. I may know a lot, but the book keeps me on my toes." There was a brief pause, and Balinas looked at Hugh, smiling an uneasy smile.

"Well? What is it then?" said Emily.

"What?"

"What the book said? Come on, Balinas, you said we had to work as a team."

"Alright, the book is saying that you must undertake a perilous journey, one which all sailors dread. It is said that those who enter may never return. But if that's true, I cannot say."

"Sorry, but I'm lost," said Adelia. "Surely no such place exists."

Barrington appeared to have broken out into a cold sweat.

"Balinas, my dear man, there has to be another way."

"If you are to retrieve the next book of lore, that is to say the book of water, then I'm afraid you have no choice."

Barrington slowly shook his head, walking backwards. He stumbled, landing on an old chair in the corner. It seemed to want to swallow him whole, giving him no way to escape.

"What is he talking about, Balinas?" said Hugh. "What is going on?"

"I'm afraid to say you are going to have to take a trip into the Sea of Lost Souls," he said, swallowing hard, "and then, well…"

"And then, what?"

"Well, if you survive that, you only have to get around the Cape of No Hope!"

Emily looked at him, slowly digesting what she was hearing.

"Hang on, are you saying that this *sea of no hope* exists?"

"Yes, it's the Sea of Lost Souls. That then leads to the Cape of No Hope, please try to keep up. That's where you will have to go, but we must study the maps and see why you must go there. Adelia, would you mind helping me for a minute?"

She nodded, and they went off to leaf through a pile of maps, leaving Hugh and Emily alone.

"So, this is … different," said Hugh, struggling to string a sentence together.

"What's that? We're here in the Chamber of Prophecy, getting scrambled messages foretelling doom and gloom, just before we head out into the unknown? There's kind of a pattern forming here."

"Yeah, well, when you put it like that …" He was rocking back and forth on his feet, twiddling his fingers. "Look, Emily, I really meant it when I said that—"

"Here we are," said Balinas, coming back between the pair with a pile of maps.

But Emily was looking at Hugh.

"What?"

"Nothing," he said. "Let's look at this map, then."

Barrington got back to his feet, and they gathered around the table. Balinas was busy tracing an invisible line with his finger.

"So, we're *here*, and the Sea of Lost Souls is *here*. Then it's the Cape of No Hope, and then jump the Demon's Gap to get there." He pointed to place on the edge of the map.

"But that's the edge of the map," said Hugh. "What is there after that?"

"Well, that's the whole point. Nobody knows. If I had a krune for every ship I heard of that sank around there …"

Everyone stopped and looked up at him.

"Well … I mean … I'm sure it's perfectly safe…"

Emily tutted and shook her head.

"This Sea of Lost Souls, is that where the Minch's home is?"

Barrington looked up at her.

"You know about the Minch?"

"Of course I do. I've been reading up on the mystical sea creatures, along with a few other things to do with the sea. It's amazing what you can learn from books."

"Listen, Balinas, I've patrolled that area numerous times. It's the one area nobody ever wanted to navigate, but the senior crews took it in turns to do our time in the barren seas. I can assure you, there is nothing out there apart from broken ships and souls without a home. As for the Cape of No Hope, even we dared not venture that far. I'm afraid of what lies beneath the waters in the area. I lost many a friend to the cape, and I don't wish to join their number." Balinas looked at Barrington and then back down at the map once more.

"Barrington, I understand your feelings about visiting such a place, especially with all you've been through. I wouldn't send you there if there were another choice, but you have to go there to get the job done. If this is the lore book of water, then it will be in your best interests to take this route, especially as you want to get there before the Elf King or Smithson. Besides, you are one of the battling trio now. You wouldn't want to miss out on another adventure." He paused then. "Yes, Adelia, my dear."

She stood with her hand up in the air.

"Maybe I could take his place. Then Barrington wouldn't have to go."

She looked at Hugh, and Emily shot her a look so deadly that Hugh was amazed Adelia was still standing. Balinas also sensed the change in Emily's mood and jumped in.

"I think it would be best for all involved if you stayed with me. I'll need a hand around here, especially as Barrington will be taking his clock with him. You'll have a lot of free time to fill."

"I'm taking the clock with me?"

"Why, of course. We don't want it here, cluttering up the library. Besides, I think it could do with some sea trials, don't you?" He looked at Barrington, who stood with his mouth opening and closing like a fish. "Good, that's settled then. I shall ask the rest of the team to dismantle it on your behalf."

Hugh looked to Balinas.

"I really don't think we are ready to leave. We haven't even got a destination."

"Nonsense," said Balinas. "I have a map right here."

He pulled out another large sheet which showed an island. Hugh gasped.

"Ladies and gentlemen, may I present to you the Isle of Fey."

Chapter 6

They stood in silence, looking at the new map that Balinas had just produced. Hugh realised how similar it was to the one in his father's book, but he was currently being distracted by the colourful images dotted around the map in front of him, to look at that right now. The map was covered in symbols — its shoreline showing mythical beasts that Hugh only knew from books of lore. They stood in awe, taking in the place names, except for Barrington, who chuckled to himself.

"I'm sorry, but I don't see what is so funny," said Balinas, looking confused.

"I'm sorry to inform you, old boy, in all the seas I've sailed, and all the charts I've looked at over the years, not once have I come across a place with that name. It's my belief that if we go on this trip, we're going after a lost cause. I mean, look at this — Androssan, Syreni Bay, the Forest of Fey?"

"*The Book of Prophecy* mentioned Syreni Bay," said Hugh, "so anything's possible, right?"

Barrington looked at him through narrowed eyes.

"No the book mentioned a bay where the merfolk live, hardly the same thing. I mean, take a look at the pictures of all the aquatic beings. They're only there to scare the wary sailor, no doubt. These names and pictures are as fantastic as the map they're drawn on. You cannot tell me you're falling for this, Hugh."

Balinas considered Barrington for a moment before coming up with a reply.

"I think you're afraid of the truth. You, of all people, should have an open mind to these things." He stared at Barrington, who refused to meet his gaze. "Tell me, before you set sail from the safety of these shores for the first time, did you know where you were going?"

"Of course I did. I was going to the great trading city of Skellig-Krieg. I mean, everyone's heard of it, haven't they?" He looked around the room and everyone nodded, including Balinas. "I really can't see what that has to do with anything."

"Hear me out," said Balinas. "So, before you set sail, you were certain this place, with its strange name, really existed?"

"Yes, but—"

"Even though you had never been there before? Or set eyes on the place?"

"Yes, but—"

"And was it not you who also tried to discourage your friend, here, from going to the barren marshlands of Bansk to search for Hamish, even making a bet with him to prove your point?"

"Well, hang on a minute."

"Yet Hamish also turned out to be very real indeed. So, what makes you so confident that this, too, is completely made up?"

"Hmmm," was all Barrington could say as he looked to the floor.

"You can see," said Balinas, "that although there's little information on the place, that doesn't prove its lack of existence."

Barrington whipped his head up, looking Balinas in the eye.

"Well, that's it, isn't it?"

"What?" Hugh couldn't understand how Barrington could try to get out of this.

"The answer is right above us." The group all looked upwards at the rock ceiling, then back to Barrington.

"I don't see anything," said Adelia, looking as confused as the rest of the group.

"Well, not literally in this room, but the room above. The Great Library. If there's any place in this world that will have the information we're looking for, it has to be the library, right?"

Balinas shrugged.

"But if we look for those particular books …"

But Barrington was too eager to prove him wrong. He was already dragging Hugh by the arm. He scrambled his way up the staircase, leaving the rest to catch up with them. He reminded Hugh of an excitable dog, running after a juicy bone.

They were out of breath as they reached the top of the stairs, but Barrington didn't pause. He ran through the door onto the landing, then bolted towards the staircase, slipping on the carpet in his haste. He came to an abrupt stop at the bottom, causing everyone else to attempt to stop mid-stair. Hugh, who now found himself at the back of the party, lost his balance and fell forwards, taking out everyone else as if they were skittles. The resulting mess landed in a heap on the bottom step. Barrington, oblivious to the carnage behind him, had already run off into the library. He turned to look up the empty stairs with surprise on his face, before looking down at the mass of tangled bodies.

"Come on, there's no time to be resting. We need to find this information, or lack of it, so I can prove Balinas wrong."

He was off again.

"Barrington, will you stop and think for one minute," said Hugh, pulling himself from the pile. "The room is huge, and it would take a lifetime to search all the books in normal circumstances. You need to ask for help."

"*Help!* That's it. Who do I talk to around here to find a book?"

"The head librarian?"

"Marvellous, Hugh, the head librarian. And which one is he again?" He searched the sea of matching blond heads in the room.

"That would be me," said Balinas, now getting to his feet. "How on earth you could forget that is beyond me."

"That's not of importance to me right now," he said, waving the comment away. "So, where are they, then?"

"Where are what?"

"The books. The ones that relate to the Isle of Fey?"

"Well, they're not here, are they?"

"*Ha!* See, ladies and gentlemen of the jury, I told you so. I present to you exhibit A." He waved a hand over an empty table.

"But there's nothing there," said Adelia.

"Exactly, my dear, thus proving my point that the place is about as real as fairies. It doesn't exist."

"What doesn't exist?" said a voice behind Barrington, making him jump. It was Wanda, which caused Hugh great alarm.

"How did *you* get in here?"

His mind went into overdrive, as he scanned the room.

"Calm down Hugh," said Balinas. "Wanda is here at my request. She has full privileges to use the library and has some information that we require. Without her expertise, there is no plan, so consider her an honorary Collins."

"Yeah, so don't go getting all jumpy on me, big fella."

"Sorry, it's just that I panicked. I thought if you could get in here then…"

But then he tailed off, knowing it would sound foolish, but to his surprise, Wanda finished his sentence.

"If I could get in," said Wanda, "then maybe Smithson could get in, right? No need to look surprised. This strapping fella has been kind enough to keep me in the loop." She slapped Balinas on the top of his arm, and he rubbed the pain away. "I understand you're worried about Smithson and the books."

Everyone looked to Balinas, wide eyed.

"It's alright," she said. "He's also explained that it's all hush, hush."

"And that goes for in this room too, Wanda," said Balinas. "Do try not to speak too loudly of the plans." He turned to the rest of the group. "I trust Wanda, as I'm sure you do too, Barrington. After all, your shop is under her supervision. Your relationship goes back a long way, if I am not mistaken? We need her onboard if we're going to get to the Isle of Fey and beyond."

"That is true," said Barrington. "Wanda, we didn't mean to show you distrust. On behalf of the group, please accept our sincere apologies."

"I should think so too, not trusting me indeed. So what was it you were saying doesn't exist?"

Glad for the change in conversation, Barrington jumped headlong back into his previous train of thought.

"Ah, yes, well remembered. You've joined us at a crucial moment, one where I'm about to be proved right."

"And what might that be, luv?"

"That the Isle of Fey doesn't exist."

"You're completely bonkers, mate."

"See, there we go, you're all bonkers in believing Balinas and his wonderful tale."

"Nah, not them, *you!*"

"What?" Barrington's smug smile faltered. "Hahaha, hilarious. She's good this one, eh? Always the joker." He softly punched her on the arm.

"The Isle of Fey is not only real, but I've visited there. You know that. All the pictures in my shop are from there, ya great drongo," she said, now laughing, punching Barrington hard on the arm.

He looked back in alarm, rubbing the spot where she had just hit him. Hugh could spot the tell-tale signs of his friend's reality breaking apart as the light of truth shone through. He was grasping the last of the straws.

"Well … well … tell me this, then. Why are there no books on the subject, eh?" He was staring like a madman at the group.

Balinas let out a sigh.

"If you had let me finish what I was saying before you butted in, I would've informed you that all the books on the subject were removed just two days ago."

Hugh stared at Balinas, open-mouthed.

"What do you mean? I thought you said that you recalled all the books here for safekeeping. How have those books been taken out?"

He suspected he may already know the answer, but he feared to hear the truth.

"Your worries would be on the money with this one," said Balinas, who was on form reading Hugh's mind. "The head of the Collins family came in and requested all information on the Isle of Fey. His authority is greater than mine when it comes to the building or anything Collins related. He liaises with the team searching for the Elf King, so has the power to request knowledge as and when they need it."

"But that means Smithson will have access to the books."

"Yes, I'm afraid so. I found out these recent developments before our meeting. By that time, it was too late. Had I known that we needed the same information, I'd have done my best to prevent the books from leaving this room."

"If Collins is in touch with those after the Elf King, they'll have informed him of the Elf King's plans," said Emily. "If they're heading to the Isle of Fey, that only means one thing."

"That Smithson will also want to try to beat the Elf King to the book," said Hugh. "Balinas, we'll need to stop them leaving, can you get some of the family to prevent it happening?"

"Whoa there, fella," said Wanda, "hold yer horses."

"*What now?*" said Hugh in desperation.

"Well, you're too late, mate."

"What do you mean?"

"Smithson's already left here with a large party. They've already gone, hence *you're too late, mate.*"

Hugh's world descended into panic. He could see it all now. His mouth went dry, and he began hyperventilating.

"It's all my fault." He clasped a hand to his mouth, then ran his hands through his hair. "I spent too long procrastinating, too long avoiding what needed to be done. Smithson's ahead, the Elf King is probably already there, and we're stuck here, and … and …"

'*Hugh…*' Emily's touch was warm on his back, her voice loud in his head. She spoke only to him, so that no-one else could here. '*Breathe, go to your calm place.*'

The Firestone glowed warmly on his chest, soaking up the blast of the anxiety that had just exploded inside. It faded away to quiet background noise. He looked Emily in the eyes, unable to speak. Understanding the silent message, she spoke to the room at large.

"We're all to blame for this. It's not just you, Hugh, even though you procrastinated for too long. We all had a part to play. I shouldn't have been so stuck in the lore book of magic. You, Barrington, should not have been so engrossed in your toy clock."

"Hey now, it's not a toy."

"That's not the point. Adelia, yes, I'm talking to you in a civil tongue. You've been doing your best to win Hugh's heart, and it's been confusing him. His mind's been elsewhere when we should've been focused on the task."

Hugh looked at Emily with surprise.

"You know?"

"Yes, I know about it, Hugh. It's not nice to see everything that goes on inside your head, and I wish you would learn to lock certain things away. But that's where you should've stepped in, Balinas. You knew all this was happening, yet you let it continue. Then you have the audacity to blame us."

Balinas bit his lip and looked away.

"We're all to blame," said Emily, "but we all owe Hugh an apology." She looked into his eyes.

The rest of the group looked stood, fidgeting awkwardly.

"We have made this task yours to bear," she said, "and that was wrong. We've blamed you for not putting in the effort when we've all hidden away from our responsibilities. Now is not the time to feel sorry for ourselves. It's time to pull together and work as one. I'm certainly not going to let Smithson get away with this, and I'll be damned if the Elf King is getting his hands on the books before we do. Now who's with me?"

Chapter 7

The guard presence outside the university grew in number by the day as they prepared to capture Hugh, Barrington and Emily. The New World authorities were pulling out all the stops to catch the trio. They had managed to gain access to the atrium and now lay in wait for their prey.

Trapped inside the library, the group spent their waking hours planning for the trip to the Isle of Fey. Using the map from Balinas, and notes deciphered from Hugh's father's book, they came up with a plan. The Collins family helped to take apart Barrington's clock and gather the supplies needed for the journey ahead. These were disguised as bags of waste, then smuggled to the dock and loaded onto a ship, organised by Wanda. Hugh expressed his concerns to Balinas about trusting an unknown captain.

"I'm sure all will be fine," assured Balinas. "Besides, given the circumstances, we have little choice."

"Alright," said Hugh, "I'm just wary about involving too many people."

"I understand your concern, and it's totally natural. I'm not happy with the situation either, but we must trust those close to us, for they are all we have. If we lose trust in them, then we have nobody. Now, if I were you," said Balinas, "I would prepare yourself for the trip. You leave here at nightfall."

And of course, Hugh knew the elf was right.

"Can you join us on our journey to the dock?"

"Alas, I would dearly love to, but I am chained to this place in ways I cannot explain right now. You must go on without me. You can always contact me via the sight if needed. I may only be able to visit in spirit, but it's better than nothing. Oh, and don't forget to use the protection rune on future trips."

He looked at Hugh with raised eyebrows.

Hugh remembered his close call in the sight the last time he fully entered it. He had been happily stepping in and out of the plane without using the rune for protection. This left him open to attack from darker forces that hide within the infinite space. He looked at Balinas, suddenly realising he had still yet to learn the correct rune. As if reading his mind, Balinas looked into Hugh. He saw a shape appear in his mind.

"This is the missing rune from your armour. Picture it and use it each time you wish to enter the sight."

Hugh nodded.

"Thank you, Balinas. I'm sorry I wasn't a better pupil."

"It's alright, Hugh. We covered a lot in the time we had, but now it is up to you to put it into practice. Now go and get packed. The sands of time are ebbing away."

Hugh turned on his heel and headed to his room. He thought Emily was there but was surprised to see Adelia.

"Hugh ..." she looked at him, her eyes watering up, then threw herself onto him.

"It's alright," he said, leaning back to look into her eyes. "I'll be back before you know it."

"What about us?" she asked.

"What about us?"

"I need to know, Hugh. Is it going anywhere, or are we just playing?"

Hugh felt put on the spot. His feelings for Emily were strong. But here, alone in the room with Adelia, his loins yearned for something else.

"I don't know, Just can't seem to … seem to …" He realised he couldn't find the words as he looked into her eyes. His breathing was unsteady, and he swallowed hard. He couldn't do this to himself or Emily. Then it happened.

He couldn't say how, but one moment they were standing still, the next they were on the bed. He was all over her and she over him.

But his mind was begging him to stop. He pulled away.

"What's wrong?"

"I can't," he said, looking away. "I'm sorry, I just can't."

"Oh, so that's it then? I really am second fiddle."

"Adelia, it's difficult to explain. Em and I have a bond going back decades."

But there was no point. She'd already stood up and was heading to the door, adjusting her skirt.

"You know, just for a moment, I thought maybe. Maybe he has remembered, has finally come to his senses … but … no." She turned, heading out of the door, stifling sobs as she went.

"Adelia … *Adelia!*"

But she was gone. Hugh sat on the bed, resting his head in his hands. It was all so confusing.

"What's confusing?"said Emily, who had appeared in the open doorway.

"What? Oh, nothing."

"No, come on, tell me about it."

She was frowning at him, and he could feel her searching inside his head.

"Hey, that's not fair. You know looking into people without their permission is crossing a line."

"Alright, sorry, but it's not fair to keep stringing me along like this – or *her* for that matter."

"You can refer to Adelia by name."

"I know, but she's the one trying to steal my man's affections. I know we have to sort things out, but it doesn't mean I have to like her."

There was a void where nobody spoke, but so much was said.

"So are you ever going to finish telling me what you were saying in the Chamber of Prophecy?"

"What? Oh yes." There was so much going on inside his head, that he had forgotten all about that. He opened his mind to hers so she could see his true feelings. "I was wanting to say that I truly am sorry for everything that has happened since our return. Adelia being here really threw me off my stride."

"Is that why Adelia left here in tears?"

"Oh, you saw her did you?"

"Saw her, she was a blubbering mess. What happened?"

Hugh's mind flashed back to the moments before Emily came in. He realised his attention had slipped to the moment where he and Adelia had come together, but not the conversation after. Sadly, he had also forgotten to close the link to his mind with Emily.

"Ah, I see. Well, I tell you what, when you have finally decided, please feel free to let me know."

"But, Emily, it's not what it seems ..."

"Isn't it? Then tell me what it is."

Hugh tried to find the right words, but none seemed to fit the moment. She took in a deep breath, huffed, turned and left the room.

"Emily!"

But she too had now disappeared out of sight, leaving Hugh to wallow in his own thoughts. He didn't have long, before more footsteps signalled the arrival of Barrington.

"Goodness me. The number of people coming from this room is like Main Street at lunchtime. I take it you've tied up your loose ends?"

Hugh looked to his friend, totally lost for how to explain what was happening inside his head.

"I just don't know what to do, Barrington." He put his head back in his hands.

"It appears all your chickens have come home to roost at once. The only problem being there's not enough space in the coop."

"But I've made my decision, but it seems to have gone pear-shaped again."

He explained to Barrington what had happened with Adelia, the subsequent conversation, then what had happened with Emily. He finished and looked to his friend for advice.

"What a tangled web you weave, my friend. I think Adelia may now have the message, cutting her off mid flow and all that. As for Emily, well you will need to make things up with her, again, but right now is not the time. I think you need to shelve your current issues and concentrate on the job at hand. It's impossible to decide here and now. There'll be plenty of time to mull it over on the journey."

Hugh nodded, looking up to Barrington.

"You're right as always, my good friend. Where would I be without you, eh? When do we set off?"

"That is the reason that I'm here, dear Hugh. Wanda has come to retrieve us. Apparently we are to leave on the next tide."

"Alright, thank you for letting me know."

"You're not quite getting it," said Barrington, now looking at his watch. "We have an hour before we lose the tide, and the captain is an efficient fellow. He wishes to leave right away. Apparently there have been some official folk knocking about, asking questions, and he's the kind of man who doesn't like questions. So, come on. Chop, chop."

Hugh looked at him in alarm.

"But I haven't packed!"

"Well, then I suggest you hurry. See you in the library in five minutes."

He turned and left the room, leaving Hugh flustered, stuffing what he could into his bag. Grabbing his father's book, he ran from the room, making it to the library to find everyone waiting for him.

"Ah, there you are, at last," said Balinas. "Have you seen Adelia? I thought she'd like to see you all go."

Hugh looked over to Emily, who stood tight-lipped, eyebrows raised, looking at Hugh.

"Errrm, I think we had best just get going."

"Very well," said Balinas.

A Collins family member marched up to him, carrying a large seal-pelt coat. He passed it to Balinas, uttered something in his ear, then walked off quickly.

"Barrington, your coat. I had one of the Collins retrieve it for you from your shop."

Barrington looked less than impressed.

"What wonderful thinking, Balinas. How can I *ever* repay you for such a thoughtful action."

"You can thank me later," he said, passing it to him. "I really think you will need it."

"Whatever. This thing brings bad memories, ones which I would like to forget."

Hugh thought he wasn't sounding ever so grateful, as it looked like an expensive coat. Barrington hung the coat over his shoulders, like a cape. Emily was paying him more attention, with eyebrows raised again, but Barrington let out a sigh and shook his head. Before Hugh could ask what the problem was, Balinas spoke once more.

"Oh, good here's Wanda."

"Alrighty folks, let's get this party rolling. Barrington, we will keep an eye on your shop whilst you are away. Balinas, the last of the provisions are aboard the ship, including your clock, Barrington. Oh, there's also more of the guard standing in the atrium. It's packed. They've been following me all day, and I can't seem to shake the buggers off."

"*What?*" said Hugh, Barrington and Emily in unison.

"It's alright, Balinas explained you have a tunnel to escape through, so they won't see us."

"The tunnel is in the east wing below where the fire was. The only route there is via the atrium," said Barrington, turning to Balinas.

"So, what now?"

"Never fear. I've planned for this very scenario."

"You have?" said Hugh.

"Of course. It was only a matter of time before the guards outside became braver and set foot inside the university. That and the fact I was handed this warrant five minutes ago. I'd say we've only a matter of minutes before the guards start to use their newly found powers and try to force entry into here."

"Then what do we do?" said Emily.

"All in good time, Emily," he said, still sounding not the least bit worried.

"If that good time could be sped up, we'd be rather appreciative," said Barrington, looking towards the door.

Balinas whistled a tune and the library, a hive of activity moments before, became still enough to hear a pin drop.

"Collins family. Never, since the Great War, have we needed to defend our way of life. Once more the enemy is at the gate, but this time we must stand and face them. Protect these fine people here and aid them to the east wing. Guard this room as is true to the family oath. Collins family, to your duties, if you will."

As if someone had pressed a button, the entire Collins family activated as one. They were busy picking up stacks of books, piled unbelievably high, and were heading to the main doors to the room. Balinas turned to the group.

"For now, we say goodbye here. You need to get into the scrum. The family will aid your exit to the tunnel. From that point you'll be on your own. Good luck!"

They bade each other the briefest of goodbyes then headed into the mass of books and Collinses. Hugh had never really appreciated how *many* they were. And they kept on coming, surrounding the trio plus Wanda in a moving wall of books. Somewhere in the background, they heard Balinas call out.

"Open the doors!"

The cool air of the atrium wafted through the room overhead, as the crowd surged forward as one. There were sounds of confusion, with calls from someone looking for Balinas.

"I'm telling you I *gave* him a warrant. Now let us through!"

The chaotic sound of guards attempting to push their way through the myriad of spines and parchment made it through to the escapees, followed by the sound of books dropping. From between the gaps of the tightly grouped Collinses, hands grabbed at the group, dragging them roughly through the scrum. Hugh feared they were done for, until he realised they belonged to more members of the family, pulling them away from the guards and towards the east wing. In the background Hugh heard Balinas call once more.

"Collins family. Book evacuation drill over. Return all books, and let our learned guests into the library, if you will."

The fugitives made it safely into the lower corridor of the east wing, escorted by a Collins, towards an ominous hole in the floor. The sound of muffled chaos could be heard in the atrium, and Hugh knew it wouldn't be long before someone noticed their disappearance. He saw a flagstone set aside next to the entrance of the newly formed tunnel, ready to seal the entrance at a moment's notice. The sight of rungs of a ladder disappearing into the darkness made his stomach churn, and he groaned.

"Does it really have to involve drops and ladders?"

"It does if you wish to get out of here," said their Collins guide.

"Come Hugh, it's only like the ladder at the greenhouses," said Barrington.

"Yeah, try not to fall this time," said Emily, tersely.

"Thanks, Emily, I'll try not to."

Barrington looked from one to the other.

"This is not the time for a spat!"

The sound of voices coming back into the atrium grew louder and more distinct and they jolted into action. Barrington swung round, knocking Hugh off balance, and he found himself in mid-air over the hole. He was grasping for anything, his hands finding nothing but damp air. He closed his eyes and prepared himself for the pain of a heavy landing, but it never came.

–POP–

Hugh opened his eyes, finding himself in a familiar place. He was back in the chill of the sight again. Annoyed with his lack of control, he quickly searched inside himself, looking for the runes of protection, including the new rune that Balinas had shown him. He was now surrounded by a bubble of golden protection and looked around, seeing that it appeared brighter than the last time he visited. He considered how to get himself back into the plane of the living, when Emily appeared next to him, her life link disappearing into the distance. She was still yet to learn how to enter the sight, full body.

'Thought I would find you hiding in here. You need to watch your step.'

'But Barrington knocked me in!'

'Hrmmm.'

'Em, can we at least agree to talk to each other? This is going to be a long enough trip without us quarrelling. My feelings are strong for you, but everything's been muddled since we last got back. I've barely had time to think.'

'I didn't realise I was such a distraction to you.'

'You know what I mean.'

'You know what? I don't understand anything, Hugh. Back in Morcarthia, I thought we actually had something special.'

'Oh, please don't you start as well.'

'Well, I'm sorry to be an inconvenience to you!'

'That's not what I meant.'

'Whatever. Come on, the others are waiting.'

With that Hugh felt the sensation of being pulled by his navel.

–POP–

They were back in the tunnel that Hugh nearly landed in. Barrington was leaning against the wall, chatting to Wanda.

"Ah, good, you found him. Right we need to get a moving if we're to catch this ship."

Emily marched off down the tunnel without looking back.

"What's *her* problem?" said Wanda.

"Don't ask," said Hugh. "Come on, we should get going."

The tunnellers had done an excellent job, and Hugh noticed it was easy going underfoot. As he and Emily lit their firestones, the light bounced off the surrounding walls with an eerie glow. It was a completely different experience from when they used the sally port. With its narrow passages and tight points where they needed to squeeze through, it had made the simple task of walking hard going. In comparison, this hand-hewn tunnel was a walk in the park. As they continued along, it opened up into an old lava tube. Hugh saw several more going off in various directions either side from the one they were in.

"How do we know where to go?"

"It looks as though the tunnellers have left their mark, my dear friend," said Barrington, pointing to an arrow carved into the wall. "We should be there in no time."

Hugh was grateful for the arrows, for without them, they would surely be lost. The lava tubes were rough and jagged, yet he saw tell-tale marks of the tunnelling team. The walls had been smoothed off, making the journey easier through the network. They were moving at a steady pace, having to jog through the unearthly environment.

The city's streets appeared to drain into the system from above. Sludge and effluent trickled down the walls, making the smell abhorrent. A stream ran through the tunnels, washing the remnants and stench of the world overhead toward the sea. The light from their firestones was joined by that cast down through the grates from the street. Now and then, Hugh caught the sight of something scurrying away in the shadows.

"I wouldn't want to get caught down here in a rainstorm," said Barrington.

He talked without breathing though his nose, which made him sound as though he had a cold.

"No, me neither," said Hugh. "Let's get a move on, in case it does rain."

The sound of the runners' horn echoed their way down into the alien environment. Hugh listened to the crowds cheering and thought he heard the dull thudding of the runners as they ran overhead. The stream deepened and became wider, resembling a river of slurry from the daily life of the world above. Another arrow pointed to a tunnel off to their right, away from the wretched flow. Hugh wasn't sure, but he thought he was picking up a more welcoming scent, something sweet tainting the grotty air of the city run off. As they moved onwards, he could see a pinkish glow casting down the wall, with a ladder leading up to it. Emily was already there and climbing up to the surface above. They reached the bottom of the ladder, and Barrington hesitated momentarily. Hugh looked at him.

"What's wrong?"

"You know as well as I do what lays at the top of this ladder."

"Yes, well, we all have our weaknesses."

"I know, but going there with the ladies, well, it just seems wrong, doesn't it?"

Wanda had come up behind them.

"Come on fellas, don't be shy."

She pushed passed the pair and climbed the ladder. Hugh looked at Barrington and shrugged.

"Here goes nothing," he said, before climbing up to the exit above.

Chapter 8

The Madame Domina-Noctis Tea Rooms were infamous around the city of Portis-Montis. Mme Domina-Noctis – Maud to those who knew her – was a streetwise, no-nonsense woman. She had worked her way up through the ranks of street life to become the head of her district. Anyone working in the area in any job had to be cleared by her first, and woe betide you if you got on the wrong side of her. She was currently welcoming the latest would-be clients into the tea shop.

She could easily have blended in with the walls, wearing a flowing pink number. But she stood out, bedecked from head to toe in jewellery. Leaving nothing to the imagination, her corset bulged at the seams. She wore the sweetest scent that money could buy, purchased for her from the finest Portis-Montis perfumier – a gift from a regular customer in port. Her face was caked in enough to make-up to give the local acting troupe a run for their money, with lips that were painted a glossy rose red, and she had eyelashes that would not look out of place on a camel.

"Well, my dears, it's a lovely surprise to see you here so early. I was told to expect you around nightfall. This is most unexpected." The sibilants sounded sharp on her teeth, and it was as if it were impossible for her to talk without her lips being pursed.

"It came as a surprise to us, I can assure you," said Wanda, looking around the room.

They were standing in a waiting area of sorts. The walls were draped in loose flowing material which covered the lights. The room was lit with a pink glow, and the air was heavily scented. Wanda and Emily stood in awkward silence, the only sound above the music was a strange cracking noise. Then someone somewhere let out a howl. Hugh and Barrington finally clambered out of the hole and took in their surroundings.

"Oh, how nice it is to see some familiar faces," said Maude.

"Ah, Maude," said Barrington, clearing his throat. "What a pleasant surprise."

If it weren't for the pink light they were bathed in, Hugh could have sworn that his friend was radiating with embarrassment.

"Wait, are you telling me you have both been here *before*?" said Emily.

Maude looked genuinely amused.

"Well, obviously they've been through my doors, what man hasn't? Though I wouldn't drop them in it by name. It's a customer confidentiality thing." She turned to Hugh and Barrington. "I was just saying to these two fine ladies that I was surprised to see you. Not to worry, I'm sure we can rustle up some ladies for you two."

She turned to Emily and Wanda.

"I'm afraid we won't have nothing for you, my dears, unless you like the female persuasion?"

Emily look annoyed.

"Erm … no thank you."

"Not to worry, not to worry. I only ask, because … well you never know these days, do you?"

Emily and Wanda looked back, open-mouthed.

"Careful standing like that in here. Some of our clientele might mistake you for two of my girls. Of course, you can always join the workforce."

Wanda shook her head.

"You have to be joking, luv."

"Oh no, my dears. With such beautiful faces, you two would go down a treat with our regulars." She rubbed a hand down Wanda's smooth face, and Wanda shivered.

"No? Well, keep us in mind, if you're ever short of work."

She left the two ladies looking aghast, turning to Hugh and Barrington.

"Now then boys, can we serve you anything today?"

She rang a little handbell on the counter, and a gaggle of scantily clad, giggling women came through from the back.

Hugh coughed and loosened his collar with his finger.

"Well, I suppose—"

"Don't you dare, Hugh Geber!" said Emily, grabbing Hugh by the ear.

"You neither, Barrington Delphin!" said Wanda, following Emily's lead.

Anyone walking down the Alley of Iniquity would have seen two men being led out of the Mme Domina-Noctis Tea Shop by their ears, a not entirely unusual sight for this street.

"Ow, ow, ow, *ow*! Stop it, will you?" said Hugh.

"Wanda, gerroff me!" said Barrington.

Emily rounded on them both.

"You should be ashamed of yourselves, the pair of you!"

Hugh and Barrington looked at their feet. A gaggle of women had made it onto the balcony above the shop. They were giggling at the pair whilst Emily berated them.

"But it's not as bad as it seems," Hugh pleaded.

"Is it not? Why don't you enlighten us," she said. "What it is then?"

She stood, tapping her foot, moving her tongue around her mouth. Barrington also fell mute.

"No? I thought as much. You listen to me now. Is it not bad enough that we find ourselves dragged off on another adventure to god knows where, only to discover that the tunnel comes out in a … a … *knocking shop*!"

She practically shrieked the last words out, causing more attention to be drawn in their direction.

"Tea rooms, if you will me dear," said Maude from within the tea rooms. "Knocking shop is so last century."

Emily looked through the door, tight lipped and wide eyed, before continuing.

"It's bad enough that we surfaced here, only to find out you are a *frequent customer*. You do realise these places are outlawed in Skellig-Krieg. Many lives have been improved because of it."

"Em, please. Try and keep your voice down. If you'd just listened to me for a second."

"Don't you dare call me *Em*, Hugh Geber!" Hugh winced at each word. "What? Am I embarrassing you, eh? You disgust me."

She folded her arms and turned her back on him.

"Emily, please, hear Hugh out. I think you've got the wrong angle on this, and you're overreacting just a little here," said Barrington, causing Emily to turn round and give him a look of indignation.

"Oh, you can keep you trap shut, Barrington," said Wanda, beating Emily to a response whilst jabbing a finger into his chest. "I wouldn't associate you with this kind of so-called *tea shop*. Frankly, I thought more highly of you than that. I wouldn't be seen dead around here. To think I was looking after *your* shop for you, whilst you attended to *urgent business*. The cat's out of the bag now, eh?"

Emily tutted in disgust.

"Well? What have you got to say for yourselves?"

She and Wanda stood with their lips pursed and arms tightly folded.

"*Run?*"

"What?" said Emily, before hearing the barrage of whistles coming down from Main Street.

Before they could move, a man stumbled out of the open doorway, mid-way through getting dressed.

"I'll see ye next time I'm in port, luv!" he shouted to the half-dressed woman leaning on the doorframe and holding a whip.

"I'll look forward to it," she said with a wink. "Oh, hello, Mr Delphin, long time no see. I can hide you in here if you're quick."

Barrington politely smiled at her.

"He'll do no such thing," said Wanda, clipping him around the ear.

"Ow!"

"Suit yourself," said the woman, returning into the tea rooms.

They watched the man who had pushed past them run down the street, weaving from left to right. He stumbled and dropped something – though they couldn't see what it was. He deftly picked it up, rubbed it on his shirt and then seemed to hit himself in the face with it, before resuming his run from the approaching guards.

"Wait a minute," said Barrington, "was that—"

"No time, Barrington," said Hugh, grabbing his friend by the collar and dragging him away from the city guards. "We need to get out of here."

"What are the city guards doing inside the Den of Thieves?"

"I don't know. But if you stay here long enough, you'll be able to ask them! *Run!*"

The group ran towards the docks followed by the sound of whistles. Everyone in the area stopped to watch the commotion. They reached the quays, out of breath and with no time to stop. As his feet skidded across the cobbles, Hugh took in the great steamers in front of him. They all looked grand in the evening light.

"So which ship is it?"

"This way," said Wanda, leading the group away from the larger vessels towards the smaller piers.

"Where are you going?" said Barrington. "Won't we need one of these big ships for where we are heading?"

"Nah mate, none of those crews were willing to do it, even with the large amount of money on offer. But I found someone who agreed to take you. It's just down here."

They rounded the corner and saw a ramshackle, wooden sailboat which looked way beyond its certificate of seaworthiness. The man that ran out from the tea rooms was also heading for the same boat, shouting orders to the crew members as he jumped aboard. Hugh was the first of the group to reach the gangplank and stopped to catch his breath.

"Don't just wait there, m'lad, step aboard, hurry!" said the man.

Hugh did but tripped, falling headlong into the waiting man. Something popped out of his face, bounced, then rolled across the ship's deck.

"Dang and blasted barnacles! Don't let it roll off the edge!"

A crew member dropped the rope he was pulling.

"Aye, aye, Captain," he said and saluted the man.

The rope he dropped whipped back, catching the crew member around the ankle. He was whisked upwards, dangling by his ankle, screaming all the way.

"Ye blitherin' idiot!"

The captain jumped onto the end of the rope before it disappeared. "Will someone stop that ruddy thing rolling away?"

Emily, who was following Hugh, stopped it with her foot. It turned out to be a glass eye, and Emily grimaced as she passed it back to the captain, whereupon he put it in his mouth to clean it before replacing it into his empty socket. Barrington and Wanda were still standing on the quayside.

"Come on, get aboard," said Hugh.

"I have to stay here," said Wanda. "Someone needs to look after the shops."

"Well, thank you for all you have done for us. We owe you a debt of gratitude," said Barrington. "I will do my best to keep you posted on our progress."

"I'm sure you will. Now hurry," she said urgently, the sound of whistles getting closer. "In fact, I'm going to scarper out of here m'self. See ya, mate!" She darted from the quayside into the bustling dockside.

"Quickly, Barrington," said Hugh, who was panicking about the city guards heading into the pontoon. He didn't fancy the outcome if they were caught. "What are you waiting for?"

Before looking at Hugh, he waited for Wanda to disappear.

"I'm not getting on that thing, especially not with him." He pointed to the captain. He appeared to be looking at them, whilst not looking at them.

"Well, yiv a choice. Sail with me or get arrested by them." The captain, pointed vaguely towards the dock, to the right of where the city guards were now amassing. "Hoist the mainsail, lads, cast off. Lift the gangplank!"

All around Hugh, the crew jumped into action and prepared to raise the gangplank. Hugh turned to Barrington.

"*Well*?" he said in desperation.

"Oh, *dang it!*" said Barrington, as he ran up onto the ship.

The plank was lifted, the sails billowed out, catching the evening breeze coming from the mountains. The ship lumbered and creaked to life, and the quayside drifted away, along with the threat of the city guards catching them. It wasn't long before they passed the safety of the harbour wall, and the smooth sensation was replaced by the gentle swaying of being at sea. Hugh was sitting on the deck with Emily and Barrington, looking for an answer to his friend's behaviour.

"Do you want to explain what happened?"

"I'd rather not."

"It'll be a long trip if nobody talks to each other." He looked at his friend, waiting for an answer.

"Alright, but you probably won't believe me."

"Try me."

"Fine. The person who we saw running out of the tea rooms—"

"Knocking shop," Emily cut in.

"Alright, *knocking shop,* was a face I didn't think I'd have to set eyes upon again. We kicked him out of the navy for being incompetent.

There was little chance of him progressing from the basic training, let alone being a captain of a vessel. Today has shown me to be wrong once more, and now, well …"

"Now yer stuck on me ship." The captain had come over to peak to his latest cargo, a toothless smile plastered across his face. "Monty Shackleton, at yer service."

He held out a hand for Hugh to shake, except it was about two feet to his right. Hugh stood to shake it, and the captain moved again. He looked at Barrington, who shrugged. Hugh grabbed the captain's hand, before he could move it any further, shaking it firmly.

"Hugh Geber, I uh…"

He attempted to make eye contact, but they seemed to move around. The glass eye had a mind of its own, wandering off somewhere of its own accord. His good eye seemed to struggle to stay focussed on any single point, at any given time. The captain had scraggly hair sticking out from under his tricorne hat, and a face worn away by many years spent at sea. His leather boots were cracked, and his long coat needed a good waxing. He was one wooden leg away from being a fully-fledged pirate. Hugh released the hand, sitting back down. He was starting to feel rough from the swaying. Shackleton turned to face somewhere over Barrington's left shoulder.

"Well, well, well. Ain't you a sight fir sore eyes."

"Hmmm," said Barrington, trying to lean into the man's gaze. "If this is your ship, which I highly doubt, then would you kindly tell me its name? I was under the impression that an unregistered captain could not sail a named ship from this port."

"Ah, that's where you are wrong. I have a licence … of sorts, and you're on *A Ship With No Name.*"

"What? That's preposterous. You can't have a ship with no name; it's bad luck, I tell you! We need to leave this ship immediately. If you can call it a ship."

He looked around in disgust.

"Barrington, we're at sea now," said Hugh. "If we go back, we'll be arrested, which leaves us with little option but to go forward. I'm not overly keen on this trip either, but it looks as though our fate has been sealed."

"Hugh, this ship has no name. Don't you see the danger we are in?"

He looked at Hugh, who stared back, confused.

"If we go to sea on a ship with no name, it's bad luck, and we'll need all the luck we can get, especially if this is our captain."

Hugh looked at Shackleton, who gave the door two feet to his right a nod and a wink.

"The captain just told us the ship's name. You're just not following it, and I can confirm that I saw it before we boarded. We are on, if I am not mistaken, *A Ship With No Name.*"

The words slowly sank in, as Barrington stood open-mouthed.

"Oh, I don't believe it," he finally said in dismay.

"Thas right, I found a little loophole in that system of yers, which let me name me ship, without naming it, if that makes sense. Some might say the tables 'as turned. Yer my ship boy now!"

"I'm nobody's *ship boy,* and I ain't, I mean, I'm *not* taking orders from you."

He sat down and pulled out his pipe and began roughly packing it.

"Put that away, now!"

"*No!*"

"This is my ship, and if I says put that away, you'll bloody well do so!"

He went to grab the pipe, missed, swiping Barrington across the face, sending the pipe flying. The captain smiled another toothless grin and laughed a raspy sort of chuckle, pleased to have made his point, whilst Emily and Hugh did all they could to stop Barrington fighting back. The action stopped as the pipe bounced off the deck and into the air. Everyone watched as it seemed to move in slow motion.

"*Nooo,* not my pipe!" said Barrington, breaking free of the hold that was upon him, and he lunged towards the moving object. He nearly made it, yet his fingers clasped at the fresh air. The pipe was going to be lost to the sea when someone grabbed it. Hugh and Emily lunged after Barrington to prevent him form going overboard. He landed chin first at the holder's feet, with Hugh and Emily landing heavily onto the deck bedside him. Barrington looked up and gasped. There on the deck, holding the pipe in her hand, was Heather McDougall.

Chapter 9

Smithson ran for the side of the *Fey Flyer,* heaving up over the side, as the spray from a wave splashed him across the face. He spat the salty, vomit taste from his mouth, before heading back to lie on he floor. It had been a day and a half, and he was not a lover of sailing. They were just entering the area that Captain Johnson called the Sea of Lost Souls. Initially, he thought the captain was making a fuss when he said he was not happy with the itinerary, but seeing as the money was good, he decided it was worth the risk.

Smithson made it back into the safety of the area clean enough for passengers. Collins was in deep conversation with Captain Johnson, who looked up at Smithson.

"I see you are still yet to find your sea legs, Mr Smithson. We'll make a sailor out of you yet, there's plenty of time."

"If this is the Sea of Lost Souls, I can see why you were hesitant to come," said Smithson, swallowing hard.

"This? Why, this is nothing. We are another good day's sailing from the Sea of Lost Souls. No, this is just the Bay of Mariners Past."

"The Bay of Mariners Past? These names must be made up, man."

"I wish they were, Mr Smithson, but like I said at the onset, this trip is perilous, not to be taken lightly. No, I'm afraid the worst is still yet to come."

Collins stood, shaking his head.

"You will have to forgive my *overlord*. He's nowhere near as well travelled as he thinks."

"I beg your pardon, *Collins*. I may be a little seasick, but that does not give you the right to insult me in that way."

"Of course, sir. My sincere apologies."

"Get back to the cabin and find that damn apprentice of yours. He was last seen on deck, sending his lunch into the sea."

Johnson stood between Smithson and Collins.

"I think you will find I was mid-conversation with Mr Collins, before you walked in."

"Yes, well, he's my servant and shall do as *I* ask."

"Maybe in normal times, yes, but we are at sea. Therefore, I am in charge of everything and *everyone*. If I wish to finish my conversation with Mr Collins, then that is what I shall do, have I made myself clear? And one more thing. He may be here to assist your needs, Mr Smithson, but I assure you, I will not tolerate any abusing of staff whilst aboard *my* ship."

He stood wide eyed, giving no ground.

Smithson stood like a goldfish, his mouth noiselessly opening and closing. Collins stood smugly behind the captain's back. Lost for words, Smithson stormed from the room, leaving Collins to finish his conversation with Johnson.

Chapter 10

Hugh, Barrington and Emily were piled up on deck, with the first and latter still on Barrington's back. They were all staring in amazement at Heather.

"Are ye going to say hello? After all, I travelled all day to join in with yer wee trip."

"Heather? What are you doing here?" said Barrington, his face turning into a full-blown smile.

He shook Hugh and Emily off and stood up. They embraced, whilst everyone looked in the opposite direction. They parted with a loud suction noise.

"Oh, it's great to see you again."

"Aye, I can see that," she said, looking flustered.

"How on earth did you get here?"

"Oh, I arrived on the morning flight from Bansk. Balinas said to come straight to the boat, said something about half the city guard camped outside the university? Anyways, it was nae hard to find, nae compared to all the other ships. Captain Shackleton said to make myself at home, as he had some business to tend to whilst in port."

"I think 'captain' is a strong word to use for Monty."

"Why? Oh, yer referring to his eye issues."

"They're a bit more than issues. The damn man can't see straight."

"Don't judge a sailor by his pipe. The rest of the crew have reassured me he is fine. All yiv to do is point him in the right direction. Besides …"

"What?"

"Oh, nothing."

"No, you were about to say something," said Barrington. "Come on, you can tell me."

"It was nothing really," she said, "just superstition, thas all."

"Ah, I see now. Well, I don't believe in the 'no women on boats' rule. You silly sausage, you shouldn't have been so afraid to tell me that."

She looked back with regret.

"There's more, isn't there?" he asked.

Heather nodded and let out a sigh.

"This is the only working ship willing to take female passengers, plus those who …" She took in a deep breath. "… who've sunk at sea."

"Ah, I see."

"Thas all it was really, I'm sure naebody meant any offence."

He turned to look away from her.

"Anyway, I've just been waiting for all of yese to turn up. I take it all the noise earlier was yir arrival, then?"

"Errrm, yes, it was," he said, turning back to face her, looking relieved to be talking about something else. "We seemed to have attracted the attention of the local authorities again."

"Naething changes, eh?" She looked at Hugh and Emily. "It's alright yese two. Ye can look again."

They were doing an excellent job at not looking in their friend's direction, whilst also ignoring each other. They turned to face the reunited couple. Emily walked, slow at first, but speeding up as she reached her half-sister. They hugged and giggled.

"It's great to see you, Heather. Thank you for all the letters."

"Aye, ye too, Em. Oh, Dad says to give ye a wee extra hug for him and to remind you to stay out of trouble."

"What's he like, eh? He's always looking out for us, even when he's hundreds of miles away."

"I know, but he cares. Ye know how he is about his daughters." Heather turned to Hugh, and her manner seemed to change. "Hugh."

"Hi Heather, how are you?"

"I'm good, thank ye." She looked around, as if expecting someone else. "Just ye is it?"

"Yes, why do you ask?"

He looked at Emily. She folded her arms and cocked her head to the side.

"Oh, I just thought you may have had yer new girlfriend with ye, thas all." Heather went and stood next to Emily, mirroring her position.

Barrington looked on in amusement, as he watched his friend attempt to get out of the corner he was backed into.

Hugh took a deep breath in, then faced up to the challenge.

"Right, now we're all reunited, let's get some things straight. First, Adelia is not my girlfriend. Yes, she and I may or may not have a history, but that's nobody's business but ours. Second, I've been so choked up these past few months with both Adelia and Emily both vying for my attention…" – Emily scoffed – "No, let me finish. When you don't get the required answer, you both storm off, or don't give me time to think. Is there any wonder I've been confused?"

"Aye, but yer loyalty should lie with Emily."

"I can't wipe out my past, as though it never happened. Whatever occurred between Adelia and myself is over, not that it was anything to begin with. If you had let me finish before you left the room at the university, I was about to tell you I sorted out where I stand with Adelia, and that I really do love you. It always has been you."

Emily and Heather stood in stunned silence. Barrington frowned at Hugh.

"You've always sworn that nothing happened between you and Adelia. Is this not the case, then? If so, why lie to me?"

Hugh turned to Barrington.

"Thank you for your support," he said before turning back to Emily. "Nothing happened between me and Adelia in the past. She wanted to, but I said no. Does that clear up any situation that may be outstanding?"

"I suppose," said Emily. "But it doesn't clear up the situation after our return to Portis-Montis."

"Oh, for goodness sake! If anything happened, it would be through no fault of mine. You try fending off two women at once."

"Ach, it must be so hard to fend them all off. Yiv got a brain, Hugh. Why not try using it once in a wee while? Where does Emily stand in all this? Ye hivnae been truthful with her. Just a bit of honesty is all thas required, nothin' else."

"She makes a good point there," said Barrington.

"You can hardly claim the moral high ground, Barrington Delphin," said Emily. "What about the knocking shop?"

Heather turned to her.

"What are ye talking about, Em?"

"Oh, did Barrington not tell you? Let me fill you in. The men have a penchant for ladies of the night."

Heather turned to look at Barrington, open-mouthed.

"What?"

"Now… err… hang on one moment. Let's not forget, this is about Hugh and Emily, not me."

Heather raised her hand and slapped Barrington across the face. This was quickly followed by Emily's hand coming across Hugh's cheek. Heather and Emily stormed off, leaving Hugh and Barrington to nurse their wounds.

"Thanks, mate!" said Hugh, who turned and walked off in the opposite direction, leaving Barrington on his own.

Monty, who had been watching the ensuing fight with interest, now made his way across the deck. He lit a pipe. Barrington went to protest, but the captain cut him off mid breath.

"My ship, my rules. I know how much ye love your pipe, so it gave me great pleasure to say no, but I'm no heathen. Ye can join me fir a smoke."

Barrington's eyes lit up with the prospect of finally being able to light his pipe. He reached into his pocket, then looked shocked, as he patted down the rest of his body. He slapped a hand to his forehead.

"I don't believe it."

"What's wrong now?"

"My pipe. Heather has it!"

"Ah, Delphin's luck comes back to haunt him again. I see yer still up to the same old shenanigans, eh?"

"What's that supposed to mean?"

"Which part? The luck or the shenanigans?"

"Both, actually."

"It's well known that a crew that sales under a Delphin normally ends up in some sort of trouble. Looks like the same theory goes with possessions too."

"I'd rather not talk about that right now."

"Heh, I bet."

"And the other comment?"

"Oh, that, yeah. Ye can't deny that, even in the short time that I was working under yerself, ye had a fair number of, well, liaisons, shall we call them, who were keen to get their point across to ye and leave their mark."

Barrington rubbed his cheek.

"But I'm not one to hold grudges," said Shackleton, "even if ye were key to my naval career ending."

"You fired a gun at one of our own ships!"

"Hrmmm, good point. But the fact is I didn't do it on purpose.

Honestly, I was really aiming for the pirate ship to the right. It's just the gun wasn't calibrated to my eyes," he said, and Barrington watched as they split apart, and then came back together.

"Tell that to the crew of the SS Bansk. Poor buggers never stood a chance. That was a nice ship, too. Surely you can tell the difference between a navy ship and a pirate ship?"

"Anyway, what I'm saying is I have me own ship now, with a crew that's willing to listen to me. Let bygones be bygones, I say. Here…" He pulled out a spare pipe and handed it to Barrington. "Think of it as a peace offering until ye get yers back."

Barrington hesitated before taking the pipe. He wiped the mouthpiece thoroughly and inspected it. It was longer than his own pipe.

"My, is this a real Phoenix long smoker?"

"Certainly is."

"Wow. I've always wanted one of these. Where on earth did you find it?"

"I inherited it but never got to grips with the thing. It stays alight in all weathers and underwater too. It's still packed, if I remember correctly."

"Well, I am honoured to be its next keeper," he said, taking the small lid off the end. On first inspection, it looked as though it was full of ash, but the glow at the bottom told him otherwise. He admired it and prepared to smoke it.

"Uh oh, here comes trouble," said Shackleton, pointing over Barrington's right shoulder.

He followed the finger to an empty deck, then looked to the left and saw Hugh coming towards him.

"I will smoke you soon, I promise," he said to the pipe, as he replaced the cap and put the pipe away. "Come back to grovel, have you?"

"No," said Hugh.

"Oh, then what do you want?"

"I was just over there, sitting, when it came to me. We're both in the same boat."

"Well, technically it's a ship, and yer on it, rather than in it," said Shackleton.

Hugh and Barrington stopped to look at him.

"What? Don't let me get between a good argument," he said, with his hands raised in the air. He turned to look at the passing view as Barrington and Hugh walked off to talk.

"Go on then, I'm all ears," said Barrington.

"First, we shouldn't be fighting. We have known each other a long time. I know everything's been stressful at the library, but things are not as clearcut as they first appear."

Barrington let out a deep sigh.

"Alright, maybe things have got out of hand, and maybe I could've been a more supportive friend, but you haven't helped yourself much these past few weeks. I've had Emily in tears on my shoulder more than once. Oh yes, it might be news to you, but there have been many times I have had to console her. You know you talk in your sleep? Well, anyway, you revealed a bit more information than Emily wanted to hear, and she's taken it to heart. Not only that, but you seem to have the ability to project your thoughts into her head when sleeping, so there's no wonder she's opted to sleep in a different room.

"Now I support you with the fact that troubles of the heart are never easy to deal with, but they're also something that should not be ignored. You've made you're decision, but I think Emily will need more than words. It's been tough for all involved."

Hugh nodded, letting out a long, steady breath.

"I know it's been hard. Nothing has ever really happened between me and Adelia, all bar the odd moment."

Barrington looked at him with raised eyebrows.

"No, nothing like that. A hug and kiss is all. When times were hard, we helped each other. Sometimes we were the only people we had to talk to. I know you were always there for me, but it wasn't the same. One night she left with the children, no note, no goodbye. It hurt, almost as much as Emily leaving. Seeing her again at the university, in familiar surroundings, sent my world into a tailspin. Does that make sense?"

"It does; however, it doesn't make it any easier on anyone, including yourself. You have a lot of soul searching to do. I apologise for being petty earlier. I should've enquired further about your troubles, rather than taking just one side of the story. Remember that I'm here for you, my friend. Now then, you mentioned something about being in the same boat?"

"Yes, regarding the tea rooms. I don't know about you, but it has been many years since I frequented that place. I never thought I'd return there. But here we both are, after an unexpected trip, with ghosts from our past. What?"

"It may have been many years for you."

Hugh raised his eyebrows. Barrington glanced away.

"Nothing since Heather, of course, but still…" He momentarily disappeared off into a thought. "Ha, there was this one girl, blonde hair, beautiful eyes, can't remember her name though?"

"Janie!"

"That's it, Janie. She was good …"

"She sure was …"

There was a pause whilst the realisation set in. They looked at each other and grimaced. Barrington eventually broke the tension.

"We never speak of this again. Agreed?"

"Agreed," said Hugh.

Barrington moved the conversation on as quick as he could.

"So what to do about the ladies?"

"I think we tackle it head on. I'm not willing to let it fester."

"Right you are," said Barrington. "Shall we find them?"

"Yes, they went through that door."

Barrington marched up to the door and opened it.

"After you."

"No, no, you can go ahead."

"Really, I insist."

He placed a firm hand into the middle of Hugh's back, pushing him through the door. Barrington followed, and the door closed behind him, plunging the small room into darkness. Hugh's eyes slowly adjusted to the light. A lamp was gently swinging on its bracket, all sooted up with smoke. Hammocks lined the walls, swaying gently with the ship's motion. They walked towards a door at the far end, with bright light streaming in through the edges. Over the creaking of the ship, they heard muffled voices, showing that Emily and Heather were in there.

Hugh and Barrington looked at each other. Then down at the door handle. Both came to the same realisation. They fought each other to reach the handle first, after a small scuffle and a kick in the shin, Hugh won the battle. The talking in the room ceased at the disturbance, showing the occupants were awaiting their entry.

"After you," said Hugh, holding out his free arm as he opened the door.

Barrington flared his nostrils before walking in and changing his face to a pleading smile. The bright light was a contrast to the previous room they had been in, both men having to shield their eyes until they adjusted. What they revealed was a daunting scene. Emily and Heather were sitting at a table in front of a window, bathed in the evening light. He had to admit that, if it weren't for the stern look they were giving him, Emily looked beautiful.

"Well?" she said, making them jump.

"I … erm … I mean to say … Well, look here …" Barrington began.

Hugh didn't want to say anything, but he thought his friend's opening gambit was, thus far, a tad weak.

"Hugh would like to say something. Hugh."

He bowed out of the way, leaving Hugh to take the floor. He gulped as the two women looked at him, tight-lipped. He looked at Emily. In this light, with the sun shining through the window, she looked amazing.

"Hugh, pull yourself together and get on with it," she said aloud.

Though she was stern, he couldn't help but notice she had turned the slightest bit rosy.

He tried to use this to his advantage. "Emily … dearest Em…"

She rolled her eyes.

"Emily, we have known each other for many years and there are many secrets we hold. You had a secret unicorn—"

"And you slept with prostitutes. I hardly see how these marry up."

"Alright, when you put it like that, it sounds, well, a tad …"

"Dirty?"

"Well …"

"Ghastly?"

"Yes, but …"

"Grim, worthless, degrading? Taking advantage of women who are in a bad situation? It doesn't matter how you word it. It's wrong."

"Emily, you must understand," he said. "I was younger back then; I had needs."

"Oh well, if it was only needs, that makes it all okay."

"No hang on, let me reword this. Are you telling me you have never strayed off the beaten track? Never spent a night with someone?"

When Emily turned and looked out of the window, Hugh took a step forward.

"See, we're not so different."

"But it wasn't that person's job. Who knows who they've been with?"

Hugh glanced quickly at Barrington, before Emily turned to face him again. He quickly closed his mind, hoping she didn't choose this moment to look inside.

"You'll have to go a long way to prove I can trust you, Hugh. You too Barrington, Heather is really hurt by what she heard today."

The pair looked at the floor.

Heather cleared her throat awkwardly.

"Well, whilst we are clearing the air, there was this one man …"

Chapter 11

The trip to the Sea of Lost Souls was still over two days' sailing away. As the group of friends had come to an uneasy truce, they started planning for what might come their way. However, as they approached the Sea of Lost Souls, Barrington was becoming more fretful. He had taken to hiding away below decks, spending more of his time working on the clock, attempting to avoid thinking about the upcoming events on their journey. They were passing through the Bay of Mariners Past. Hugh was struggling with his breakfast, which was attempting to make a second appearance. He tried to take his mind off the sensation by helping his friend with the clock.

It was reassembled and now looking as it did in Portis-Montis. Hugh was amazed, for Barrington had not only got it working, but it was almost accurate. His friend was running between the clock and a large sea chart on the table next to him. Hugh saw a red line, marking their progress across the seas, noticing the Sea of Lost Souls was coming ever closer. The ship took an uneasy lurch downwards, and Hugh held a hand to his mouth, swallowing hard. He couldn't help noticing that Barrington had the shakes.

"Are you alright?"

"Yes, why?"

"You seem a little preoccupied with the clock, that's all."

"Well, it won't build itself, Hugh, will it, dear boy?"

"Hrmmm. You've missed three of the planning meetings. From a friend's perspective, I would say that you're trying to hide away."

"What? Come on, Hugh. What do I have to worry about?" He didn't sound too confident in his words. "No, I have to get this finished. This will change the world of sailing forever."

He carried on, beavering away. Hugh pulled out the watch that Balinas had given to him in the library, checking its time, with the large clock face in front of him.

"My watch reads one minute past the hour, yours is one minute to."

"Yes, well, maybe your watch is wrong. Have you thought about that?"

"But mine's an Ever-Right. You can't get more accurate than that."

"Ridiculous. This is the greatest clock the world has ever seen. I'm able to mark out on the charts where we are. You're just jealous that my clock is more accurate than yours!"

He was looking and sounding like a madman.

"Are you sure you're alright. It's normal to feel uneasy about the current situation, given all you've been through, but you can talk to me about it."

He was cut short by the clock whirring into action. The fanfare struck up, and the mini-Collins family figures appeared.

"Blasted figurines, climbing over my ruddy clock," said Barrington over the racket.

His ranting disappeared as the fanfare reached its usual crescendo. Hugh had already covered his ears, in preparation for the donkey bird's call. This was fast becoming a bone of contention aboard the ship. Whenever the clock chimed, the crew threatened to destroy it, especially in the middle of the night. Eventually, the hourly show came to a stop, and Hugh released his hands from his ears. The sound of footsteps on the stairs into the room was followed by someone falling down the stairs, swearing loudly.

"Bugger!"

It was Shackleton. Hugh rushed to his aid, but the captain pushed him away.

"It'll be alright, get yer hands off of me. This ain't the first time I've fallen down these stairs," he said, showing his toothless smile once more.

He got up and looked at Barrington.

"Can't ye disable that thing? It's making the crew restless, which in turn makes me restless."

"I'm yet to find the lever installed to switch it off. My home help thought it would be fun to hide it somewhere in … *there.*" Barrington gestured at the whole clock.

"Wossit supposed to be, anyway?"

"I was wondering when you were going to ask. This is the clock that will revolutionise sailing and shipping as it stands today."

"Oh … right. Wossit called then?"

"Eh?"

"It's got to have a name, ain't it? *The clock that will revolutionise sailing and shipping as it stands today* is a bit of a mouthful, doncha think?"

"It's called … a DST clock."

"What the hell does that stand for?"

"Donkey Standard Time," he said proudly.

"Oh, right," said Shackleton with a shrug. "If it's all the same, I'll stick to me pocket watch."

He pulled out a grubby timepiece and opened it. As he did so, the watch Hugh was holding onto started to vibrate.

"Is that an Ever-Right?" he asked Shackleton.

"Sure is. I take it yers is too, judging by the way mine's quivering." He then did a double take between Barrington's clock and his watch. "It's two minutes out, just thought ye ought to know. He turned to leave the room, walked into a support post, swore, then realigned himself for the stairs.

"Two minutes out. Huh, what does he know?" said Barrington.

"Well, that's two of us," said Hugh, "so there might be something in it."

"I think it's accurate."

"What are you talking about? It can't claim to be the most accurate clock in the world, when it's obviously not."

Barrington huffed and his shoulders dropped in resignation.

"Come on, let's go find the ladies."

He rolled up his charts, and they headed upstairs. The deck was slippery underfoot and the air full of the smell of seaweed. Hugh had to grip onto the deck rail to prevent him sliding around. The wind was strong, and the rain was coming sideways. They struggled to the door leading to the sleeping quarters.

As soon as they were out of the weather, Hugh felt instantly warmer. He reached into his shirt, pulled out the firestone, and activated the heat mode. As he and Barrington walked quietly through to the back room, passing sleeping sailors in their hammocks, they were dripping wet and giving off a misty haze. When they entered the cabin, Heather looked up.

"Yese two look wet," she said with a chuckle.

Emily sat, nodding.

"You certainly do. Barrington, why aren't you using your coat? It's *perfect* for this weather."

Barrington stood tight-lipped, staring at Emily, thinking up a suitable retort.

"Wouldn't want to get it wet, *would I?*"

Hugh and Heather looked at the pair, confused as to what was going on. Hugh decided they wouldn't be getting any information and sat down at the small table.

"What have you found out so far?" He suppressed a burp. Emily leaned back in her chair, looking under the table.

"You alright?" she said, scrabbling around on the floor for something.

She pulled out a bucket and passed it to him. The sight of this was enough to trigger his system into action, and he left the room, retching. He came back five minutes later, looking pale and wet.

"Did that do the job?" she asked.

Hugh nodded, wiping some excess water off his face.

"I went to tip it out overboard, got drenched."

Emily wrinkled up her nose.

"Best keep hold of the bucket." She tapped him on the leg, and it squelched. "The captain says we are close to the Sea of Lost Souls."

"What?" said Barrington, unfurling his charts. "But according to my calculations we're at least half a day away?"

"Yes, he said not to rely on your charts."

She gave him a sympathetic look. A vein throbbed on the side of Barrington's head. He took the charts, screwed and ripped them up, screaming. The others flinched. Once the sheets were suitably destroyed, with bits of paper slowly fluttering to the floor, he retook his seat at the table, breathing deeply. Everyone sat staring at him, not wanting to trigger another outburst. Hugh looked at his friend warily.

"Better?"

Barrington nodded but said nothing. Emily took in a deep breath and continued.

"Alright, well, the captain says we'll know when we enter the Sea of Lost Souls. There will be a brief time when all goes calm."

Hugh looked at her in confusion.

"Calm?"

"Yes, calm. It's hard to believe going through these waters."

"Oh, that'll be much better."

"Hrmmm, you may want to re-think that. We'll have to pass a test if we are to be guaranteed safe passage."

"What *sort* of test?"

"He said we may have to step up to the mark. He insisted that neither he nor any of the crew will do it."

"But, surely they are the best suited for the job. Any test out here must involve water or the sea. I can't envisage anything too hard for them."

Barrington begun laughing, making them all jump.

"There's so much you all have to learn. There's a reason I dislike travelling this route, and why other sailors avoid the area like the plague. The Rhyming Minch."

"The *what*?"

"The Rhyming Minch, Hugh. Once we enter their waters, there'll be no turning back. You either pass their test or follow the rest of the poor souls who sailed here and were lost."

"That explains why the captain was annoyed they couldn't find the Portis-Montis poets," said Heather.

They all turned to look at her.

"What? I told ye earlier, Barrington, he went to run some errands on shore. He told me he had no luck, that they'd all gone."

"What, all of them?" said Barrington.

"Aye."

"But there's fifty of them. They can't all have gone?"

"Apparently, they left on an earlier voyage. Someone wanted to be sure they'd get a clear passage."

"Egads, that spells doom for us all!"

"I wouldn't be so sure of that, Barrington," said Hugh.

"If you think there's a poet within that motley crew, then be my guest, go find him. This is ridiculous. We need to turn this ship around before it's too late." He banged a fist on the table, making the goblets rattle.

"I fear we may be past that point," said Emily, her eyes widening.

"How so?"

Emily didn't need to answer the question. It was clear to all that the swaying motion of the ship had eased. Heather grabbed a hold of Barrington's hand.

"We're all doomed!"

"I wouldn't say that," said Hugh, waggling a finger in the air.

"Oh really? I suppose yer hiding a wee poet in that bag of yers, are ye?"

"Not exactly in the bag," he said, gesturing to himself.

"Hugh, my dear friend. You aren't seriously telling me, that you class *yourself* as a poet," said Barrington.

He, Heather and Emily burst into laughter. Hugh looked affronted.

"I used to be part of the PMPPS, I'll have you know!"

"What the hell is the PMPPS?"

"The Portis-Montis Professional Poets Society. I was one of their top poets."

There was a brief pause, before the hysterics continued.

Hugh was annoyed.

"What?"

Barrington was banging the table with the flat of his hand.

"Portis-Montis Professional Poets Society?" he said between gasps. "Pull the other one. Surely you mean the Portis-Montis Society of Professional Poets?" he said between gasps.

"How dare you! I would never associate with the PMSPP, a pompous group. The PMPPS is a more refined society of poets."

"Never heard of them." He wiped a tear away from his eye.

"We weren't as well known as the PMSPP, but we could give them a run for their money any day."

"How big was this *society?*" said Emily.

"Well, there were at least three of us. We had big plans, really going to bring poetry into the mainstream."

"*Three?*"

More laughter followed, and Hugh waited for them to regain composure.

"Hang on?" said Heather, who was flushed. "Ye said at least? Surely ye must know how many were in the society?"

"Well, it was a secret society, so it was hard to be sure how many—"

He was cut off by more laughter.

"*Oh, it hurts…*" said Barrington, tears rolling down his cheeks.

Before anyone else could speak, a noise brought them down to earth with a bump. The sound of scratching was reverberating through the ship, and Barrington's face went from joy to fear in one fell swoop.

"Dear sprites, they're here!"

"Leave this to me," said Hugh.

He walked the room, slipping awkwardly in the puddle that had pooled out of his clothes. The rest of the group stood and followed him. The sound of scratching was eerie and filled all empty spaces in the silence. Other footsteps, panicked ones, were now joining the scratching. Just before Hugh went to step out onto the deck, Barrington placed a hand onto his shoulder.

"Hugh, there's one thing you should know before you put yourself up for this. Say nothing unless it is in rhyme."

Hugh nodded, swallowed hard, and headed out onto the now bright, sunlit deck.

Chapter 12

Hugh shielded his eyes once more as they adjusted to the bright light of the outside world. He faced an unnerving sight. The sails hung limp upon the mast, without a breath of wind in the air. At first Hugh thought the sun was out, before realising they were surrounded by a bright backlit mist. He took in the deck in front of him, and a shiver went down his spine.

The crew had assembled with whatever weapons they had to hand, which was quite disconcerting. A cutlass or two wouldn't go a miss, as they all stood there with mops, buckets and feather dusters. But that wasn't the worst of it, they were all dressed in pinnies. It appeared the crew were mid-way through a deep clean of the ship and had been caught off guard. Hugh leaned back to mutter to Barrington through the side of his mouth.

"Why are they all wearing pinnies?"

"I don't know."

A sea of hopeful red faces stared back at them, looking about as battle ready as a dead slug. The only person looking even vaguely ready for action was the chef, Tinker – though how much damage one could cause with a whisk, Hugh wasn't sure. What he lacked in weapons, he made up for in bulk. In front of the crew, leading the pack, was Captain Monty Shackleton. Between the two teams of people, towering above the tallest man on board, were the Minch.

They were tall, blue-skinned creatures, with webbed hands and feet and had spiked fins on the sides of their faces. The smell coming off them reminded Hugh of the fisheries warehouses, back on the dock in Portis-Montis, causing everyone to keep their distance. They looked immensely strong, and though the crew outnumbered them two to one, Hugh didn't fancy their chances with them in battle. The tallest of the blue creatures stepped forward to speak to the captain. Shackleton's second mate, Raddershins, stepped forward, turned the captain thirty degrees to port, then stepped back into line, keeping his head bowed.

"Captain Shackleton, we meet again," said the blue creature, its voice raspy, with a hint of fingernails being dragged down a blackboard. "You think you can escape me with your band of *pretty men?* Send forth your chosen one, let me look them in the eye. Show me the person who has the skill to get you by."

Hugh watched on as the captain's eyes moved in all directions, as if they were scanning the ship for an exit. Hugh felt a hand shove him forward. The eyes stopped roaming and homed in on him. He felt his heart flip in his chest as, unseen behind him, Barrington was gesturing to the captain that Hugh was the one to choose.

The tall, blue figure slowly turned to follow the captain's gaze. As he looked at him, Hugh felt as though he were gazing into his very soul. He wanted to run, to hide, but his feet appeared to be stuck to the deck. All the gusto he had had moments before washed away. The crew looked on in hope. The blue creature let out a raspy, clicking laugh, and the rest of the Minch joined in. The clicking went through Hugh, each one making his bones jump in his skin. The leader stepped forward, looking Hugh up and down through his blue frill that covered most of his face. As he bent down to assess him, the frills swung out, bouncing off Hugh's nose.

"So, this is your choice for our little rhyming match."

He appeared to be assessing Hugh for his worthiness as an opponent.

He let out another evil laugh and took in a deep, raspy breath, as he stood upright once more.

"Very well. Chin up boys, it looks like today we'll be having ourselves a mighty catch."

Hugh made an audible gulp.

"So, here's how it will be," said the blue figure. "We have ourselves a match, let's say we get to three. So come along, my little human friend, let us have our battle to the very end."

Hugh looked back, his mind going blank.

"Well … I … erm …"

"That's one to me straight away, only two more before we get our pay. If you wish to pass safe through our water, harder you must try, or all of you we'll take to the slaughter. Be sharp and to the point, or your souls will live for eternity under the water."

Barrington leaned in from behind Hugh and whispered into his ear.

"Don't talk unless it's rhyming—"

"No help from the back please, that's cheating. Now come little human, time is fleeting. I'll let you off just this once, but cross me again, and I won't be so kind." He stared at Barrington. It looked like he wanted to kill him. Instead, he returned his attention back to Hugh.

Hugh's eyebrows rose in surprise.

"Here you are talking of time, and yet you forget to rhyme. I think it's not me that needs to worry, but you. Here's what I plan to do. I'll accept your challenge for a little game, and I'll beat you each time, finding words that … that …"

The Minch began clicking with glee.

"…that sound the same?"

"Really? Is that the best you can do?" muttered Barrington.

"Shut up and let me finish this."

"I said no conferring, that is true. So now it's two to me, and one to you."

He leaned close to Hugh, bearing down on him from above. Hugh stepped backwards, moving away from the fishy breath which was emanating from the mouth of the unearthly beast.

"Why, that's not fair, we were not cheating. It is now you that is reneging on the rules of our meeting."

"I make the rules and say it's a crime. So it still stands that I have one more to get, and then you will have lost our little bet." There were a series of clicks and rasping behind him, as his party were getting keen to take away their prey. "Settle down you lot, I don't need your help, I think these will taste nice with a bit of sea kelp."

Hugh cocked his head to the side.

"I believe that is one point to me, which makes me even with the sea."

"I don't think so, little human, for I did rhyme, you'll have to try harder, better luck next time."

"Ah, but that is where you are wrong, my blue Minch friend. You just refused the help, thus you were conferring, so that's two all I think, and only one can reach the end."

"Dang and blasted humans, you haven't won yet. I will get you in the end, and I think you'll make a nice addition to my set. Let's end this match over, put your tricks away. I wish to be getting on with my day."

Hugh stood, the last words running through his head. The Minch were getting restless.

"Well? Don't you have something to say?"

Hugh looked up, a wry smile on his face.

"Alright, I'll take a punt. What is this spilled down your front?"

He dared to walk up to the Minch, poking him in the chest.

"What? There's nothing there."

"Ah, how very true, but alas there shall be no catch for you!"

On his last words, Hugh jumped up and flicked his finger up to a barnacle where the Minch's nose should be. It was cold and slimy, but it didn't matter. He had outwitted his opponent in the simplest of ways.

The deck of the ship erupted into cheers of raucous applause. The leader of the Minch stood aghast at falling for such a trick.

"Bloody humans and your evil ways. Stand down men, we're not getting our catch today."

The rest of the Minch boarding party puffed their chests out to the sea of dusters and mops.

"We must abide by the laws of the sea. My men, you must come with me." He turned to Hugh. "This isn't the last you have heard from me, Hugh Geber."

Everyone on deck went deathly silent, the Minch's words cutting through the frivolity like a knife. Hugh stood frozen to the spot.

"You know my name? How?"

"Yes, I know your name, there is a party ahead of you, and they have gone much further. Whatever you seek is doubtless lost, so turn around or rue the cost."

"We must go on," said Hugh. "We have no choice, for our enemy is strong and we mustn't give them a voice."

"Then go you must, I will grant you safe passage. Now be on your way. Let us hope, for all our sakes, that you win the day."

The Minch ran for the rail, diving back into the depths of the ocean.

Hugh turned to Barrington.

"That was close."

"Too close, my friend. I apologise for nearly dropping us in it back there."

"At least we can now get moving. It sounds like Smithson has already been through here."

"That is troubling news, but not unexpected. If they couldn't get past with all those poets on board, we would stand no chance."

Shackleton walked over to the pair, giving Hugh a large pat on the back of the head.

"Well done there, lad. Ye did us all proud."

"You certainly did," said Emily. "I apologise on behalf of us all for not having faith in you to rhyme."

Hugh smiled back.

"Well, what can I say? It's all in… uh, the work of a day?"

They all looked at him.

"Dinnae go giving up that day job just yet, will ye, Hugh?" said Heather.

There was a brief pause, before they all started laughing.

Hugh shrugged.

"Right, just the Cape of No Hope to pass, then we are on the home straight."

"Oh, as simple as that is it, my lad?" said Shackleton, shaking his head.

"If that was the Sea of Lost Souls, the Cape of No Hope can't be any worse, surely?"

"Dearest Hugh, if only you were correct," said Barrington, patting him on the shoulder. "No, I'm afraid that we sailors fear the Cape of No Hope more than the Sea of Lost Souls. Not one boat that's sailed to the cape has ever returned, and don't get me started on the Demon's Gap."

Emily looked confused.

"Are you saying that they sink?"

"I wish it were true, me dear," said the captain, "but the fact is nobody knows. The ships never return. If we do it, then it's more than likely a one-way trip."

"Hang on a minute, if we're going to retrieve what we need and then *return*, how are we to get it home? We must return to Portis-Montis."

"Then that's a bridge we'll have to cross when we get there. Are ye still willing to do it?" Shackleton looked at them in the eye as best he could.

"Of course it's a yes, isn't it?" said Hugh, looking at the rest of the group. "We're still going through with this, aren't we?"

"I tell ye what," said Shackleton, "we're over a day away from the point of no return, so I'll give ye till then to make yer mind up. Now if you'll excuse me, I've to get me ship ready fir presentation.

Oh, and I'd appreciate it if ye didn't mention the pinnies, mops and dusters. Me men get a bit touchy about it."

He turned on his heel and zig-zagged his way back down the deck, leaving the rest to contemplate their fate.

They headed back to their cabin, spending the rest of the day in heated conversation, debating the pros and cons of continuing their journey into the unknown. Hugh threw his arms up in the air.

"There must be land beyond the cape. People can't disappear without a trace."

"Hugh, that is the point that I keep trying to make. We haven't any evidence to prove what happened to anyone who travelled past this stage. The navy patrols only made it this far before turning around, fearing death beyond the cape. We used to take it in turns to pick up a poet from Portis-Montis, then head out to meet the Minch. The poets were more than happy, as they were paid handsomely, considerably more than on the mainland. But that's beside the point. I think it's a dangerous idea."

"Listen, Smithson is after the same book as us. The Elf King may already be there. We either sit here and let them get away with it, or we attempt the impossible and go after it ourselves." He turned to Heather and Emily for support.

Emily took in a deep breath.

"I think, for once, Hugh is talking sense, and that's a lot coming from me right now. I say we crack on and get the job done. What's your opinion, Heather?"

"Aye, I say let's do it. We need the book, and Dad always says to do yer best, even if ye die trying. You cannae try harder than that."

Barrington scoffed.

"Hardly reassuring, though, is it?"

"No," said Hugh, "but it's all we've got right now. So, that's decided. We're going around the Cape of No Hope."

Barrington stood up roughly, knocking his chair to the floor.

"You're all mad. None of you have a clue what we're blindly sailing into. It's a suicide mission!" He left the room, slamming the door.

It was midnight, and the Donkey Bird clock was beginning its chime of the hour.

"That bloody clock!" said an unknown voice into the night.

The sound of somebody running across the deck was followed by the chime being cut short.

Hugh awoke to the sound of screaming. At first he feared it was Emily or Heather, but as he came around further, he could hear angry ranting out on deck. He jumped from his hammock, shielded his eyes from the sun and scanned the deck for the disturbance. Barrington appeared to have finally lost it. He was running around, shouting garbled words at the crew, who were looking at him like a man possessed. Behind him, Heather was trying to calm him down with little effect. Emily came out on the deck next to Hugh.

"What the hell is going on?"

"It's Barrington," he said. "I fear our friend has finally lost it. It must be all this time at sea. I fear it's bringing back old memories locked away for all these years. Come on, let's try to help Heather."

They ran over to where Barrington was pinning one of the crew to the port side rail, threatening to throw him overboard. His eyes were wide and bloodshot, and as he spoke, bits of foam were forming at the edge of his mouth.

"Was it you, eh? Was it?"

The quivering man shook his head with fear, and Barrington turned his attention to the rest of the ship's crew, who had encircled him, trapping him like a rabid animal. They armed themselves with what they had to hand. Some came straight from their beds to investigate the commotion and were wearing an assortment of bedclothes – or lack thereof – looking red in the face. Emily and Heather stood open-mouthed. Hugh didn't know where to look. He spotted Tinker, who had come straight from the kitchen, this time armed with a wooden spatula.

"C'mon then! Who was it, eh? Which one of you stinking bastards destroyed my clock?"

Hugh edged closer.

"Barrington, you need to calm down."

"Was it you? Did you touch my clock?"

"What? No, I didn't touch your clock."

"Then one of them touched my clock. Own up! Who was it?"

"Enough!" bellowed Shackleton, arriving on deck. "I will not have this mutinous behaviour on me ship!"

His eyes appeared dead straight, his voice so loud that it shook Hugh, and everyone else on the deck, to the core. They all stopped still where they were standing, partly because of the captain's words, but more because he seemed to emit some sort of unseen and heretofore unrevealed power.

"Take this man to the brig. We'll deal with him shortly."

Though he attempted to fight, Barrington was no match for two of the crew. He made himself as limp as possible as they dragged him off with a lot of grunting.

"Sorry about that. I hate having to carry out such manoeuvres at sea, but the man had to be stopped. I thought he was gonna to throw old Enis overboard."

Shackleton's eyes had returned to their usual wandering ways. He tuned to the young crew member who had sunk to the floor in shock. He spoke gently and calmly to the poor man, reassuring him that was all safe.

"It's alright, Peter. Yer safe, I promise. My word to ye is as strong as it was when ye first came aboard."

He stood to address the rest of the crew.

"That goes fir all of yese. I gave you my word as captain that I would protect ye from danger the day ye all stepped aboard me ship. I recognise we may not be the most usual crew on these seas, but by sprites, we're the best."

The crew replied to this with a seaworthy cheer.

"I don't think I need to remind ye we have all been in our newest crew member's position, some of us more than once," he said, attempting to eye up the cook.

The crew chuckled.

"Now, I ask that ye carry out your morning tasks and get yerselves ready fir breakfast. We wouldn't want to upset Chef Tinker. Oh, and for goodness, put some bloomin' clothes on, will ye! Dismissed."

The crew chuckled once more, then dispersed to carry out the captain's orders. He turned back to Hugh.

"Good mornin' to ye. Have ye decided on what ye want to do about sailing onwards today?"

"Errrm, yes, but first, can you tell us what you intend to do with our friend?"

"Him? A couple of hours in the brig should show him right. We normally get one per trip, though I wasn't expecting it to be him, that's fir sure. What was it that set him off?"

"I think someone has destroyed his clock, but we don't know who."

Shackleton chuckled to himself. Hugh looked the captain up and down.

"Do *you* know who was behind it?"

"Nope, but I don't see the issue. It was only a clock."

"To you, it was a clock, but to Barrington, it was more. It was helping him come to terms with a lot of stuff, and it was also helping to take his mind off this trip."

"Well, like I say, he won't be in there fir too long. I can't let behaviour like that go unpunished. Poor Peter's had it hard, what with 'is parents naming him what they did. Boy never stood a chance. Ye do understand what this ship is? It's a place where people who've had a rough start in their lives can move forwards. It doesn't bother me. I want to give them a safe place where they can do a good job without prejudice."

Hugh was viewing Shackleton in a new light. Until now, he had thought him and the ship's crew odd, perhaps not as good as the usual run-of-the-mill crew.

"I feel as though I should apologise to you. What you are doing here is amazing."

The captain batted the comment away with his hand.

"Nah 'tis nothing, all in a day's work for me and the crew. I know all about not fitting in. Anyway, too much talking like this will make an ol' sea captain like me go soppy. What's yer decision for the Cape of No Hope and Demon's Gap?"

"We have agreed," said Hugh – then Emily coughed behind him. "Alright, nearly all of us have agreed to go ahead and sail the cape."

"Well, thas good news. I take it ye faced resistance from Barrington."

Hugh nodded.

"Tell ye what," Shackleton said, "let me talk to him. Maybe I'll be able to change his mind?"

"You can try, but I don't know how far you'll get."

"I've got me ways," he said, tapping the side of his nose. He turned and headed off towards the brig.

Hugh turned to Emily and Heather.

"I doubt he'll be able to convince him. How are you two doing?"

"I'm a wee bit shaken," said Heather. "I've never seen him like that. I thought he was about to throw that poor boy over the rail."

"I can understand his apprehension. There's a lot he's going to have to face on this trip," said Emily.

Hugh and Heather looked at her, eyebrows furrowed.

"He nearly died at sea, remember? Along with everything else he's going to face, it's going to be a long trip."

"I suppose, when you put it like that, it's a lot for one person to take on." Hugh couldn't help thinking Emily wasn't revealing all. His thought was disturbed by Heather.

"What's that?" she said.

They looked at the horizon, where she was pointing.

"It looks like another incoming storm," said Emily, seeing flashes within what looked like dense cloud.

A crew member walked past as they were discussing what lay upon the horizon and shook his head.

"Nah miss, that ain't no storm. That's the Cape of No Hope."

Chapter 13

Throughout the morning, the fog bank that surrounded the Cape of No Hope loomed larger and larger until it filled the horizon. Hugh couldn't help wondering if their decision to carry on was the right one. Even the crew seemed subdued in the presence of such a dense wall. Barrington was now back on deck. The captain's words had convinced him to calm down to a point, but he was still edgy. The sea was becoming choppy once more, which only added to the tension.

Barrington looked from the fog bank to Hugh, his eyes wide with fear.

"I don't like this, Hugh. I don't like it one bit."

Hugh didn't want to admit to his friend that he, too, was having second thoughts, but he knew Barrington would jump on any idea of retreat.

"I know, but if we are to get the book, then we need to face our fears. Why are you carrying that coat?" He looked at the seal pelt coat his friend was holding onto like a comfort blanket. "It's as hot as hell out here."

He had expected it to feel cool as they approached the weather front, but it appeared to be emitting heat.

"I just want it nearby," said Barrington.

Heather came and stood next to him and held his hand but said nothing. Emily went and stood next to Hugh, resting her head on his shoulder as he put his arm around her.

Captain Shackleton stood at the prow of the ship and cupped his hands.

"Hold tight, lads and lasses, we're going in!"

Tendrils of fog seemed to come out to meet the ship, as if attempting to pull the vessel in by the bow. The sea appeared to boil around them as it frothed up the sides, splashing onto the deck. Hugh's heart was thumping in his chest, and the firestone was glowing brightly. He noticed Emily's was doing the same.

The air crackled around them, and the hairs all over Hugh's body were standing on end. He looked around and saw that it wasn't just him – the hair on Emily's and Heather's heads was standing upright as well. He felt his own hair, and it zapped him with static. The same was happening to the rest of the crew as the fog around them seemed tinged with purple. The ship was crackling underfoot and felt as though it would break under the tension. The air smelled strongly of burnt metal; Hugh could taste it in his mouth.

"Captain, is this expected, or ought we to turn around now?" He had to shout to be heard over the noise around them – the air was now humming, as if the particles were bouncing against each other.

"Too late now, lad! We're in the belly of the beast."

Barrington was visibly shaking next to him, and Hugh put a hand to his friend's wrist to reassure him. As they continued forward, Shackleton unfurled a scroll of paper, and his voice boomed out as he read the words aloud.

"This is Captain Monty Shackleton of *A Ship With No Name*. I request that the powers that be let us pass with ease; and may the fortunes of the world that once was be forever on our side." He waited, as if expecting something to happen. After a long pause, he added, "Please?"

For a moment, Hugh thought nothing was going to change, but then he felt the ship surge forward. Once more, everyone's feet were held fast to the deck by some unseen force. They were moving faster and faster, with the purple lights flickering and arching all around them.

Hugh feared he would be flattened by the force of the movement, but as he leaned backwards, something pushed him upright. He attempted to speak, but his voice was gone. His nostrils stung with the smell of raw power, and his firestone was glowing so brightly and giving off so much heat that he feared it would ignite his clothes. He saw Emily having the same worry, but he was in no position to help.

The captain threw his hands into the air, letting out a wail of euphoria. The purple lightning arched towards them, flowing through him and into the ship. Hugh's entire body fizzed, his hands tingling on Barrington's wrist and Emily's shoulder.

Ahead of them, he could hear the roaring of water. He attempted to look ahead, but he could not see anything. It then dawned on him very quickly that this was because there was nothing there, apart from a very large gap. It looked as though they were about to drop off the very edge of the world. He had no time to think, as in one enormous movement, the ship surged forward so fast that everything went blurry. They had to be falling, there was no other explanation for it, but his senses told him they were moving forward. He had one last moment of panic before the world around him fell into darkness.

They regained consciousness, laying on the deck of the ship, drenched in water. The sun was beating down on them, the air blisteringly hot. Hugh opened his eyes into a cloudless sky. For a moment, he did not know if he was dead or alive. He propped himself up on his elbows, seeing the rest of the crew in various stages of coming to. Emily was next to him, sitting cross-legged in a daze.

"What happened?" he asked her.

"I don't know, but I feel amazing!"

Hugh sat himself up and realised that he, too, felt energised and alive. Barrington and Heather were now waking up and looking wearily around the deck.

Barrington turned to Hugh. His eyes were bloodshot.

"What …? Where are we? Where's the fog, the lights, the roaring water? Are we dead?"

"I think not, my friend. I think we know why it's called the Demon's Gap, and it would appear we have survived to live another day. Where we are, I could not say, other than we made it through the fog."

He turned, seeing the fog bank some distance behind them. They must have been out cold for some time. Shackleton came down to see them, looking exuberant.

"A-maz-ing!" he said, helping them all to their feet.

His hand tingled as he grasped Hugh's outstretched palm. His eyes had also appeared to be corrected, now looking directly into Hugh's gaze.

"Wow! Your eyes…"

"I know. I can hardly believe it. This place must be teeming with power."

He disappeared to check on the rest of the crew, helping those who were not already back on their feet. They were all now looking around, trying to understand where they'd emerged and discern where to go next. The sea was calm, and a haze blurred the horizon. There was nothing, apart from the fog behind them – which Hugh did not want to return through.

"Now what?" he said, looking around him.

"I'm not sure," said Barrington, "but there's nothing here to aim for."

"Nonsense, we'll follow our noses," said Shackleton pointing to the horizon. "Out there me friends, is a world to be discovered. It is in that direction that we shall go."

"Monty, dear boy, we cannot just go off gallivanting into the unknown without point of reference or bearing. It's suicide!"

"Pah! Live a bit, won't ye, Barrington? This is me ship, and I'll take her where I see fit."

"But what makes you so sure *that* direction is the correct one? Why not *that* way, or *that*?" Barrington was pointing all around him to various points on the empty horizon.

"Because I know. Plus, there's a bird flying in that direction, and I can guarantee you a bird like that is heading for dry land."

Hugh looked skywards and saw a multicoloured bird heading out ahead of them. It was unlike any bird he had ever seen. The water was a startling aquamarine and looked inviting, and if he could swim, he'd have jumped in there and then.

Emily came over to join him, peering over the rail.

"Amazing, isn't it?" he said.

"Yeah, but you couldn't get me within ten feet of it."

"Why not?"

"Don't get me wrong," she said, "I like the water well enough; I just don't like it above my waist. There wasn't much chance to learn how to swim when we lived in the mountains."

"You neither, eh? Listen, Em, I really am sorry. I wish I could take back the things I have said and done, but I can't. What I can do is ask for your forgiveness."

"I get that Hugh, but you have to be serious. Call it self-preservation, but I can't afford to get hurt."

"Nor I. You really are everything to me. I realise I was a fool to have my head turned, but it was unfinished business, and that's finished now. I think."

"Oh, well, that's totally reassuring."

"Emily, I didn't mean it to come out like that, please ..." He went to give her a hug, but she shrugged him off.

"No, Hugh. I need to know you're totally clear in your head that you are over Adelia and nothing else will happen between the pair of you."

"But I've told her. There's nothing for her to gain in pursuing me."

"And your feelings to her?"

"Like I said before, it's you that I love, not Adelia."

"Words are one thing Hugh, but I need to see it in your actions, amongst other things."

"But…"

It was too late. Emily had already turned and headed back inside without so much as a backwards glance. Heather looked at her – then at Hugh with a frown – before chasing after her. Barrington headed over to his friend.

"Issues?"

"Can we not talk about it right now?"

"I think this is part of your problem, my dear friend, your unwillingness to say what you are really thinking. If you aren't honest with Emily, she will never trust you."

"How are we ever supposed to understand women?" Hugh said. "One moment it's fine, the next it's all up in the air again."

"You forget the bond you share lets her see more than just what you are saying."

Hugh gave him a deadpan look.

"Since when have you been an expert on women? I've already made it clear to Emily that I don't like her rooting though my mind."

"I'm not saying I'm an expert. I'm just repeating what Heather said. As for Emily looking at your most treasured thoughts, sometimes it isn't that easy. You are so loose at times that even I can sense what's happening inside your noggin."

"But what I'm thinking isn't necessarily how I feel. Occasionally my thoughts may wander, but that doesn't mean I don't care for Emily. If she, or anyone else for that matter, chooses to see more than is actually there, then more fool them."

They both stood in silence for some time, looking out at the sea stretching in all directions to the horizon. There was nothing to be seen except the bird, still flying high above the ship cawing to itself.

"So, where do we think that fella came from then?" said Barrington, looking puzzled.

"I'm not sure. I can't see how or why a bird like that would be out at sea."

"Birds."

"Sorry?"

"It's *birds* now, look."

They both looked up to see another multicoloured bird joining the first.

"How very peculiar."

The ship was cutting through the calm waters with ease. Hugh suddenly realised there wasn't a breath of wind, yet the sails were still full of air. Barrington nodded towards them.

"You've noticed that too, have you? This really is the most peculiar sea I've ever seen. It's just, well, it's hard to explain."

"That'll be the magic," said Hugh.

"Magic?"

"Yes. That fog bank we came through back there was full of it. Couldn't you smell it or taste it? It must be stronger on this side of the bank."

Barrington nodded but said nothing.

"Land Ho!"

Hugh and Barrington ceased their conversation, running with the crew to the front of the ship, and there, emerging from the misty horizon, was the top of a distant land mass. The birds above them began cawing loudly, and Hugh saw there were many more joining the flock.

"Looks like Monty was right," said Barrington.

They were soon joined on deck by Emily and Heather, who had emerged to see what all the commotion was about. Everyone was at the bow of the ship, looking to the horizon.

"Steady as she goes, lads, and keep those eyes peeled. It's land alright, but we don't know what we'll find there. Friend or foe."

Hugh didn't like the sound of that, and Barrington read the look on his face easily.

"Come on, we need to get back to the cabin," said Barrington. "We really need a plan for what we are to do next."

Hugh nodded and followed the rest of the group across the deck. Barrington held the door open for him to walk through and closed it behind them. As they entered the cabin, Hugh could see that Emily's eyes were red and puffy. Barrington closed the door and turned to address the room.

"Alright. Here's what we need to do," he said quietly. "Hugh, you need to apologise to Emily."

"What? But I've already done so, numerous times."

"Don't question it, just do it. You need to not only say it, but feel it, keeping your visions of Emily strong in your mind's eye. Think of the current situation we're facing and the damage that's been done these past few months. It's the least you can do right now."

He ushered Hugh up to the table where Emily and Heather were sitting. Hugh turned back to his friend, but Barrington placed a firm hand on his shoulder, and faced him forward again.

"Emily, I'm sorry."

Barrington squeezed his shoulder.

"For…"

Hugh looked into Emily's eyes. He filled his mind full of images of Emily, and the time they has spent together.

"Emily, I've been a fool these past few months. I should have been more honest with you and Adelia. I should not have let the situation get this far, and for that, I am truly sorry."

He chose to hide the next part of the conversation, and they spoke directly into each other.

'I love you, and I mean it. I wish I hadn't been so stupid.'

'At last, a bit of honesty. This goes some way to fixing things, but it doesn't make up for all the pain and hurt. It's been hard seeing your conflicting thoughts, and before you say anything, I haven't been snooping around in your head.'

'It's alright, Barrington has had a good chat with me, and I can see where I have made mistakes. I know talking honestly with you is the best path forward from here.'

'Well that goes some way to help things, but it will take a lot more to fix this. You will need to prove your love for me, Hugh Geber.'

Hugh nodded silently.

"All sorted?" said Barrington, who understood the situation.

"For now, yes," said Emily, wiping her face on her sleeve.

"Good, at least that's sorted. We really are going to have to pull together as a team. I realise my own actions haven't been conducive to this point, and for that I apologise. But from here on in, we are in this together, agreed?"

They all nodded.

"Alright, then let's get down to business. We need to know if what we are searching for is in this direction. Hugh, could you get the Orbis out of your bag, please."

Hugh walked over to his bag, reached in and found the Orbis first time. He pulled it out and walked back to the table. Hugh opened up the Orbis and cleared his mind, watching the outer needle go steady. He had almost focussed on the lore book of Water when his thoughts drifted, and he searched for the book of Alchemy once more. The inner needle went crazy, spinning around at such a pace, that he couldn't focus on it.

Barrington looked down at the whirring needle, then back to Hugh.

"That's a worrying sign."

"Did you think of the right book, Hugh?" said Emily, looking him in the eye. She let out a large sigh. "You must concentrate, Hugh, or this plan will never work."

"But it wasn't intentional."

"Hmmm…."

Barrington slammed a palm down onto the table, making them all jump.

"I don't think either of you are grasping the situation here. You need to put all personal feelings to one side and focus on the task at hand. We are fast heading to the Isle of Fey, and we still have no plan to speak of. Not only that, we have no clue of what to do once we set foot in this foreign land. Who knows how they will receive us? Smithson and the Elf King are making their way to the book we need. They may already have it for all we know. We don't have the time to deal with our own personal agendas now."

"Sorry, Barrington," Hugh and Emily said in unison.

Hugh wasn't liking this new and enthused version of his friend. He looked back to the Orbis and steadied the outer needle. He moved his mind to the lore book of Water, trying to think of things relating to water. The inner needle slowed, stopping at a point somewhere beyond the front of the ship – in the direction they were going.

He looked up to the rest of the group, who were transfixed by the needle.

"There's our answer. It's somewhere in that direction. Let's hope it's on the island and not further out to sea."

Barrington shook his head.

"No, I think we are close. I don't know why, but there is something telling me it's not too far from here."

They were disturbed by a knock at the door, and Shackleton came into the room.

"Sorry to disturb, but I thinks ye'll all want to see this."

They followed the captain out onto the deck and gasped at what they saw.

"What the devil is that?" said Barrington, looking at Hugh.

"I have absolutely no idea, my friend."

Chapter 14

They all looked out towards the island, which was now fully in sight and filling the horizon. But that wasn't what was troubling those aboard *A Ship With No Name*. It was the statue they were passing which was the cause for concern. At first, Hugh thought it to be some sort of oddly shaped lighthouse, but as they neared it, he saw it was indeed a light green statue. Towering over the ship, it depicted someone holding a book in one hand and a torch in the other. He took in its large crown, then noticed there was a purple light flowing from the torch, which arched up into the sky, far beyond his field of vision. Barrington tapped him on the shoulder as they passed the colossus, pointing to his left. There was a second enormous statue on the far horizon and a third to the right.

As they passed the colossus with its blue haze, Hugh's hair momentarily stood on end.

"I think it's some sort of magic, but I can't think what its purpose is."

"I'm not worried about *that*," said Barrington, for he was looking at a boat that was coming to meet them. "Let's hope they're friendly."

Shackleton called the crew to order.

"Men, to yer positions. Mullins, hoist the Ranthinian standard; let 'em know we mean no harm. Lower the mainsail to slow us down. Throw the water break off the stern."

Hugh watched two of the crew lob a large sheet attached to two planks of wood and two ropes off the back of the ship. He heard it splash into the water, then sensed a slowing of their speed.

Barrington looked to the captain, open-mouthed.

"Are you mad? Why slow down? We can outrun them easily."

Shackleton let out a sigh.

"I knew ye were rusty, but surely ye must know where one ship sails from port, there will be twenty and two that will follow. I remember some of the naval training, small though it was. We've no weapons, and though she may not be as magnificent, she is still me ship, and I intend to keep her in one piece. Drop anchor!"

The whole ship seemed to rattle to its core, as the chain was released, and the anchor dropped to the ocean floor.

The ship slowed further, coming to a stop as the foreign ship, the SS *Orthina II*, came alongside. It was a sleek model, its metal hull cutting through the water with ease. Lines were thrown between the two ships, mooring them together, and a gangplank was lowered. It wasn't much bigger than *A Ship With No Name*. Through the tiny portholes on SS *Orthina II*, Hugh could see small faces looking out at them. A boarding party was gathering, making ready to cross.

An officer of some sort stood at the top of the plank. He had a pointy nose to match his chin. His pencil moustache was waxed with precision, and his thin eyebrows pointed downwards as his brow furrowed.

"Prepare to be boarded, you Ranthinian scum!"

The man spat into the sea, but then a more polished man appeared next to the first.

"Number Two, no need for that tone. Let's show our fellow seamen some respect. I suspect they have had a long journey." The crew of *Orthina II* stood to attention. "At ease, at ease."

Hugh watched this newcomer make his way down the gangplank.

"Permission to come aboard, Captain?" he called.

He smiled and winked at Shackleton, his gold teeth glinting in the sunlight. The man was rather rotund and wore a white suit with a cummerbund. There were many rows of colours pinned to his chest and medals that swung as he walked. He had oversized epaulettes with long gold tassels hanging down from them, which swayed in the breeze. His polished boots were mirrored enough that Hugh could see the sky reflected in them, and he had a cloak over his shoulders, held down with gold buttons. He also brought with him the strong smell of aftershave, filling the air with its spicy scent.

"Why, of course," said Shackleton, attempting to hide his own smile.

"Marvellous, saves the need for violent intervention. Stand down, men," he called back to his ship.

Hugh saw that more people crowded the gangplank, looking marginally disappointed. They saluted and walked off.

"Are you sure, Captain? Not even a customary orb of compliance, just to show these *New Worlders* that we mean business?"

"Come now, Number Two, let's be cordial to our new arrivals," said the captain with raised eyebrows. "We wouldn't want a repeat of earlier. Please excuse my number two, he's not as civilised as you or I. Has a tendency to be violent. It's ingrained into him, poor thing."

Number two spat onto the deck once more, muttered something under his breath and walked off.

"Well, how can we help you today? I must say, you wait all this time for some action, and three boats turn up in the same week."

Barrington urgently pushed to the front of the queue, looking the captain up and down with surprise.

"Cavendish? Is that you?"

"My goodness, Delphin?"

"The one and only." There was a momentary pause, then the pair carried out a secret handshake of sorts.

"Bish, bish, bash, bash, Shack-nee, Shack-nee, make em crash. Take those blighters by surprise, till you see the whites of their eyes. Tinkle, tinkle all the way, till the trophy's ours, hip-hip-hooray!"

They finished with a large chest bump, before giving each other a manly hug, patting each other hard on the back. Everyone else stood staring, not sure how to take in what they had just witnessed.

"I haven't seen you in sixteen years," said Cavendish, releasing Barrington. "Please tell me, you didn't pass through the defence to get here?"

"What defence? The last we knew you of you and your crew was when you went off onto the fateful journey to patrol the Sea of Lost Souls. We thought you were all dead. What happened?"

"I thought it was time we took on the Cape of No Hope, see what lay beyond. Of course, we knew of all the stories of missing sailors taken to their deaths, but we wanted to investigate further. I needn't go into detail about the fog. I'm sure you're now aware of that. It's a security measure to prevent us *New Worlders* getting out. Occasionally, we slip through, which is how we accidentally crossed. Since then, measures have been tightened up. How did *you* get through?"

"I don't know, to be honest with you. We aimed for the fog and sailed in. Is it related to the statues?"

"I see you're as astute as ever. Yes, the statues help to keep the two worlds separate. There is one area inside the ring of defence, and that's Morcarthia, oh and we mustn't forget about the university, of course."

"Hang on?" said Hugh. "Did you say that Morcarthia is inside the ring of defence?"

"Yes, and who the devil are you?"

"Ah, sorry everybody," said Barrington. "This is Captain Cavendish, and my very good friend. He was a year ahead of me at the naval academy, and also the person who got me into Shack-nee dancing."

Emily and Heather smirked.

"You may well be laughing, ladies, but it was under his careful guidance that we made it to the finals three years running. Of course, that all ended when Augustus waded in to steal our crown. Cavendish, this is Hugh Geber. You remember I used to tell you about him?"

"Oh, one of the Gebers, eh? Well, it's a pleasure to meet you. So sorry to hear about your father."

This took Hugh by surprise.

"How do you know of my father?"

"Who, Frederick? He used to visit here regularly. When I first came here, I integrated myself into society, working my way up the ranks. Your father helped me out along the way, I can tell you."

"Whoa, hang on a moment. So you're saying my father used to visit here regularly? Why?"

"Oh, he was after some books apparently, we don't know why. Anyway, there were two other ships that arrived before you, and they both said they were here to pick up where the trail had died off … sorry, how heartless of me," he said, looking at Hugh's reaction.

"How did he get past the defence barrier?"

"There are ways and channels. Mainly from the landing point in Morcarthia at King's Seat. It's a sort of checkpoint, though you wouldn't know it was there unless you knew what you were looking for."

"Just a minute, two boats came to pick up where my father left off? Do you mean Smithson openly spoke about what he was doing?"

"Yes, two boats. When we heard that the son of Robert Smithson had made his way here, I came to greet him. It's rare for people from the old stomping ground to visit, so I had to find out how he managed it. We don't need that secret slipping out. I'm still puzzled as to how *you* got through."

"The captain," said Hugh, thumbing over at Shackleton, "spoke from a scroll, and we seemed to jump through."

"Did he really? I'll have to be questioning you in a moment, Captain…?"

"Shackleton, Captain Monty Shackleton, at yer service."

He went to shake Cavendish's hand, but the man frowned and turned back to Hugh, leaving his hand empty in mid-air.

"Hrmmm, anyway, we were saying?"

"You were filling us in on the two ships which arrived ahead of us."

"Oh, yes, right. Well, I sensed Robert's son is on the right path, not that we are entirely sure of where the books are. We know your father was heading up to the north of the island, wanted to talk to the merfolk up near Killinsfolk in Syreni Bay."

"Merfolk?"

"Yeah, that's one of their main haunts. Anyway, Robert's son wasn't too interested in the mer people, but seemed more interested in the other boat. We didn't see the chap who ran that crew, he left it to one of the lower ranks to negotiate with us. Anyway, both parties set off yesterday. There's not a problem, is there?"

"Only that they are seeking the books for nefarious reasons," said Hugh.

"Really? Goodness me, I didn't know. I assumed that Robert's son would pick up the task his father had started."

"Well, it was *my* father actually," Hugh said, wanting to set the record straight. He turned back to his companions. "If Smithson is already on the path, then we can bet the Elf King is also amongst them."

"Sorry, did you just say the Elf King?" Cavendish looked incredulous. "I thought tales of him kicking about were just that. Some story to scare small children with."

"He certainly did, my old friend, and they are no mere tales," said Barrington. He turned back to Hugh. "Maybe Smithy took two boats with him, have you considered that?"

Hugh pondered the question.

"Possibly, but the Elf King is a shapeshifter. He could be running that ship, and we would never know. We need to handle this situation carefully."

Heather nodded.

"Once we get into dock, I'll need ye to take me to the nearest mapping room, Captain Cavendish, if thas possible?"

"Please, call me Geoffrey. I'm sure we can arrange that for you," he said solicitously. "Sorry, I don't believe I caught your name."

"Heather McDougall."

"Very nice to meet you," he said, taking her hand and kissing it. "You wouldn't be related to Hamish by any chance?"

Heather blushed.

"Aye, he's me dad. Do ye know him?"

"Not personally, but I've heard of him. May I say, you have beautiful eyes?"

Barrington moved in and put his arm around her.

"Shall we keep our eyes on the task in hand?"

"If we must," said Cavendish. "So, what do you require from me?"

"We'll need access to the maps, as Heather said. We'll also need to prepare for a trip up to this Killinsfolk place."

"Alright, I take it you have all the relevant gear with you?"

"We have food, we can pick up the rest along the way and ..."

But Cavendish was giving him a slightly incredulous look.

"What?"

He began laughing.

"One doesn't simply take a stroll up through the Isle of Fey, like it's a Sunday afternoon stroll in the park. No, you must get permission from the High Enchantress."

"What? Do you mean to say the other parties passed through with ease?"

"Errrm, no. That's not it at all. They simply messaged ahead and got their relevant paperwork in order first. If you had used the normal channels, this wouldn't have been an issue. Dear me, if only you had known this in advance, it would've saved a lot of the hassle."

"How long will this take?" said Emily.

The captain puffed his chest out, blinked, then looked at Emily.

"Excuse me?"

Hugh didn't think the captain's tone would sit too well with Emily.

"I think what she wanted to say was—"

Cavendish held up a hand.

"I think the young lady can surely speak for herself. Now, you were saying …"

Emily fixed him with a level gaze.

"I wondered how long this would take. I would like to know, *please.*"

"I'm sure we can sort all this for you soon, my dear. No need to worry about it."

"I beg your pardon?"

The waters around the ship simmered.

"I said there's no need to worry about it, my dear. The men will sort everything—"

He was cut off mid-sentence, as a purple flash hit the ship with a crack, arching off the statue behind them. It left a scorch mark on the deck and filled the air once again with the smell of burnt metal.

"Oi, that's me ship yer hittin'."

Emily swung around to glare at Shackleton.

"Never mind …" He chuckled nervously.

She swung back to the captain.

"You were saying, *Geoffrey?*"

He swallowed hard, unable to release himself from Emily's glare. She appeared to be growing in stature once more.

"I, uh yes, well, I will get my men to assist you with your plans."

Emily stood down, smiling smugly.

"Thought you might change your mind."

"Righto," said Cavendish. "We will need to get ourselves back into port. Are you alright to follow us in?"

"I should say so," said Shackleton. "I'll get me men to prepare the ship."

"Good man. Oh, a word to the wise, I would go steady on the locals if I were you. They're already jittery, what with the other ships turning up. The liminal line is supposed to keep the New-Worlders in."

"How so?"

"The world was split after the war. Those who sided with the Elf King were held within the liminal line. This was to separate them from everyone else, like a punishment. It was bad enough when the powers that be negotiated to open the passage from King's Seat. Now you all turn up, jumping the liminal line itself. Folk are pretty angry with the situation. If they hear about the Elf King, it might send things over the edge."

"Why?" said Hugh.

"My dear man, please understand, these people were taken to the brink during the Great War. They thought the problem was dealt with, especially with the defences. Any whiff of the Elf King and they are bound to worry. If he's back and real, as you say, then we are in for turbulent times."

"Why would that affect people here? They are miles away from Morcarthia."

Geoffrey sighed into his hands.

"Do think it through for one moment. If you were locked away, had your lands stripped from you, how would you feel? Who would you go after first?"

"When you put it like that ..."

"Factor in world views on the human race, and it would only need a spark to light that powder keg. They were always snubbed by the other races due to a lack of powers."

"I'm sure the New World wouldn't want to join the Elf King, would they?"

"Not at all. They were only forced to live together in exile, start again from nothing. I mean, that would leave a chip on anyone's shoulder."

"You aren't one of those people?"

"Not all of us wish to rage war against the Old World. Besides, there are reasons I wished to stay on this side of the border, eh Barrington?"

Emily looked at Barrington, who looked away.

"Naturally," said Cavendish, "we have people on the inside keeping the peace. That's why the navy was set up."

Hugh looked at him in disbelief.

"So the navy is an Old World institution?"

"The navy's roots can be traced back to the Old World, along with the university. We must remember, though, the New world continues well into the southern hemisphere. Ranthina and Morcarthia sit above the great landmasses to the south where living is not so easy. This needs to be managed carefully."

Barrington took in a deep breath, letting it out slowly, making his cheeks puff out.

"Well, we ought not to keep you here. It looks like there's work to be done on all sides." He was now ushering Cavendish towards the gangplank.

"Hang on," said Hugh. "What did you mean when you said there were reasons you wanted to stay on this side of the liminal line?"

"Now, now, Hugh," said Barrington, "let's not keep the man busy with lots of questions. Didn't you hear, there's work to be done."

"But I want to know why."

"No, the man said there's work to be done." And Barrington gave Cavendish such a push up the plank, he nearly lost his footing.

"My you are keen to get on, aren't you?" said the captain, stumbling up the plank and onto the *Orthina II*. "We'll see you on shore."

Before Hugh could question any further, the order was given to lift the gangplank, and the tethering lines were released. He watched as the two ships parted ways, knowing that his questions would have to wait.

Shackleton's crew was retrieving the water brake and raising the anchor. He sensed the ship move forwards once more, and they followed in the wake of the *Orthina II* towards the foreign island. The port with its colourful buildings lining the harbour walls came into sight. The surrounding hills melded into the city, the houses appearing to cling to the rocky outcrops. In the distance, on the highest point, stood a glittering palace, and Hugh's thoughts turned to the unexplored land they were about to set foot upon. He was brought back to the present by Barrington, who nudged him.

"What?"

Barrington pointed to the harbour wall, and Hugh saw what was worrying his friend. The walls along the quayside were lined with people. It was as if all the locals had stopped what they were doing, just to catch a glimpse of the latest arrivals coming into dock. Hugh looked around the ship at the others and the surrounding crew. All were afraid because the feeling coming from the harbour wall was one of simmering hostility.

The ship passed by a swing bridge which closed behind them like a massive sea gate, trapping them into the harbour. One thing was certain, there was no backing out now.

Chapter 15

The crowd jeered as they came alongside the dock, the noise so horrendous, Hugh was unable to converse with Barrington. He was beginning to wonder if it was a good idea to step off the boat. Captain Cavendish had already alighted from his boat and was receiving a hero's welcome. Captain Shackleton held back from mooring to the quayside, unsure if it was safe. They watched as Cavendish negotiated with the officials on the dock. He appeared to be in a heated debate with his opponent.

Hugh stood on the deck of *A Ship With No Name* and attempted to calm his nerves. He blocked out the noise of the crowds, trying instead to focus on the multicoloured birds flying overhead. He closed his eyes, breathing in a deep lungful of fresh sea air. He got hints, from the city, of raw fish mingled with garlic and spices. His mouth was watering.

The ship jolted underfoot, and he opened his eyes, seeing they were now mooring. Lines were thrown to the dock workers and were being tied off. Officials had boarded the ship via a rope ladder, taking the decision not to moor out of the captain's hands. They liaised with others on the dock, who were busy clearing an area for the gangplank. They appeared to be pushing the crowds back, making extra space, so the crew could step ashore without being accosted by the rabble.

Captain Shackleton insisted he was first to head off the ship, followed by Hugh, Barrington, Emily and Heather. The crew brought up the rear. It was now so noisy that Hugh was disorientated. He let himself be guided by port officials as they led everyone from the ship into a building decorated with flags.

The atmosphere inside the building was markedly different. The noise of the crowds was muffled by thick walls, and the air smelled of dust and damp. They stood at the end of a large arrivals hall, facing a group of guards who were conversing around the security desks. Between them, stood a maze of barriers ready to guide them back and forth in an organised queue. Barrington assessed the situation and took the easy route by ducking under the wooden blockade.

A guard saw this and began running back and forth along the rows. His uniform was blue, yellow and red with puffed sleeves and trouser legs that rubbed against each other as he moved, making a swishing noise. He wore a ruff around his neck and had a black helmet, pointed at the front and back. It had bright yellow feathers sprouting from the top. As he approached, Hugh saw he wore leg gators in the same pattern as the rest of his uniform. His black hobnail boots, which were polished to a mirror shine, had seen a long service life. This was given away by the sparks coming off the bottom of them as he marched towards the group from the far end of the queuing system. He also carried a large wooden pike stick with a finial on the end that had been sharpened to a point.

"'Scuse me sir, *yes you,* no not you … or you … *him!*"

He pointed to Barrington, who stopped making his way forwards and waiting for his security guard foe to make his way towards him. He watched him zigzag his way through the system, refusing to duck under at any point. After much fuss, he finally reached Barrington.

"You'll have to move back to the start, sir. No queue jumping, please." He pointed to a cobweb covered sign which read:

QUEUE JUMPERS WILL BE SENT TO THE BACK OF THE LINE.

"Now move back please, go on with ye, lad." He poked Barrington with the stick.

"Ow. That hurts. Ow! Stop it!"

"Then ye'd best be gettin' a move on."

Barrington ducked back under the barrier.

"Oh, for the love all things, not like that for sprite's sake," said the guard. "Follow. The. Designated. Route. For goodness' sake. Talk about leading horses to water."

He ran around the barriers to Barrington.

"Why not?" He didn't take his eyes off the stick. The guard pointed to another sign.

NO PASSING UNDER THE BARRIERS.
THEY ARE THERE FOR YOUR SAFETY.

Barrington was about to protest when he was pushed back by some invisible force. The guard was pointing his pike stick at him. Hugh thought he saw the finial glowing. Barrington appeared to be pushing back, but the harder he resisted, the more he was rebuffed. His shoes squeaked on the floor, as he slid backwards. Eventually they returned to the main party and Barrington came to a halt.

"Is this alright?"

"Would you like to read the sign again, sir? Or do I have to spell it out for ye?"

"Why do I have to go to the back?"

"Queue jumpers never prosper. Now back ye go please, go on with ye."

"But it's really long."

"Not my problem, is it, sir? Perhaps next time ye'll be thinking twice before breaking the rules, won't ye? Now *move!*"

Once again, Barrington found himself unable to resist the security guard's instructions. He eventually yielded, heading to the back of the line, whilst the guard returned to the front. He pulled something out from the front of his uniform and held up a paddle with the words "follow me" on it.

"This way, if ye will."

The sound of grumbling made its way down the queue. The guard stopped, causing a pileup of people.

"Does someone have something to say? Speak up, I can't hear you down the front here."

Silence followed.

"Good, now— wait a minute?"

He stopped and sniffed the air, wrinkling up his nostrils as he did so.

"Is somebody carrying *tobacco*?"

Another silence followed, and the guard looked down the line. Nobody owned up.

"Right, that's it. Bring forth the glawackus."

"What's a glawackus?" said Hugh, not sure if he wanted to know.

"Ye'll find out soon enough, sonny."

Hugh looked at the wall to his left, seeing a metal barrier being lifted. A strange cackling noise reverberated off the walls, and two more guards appeared. They had metal armour covering the top half of their bodies. Hugh watched as they tugged on the ropes they were holding, trying to encourage whatever lay within to come out into the room. The sound of whips could be heard, and slowly, the beast stepped out into the room. A high-pitched shriek came from up the line followed by a thud. It was the ship's cook. He'd fainted.

The cackling beast was the size of a bear. It had the mane of a lion and was black like a sleek feline. It made its way towards the new arrivals, and Hugh felt its cackle reverberate off him. Its eyes were covered, and it seemed to use its voice to find its way through the room. As it headed up the line, it sniffed the air, seeking something. It stepped over the cook, paying him no attention, and finally reached the end of the line where Barrington was standing. It nudged him, took in a large sniff and howled by his leg. Barrington tried to push the creature away, but it wouldn't desist.

"Leave me alone, get away, you foul beast."

The guard smiled a sinister smile.

"Well. What, a, surprise. If it isn't the chap who thought he could jump the queue? There's always one trying to sneak forbidden contraband through. I think we'll take you off for *extra* security checks."

"But I haven't got anything on me. Why isn't it smelling them?"

"Ah, yes, but it's not them the glawackus is sniffing. It's you. Oh dear me, it really isn't your day now, is it, sir?"

"It's just the smell … the remnants from … half this crew must be carrying …"

Hugh thought the guard was enjoying the power trip a little too much.

"Too late, mucker. Take him away, chaps."

"But … but …" was all Barrington could say.

It was no use. Extra guards appeared, and from the smell of rotting onion mixed with week-old worn socks, they were trolls. Hugh watched as they hoisted his friend up by the armpits, ignoring his protests, and carried him off to a side room. The glawackus followed closely behind, its howling outweighing Barrington's pleas. The door slammed shut behind the party, leaving only the echo in its wake. Hugh looked from the door, back to the guard.

"Where have they taken him?"

"Your friend will be fine," he said. "I can assure ye of that."

"He has done nothing wrong."

"And I assure you, we shall be very thorough with him."

"Hugh, I really think you should listen to me and stop talking," said Emily, not hiding the annoyance in her voice.

"Emily, I think I'm more than capable of handling this little chap. After all, this is what Barrington would do for any of us. Leave this to me."

"Who are you calling little?" said the guard.

"Maybe I should do the talking?" she said.

"Let the lady do it," said one of the crew members. Hugh looked down the line, to see who had spoken. He was met with a sea of faces looking back at him, many of them were nodding in agreement.

"No, I insist. I've been watching Barrington and how he conducts himself. I'd like to think I've learned a trick or two."

"That's what I'm worried about," said Emily.

Hugh turned to face the guard, ignoring the chatter from the crew behind him.

"Now then, Mr…"

The guard looked up at him, tight-lipped. Hugh cleared his throat awkwardly.

"We can find that out later. I'm sure you'll agree with me that there's been a misunderstanding of sorts. Maybe we could come to a gentlemen's agreement over this issue."

He sensed Emily and Heather's glares drilling into the back of his head.

"And what *misunderstanding* might that be?"

"Well, this whole thing about the tobacco. Where we are from, it's no big deal. I mean, it's just something we New Worlders do – well not all of us; I can't stand the stuff, absolutely awful habit if you ask me. Now I'm sure we can find a resolution to this situation," he said, patting his pockets down. "Would you believe it, I left my money aboard the ship, but my friend in there has plenty. Erm, what are you doing?"

The guard had placed a pair of spectacles on his nose, pulled out a pad and was writing down everything Hugh was saying.

"Add trying to bribe a border official to the charge sheet …" he said as he wrote.

"Hugh!" Emily snapped behind him. He ignored her and carried on.

"This is how I see things. You Old Worlders have been out of the loop for a while …"

At this the guard nodded and rolled his tongue inside of his mouth.

"Thinking they are better than the Old World … giving the air of looking down on us …"

"But I am looking down on you!"

"… also agrees with statement …"

"No, I meant you are small, so it's obvious that I am looking down on you. Look, all I am trying to say is times have changed, so if you could view it from our perspective, it's not really that big a deal. You don't have to write that down … please stop writing …"

"*Hugh…*"

"I mean, what's a bit of tobacco between friends, eh? I mean, it's just a cultural misunderstanding, that's all…"

"Hugh, stop talking."

"Our new ways, verses your old, outdated ones," said Hugh, still ignoring Emily. "It's perfectly acceptable in Morcarthia, also in the Old World, I might add," — the guard stiffened — "and we were there only three months past, so the rules can't have changed that much."

"Morcarthia is as Old World as you. There's a reason why that lot were left inside the liminal line," said the guard.

"Okay then, hear me out. When I say that my friend really has nothing to hide, it's true. Where on earth could he hide anything?"

He smiled at the guard, hoping this would be enough to change his mind. The guard looked at Hugh, then called out to one of his associates.

"Argus, make sure you give our latest visitor the full treatment, will you? I think this one is trying to cover his friend's tracks."

"Absolutely, sir," said the guard, running to a cupboard, pulling out a pair of thick rubber gloves long enough to reach the man's elbows. He ran back into the room to an audible cheer before the doors closed.

"What are they for?" asked Hugh.

"The next level search, of course. We Old Worlders like to be thorough. You could make it easier for your friend and tell me where he's hiding the goods."

"But I've told you he has nothing to hide. It's hardly a civilised approach. I mean," Hugh let out a little laugh, "what kind of heathen country is this?"

Another howl made its way from behind the doors.

"Hugh, would you shut up!" said Emily.

"At last, someone who speaks sense. I would take your friend's advice, or would ye like to join your friend in the search?"

Hugh wisely kept his mouth shut, looking to the floor.

The guard nodded.

"No? I thought as much. Right, if you would all follow me please and we'll get this process underway."

The man removed his spectacles, pocketing them along with his pad. Hugh watched him walk back and forth through the queueing system. He turned to Heather and Emily, who shrugged. Hugh followed in the footsteps of the guard, who had reached the front. When they finally caught up with him, the guard was already sitting in a security booth, giving him a high perch to look down upon the group.

"Papers," he said, holding out his hand. Hugh craned his neck to see the guard's face.

"Erm, will these do?" he said, pulling out his identity papers.

"It's a start. Hand over the rest of the permission forms, then we'll get you moving to the next stage."

Hugh stared at the guard, unable to think of what the guard was talking about. A howling noise made it through from where they were holding Barrington.

"Come along, we don't have all day."

"I don't know what you are talking about. What papers are we supposed to have?"

"Listen, it's very simple. When ye left King's Seat, your relocation agent would have handed ye the relevant documentation. This allows ye to travel in the Old World. Those are the papers I'm referring to."

"But we didn't leave from King's Seat. We left from Portis-Montis."

"Ye left from Portis-Montis? Then how did ye collect the papers from King's Seat?"

"We didn't come that way. We came via the Cape of No Hope through that magic fog stuff."

Hugh moved uneasily on the spot, and he could feel the moisture trickling down his head. The guard looked him up and down, before leaning out of the booth, taking in the rest of the crew.

"D'ye mean to tell me that ye *didn't* come via the normal channels? That ye *don't* have the correct paperwork? And are ye also openly admitting that ye've not only entered Old World waters by *jumping* the liminal line, and ye did so knowingly and willingly?"

"Errrm, yes."

The guard gasped. Hugh watched his hand move towards a large red button on the desk.

"What are you doing? Please, don't push that."

"I'm afraid this is far above my pay grade. This number of illegal immigrants is equivalent to a full-scale invasion." His hand appeared to be shaking. "Now, don't go making any sudden movements, d'ya hear me lad? The boat we sent out should have taken ye all into custody before ye even docked."

"Please, we mean no harm."

"*Mean no harm?* Do ye realise that ye've contravened the official peace treaty, 1336B, line five*?*"

"You mean 1356D, line eight," said Tinker. Everyone turned to look at the cook.

"What? I studied the rules for my food exam. 1336B, line five states 'No child is to handle fruit from the New World, unless it's been thoroughly washed.' You mean 1356D, line eight, 'Any groups larger than the number of three that cross the border, known as the liminal line, at any unofficial point, shall be deemed a full-scale threat and an act of war.'"

"Thanks, mucker. I stand corrected."

"But that's not true," said Hugh. "We're not declaring war!"

"I haven't finished. It saddens me to say that in violation of treaty 1356D, line eight, we've no choice but impound yer little vessel."

"But that's me ship!" said Shackleton.

"Not anymore. We're going to have to commandeer it for the upcoming war effort."

"But we haven't arrived here to invade. Far from it. We're not at war!" said Hugh, now pleading with the guard.

"Ah, that is where you are wrong. We are at war – or will be once I fill out the relevant paperwork, file it with the elder council, get it signed and filed under the relevant department. We will take you into custody until the money is paid for your release. Never in my wildest dreams did I think I'd be the one to press this button!"

The guard raised his hand above his head and slammed it down hard on the red button in front of him.

Chapter 16

Pandemonium ensued. The alarms were deafening as the noise bounced off the hard walls. Dust fell from the rafters as doors were flung open with guards pouring into the hall as if they were flowing out of the room's solid stone walls. The ship's crew put up a valiant fight, but they were quickly overwhelmed and soon surrendered.

Hugh's arm hairs stood on end, with the amount of power being drawn in from the world around them. He felt pairs of hands grabbing at him, and he fought back until a kick to the back of his knees sent him tumbling towards the floor. The wind was knocked out of him. Guards landed heavily on his back, preventing him from escaping, not that he had anywhere to run. A sharp blow to the back of his head rendered him unconscious.

Hugh was in a place he had visited many times before. The dark coldness of the sight penetrated deep into his bones. He could hear a quiet conversation happening nearby. Hugh rose and realised he was shivering. Remembering his recent lessons with Balinas, he set to calling forth the runes needed to protect his life-link. He could make out Emily's voice.

'*… told him to listen to me, but would he listen? Of course not.*'

It turned out she was talking to Heather.

'Aye, I knew we should've intervened before he got that far. Talk of the wee bugger, here he is. I see ye decide to leave yer body behind this time, eh?'

Hugh looked at the pair moving towards him.

'I didn't have time to react. How have we ended up here again?'

It seemed lighter than usual. Emily was as clear as she had ever been, compared to the previous times that he had entered the sight.

'You're kidding, right? We said let us do the talking. But you had to be the man, didn't you?'

She looked at Hugh, and he looked away into the emptiness of the sight.

'Sorry. Look, can we set this aside for the time being? What are we going to do now, and where are our bodies?'

He looked back over his life-link, seeing it follow the golden lines of Emily and Heather's, back in the same direction.

'Can I assume we're all in the same place, then?'

'Aye, that we are. I'm impressed. Ye put up a good fight back there. It took six guards to put you down.'

That surprised him.

'I did? I wasn't aware of that. One minute it was all noise, guards and fighting, the next, I'm waking up here.'

Emily was less impressed.

'Yes, well, despite your lack of negotiation skills, it would appear there's more inside you than meets the eye. You were out cold when they dragged us all to the cells. We took an educated guess that you may have fallen into here again, and we were correct. You came around as we arrived.'

She examined his protected life-link.

'*I'm pleased to see that at least you have some common sense.*'

'*Well, given that I nearly died in Skellig-Krieg, I think this is much improved.*'

Emily said nothing but looked grieved. Hugh thought back to the cell in Skellig-Krieg to when he nearly lost himself to the sight. Emily had omitted to teach him an important rune of protection, meaning that each time he entered the sight, malevolent spirits could leech away at his soul.

'*Listen, you know I don't blame you for all of that. It was a simple mistake.*'

'*Yes, but it was one that nearly cost you your life.*'

'*That's in the past now. We're missing the bigger issue, which is where are our bodies?*'

Heather spoke up.

'*They're in the cell, of course, ye wee ninny. Where else would they be? Ye were the one who got us arrested.*'

Hugh thought about fighting his corner, before deciding against it. He coughed awkwardly before moving the conversation on.

'*Yes, right. Shall we get back and see if I can't make amends?*'

'*Aye, but this time, can we agree that we do the negotiating from here on in?*'

'*Yes, alright. I get the message.*'

'*Good. Alright, let's get back. The others will wonder where we are.*"

Hugh felt the tug of Heather's force, willing him back towards his body, and he went with it. With the usual sensation of pulling behind the navel and a

–POP–

They were back in the plane of the conscious. Hugh opened his eyes and rubbed the back of his neck. He was at one end of a large cell, slumped up against a cold stone wall. A salty breeze fell on his face, and he looked up to a window. Bright sunlight shone through, casting the shadow of bars along the cell floor. At the other end of the space were Captain Shackleton and his crew, who surrounded Emily and Heather. The women were laid out on benches on either side if the room, with fingers dipped into water. Hugh knew most people needed to be close to water in order to enter the sight. He, however, had been gifted a special skill through his family bloodline, meaning he didn't have to be near water to cross over.

The crew of *A Ship With no Name* turned to looked at Hugh as he adjusted how he was sitting. He gulped and let out a nervous laugh.

"Hi …"

"I think," said Captain Shackleton, "that ye owe me, the lads and these two fine ladies here an apology."

"It's alright," said Emily, making the crew jump as she sat up. "Hugh has already apologised to us."

"Aye, I'm sure he has, but I think meself and the lads would like to hear it for ourselves."

They turned back to look at Hugh, whose mouth had gone dry.

"Well … I … Um, I'm sorry."

"Fir?" said Shackleton, all niceties dropped from his voice.

"For … not listening."

"*And?*"

"And for getting us into this situation and not taking the advice of Emily and Heather."

"That's better," said the captain. He turned back to his crew. "Mr Geber has apologised now, so I don't want to hear another peep out of yese lot about the situation."

The crew gave him a silent stare and Shackleton glared back at them.

One by one, they murmured their agreement – though Hugh was unsure if it was willingly done, or if there were other forces at play.

The scene was broken by the sound of keys jangling. A jailor appeared at the barred door. He opened it, thrusting a dishevelled Barrington into the cell, then slammed the door shut behind him. The crew parted as Barrington limped towards a bench and looked at it, before opting to stand. Hugh, Emily and Heather stepped forward to help him.

"Barrington, what happened?" said Hugh. "You look awful. Quick, take a seat here."

He tried to guide his friend down to the bench, but Barrington shook him off.

"Please, no. Not right now."

"What happened to ye?" asked Heather, as she stepped up to embrace him.

He let out a little whimper but did not rebuff her as he had done Hugh.

"Horrible, unspeakable things. Why didn't any of you try to help me?"

All the eyes in the room swung around to Hugh, who loosened his collar. Barrington turned wide-eyed and glared at this friend. Hugh rubbed the back of his neck, not knowing where to start.

"Well, it was like this …"

He set off, filling his friend in on all the events that had occurred in his absence. Barrington listened with a furrowed brow, leaning against the wall for support. When Hugh had finished, he waited with bated breath for Barrington's response, along with the rest of the room.

"So, what you are telling me is that not only did you make my situation worse, you also destabilised the world and started an international war?"

"I didn't start the war," said Hugh. "*We* started the war when we crossed over the liminal line."

Barrington looked at him, gobsmacked. Hugh thought his friend was about to clobber him. But instead, he sank down onto the bench, deflated.

"Ow!" he said and rolled onto his side.

"Well?" said Hugh.

"Well, what?"

"What are you going to do about this situation?"

"Why is it down to me?"

"Because you're the one who got us into this mess," Hugh said.

"I told you smoking that pipe was a bad idea."

"I hardly think I am wholly to blame for this. You didn't help matters." There was a silence, during which Barrington closed his eyes to muster some energy.

"I didn't have my pipe with me, only the one that Monty gave to me on the boat," said Barrington. "That has since been removed from my person. A loss of a thoroughly good pipe, I might add. I have

been threatened with some beast called a glawackus, questioned and searched – *thoroughly* searched. I think I've paid in full, and then some, for my mistakes. You've been knocked out and woken up in a cell relatively unharmed."

"Actually, I have been harmed, attacked by numerous guards," said Hugh. "And I too have lost my possessions, including my firestone, so you are not the only one to have lost something you hold dear."

"Be that as it may, you only have yourself to blame."

"Your so-called *friend*, Captain Cavendish, could have at least helped out," said Hugh. "Why did he not warn us about the situation before we arrived. As for the pain, my neck really is sore, I'll have you know."

"Really is sore …" said Barrington to nobody in particular, then looked Hugh in eye. "I have had someone's hand around, and in, regions I never wish to have touched again. Would you like a stranger's hand rooting around where the sun doesn't shine?"

"Well … I mean … when you put it like that …"

Barrington said no more, staring vacantly in silence at the floor. The rest of the room stared at Hugh. Emily looked to Hugh and cocked her head.

"Well, would you like me to hold your hand?" she asked.

He looked at her and, knowing what needed to be done, held out his right hand for her to take. It felt warm, and his chest fluttered with excitement. Her voice sounded in his head.

'Concentrate, Hugh.'

"Right, yes, I better had," he said aloud, causing some confusion within the room.

He concentrated on his entire being and focused on clearing his mind, attempting to bring Emily with him, but something was blocking his entry.

"What's wrong?" asked Heather.

"I can't step over full body. Something's stopping me. How did you manage it?"

"We didnae step over full body, only via our life-links."

"But I normally just fall in. This feels different, like there is something barring me from leaving this plane fully."

"Maybe it's an Old World thing," said Emily. "Let's see if we can make it over, using our life-links."

They went to sit down on one of the benches, so they wouldn't lose their balance once they had crossed over. Hugh concentrated on the sight, clearing all thoughts from his head, and attempted to get his life-link activated. He felt Emily's hand in his, and the usual sensation of being sucked through a keyhole backwards took over. They were in. Hugh immediately began calling out the runes for protection, feeling the warmth envelope him as he worked. He turned to see Emily had been pulled through with him, and he combined his runes with hers.

'I wouldn't want us to get separated. We need to stay together.'

Emily gave him a smile.

'What do you suggest we do now?'

'*I guess we need to see who we can find. HELLO … Is there anybody there?*'

They waited for a response, but none came forward.

'*Seriously?*'

'*I think we are on our own.*'

'*Of course we are on our bloody own!*'

Hugh looked around to see if there was anything that may give him some of idea of what to do next. He saw, off into the distance, a darker area and headed towards it. It seemed like the right thing to do, as though he were being somehow compelled.

'*Where are you going now …? Hugh, are you listening to me?*'

'*Yes, of course I am. There's no one else to talk to, is there?*'

'*Don't take that tone with me, Hugh Geber. Where did you disappear to back there? I was talking to you, but you didn't respond.*'

'*You didn't give me a chance to answer. You only asked where I was going.*'

She shook her head.

'*No. I called your name repeatedly, but you seemed to have tuned out. You must pay attention while we are here, Hugh. It's a good thing we're linked together, otherwise I would have lost you for good. So, where were you going?*'

'*I was interested in that dark area over there.*'

'*Hugh! I've warned you before, not to pay attention to things like that while we're in here. It will only lead to danger.*'

'*Alright, what ideas have you got then?*'

There was a pause whilst Emily thought what to do next.

'I think we should go this way.'

She pulled him backwards.

'But that's away from the dark area.'

'Exactly.'

Hugh felt himself being pulled back. Unable to resist, he gave in and went along with her plan. However, they didn't get far before they found their way barred. They walked into something solid, and it crackled as they touched it.

'Ouch! What was that?'

They had walked into an invisible barrier.

Emily was just as confused.

'I don't know, but it hurt.'

Hugh watched her as she reached out into the open space again. The same thing occurred, yet Hugh still felt the pain, even though it wasn't he who touched it.

'Ow! What is that, and why did it still hurt me?'

'I've said I don't know what it is, but we're linked together. I guess whatever happens to me, happens to you, and vice versa.'

Just then, someone joined them on the other side of the invisible barrier, with a

–POP–

'Aright there. Now then, what are ye up to? Trying to escape there, were ye?'

It was the guard that they first met on their arrival. Emily turned to him.

'What is this?'

'*This?*'

He tapped the invisible wall with the finial on the end of his stick. A web of runes lit up in front of him, blocking Hugh and Emily's way. Hugh looked around into the infinity of the sight, seeing the wall going off as far as he could see in all directions.

'*This keeps you in, and us safe. It's a life-link locker net. Ain't nothing getting past this, that there won't. It's a good thing too, otherwise ye might've escaped, wouldn't ye now? So, why don't ye head back to yer bodies, as there ain't no way you'll be getting past this.*'

He chuckled, then disappeared with a

—POP—

Hugh and Emily stood in silence, dumbstruck at the situation they were in.

'*Hugh … Hugh … Is that you?*'

'*Father?*'

Before Emily came back to her senses, Hugh pulled as hard as he could. He could feel her attempting to pull back against him, but his will to see his father was strong. It was coming from the dark area – he knew it, and he could feel it calling to his soul.

'*Hugh! Stop! I said stop it, damn it! You're scaring me!*'

There was fear in her voice. Hugh stopped, as he was brought back to himself.

'*Oh, Emily, I'm sorry.*'

'*Don't, just don't! I wish we weren't linked, otherwise I'd leave you here, Hugh Geber. What the hell do you think you are doing? I warned you not to follow that …*'

But something had now grabbed her attention. Hugh turned around. There in front of him, he could just make out the faint outline of someone coming towards them.

'Father?'

'Hello, Hugh.'

Chapter 17

The Elf King was sitting in his cabin. It wasn't ostentatious, by any means – a small room, being only a foot longer than the bed, and only twice it's width, but he wanted nothing bigger. Staying undercover was the most important thing right now, and if that meant making a few sacrifices, then so be it. He disliked travelling by sea but knew that needs must if he were to get the book before Smithson. He was hot on the man's heels but still keeping his distance. With any luck, the man would lead him directly to the next book without too much effort from his side. He just needed to wait for Smithson's boat to drop anchor, then ambush his team of divers. It was all too easy. His new servant boy walked in, and the Elf King beckoned him to take a seat. Tavish sat awkwardly, unsure if it was the right thing to do.

"Don't be afraid, boy. I don't bite."

"Yes, sire … I mean, no sire."

"It's okay, I've told you to dispense with the usual customs. We don't want anyone hearing those words and finding out our true identities. You must remember, we are unknown to all on this ship, and that's how I would like it to remain."

Tavish nodded but said nothing.

"Tell me, do you know why I rescued you that day from the water?"

"No, uh …" – he stopped himself from using the word sire – "No, I don't."

"Well, let's see if we can make this any easier." He pondered on how to deliver the next part, as he didn't want to scare the boy away. "Tell me, what do you know of your parentage?"

"Nothing. I don't think they were interested in me. They dumped me in an orphanage when I was a baby. I never saw them, and they never came back for me, so I remained unloved."

"I think that's not *quite* true, do you?"

"Alright," said Tavish, "not everyone gave up on me, but I always felt like I never fitted in, a misfit in life's great tapestry. That's why I ran away from the orphanage and then ran from a life I never wanted to be a part of. I do know that if you hadn't found me when you did, I wouldn't be here now. I owe you a debt that I will repay in servitude."

"How loyal, for one so young. What if I were to say that you have no debt to pay? I did what anyone would do in that situation, or should I say, what any father would do for his son in that situation."

There was a long, uneasy pause, whilst the servant looked agog into the king's face.

"Yes, it's true – though to be fair, I thought you lost along with your mother. I was surprised to realise that I was given a gift from the sprites themselves."

"But, how, why? We must have crossed paths numerous times. Why did you never look for me as a child or when I was growing up? You left me there, to suffer in silence." The boy went to stand, as if to leave the room. "I can't believe this, it's not true."

"Wait, Tavish, don't leave. We have much to discuss, my son."

"Don't call me that!"

"Why not? It's the truth."

"No, it's not true. This is one of your sick and twisted jokes, isn't it?"

He went to leave, but the king placed a hand on his arm, stopping him in his tracks.

"I assure you this is no joke. You can't run from here. Where would you go? Who would you tell? One of the ship's many crew? Is that what you would do, blow our cover in one fell swoop? Or would you jump ship, take a dip in the nice fresh sea? I hear you like the open water. Rescued twice now if I'm not mistaken?"

A look of fear flashed across his son's face before he regained his composure.

"That's right," said the Elf King, "there is nowhere for you to go, no-one you can tell. For if you reveal our little secret, then you would be in as much trouble as me, if not more. Hiding a known criminal, one such as myself, would not go down well with the authorities, I can assure you of that. Though if you want to, go ahead. It would be a lengthy prison sentence at the very least – and death at worst."

His son looked at him, then towards the door, as if assessing which would be the better fate to face. He sat back down on the bed.

"That's it. You know it's the better option."

"This is impossible."

"Impossible, but real. I can see that you are still in need of more proof."

He unbuttoned his shirt and rolled it off his left shoulder, revealing a tattoo in the shape of Morcarthia. His son's eyes opened wide.

"Yes, it's true. I've shown you mine, so let me see yours."

Slowly, the boy undid his shirt and pulled it down over his left shoulder, revealing a matching tattoo.

"There we are, that should be all the proof that you need. These are given to all royal children at birth. Now, come sit with me, my son, we have much to plan."

Chapter 18

Smithson was sitting in a bar in Killinsfolk, watching the sun set over the bay. He was busy digesting the latest message from his contact. Word was that Geber and his band of not so seaworthy followers were due in court the next morning. The chances of their release were slim to none, and a smile spread across his face. This was turning out to be the perfect evening, and there was nothing that could spoil it.

"Mr Smithson, sir."

It was Collins. Smithson let out a sigh.

"What is it, man? Can't you see I'm busy?"

Collins looked from the drink to Smithson, then to the bay he was looking out over.

"Well, I wouldn't want to disturb sir's busy work; after all, it looks very important."

"Go ahead then, you've ruined the moment, anyway."

"If you are not interested, then I can take my news elsewhere. I hear the Elf King is on the move, and I'm sure he would appreciate the information."

"Oh Collins, I don't know where you're getting your information, but you really need to work on those contacts."

"And what is that supposed to mean?"

"Well, let's say that the Elf King and I have a mutual understanding. I'm sure it's something that you wouldn't understand, and I wouldn't want to worry your little brain with such complexities. Now, have you come here to tattle on the Elf King, or do you have some actual information for me?"

Collins looked at Smithson, seething but refusing to let it out. After a deep breath, he delivered the update.

"We have an underwater ship that will get us to the desired area we are looking for. I need you to sign off on the hire payment for the captain and the insurance."

"Insurance?" said Smithson, taking the paper from Collins and examining it. "What an absurd amount of money. We're only looking for a book. Can't you get them to lower the fees?"

"I'm sorry, but I don't think you're on the same page as the rest of us. You realise that, to get to the book, you have to sail through waters protected by magical rites, don't you? Rites that will have to be overcome."

"Magical rites, indeed. Collins, you do like to overdramatise these things somewhat. All they have to do is go swim amongst some fish and retrieve the book we're looking for. You're fully aware these aren't any old books we're after. It's vital the New World gets them *before* the Old World realises what I'm up to."

Collins gave him a level stare.

"It's high time you looked at the world we are in. It's not just going down to the fish, as you so crassly put it. The merfolk are an ancient race, one so old that it is said the human race may well have their roots embedded in them."

"Piffle, as if we could be related to some fish."

"*Merfolk.*"

"Alright, keep your hair on. Whatever you wish to call them, you cannot stand there and tell me you believe in these *children's stories?*"

"Have you not seen what is happening around you? Can you not remember crossing over the liminal line?"

"Collins, you know as well as I do, that was just a bad thunderstorm. I chose to sleep that one out in my cabin. All these parlour tricks, and that's all they are, well, they are being performed as a way to try to scare otherwise clear thinking New Worlders. They're clinging onto outdated ways and beliefs. The sooner the New World can sort this mess out and get some law and order around here, the better."

"Do you really think the New World has that much power? You'll be eating your words by the end of all this, I can assure you of that. Just you wait until we're down there, then you'll see what the Old World really stands for."

"Hang on?" said Smithson, scoffing. "You don't seriously think I'm actually going down there in that leaky bathtub with those crackpots, do you?"

"How else do you intend on getting this book?"

"I was going to send you, of course, and your little apprentice. Where is the boy, anyway? Is he shaking like a leaf in the corner, still afraid of his own shadow?"

"I might remind you to show Maso the respect he deserves. He's a Collins, and don't you go forgetting it."

"Oh please, don't tell me you actually care for the boy?"

"We Collinses must stick together and stay true to our family oath, though that's something I doubt you'd understand."

"And what is *that* supposed to mean?"

"Do I need to spell it out for you? Your idea of family is sketchy at best. Why, I sometimes doubt if there's a caring bone in your body."

"Excuse me, but who do you think you're talking to?"

"Seeing as you're the only person propping up the bar, I would think it's quite obvious, well, at least to the non-apes in the room."

Smithson slammed his drink down on the bar, smashing the glass.

"How dare you! I am your boss, and don't you go forgetting that!"

"You just keep telling yourself that. Now if you don't mind, I've a trip in a leaky bathtub to take, wherein I'll see some old friends that you don't believe in. Good day to you, *sir*."

Collins turned on his heel and strode away from the bar. Smithson slammed his hand down, momentarily forgetting about the broken glass.

"Damn you, and damn your family, Collins. Ah, shit!"

He pulled the shard of glass out of his hand and wrapped it in a napkin to stop the bleeding. Furious with himself and Collins, he turned back to look across the bay, only to see that the sun had disappeared below the horizon.

Chapter 19

Hugh stood looking into the broken image of his father. The empty darkness of the silence was bearing down on him, and he was finding it too much to take in. Emily, who was equally shocked, was the first to break the stalemate.

'Frederick? But how, why …?'

'I know this is hard for both of you, and I apologise for taking you by surprise.'

Hugh found his voice.

'See, I told you he was alive. You told me not to follow the voice, said it was malevolent, yet here he is.'

Emily turned to him, but it was Frederick who spoke.

'Hang on a minute, Hugh. Emily is not to blame here. She was right to be cautious, there are many things out here that would happily do you harm, given the chance. You of all people should know the importance of this, having experienced the effects of those malevolent beings first-hand.'

'But you're supposed to be dead, father. Those voices were supposedly guiding me astray, and yet you're here, standing in front of me. Where's your body? We can get out of here, come find you and see you in person.'

'*Steady on, Hugh. Let's take a few steps back. I'm technically not alive, but I also cannot reveal where my body is.*'

'*Why not? We can help you, bring you back. We've done it before.*'

Emily was shaking her head.

'*No, Hugh. Look at your father. His image is broken. I don't think this is like the other time when we rescued Hamish or when you rescued Heather.*'

'*Emily is correct, Hugh. I'm beyond saving, but I cannot pass over for a couple of reasons. First and foremost, I am still holding onto something dear to us both. But there is something else. It seems the one who guides those over is currently not in the right place. There is so much to explain, and there is not enough time right now.*'

'*But I just want to see you. Have you got the book of lore for alchemy?*'

'*Again, all in good time, Hugh. The book of alchemy is in a safe place, and I feel that now is not the time for me to reveal its location. You have more steps to complete first and must continue to find the other lore books.*'

'*So it is true then? You were searching for the other books of lore as well, not just the one for alchemy?*'

'*Yes, but I was side-tracked by something else. We, that is Robert and I, were being followed, but we never saw who it was. They are after the item I removed from behind the waterfall in Dallum, and it was only with Robert's help I got away. I removed a box and hid it in the Hotel Alpine for you. I take it you found the box under the floorboard, as I explained in my letter? You must keep it safe. It's imperative the box does not fall into the wrong hands. You'll have to find the other books of lore before the Elf King does, otherwise it will spell danger for the world at large.*'

'*We are looking for the books of lore, in fact, we've found two already. Smithson has the box.*'

'*What, how? Why did you give it to him? I didn't realise he was helping you, otherwise I would have advised caution there. He never like me and his father working together and resented when Robert joined me on my trips away from the university.*'

'*We're not working with him, and we certainly don't trust him. It's a long story, too long to tell now.*'

'*Then you need to get the box back from him.*'

'*Well, that's easier said than done. If we ever get out of the cell we're currently in, we can resume the task we've been set.*'

'*The cell?*'

Here Emily decided to speak up.

'*Yes, we're currently locked up because of some smart talking from your son.*'

'*Hang on a minute, it's not all my fault. Barrington was also partly to blame.*'

'*I'm not going there, Hugh. We can agree to disagree.*'

The sketchy outline of Frederick shook its head.

'*Sorry, are you saying that Barrington is also with you?*'

Hugh decided to briefly fill his father in on the events which led to them being locked up.

'*… so now it's up to me to fix all of this. I tried to enter the sight full body, but I didn't seem to manage it, which is confusing because I couldn't stop falling in here a few months ago. Just the slightest jump and I was in.*'

Frederick stood motionless, as though he were computing what Hugh had just recalled.

'*I know the reason why you can't enter the sight full body, and why you met that barrier. The cells at Androssan are heavily fortified and designed to hold those with access to the sight. If you could just enter the sight full body, then anyone could escape. As for the extra security within the sight, well that is an extra protection, designed to stop those who enter the sight from contacting the outside world. It's a testament to how well you two are trained, to see you both here together.*'

'*But how can we see you?*'

'*Ah, well, that's a little more complicated to explain. I've got myself stuck between the two planes, neither being in the sight nor in the world of the living. I'm in a holding pattern of sorts, waiting for the right time.*'

'*Is it something to do with the dark area over there?*'

'*Yes, that's right, though again, Emily is correct when she says you mustn't go near that place, at least not until the right time. I cannot tell you when that will be – only you'll know when. Follow your instincts on that one.*'

Emily nodded.

'*So, now what are we supposed to do?*'

'*Well, you'll need to contact someone to get you out of the situation you've found yourselves in. They will also need to counteract the catastrophic sequence of events that has been triggered.*'

'*But didn't you say we wouldn't be able to reach anybody from within the cell?*'

'*Correct, you cannot contact anyone, but I can. You'll have to trust me on this one, and I'll need a little time to get to the right people.*'

'*So what do we do in the meantime? I don't think we have that much time left to wait.*'

'It shouldn't be too long, I hope, and if things get sticky, try to keep them talking, though I suggest you leave that bit to Emily, Hugh.'

Frederick looked into Hugh's eyes, but Hugh did not return Frederick's faltering gaze.

'For now, I suggest that you two get back to the cell. If the guards realise you're not back yet, it could lead to more trouble.'

'No wait …'

Hugh moved towards his father as if preparing to give him a hug.

'Stop! We must not make contact. I'm unsure what will happen if we do. It may have irreversible implications. Trust me when I say there is nothing more I want than to hug you, but we can't. Now please, go back to the cell and leave the rest to me.'

His outline faded away before Hugh even had a chance to fight back. Emily was already pulling on Hugh, drawing them both back down their life-link. Hugh felt the sensation of being dragged through the keyhole once more, and he realised he was back in his body. The smell of stone, metal and body odour came through, and he opened his eyes.

—POP—

"Ah, excellent, you're back in the room with us," said Barrington. "We were getting a little worried that you wouldn't return to us. What's wrong?"

Hugh sat up and was wiping the tears away from his face. Emily filled in the room at large with all the events that had transpired within the sight. As Hugh looked around, he realised that the sun was setting in the Old World outside their window.

"What time is it?"

"It's past teatime now, my dearest Hugh. We saved you some food, but don't get your hopes up. It's nothing to write home about. You were out for a long while, I must say. The guards were most startled to see you had both entered the sight, they were going to send someone in to send you back here. We could hear them discussing the situation. They were most perturbed that you had entered the sight again."

"Well, father said that we were lucky to be there. All we have to do now is sit and wait and hope that he finds a solution to get us out of here."

Barrington rolled his eyes.

"Is there any help on the way, or not? Emily said that Frederick was sorting it, so he must have hinted at something?"

"Look. I wish I had some answers, but the truth is that I don't. He didn't say what he was going to do, only that he would sort it."

"So, what are we supposed to do? We can't sit around here whilst Smithson's out there gallivanting after the book, and that's *without* the Elf King being factored in."

"Barrington, stop it," said Emily. "We're at as much of a loss here as you. We'll just have to wait and see what happens and trust that Frederick can get us the help we need."

"Well, let's hope that he can get us further than his son has," said Barrington. "Whilst you were in the sight, the lads and Heather, here, filled me in with what happened." Barrington stood shaking his head, chewing the inside of his mouth. "Well? Don't you have anything to say?"

Hugh's head hung low. He felt as though he had done ten rounds in a wrestling contest.

"Just leave it," said Emily, coming between Hugh and the rest of the room. "Hugh has been through enough today."

"Hugh's been through enough?" Barrington exploded. "I have had an internal search carried out and by the sounds of things, he played a large part in how that ghastly experience unfolded. I'm sorry that poor old Hugh here's had a tough day, but I think my sympathy tank is a tad empty."

Barrington's tirade was broken by a rap on the bars by a guard.

"Oi, do ye think ye could keep the noise down in there? You're disturbing our game of feather points."

"What on earth is feather points?" asked Barrington, thrown off his stride.

"For goodness sake, you New Worlders are all the same," said the guard, "uncultured and crass. It's where we throw small metal spikes with feather flights on the back at a square chequerboard with numbered areas."

"Oh, do you mean quill shot?"

"No. I mean feather points. Now keep the noise down, would ye? All this whining's giving us a headache."

With that, the guard walked off. The captives had to endure three hours of drunken fun as the guards got into their game and grew progressively more raucous. Hugh didn't know what time it was, but the moon was high in the sky before the noise eventually abated. He fell into an uneasy sleep filled with dreams of falling, his father berating him and the destruction of the world.

The following day, they were awoken by the sound of bowls filled with cold mush being shoved into the cell. Hugh's stomach groaned away to itself, and he reluctantly ate the gruel in front of him. Around mid-morning they heard the ominous sound of keys jingling their way towards the cell. The occupants looked up to see the guard unlocking the door.

"Are we to be freed?" asked Barrington.

"Errrm, no. Yer to be sentenced by the court for treason."

"We can't be sentenced for treason when we haven't yet been tried for it."

"Who says you haven't been tried. Anyway, you should have thought about that before you violated our waters. We found enough fulminate powder on that ship of yours to warrant a one-way ticket to Traitors' Drop."

Barrington looked at Shackleton, who shrugged and smiled awkwardly.

"What? We didn't know about the fulminate powder! You have to believe us!"

"Like you didn't know you were carrying tobacco on entry, I suppose. I think your co-conspirator's face says it all. Follow me, please."

Chapter 20

The prisoners were guided, in silence, up a spiral stone staircase. It seemed to Hugh that the stairs were never-ending, and just as he was getting to where his legs were about to give in from exhaustion, the group reached the top of the stairs and were ushered into a brightly lit, polished stone courtroom. His senses were overloaded by light and noise, for the room erupted as they entered. Hugh looked up, and he saw a wooden balcony, packed with the townsfolk who had all come out in force to watch the trial. Their guard disappeared, leaving them alone in their wooden pen. Escaping was off the cards, as they were squeezed together, with a large drop all around them, below which lay a spiked pit. Hugh stroked the stubble on his face uneasily, and he saw the rest of the group looking just as uneasy. Barrington was hugging Heather, and he thought he ought to do the same to Emily, but she shrugged him off, leaving him feeling alone and unwanted.

Hugh was packed up tightly against the edge, and his hand was resting next to a gap in the handrail next to him. He looked down, seeing it was a small door. His world spun, as he imaged the idea of it bursting open and falling to his death. Opposite this was another mini gallery, filled with guards. Between them, there was a wide plank of wood suspended out of the way. If put in place, it would provide access between the prisoner pen and the guard gallery. An aisle split this gallery in two with a door at the end. Daylight seeped in around the edges, which made Hugh feel uneasy.

Opposite Hugh and the prisoners, officials dressed in dark robes and wigs sat in their own private gallery. They looked down upon the accused with critical eyes. Behind them was a chair with a door behind it. The court bailiff entered, and the room fell silent.

"All rise. The honourable Judge Roderick Ranglestaff presiding."

Hugh looked at Barrington, Emily and Heather, who all wore the same look of surprise.

Those who were seated, stood, all eyes now looking to the door behind the chair. When it opened again, it revealed a character dressed in a red and gold cloak, round rimmed glasses and a ringed wig draping well below the person's shoulders. Hugh watched as the judge fought through his ceremonial garb and sat down. He pushed his glasses into position – left askew when he was climbing into his seat – back up his fat nose. He was sure to leave enough space to be able to peer over the top of them down at the accused. The judge banged a gavel three times on the bench. It sparked each time it struck. Hugh's body tingled all over, as the room fell silent around them. The judge cleared a large amount of excess phlegm from his throat, spitting it to the floor. He reminded Hugh of a toad.

"Thank you. You may be seated."

The gallery made an audible creak, as various bottoms squeezed onto the small wooden benches.

"Bwing fourth the charges."

A guard in colourful uniform, wearing a black hat with a white feather in it, ascended some steps up to the judge's bench. It took an age for the man to climb the numerous stairs, the sound of his footsteps echoing around the room. He was out of breath by the time he reached the bench.

"Please, do take you time. It's not as if I've anything better to do," the judge said to the man now clutching his chest.

"Well? Do wun along, I don't wemember inviting you to stay for a party."

The guard bowed, mopped his brow, then began his descent from the bench. The judge read through the sheet twice, before turning to the accused party.

"Never in my caweer of wesiding over this courtwoom" – some sniggering came from the balcony behind Hugh, and the judge paused, peered over the top of his glasses at the gallery, before carrying on – "have I been pwesented with such heinous cwimes. To not only cwoss over the liminal line which sepawates our two wealms, but …"

He stopped again, this time to peer over his glasses at Barrington, who had raised a hand.

"Yes? You wish to addwess the courtwoom?"

"Your honour," Barrington began, and the judge rolled his eyes and let out a sigh. "Errrm, I was just wondering where the jury was?"

"I beg your pardon?"

"Well, it's just in our world, we're entitled to a fair trial, with a judge and jury. I'm not sure how thing are run here in this place— ow!"

Heather had kicked Barrington in the ankle, leaving a big enough gap for the judge to cut in.

"Never in my life have I been insulted like this, especially not on my own courtwoom!" – more sniggering was heard, but this time it came from Hugh's right, from the gallery of guards – "Silence! I will not have this insolence. So, you think you are entitled to a fair heawing, do you? That maybe I'll be unjust in my wuling? Well, I don't wish to know how they do things in the New World, but here we deal with things diffewently. I am judge and juwy, and what I say goes. If we gave power to the common people, we would be no better than the wabble you associate yourselves with."

There were calls of approval from the gallery and guards alike.

"But that's not fair!" said Hugh, who was feeling the injustice of the situation. The rest of the group had found their voices and were also now joining in.

"SILENCE!" shouted the judge, his voice booking around the room whilst he banged his gavel repeatedly.

The effect was instantaneous. The group couldn't carry on with their complaints, no matter how hard they tried.

"I am appalled at the behaviour in fwont of me. This weckless act of war must, and shall, be dealt with appwopwiately. I think we should skip the boring part and jump diwectly to sentencing."

The room erupted into a soup of noise. Those on the gallery were back on their feet, shouting out things they believed should happen to the group below them, whilst the accused had broken the spell cast upon them and began hurling insults back. Many items were being thrown down, including rotten fruit and vegetables. The judge, though not audible over the noise, commanded control with his gavel once more. One rather rotten, ill-aimed tomato hit him square on the nose. There was a collective intake of breath throughout the courtroom.

"Who thwew that?"

The person in question was pointed at by everyone else in the gallery.

"Guawds, I think we should twy out the twaitor's dwop."

More sniggers came from the galleries.

"Who is that? Do you wish to join this wepwobate on his final dwop?"

Not a sound could be heard.

"Good, then we shall pwoceed. Guawds, thwow him fwom the dwop!"

Hugh watched as the closest guards pushed their way through the crowd towards the man in question. He protested and attempted to make a run for it, but found his way impeded by the crowd. The guards grabbed the man under the arms before dragging him off. He appeared a minute later, coming out of the door next to the guards' gallery. He was dragged, kicking and shouting, all the way to the door that Hugh had been looking at earlier. Those in the viewing gallery craned their necks, attempting to see what would happen next.

Hugh watched as the door was opened, letting bright sunlight stream into the courtroom, temporarily blinding him. He could make out the silhouette of the man, pinning himself momentarily to the frame, whilst the guards grappled with him, before they won, shoving him out of the door. They could easily make out the sound of his scream disappearing off into the distance before the door was slammed shut, leaving the room in an eerie silence.

"Vewy good," said the judge with a smile, whilst wiping the rest of the tomato off his face. "Anyone else fancy thwowing some fwuit and vegetables in my diwection?"

The room remained silent as the crowd in the gallery retook their seats.

"I thought as much. Wight, where were we? Ah yes, about to deal with you lot, as I seem to wemember. I think we can all agwee that you are a thweat to the state, and therefore, I sentence you all to the twaitors' dwop." He banged his gavel twice. "Guards, lower the footbwidge, if you will."

There was more commotion, this time coming from just behind Hugh. Everyone was backing away from where he was, finding whatever space there was left behind him. Hugh was left frozen with fear, as he watched the plank lowered into place. One of the guards on the opposite side tapped his stick, and the finial glowed. The door swung open under Hugh's hand, nearly taking him off the edge as it went. He was left looking down into the void, and he swallowed hard. He was now aware of the people behind him moving towards his back, and to his horror, he realised guards were now coming up the stairs to push the crowd onto the bridge.

"Come along, we don't have all day. I have a lunch waiting for me, and I don't wish for it to be cold," said the judge.

If Hugh didn't know better, he would have thought the old man was doing this purely for his own entertainment. He was pushed towards the edge as the plank was finally lowered into place. Not wanting to fall, he had no option but to step out onto the wood in front of him.

It bounced under foot, and he feared it would become dislodged, sending them to a painful death upon the spikes below. Then, from somewhere far below him, a door was flung open, nearly causing him to lose his balance.

"STOP, I say. Stop this instant!"

"What is this bwazen intewuption to the pwoceedings? May I wemind you that this is a cawt of law, and I am a wegcognised … oh, it's you Purcival. What wight do you have—"

"Just stop. You there, on the plank, don't move!"

Unsure of what to do, Hugh stopped halfway, bobbing up and down over the gap. He could feel the people behind him coming to a stop. The plank gave an uneasy creak but held firm. Hugh watched this Percival fellow ascending the many stairs to get to the judge's bench.

"This is an outwage, Purcival. You have no wight to enter my courtwoom and tell me what to do? No wight at all! You are wuining all my fun. Cawwy on with the pwoceedings!"

"Do NOT carry on!"

The plank shook beneath Hugh's quaking legs.

"Will someone make up their bloody mind around here," he said.

"Roderick Ranglestaff, as your older brother, I order you to listen to me now. I have a note from the high enchantress, ordering the release of these people."

He was nearly at the top and extremely out of breath.

"Besides, we have the dragon riders of Hassenlair outside, ready to catch anyone else you decide to throw out the door. We caught the last one, goodness only knows what he did, and I don't wish to foot the bill for anymore. You know that door is only to be used in exceptional circumstances."

"But they are warmongerwing enemies of the wealm, and the law wequires—"

"I know the law as well as you," he said. "You there, don't you take another step!"

Hugh felt the bridge bounce ominously, and someone bumped into his back, causing his stomach to drop to his boots. The plank made another ominous creak, and Hugh thought he caught sight of it moving at the other end. Percival had finally made it to where his brother was seated.

"For the love of all things spritely, just read it, will you!" He held the piece of paper aloft for his brother to read.

"We were just getting to the weally fun bit," said the judge, taking the paper. "Are you sure we can't dwop just one of them? For old time's sake?"

"Read the message."

"Oh, vewy well."

He read the note in his hands, let out a sigh, then looked up at the room.

"Appawently we are to welease the pwisoners."

Murmurs of disappointment came from the crowd on the balcony, who were all looking forward to a good execution. Percival was already making his way back down from the bench.

"I'm sorry, but it is now twuly out of my hands. Guawds, welease the pwisoners."

Behind him, Hugh felt the group edging backwards, and ahead of him he watched the plank move closer to the edge. When he turned he saw he was the last one remaining on the plank. Barrington, Emily and Heather were standing near the open drop, beckoning him towards them and safety. When he passed the middle of the plank it started to bounce in time with his steps. One step from safety, the bouncing dislodged the far end.

Everything seemed to go into slow motion.

The plank dropped away beneath him, and he was falling towards the spikes below. He was scrabbling at thin air, trying to grab hold of something. He thought he was a goner and wished he had more time to fix the bridges in his own life before his untimely death. He closed his eyes, with images flashing before him. Images of Barrington,

Emily and Heather, in happier times. He felt the pain, which he assumed were the spikes impaling him. But then why was it only in his arms and shoulders? His head was throbbing, as though he had hit it, and everything seemed calm to him.

Hugh opened his eyes, seeing the same happy image as before, but realising it was actually happening. Sore and achy, he sat up to realise that he was back on the platform for the accused. Sound was returning and he felt the sensation of people jovially patting his back, and someone's arms around his neck, trying to hug him for all it was worth. He turned and looked into Emily's eyes.

"You're safe, it's alright," she said into his ear.

"What happened?" he asked.

"The plank went from underneath you, but we caught you at the last moment, me, Barrington and Heather. The rest of the crew were quick to get behind us and help haul you back up."

"Just like a man overboard, lad," said Shackleton, patting Hugh on the back. "All those years of training came in handy."

He chuckled and went to congratulate the rest of his crew on a rescue well done.

"Thank you," said Hugh, "all of you."

He was shaken by the experience, feeling wobbly all over.

"It's alright," said Barrington. "We nearly lost you back there. It was Heather who got a hold on you first, which gave me and Emily enough time to grab on. The crew were quick to link arms and haul us all back in from the edge."

"Aye, 'twas a close call, Hugh," said Heather. "I'd rather not do that again, if it's all the same to ye?"

"That's fine by me," said Hugh, and they all let out a laugh.

"Mr Geber, Mr Delphin, Miss Le Fey and Miss McDougall I presume?"

It was Percival, who was flushed in the face and had sweat dripping from his brow.

"Percival Ranglestaff at your service."

"We're glad that you came when you did," said Barrington. "Talk about cutting it fine."

"Yes, sorry, we only got the message this morning."

"Well, thank you, Mr Ranglestaff."

"Please, call me, Percival."

He held out his hand, and Barrington shook it vigorously. Hugh, however was not so quick to take the man's offer. He looked at Emily, who also appeared to be having the same thoughts.

"How do we know if we can trust him?" she asked.

"Well, we can ask him if he is a part of the EGF."

"Great idea," she said looking at Hugh expectantly. "Well? what are you waiting for?"

Hugh let out a sigh and turned back to Percival. If he really was to be trusted then all he had to do was ask to look at his EGF symbol, and in return, he would ask Hugh to see his first.

"Well, Percival, I have a very important question for you. How do we know we can trust you?"

"After you."

Chapter 21

On the southern end of the Isle of Fey, nestled around the inlets and hills, lay the capital of Androssan. The green island stood alone in the open waters of the sea known as the Mari Populi. Steeped in ancient traditions, the city's streets teemed with life, working in a synchronised pattern following the ebb and flow of the tides it had grown up with. Over the years, the city had expanded to fill the nooks and crannies of the hills it was built upon.

Where the streets worked upwards, shops could be found either side, making use of what would be deemed as dead space of the ground underneath, nestled into the hillside like hermit crabs filling empty shells. The streets curved around the rising terrain, tempting visitors to go in deeper and explore the possibilities open to them.

The city's buildings were painted in a multitude of colours, and any of the walls which weren't painted were covered with tiles. On sunny days, the colours would gleam like a multicoloured confectionary box. On the wet days – of which there were many – the colours were a welcomed relief from the overcast skies.

There were numerous apothecaries dedicated to making various sea-based potions and elixirs made from various crustaceans, shells and seaweed, as well as the usual ingredients gathered from around the island. These were transformed into remedies for ailments from toothache to wet foot, a well-known blight for the sailors and fisherman.

Down on the quayside were many huts dedicated to the gutting of fish before moving them to the salters. They took the fresh fish and massaged salt crystals into the freshly cleaned flesh and hooked them onto canes in rows of twenty, ready for the padders to take them to the smokers' wharf, where the smell of woodsmoke filled the air. Chippers could be seen adding wood chips to the bottom of the smokers, where fish hung row upon row to be flavoured and preserved.

Where the land flattened off to meet the sea, great salt beds had been set up to mine the sea of this precious resource. Windmills had been built along the channel leading to the beds, to help pump the water when the beds needed topping up with sea water. The so-called salt kings and salt queens were in charge of divvying up the salt, or white gold as it was known locally, into the different grades needed for city life, from preserving food, to use in the magical potions of the city's apothecaries.

Many shops were dedicated to the old arts, such as *"Sights and Seer's — For all your clairvoyant needs. Your visit is expected!"* But by far the most common Old World art practised in the shops of Androssan was alchemy. In apothecaries across the capital you could find people in dark rooms, working on the latest advances in the Old World. Hugh peered through shadowy doorways, lit up by sparks and flashes as the occupants within attempted to work on the greatest of life's mysteries. It wouldn't be a normal day if there wasn't an explosion or two, with alchemists stumbling out of multicoloured, smoky doorways, covered in soot.

Moving on from there, was the area known as the Fures. Huddled into the darkest corners and hidden alleyways, was where the shady elements of the city lived. As was true of most cities of it size, Androssan had a thriving underworld, and the Fures was where it could be found. Unexplained noises arose from dark alleys, and rumours were never in short supply. The mob leaders ruled here and to cross them might well cost you your life.

Flowing through the city, cleaving it in two, was the River Dogo. Its waters were said to have magical powers, for it flowed from deep within the Isle of Fey. Its banks were lined with steps, often full of people looking to bathe in the flowing river. North of the Dogo, lay the upper city and the palace of the High Enchantress. It was from here that the day-to-day life of the city was run, with some overreaching powers over the isle itself, though most was left to the local districts to oversee.

Hugh was taking in the sights, sounds and smells as they crossed the river by way of the bridge which trapped them in on their arrival. Seabirds cawed overhead, diving at the city's fishing fleet as it sorted the day's catch. Percival led the group along the isle's Mile – the road that lead up from sea to the palace. Up ahead, on the highest hill in the area, stood a large palace. It commanded a formidable view over the city with its many towers set behind the safety of an impressive curtain wall. They were now walking uphill, along cobbled streets lined with shops. Crowds of people lined the streets, all parting as the group of newcomers walked past. Folk stood outside ale houses, smoking pipes as if to mock Barrington – who looked on aghast at the hypocrisy. As they approached, Hugh saw more of the guards marching along the crenelations, their feathered hats reflecting the midday sun. The day was warm and the city humid, and the group was slick with sweat by the time they arrived.

"Make way for the party to see the High Enchantress," called the head guard. "Make way, I say!"

They passed through a fortified gate in the great stone wall. To each side of the gate stood armoured oxen with riders to match. The air was cooler in the shade of the building, much to Hugh's relief. Once they cleared the curtain wall, they entered the first courtyard – which was a hive of activity comprising numerous market traders selling all manner of items from food to amulets.

As the guards cleared the way for the new arrivals, the area quietened down. Hugh knew all eyes were on them, and so he continued looking straight ahead. People were discussing the recent events in the courtroom with their neighbours, some agreeing with what had occurred, while others were not so keen.

They were soon up the next line of defence, in the form of an inner wall, also heavily guarded. Though this was a lower wall, it sat further up the hill, giving it more grandeur. The guards in the inner courtyard stood to attention and saluted their arrival. A large tree, standing taller than the walls, filled the space between the wall and the building. It was being guarded by four men on oxen armoured the same as those at the gates. Up ahead were a set of impregnable doors not unlike those of the Great Library back in Portis-Montis.

They had now entered the main palace of the High Enchantress. They were standing in the main hall, which was cool and had large corridors running left and right. A door in the right corridor opened up, filling the space with a clattering noise which was abruptly cut off when the door slammed shut. Up ahead was another set of doors and staircases that led off to other parts of the palace. The marble floor echoed underfoot, as the party came to a halt underneath the gaze of seven statues, each representing a different district of the Isle of Fey. Percival was talking to a guard on the staircase, who looked in their direction. Hugh could just about make out the conversation.

"… and I'm telling *you* we have it on the highest authority. The request has come from the High Enchantress herself."

"And *my* orders are to keep all visitors back until such time that her ladyship is ready."

"Listen, Bobkins, I haven't got the time to stand here and debate this with you. I have my orders and the authority, I might add, to go up these stairs. I've known you since you were knee high to a unicorn. And your mother for that matter. What would she say if she were to find out you were not only refusing to follow the orders of a higher rank but were also demoted to the duty of disposal from the latrines tower?"

He let the words hang in the air and waited for the guard to sweat it out. After an awkward two-minute silence, Bobkins finally relented.

"Fine, but I want it known that I had nothing to do with this and that I did all I could to prevent you from entering."

"You have my word," said Percival, who then turned to the rest of the group. "Alright, if you would be so kind as to follow me, please."

With that, he was off again, this time climbing up a mighty marble staircase. As they ascended, Hugh broke out into a sweat once more. The accent up the staircase seemed never-ending. He looked out the windows as they passed, seeing an amazing vista across the city.

"Come along, Hugh, keep moving," said Barrington. "We're all right behind you."

Hugh turned to see the rest of the group backing up behind him, nobody wishing to take the lead.

"Sorry," he said, "I'm just amazed at the view."

"Yes, well, can you be amazed whilst walking, please? If I stop for too long, I doubt I'll get going again."

Hugh huffed before carrying on with his journey up the stairs. Percival had disappeared further up, and Hugh picked up the pace, hearing someone rapping on a door up ahead. As he rounded a corner, he saw that the staircase opened up into a large chamber. Percival stood at some gold-plated doors. Hugh hadn't been able to take him in until this moment. He was a broad-shouldered man and wore a uniform similar to the other guards, though his had golden epaulettes with polished buckles on his shoes to match. He was clean shaven with a chiselled jawline, royal blue eyes and dark hair swept to one side. He had taken his purple beret off and was waiting to be let into the room.

"When we enter, let *me* do the talking," said Emily into Hugh's ear.

Before he had the time to respond, the doors swung open, and Percival stepped in, handing a note to the nearest guard, who announced their arrival.

"Lord Percival and the party from Portis-Montis, Ma'am."

Hugh looked around the room, amazed. From behind him came audible gasps from the rest of the group as they entered. They were in a large, round chamber with numerous ornately-gilded marble carvings. The more Hugh took in the room, the more gold he saw. Even the window frames hadn't missed out on the special treatment. There was a large domed ceiling with a viewing gallery wrapped around the outside. Hanging from the centre, there was a massive chandelier which far outweighed the one in Smithson's office. Hugh's eyes followed the large marble pillars back down to floor level. Around the room were niches, alternating with large windows and paintings depicting the different leaders from bygone eras. He heard water running somewhere in the background but couldn't see the source. Percival strode up to a chaise lounge where a lady was stretched out taking a rest. He went down onto one knee.

"This had better be important, Percy," the woman said. "You know I don't like my rest time being interrupted."

"Sybil dear, I have the party from Portis-Montis here, remember? We were only discussing them earlier."

"Ah yes, bring them forward," she said, removing the cucumber slices that were on her eyes and placing them onto a dish held out by a waiting servant, who she waved away with her hand.

Percival helped her up and into a blue velvet cloak, lined with black wool – apart from the hood, which was white fur. She turned to Hugh, beckoning him to step forward.

"This is Hugh Geber, my dear," said Percival. "Hugh, may I present to you the High Enchantress, overseer of everything that happens here in Androssan and throughout the Isle of Fey."

"It's a pleasure to meet you," said Emily, arriving at Hugh's side and taking a knee. "I am Emily le Fey."

"What's the matter? Can't the man speak for himself?" asked Percival.

"No, it's just better that I do the talking. Hugh can talk his way into trouble quicker than a hog talking its way onto a roasting spit."

The enchantress eyed Hugh up and down with a curious look, and he felt himself flush with energy.

"On any normal day, nothing would please me more than to speak to you, my dear. Believe me when I say, there is much to discuss on our part. But I must speak directly to Hugh. After all, it's his name that got you out of the dire position you were in."

"It did?" said Hugh, looking at her in surprise.

"Don't look so shocked, Hugh. You have many friends on this side of the liminal line. However, I would advise that you think more carefully before you speak in the future. We can't afford to lose you because of some misspoken words, now can we?"

"Errrm, no, but I wasn't intending on all of this happening. I only wanted to make things better."

"I understand you had well-meant intentions; however, sometimes it is better to ask for help, rather than dig yourself into a bigger hole. It takes a strong person to admit they are wrong, but it takes an even stronger one to admit they need help. It's not a sign of weakness. You're all going to need each other over the coming months, and you must learn to play to each of your strengths. But let's set that aside for now. We need to focus on the important matters that are at hand."

"Are you talking about the war that we may have started? We really didn't intend for that to happen. It was the guard who triggered all that off."

"There's no need to worry about that circumstance. I must admit, we were concerned at first, but once we received the message about who you were, it was easily sorted, so no harm was done. Any big events such as war, have to pass through me. Luckily for you, I have a calm head."

"Excuse me," said Barrington, "are you saying that Hugh's message got through to someone?"

"Why, of course. You didn't think it fortuitous that you were released mere moments before your untimely deaths? You can thank Percy here as well, for it was he who delivered the message to me personally. He was also the one who summoned the dragon riders of Hassenlair to be on standby in case he couldn't release you in time."

"Well, it helps when your wife is the High Enchantress, I won't lie, but it also appears that you have some good friends this side of the liminal line. It was the head of the Weavers Council who contacted me and explained your predicament. When I realised who you were, I moved swiftly to set you all free."

He looked to the party behind Hugh, who were looking dumbstruck at the change of events they found themselves in.

"If you all head back through those doors we came through, my people will get you sorted with fresh clothes and a decent meal."

"Can these three stay with us?" asked Hugh, gesturing to Barrington, Emily and, Heather.

"Of course," said Percival, "I wouldn't expect anything less. Let me arrange some lunch for us, then we can discuss things more civilly."

He clapped his hands twice, and the party of sailors were led from the room. Moments later, more servants appeared, with a table, some chairs and a mass of food. It wasn't long before they were tucking into the finest cuisine on the Isle of Fey.

"So, tell us," said Barrington, "who was the messenger to whom we owe our lives? I would like to buy him a drink, if he's still in town, of course."

"It was Stanley Weaver," said Percival.

Sybil nearly choked on her food.

"How dare you mention that man's name in this room! Filthy Weaver!"

"Now, my dear, let us not bring old family disputes into this.

He came in good faith, and I implore you to let it pass this once. It was he that saved these poor fellows lives after all."

"Very well, I shall permit it this once, as it is pertinent to the conversation."

"Thank you, my dear. The man in question was most insistent that you be released, putting a very good defence in for you all. It's also not in our best interests to get in the way of the Weavers." He glanced at his wife, who glared back, but said nothing. "He's refusing to leave the city until he sees you all face to face."

Barrington took a sip of some entirely excellent wine.

"Ah, so Stanley has made his way over here? That's twice we owe him for getting us out of a sticky situation." He recalled their close shave in Morcarthia and how Stanley helped them evade capture on the road to Dallum.

"Well, you have some loyal friends around you, even if it is a Weaver," said Sybil. "Your father, Hugh, was also lucky to have good support around him. It's just sad he was betrayed. You will have to be careful as you progress along your journey and trust in the family network."

"Sorry, but you knew my father?" said Hugh.

The rest of the group had stopped eating and were sitting open-mouthed.

"Of course, he was well known in these parts. He was a regular visitor before you were born, and then more recently when He was looking for the books of lore, as I seem to remember. He left me with *this* before he departed. I had a feeling I might need it today."

She reached inside her top and produced a letter, which she passed to Hugh. He took it, looking at the envelope with awe.

"I didn't realise that he came this far. I've only ever known him to stick to the laboratory in the years running up to his death. I assumed the map he drew into his book was from a book in the library. He did take some trips with Robert, but I never knew where he went. The only other trips I remember are the ones we took as a family, before my mother and Joseph died."

"Ah yes, your dear mother. It's such a shame what happened all those years ago."

"You knew my mother as well?"

"Naturally, and for your father to look after you, even after all that happened, shows true testament how much he loved you. Tell me, is Alfred still on the scene?"

"Yes," said Hugh, "he's taken up the battle in Skellig-Krieg. It was all getting pretty rough there before we set sail for here."

"Well, we all make our own beds. Let us hope he remembers which one is his."

Hugh looked at Sybil, confused, and then down to the letter in his hand.

"Well?" asked Emily. "Don't you want to open the letter?"

"Oh, yes." Hugh carefully opened the envelope, spying his father's writing on the front. He was becoming accustomed to the letters and the random way in which they seemed to make their way to him. He opened up the page and read aloud what was written within.

Dear Hugh,

I hope this letter finds you well. Let me start by saying that the company you are currently with, that is Sybil and Percy, are good friends of mine and the entire family. They can be trusted, and I know they will look after you.

n still on the road with Robert, and we have just returned
1 Killinsfolk in the north of the island. I've stumbled on an
sting find, which meant we've had to turn back, and we'll
o take a trip back to Morcarthia. If you are reading this,
ly hope that you are on the trail of the books of lore.

You'll need to head up to Syreni Bay in the north, to get the book of lore for water. I hope that you have accrued some help along the way, but if not, then I'm certain that Sybil and Percy will help.

Until we next meet, stay safe.

Love always,
F x

Hugh looked up from the letter, seeing all the eyes in the room on him. He looked back down at the letter, then back up again, trying to get the order of events correct in his head.

"So, you received this before my father's death, just before he headed to Morcarthia with Robert?"

"That is correct. Had I seen how the events were going to pan out, we would've advised him to take heed when travelling through Morcarthia. However, my visions beyond the liminal line can be hazy and hard to read."

"You had visions? You're a seer?"

"Yes, I am a seer, one of the originals, in fact. There were once three of us, but we parted company some time ago, under troubling circumstances. But that is not for us to discuss today. As things stand right now, the fate of the world appears to be in your hands."

"But, why me?"

"Not just you, Hugh, but with your friends here as well. If my sources are correct, then the Elf King is hot on your heels, and to make the situation worse, the one who they call Smithson is already at Syreni Bay, searching the area for the merfolk. We have already sent word to our people up north to do their best to prevent this from happening, but they won't be able to do so indefinitely."

Hugh couldn't believe what he was hearing, and by the looks of things, neither could the rest of them.

"Are ye saying that we've already lost the race?" asked Heather.

"No," said Sybil. "That is not what I am saying at all. If you all pull together as a team, then I'm saying that you'll still get the book …"

Hugh went to protest at this, but Sybil cut him short.

"I'm fully aware of the situation within your present company, and that all's not as well as it could be. I need you to set your differences aside, for it is the only way you will proceed. The soothsayers have informed us that the future is unclear on all these matters, and this is a critical point in time for the entire world. I myself, have seen what may come, and I refuse to let the world slip back into the old ways of power mongering and war. We are working hard to weave the future in our favour; however, input is needed from your side for the future to fall our way and not into the hands of our enemies."

The words fell around the room like a blanket and seemed to smother out all noise from the outside world.

"When you put it like that," said Barrington, "it certainly puts things into perspective."

"Which is why you must carry on with the task you've started," said Percival. "We're all concerned with the recent turn in events happening over the border. We have messages coming in from many leagues to the south – reports of fighting breaking out and mass movements of people moving toward the borders of the Old World. Old fights are being dragged out of the mud once more, and those who are still loyal or who had ties to the Old World are looking to return. We're struggling with the numbers already heading our way, and we'll be hard pressed to deal with anymore. It will be impossible for us to keep track of all the people coming across. The fear among the general populous is that we'll be overrun with enemies of the state. They are worried the enemy will use the movement of people to get here and stir up trouble.

"You'll have noticed the uproar on your arrival. This will only get worse as more people attempt to jump the liminal line illegally. We cannot, and will not, let this happen, which is why you mustn't fail at this task."

"No pressure then?" said Barrington.

"This is not a joke," said Sybil. "I can assure you the world will not be worth living in if either the New World powers *or* the Elf King get hold of the books of lore. I have seen what lies down that path, and I will do anything to prevent it from coming true. We intend to fight to the death for what we believe in, and we hope you do, too."

Again the room was left in a heavy silence, which was broken this time by Hugh.

"Well, I mean, we'll certainly do all we can to help the cause, but …"

"Good, then that's settled then," she said.

Barrington, Emily and Heather all looked at Hugh, flabbergasted.

"I asked Percy to get his men to retrieve your belongings from *A Ship With No Name*. I have the rest of your belongings which were confiscated from you when you were taken into custody" She clapped her hands.

At this, their belongings were ceremoniously brought into the room by servants of the palace. They handed over the firestones, staff, the phoenix pipe and personal items taken from them. They also carried fresh backpacks with the supplies needed for their trip into the unknown. Still in shock, the group were guided to some steps at the end of the room. They led to a marble altar on a raised platform and revealed the source of water Hugh had heard before. A staff rested on a plinth, keeping it dry from the water flowing from a standpipe, which poured across the altar top, before cascading off the sides into a drain. Sybil asked them to kneel on some cushions on the steps. She placed the staff on each of their shoulders, and Hugh felt a wave of tingling go through his body.

"I grant you all freedom of the Isle of Fey. I grant you access to all seven districts and ask that your passage is left unheeded as you carry out your work." Her voice boomed around the room, and the top of the staff was now glowing. "I send this message to all the leaders of this fine realm and ask that they respect my wishes as is expected by the powers invested in me as your High Enchantress."

Streams of light were flowing out of the staff, and Hugh saw they comprised hundreds of fireflies. They appeared to swirl above Sybil's head before disappearing into the firefly messaging system at work there.

"By now, the messages should be at their destinations."

"A bit quicker than the runners then," said Barrington.

"Yes, but they too have their advantages. For instance, if the tubes that the firefly system uses get severed, it makes the system inoperable. At least the runners' system cannot be cut off."

"Unless someone walks out in front of them," said Emily.

"Yes, but who would be silly enough to do that?"

"Nobody in particular," said Emily, who, along with Barrington and Heather, were stifling sniggers.

Hugh went red in the face.

"Yes, well, we know that wasn't my fault," he said, keen to move the conversation forward. "Anyway, it's probably time that we made a move out of here."

"I suppose you are right, old bean," said Barrington, wiping a tear away from his eye. "So how's best to get out of here, and is Stanley still waiting for us?"

"I believe he is," said Percival, "if you would like to follow me, I will take you to meet him."

"Goodbye, to all of you. Have a safe passage through our fair isle," said Sybil. "But take heed, stick to the main roads, and avoid the Forest of Fey. There are forces there that even I cannot protect you from. Stick to the lighter pathways, and you can always rely on my help and the help of the peoples of this land. You have but to ask. I can be contacted through the usual ways and means."

"Thank you," said Hugh, "and I hope the next time we meet will be in better times. I have lots of questions to ask you about my father."

"I'm sure you do. Goodbye for now."

With that, Percival led the group out of the room. As the doors were closing behind them, Hugh caught sight of Sybil retaking her place on the chaise lounge, with fresh cucumber slices on her eyes.

Chapter 22

They were led back down the spiral staircase by Percival. Hugh was expecting him to head out the main door, but he led the group up to a wall where he pressed a brass stud set in the floor, revealing a hidden doorway. He led them into a servants' staircase far less ornate than the one which led up to the chamber of the high enchantress. This was a wooden affair with well-worn treads, smoothed off by the many feet that had climbed up and down over the years. Hugh looked up and down the centre of the shaft, becoming dizzy with the myriad of handrails.

They passed a hole in the wall that opened onto a dumbwaiter shaft, with ropes and pulleys shuttling food and dishes up and down at great speed. Kitchen smells filled the air. From the trays rattling past them, Hugh could see the lunchtime service was still in full swing. Even though they had just eaten, the scent of roast chicken, vegetables and gravy made Hugh hungry again.

They had to stop at regular intervals in passing niches, to give way to the oncoming traffic making its way upstairs, ladened with all manner of items from bedsheets to cleaning gear. Eventually they made it down to the kitchens, the beating heart of the palace. There wasn't any marble to be seen here. The floors were laid with a durable flagstone, the lime-washed walls filled with numerous pots and pans and trays. Servants were bustling around the kitchen staff, who were all at various stages of preparing and cooking food. A large table filled the centre of the room, with food passing this way and that, as each stage of the production was completed. A large range, fifteen feet in length, was surrounded by numerous people with frying pans, roasting dishes and clouds of steam.

Percival guided them through the chaos to a corridor teeming with life. The smell of food was replaced with wash powder and starch, and there were rooms off to each side of the corridor stacked with linen and clothes being cleaned and pressed. The air was close and hot, and Hugh found it harder to breathe in the moist air. As they passed, the servants stood to one side and bowed their heads to Percival as he went by.

The goods in entrance was at the end of this long corridor. The space opened out, and Hugh saw different areas for storage and the largest piles of orbs he had seen to date. He was reminded of the piles of orbs they had seen in the Ranglestaff mines back in Skellig-Krieg. This explained what they were being used for. There was a delivery being backed in, with a vehicle that looked like a steam car but with no sign of steam being emitted.

"I say, Percival old chap, what do those things run on?" said Barrington.

"Runes and the natural world, of course. What else would they run on?"

"Oh yes, how silly of me."

Hugh saw *Ranglestaff's Orbs* painted on the side, and as the vehicle came to a halt, workers climbed up to start off-loading the cargo. Others were on the stack itself, moving the orbs up the pile to people at the top who fed them into metal spirals which disappeared off into the walls. As fast as they were coming off the vehicle, they were being fed into the belly of the beast. Percival explained how the pile usually got rotated once a day, and they always had some orbs spare, ready for busier days. They were used for everything from cooking and heating to lighting the vast building above.

They moved through the space out into an open courtyard, and Hugh looked up, seeing they were now at the rear of the palace. They appeared to be at the base of the hill again. A large wall protected this area, and the guards were, once again, marching up on the ramparts. They headed towards what appeared to be a large house in the corner, yet as the crowd parted up ahead of them, Hugh saw it was mounted on wheels. Percival hopped up onto a veranda, a couple of feet off the ground, and rapped on a green door. It opened to reveal Stanley Weaver, dressed in his suit and oilskin and still wearing the wooden clogs that Hugh remembered him in last time. The rest of the group climbed up to see their old rescuer.

"Now then, you lot, how's it goin'?"

"Not bad thank you, Stanley," said Hugh, and to his surprise, the old man hugged him.

"I didn't think I was goin' t'make it to you in time. When the message came through from yer pa, I fired up the ol' home here and came back into Androssan. You were lucky that I'd stopped overnight jus' outside of town, otherwise it'd have been a different story."

"Well, we're all grateful that you were here, again, to help save the day," said Barrington. He turned to Percival. "Are you able to send a message over to the New World from here? I need to let Wanda, my contact in Portis-Montis, know that we're safe."

"Naturally, we have contacts crossing the liminal line on a regular basis. Come, let's see if we can get sorted before you have to set off. Will that be alright, Stanley?"

"I'm sure we can hold off leavin' a little longer, but don't be too long, mind. Mrs Weaver don't enjoy hanging about around here. I think she jus' wants to get home."

"No worries. I'll have him back quicker than a firefly message."

Percival jumped back to the ground with Barrington hot on his heels.

"I suppose we should catch up over a cuppa of something warm," said Stanley to the rest of the group, and they all followed him into the house.

Hugh had to pause on the threshold as his breath was taken away. Though it didn't look small from the outside, nothing could prepare him for what greeted his eyes on the inside. He looked back to the courtyard, leaning through the door and looking upwards. The house didn't seem overly large, yet back over the threshold, the space appeared infinite. A staircase wound its way up into a dizzying height, with many rooms going off in all directions. Light streamed in through a large lantern, bathing the room in a warm glow, making it feel very homely.

In the background, he could hear the clacking of a machine of sorts, similar to the one he had heard in the palace. A door opened on the next floor up, it was marked The Weaving Room, and someone wearing a leather apron and wooden clogs came out, the door slamming shut behind him. From the brief glimpse Hugh got of the room, he could make out a mechanical weaving loom working away. A fine mist of cotton dust filled the air and floated down to the group below like snow.

"Ain't you got them extractors on up there?" Stanley shouted up to the man.

"Nah, it's blocked again. How long before we set off? Have we gots time sort it out?"

"Aye, you gots time, jus' get it sorted, right? We gotta keep them machines runnin', understand? We's at a critical moment in the timeline. To stop 'em now would be catastrophic."

"Right you are, Mr Weaver, sir," said the worker, a hint of annoyance in his voice.

He opened the door – another cloud of cotton being expelled – and started barking orders at the room at large, as the door slammed shut once more behind him.

"Sorry 'bout that," said Stanley, blowing an errant fluff of cotton off his nose. He sighed. "Now, where were we? Ah yes, a cuppa something warm."

He headed through a door in front of him, guiding the group into a parlour. This was a warm, dusty room, and Hugh found himself clearing his throat on a regular basis. The walls were covered in portraits of the Weaver family. Plush wing-backed chairs were set out in a circle with little side tables next to them. Stanley clapped his hands, and an entourage of people entered, carrying trays of biscuits and pots of tea and mugs that rattled and clinked as they walked. These were set down on the tables, and the servants left the room.

"That's organised," said Hugh. "How did you know we were arriving?"

"I'm a Weaver, and me wife's a seer. Our job is to know all and try to alter the weft of time. Apologies for the state of the place, but we hold meetin's in 'ere, and the lads are always covered in cotton. It's not much, but it's home."

He gestured to the empty seats, and everyone sat down, sending more dust into the air.

"Really, this is most ample, especially from where we've just been," said Hugh, coughing further.

"Oh, sorry," said Stanley, and he quickly stood up and pressed a button on the wall.

Nothing happened. He banged the wall above the button.

Hugh tingled all over, as the sound of a fan kicked into action. He saw, by the light streaming in through the windows, all the dust began heading towards a thin gap surrounding the edge of the room. Within a minute the air was noticeably clearer, though Hugh's throat was still irritated.

"At last, ruddy fans, always stoppin' at the moment. So tell me, how's it you have ended up out here?"

Hugh talked Stanley through the events they had been through whilst Emily and Heather listened. He noticed that their slurping of tea increased when he reached the part where they were captured. Hugh didn't go into too much detail, but the noises and stares coming from the two women eventually caused Stanley to enquire what was wrong.

"I do hate to spoil a good story, but Hugh here is not being quite as open as he ought to be," said Emily.

She filled Stanley in with the blanks that Hugh missed out.

Stanley looked at Hugh with raised eyebrows.

"S'all right. I already know about the awkward circumstances that you found yourselves in, and if it wasn't for some quick weaving on my side, you may've found yourself at the bottom of the dead man's drop."

"You already know about what happened? How?" asked Hugh.

"Well, for one, my wife is a seer as I've said, and second, your pa filled me in. As soon as I realised what danger you were all in, I set the lads to work, to try to counteract the unfolding events. It's safe to say they were not too impressed to be gettin' involved in the political goings on of the High Enchantress. But I told them they had no choice in the matter. Luckily we're good workers of the weft, and we managed to get you out of trouble. I dread to think of what would've happened if we hadn't made it to you in time, but we did, and tha's all that matters now." A bell rang somewhere in the background. "Ah, that'll be your friend back. At least we can get ourselves on the road again. I hates stayin' in tow for too long. People are already startin' to ask questions of me, and it gets me on edge. 'Scuse me a minute whilst I go see your friend in."

He stood up and headed to the door, back into the large entrance hall.

They all sat and listened, Emily and Heather slurping their tea, sitting opposite Hugh without breaking eye contact. The only other noise filling the room was the gentle clacking of the machines in the room above. They heard Barrington's jovial laugh get louder as the door opened and he was guided in by Stanley.

"Ah, here you all are," said Barrington. "Stanley has informed me you have been bringing him up to date on all our recent events."

He looked at the scene in front of him, reading the room in an instant.

"I hope you haven't been giving poor old Hugh here a rough time. I've seen fit to put all that happened behind me, for now at least. We need to move forward with our plans if the news is correct."

"What news is that?" asked Heather. "I hope it's nae bad."

"It's not bad, just *concerning*. Apparently Smithy has already made it to the north of the island and has commenced his search for the book. Of course, when I say Smithy, I mean he's getting Collins and his new helper to do all the dirty work for them."

"Collins has a helper?" said Hugh. "That must be the same person who attacked Hamish."

"Yes, I believe it could well be. I've some good news to report though. It would appear that it's not all plain sailing on the good ship Smithson, or should I say *the Fey Flyer*."

"*The Fey Flyer?*"

"Yes, that's the ship he's on, but Wanda has no news of the other ship, or its passengers. The news gets better. Smithy and Collins have had a falling out of sorts in Killinsfolk. It was all witnessed by one of Percival's contacts."

"That's excellent news. Let's hope that they continue to fall out and that Smithson is left on his own," said Emily, but Hugh was already shaking his head. "What's wrong?"

"The situation is not as black and white as that. They can't just fall out."

"Sorry," she said. "Why do you think Collins won't turn on Smithson? Surely that's the best outcome for all of us?"

"Yes, it would be a nice outcome, but it's not possible. The Collins family are tied to the university and duty bound to do whatever is bid of them, no matter how strained the situation is between the chancellor and head Collins. It's one of the fundamental laws of the Collins family, and this is backed up with a magical contract. If the head of the Collins family breaks any part of the contract, it would put them at risk of losing everything.

"In order to keep their jobs and their home at the university, they must assist the chancellor and keep the building running. It's as simple as that. You only have to look at the Great War to see how close their bond is to the building, for without them, there would be no Great Library or university."

"But surely it works both ways?" said Barrington. "If Smithy breaks his side of the deal, there has to be some sort of recompense?"

"Well, in that situation, the Collins family can come together to oust the current chancellor, but it has to go through the board of governors and be agreed to by the head of the family. I think that is something that Smithson will be aware of. He has to be in the building for the vote of no confidence to take place, which is probably why he has not returned in some time."

"Alright," said Barrington, "so what is stopping Collins from writing home to get the process moving? They could replace the chancellor and move on."

"Again, you are looking at this through modern eyes. When these contracts were put in place, nobody could foresee what would be happening now. The chancellor would not have been thought to be away for this length of time, nor the head of the Collins family. All parties have to be within the university for a vote of no confidence to take place. It's archaic, but this is the way things were done back then. Perhaps, when this is all over and the dust has settled, the contracts can be reformed, but for now we're stuck with the situation as it is."

"Alright so we must assume Smithy is avoiding the building, knowing that to return would put paid to his plans. We know he will stop at nothing to get what he wants. But right now we need to focus on what he is doing instead. We can't just sit here discussing it all day, whilst he is drawing close to the prize. What are we going to do about it?"

"Aye, we need to get a move on before it's too late," said Heather. "We have to leave now if we're to have any chance of stopping them getting their dirty hands on it. Perhaps we can hitch a lift with our sailing friends? It'll be nay bother for them to get us up the coast … what?"

It was Barrington was shaking his head this time.

"Apparently the guard we ran into when we arrived not only impounded the boat, but also took time to pull the thing apart, looking for extra evidence to charge us with. Monty is livid with them and is insisting the ship be returned to its previous state before sailing. Percival has got some of his best men on the job, but it will take a few days to fix the damage."

"Oh great, so now what do we do? We can't let the book fall into the wrong hands," said Emily.

A cough came from behind them, and they all turned to look at Stanley.

"I believe I can help with that."

Chapter 23

The streets of Androssan were used to diverse trade making its way to and from the docks, and in from the hills beyond the city. This, plus the island folk who came to the area every day to either make a living or purchase goods available nowhere else, meant the streets of the capital were often difficult to navigate.

Hugh currently had a front seat view of the carnage that Stanley's mobile home was causing. Once they had loaded up with a fresh cargo of food and water and orbs to power the mighty machine, Stanley readied his motley crew to their muster stations, ready for their exit from the city. He donned a pair of leather gloves as a tingle of power spread through the machine, and Hugh watched the old Weaver bring his house to life. They were all sitting up on a large, padded bench, surrounded by levers and pulleys plus the pipes he used to keep in touch with the rest of his crew.

The house rose off the ground. Stanley informed them that the house had been fitted with rune suspension to make for a more comfortable ride, though Hugh struggled to feel it. All it appeared to do was add a swaying motion to the rattling and shaking happening around them. With a lot of crunching and grinding, Stanley found the gear he wanted, and the house began edging backwards.

Hugh didn't need to see what was happening to know what was going on below. The sound of screams from the communication pipes, tied in with the yelps rising from the wildlife in the courtyard, was enough to paint a picture of the carnage currently taking place. More crunching of gears, and the goliath swung forward in the tight space, scattering people in all directions. Hugh winced, grabbing the seat for all it was worth, as they nearly hit the wall. Percival stood open-mouthed, watching the chaos unfold. Stanley looked like the captain of an unruly vessel. He winked and saluted to the man before he disappeared out of sight around the side of the house. Many awkward moves later – and after the complete decimation of the courtyard below – Stanley finally had the beast pointing in the right direction.

They were now heading towards a gate composed of stone pillars and a fresh wooden arch. Hugh pondered if this may have been a new addition to the gateposts, only to have his question answered when he saw numerous carpenters scrabbling to get off the top of the fresh structure. Even though they weren't moving fast, Hugh could tell Stanley wouldn't alter his course. He looked up behind him to see a battered metal chimney – then forward to the new wooden arch. Carpenters and guards alike called out for the man to stop, but it was no good. Stanley pulled a lever, and a protective canopy sprung out over their heads, just as the chimney took out the new structure. Bits of splintered wood bounced off the canopy, protecting those underneath from certain injury. Hugh looked up to his left to see a deflated carpenter drop to his knees, shaking his head in disbelief.

"Won't they be angry?" said Hugh over the noise and commotion.

"Nah, I'm a Weaver. They gets edgy fightin' us. I'll send 'em some money later. We needs to get movin'. Besides, I warned them I'd need to get out of here again."

"Couldn't you at least have lowered the house down a bit?" said Barrington, who jumped as a weathervane landed point first into the roof in front of them.

"What, and ruin the comfort of me ride? No thanks. I've already woven them some good fortune, and to hear how they treated you wasn't right in my eyes."

Barrington certainly couldn't disagree with this.

"Now let me concentrate on me drivin'."

Stanley's mobile home rumbled on past the gatehouse, heading towards the road that led out of the city. Ahead of them, Hugh saw the awnings and canopies of numerous shops and street sellers being hastily pulled back as the house moved towards them. Those walking at street level either had to retreat to a safe side street or run ahead of the house to get out of its way. It was clear to Hugh that Stanley would not stop for man nor beast. More instructions came through the many pipes and tubes next to Weaver's ear, and he shouted his replies over the din.

Hugh noticed that Stanley steered the building with a crank handle, though it was slow to respond to his actions, but he was navigating the streets, nonetheless. They were now heading down treelined avenues with the birds taking to the sky all around them as they passed by. They were similar to the bright multicoloured birds that Hugh had seen before, and their calls were alien and other worldly. It was a good hour before the houses petered out, and they found themselves surrounded by tropical foliage and travelling uphill.

"Hold on to your hats," said Stanley. "I'm going to let her rip!"

The rest of them braced themselves for the upcoming change in speed. Gears were crunched, and pulleys and flywheels squealed into action, but no noticeable change of speed was detected. Barrington nudged Hugh, who looked down to his left, seeing a mule and cart overtaking them. He turned back to speak to Stanley and saw he was now wearing a pair of goggles, a leather hat that covered his ears, and a scarf.

"Feel the power!" shouted Stanley over the racket.

"Errrm, yes," said Hugh, trying not to laugh. He then leaned over and spoke sotto voce into Barrington's ear. "I think the man's a tad doolally."

"Not doolally, Hugh, just getting the most out of the weave of life," said Stanley.

Hugh felt his cheeks flush with colour.

"So, what's our plan now? We need to know where we are going," said Emily.

As if to answer her question, a call came through one of the pipes – though Hugh couldn't make out what was being said, only that it was a woman's voice.

"Dee will see you now," said Stanley. "If you head downstairs, someone will take you to her parlour."

Confused by this, the group stood, wobbling to catch their balance, and made their way back into the house. They returned to the large entrance hall where they were greeted by one of the servants who led them up the wooden staircase. As they rose through the space, Hugh kept his hand on a wooden handrail, polished over the years by the many hands that had passed over it. Everything rattled, from the ornate light fittings to the pictures on the walls, to the spindles on the staircase. Dust fell gently by as they climbed the stairs. The servant led them off at the third floor through a set of drapes. Beyond this was a room which reminded Hugh of the tea rooms in Portis-Montis, its walls draped in deep purple silks. The air was hazy and filled with incense, which made Hugh feel drowsy. A set of drapes opened at the other end of the room, revealing Dee Weaver, Stanley's wife.

Dee wasn't a tall woman, but her presence filled the room with an ethereal glow, captivating all those within the room. Her deep tanned skin and dark hair were offset by startling blue eyes which matched the cloak she wore. Hugh was mesmerised by her eyes, and she seemed to look directly into his soul when he looked into them. She removed her cloak, revealing the midnight blue satin robes she wore. They flowed across the floor behind her with the edges trimmed with gold tassels. She didn't appear to walk, so much as glide across to a deep velvet chair set behind a table with a crystal ball on it. She gestured to the four other chairs set around the table, and each member of the group sat. The servant bowed his head without saying a word and left them to it.

Nobody spoke. The only sound was some far-off clinking of glass phials or jars, somewhere in the back room. The group looked at Dee, and she stared back serenely. Then, without warning, she broke the tension, her arms flying above her head, making the rest of them jump.

"So, it is true," she said. "Hugh Geber is sitting before me, wanting answers to things that have yet to pass."

She eyeballed Hugh. He loosened his collar and cleared his throat.

"Errrm … Yes?" he said, unsure if this was the correct answer.

His thoughts desperately tried to keep up with the current pace in the room.

"Yes, that is correct," he replied more confidently, his brain finally clicking into gear. "We need answers. We don't have a clue where we're heading or how we're to get there. All we know is there's a book we need to get before anyone else. Beyond that, we are lost."

He was fixed on the woman's gaze, and it looked as though her eyes had clouded over, which sent chills down his spine. He watched as her attention went down to the crystal ball on the table, which had also clouded up. He was transfixed by the swirling gasses contained within the ball, and he felt himself being drawn into it. With a strange sensation – one he recognised only too well – he felt himself being dragged through the keyhole, into the other plane.

—POP—

His eyes opened, and he was confused. It was nowhere near as dark as he expected it to be, in fact, it was quite colourful. He found himself in a green meadow, filled with bees and butterflies. A large tree stood in the centre of the meadow, its shade providing welcome cover for the flora and fauna. He tuned to see Dee, who held out a hand for Hugh to take.

'*Walk with me, Hugh.*'

'*Where are we? This isn't anything like the sight I remember.*'

'*You are in the land between the planes. We are neither in the sight, nor the plane of the living, and it is where many magical beasts roam.*'

Hugh looked around him and saw numerous animals and beasts grazing in the meadow. He saw a unicorn and realised that it was Aeolus, Emily's spirit animal.

'*This is the land of the seers, Hugh, a place where we can look forward to what may come to pass, if the current events continue in the order they are occurring at present. This doesn't mean to say they have to happen; only if nobody intervenes, they will become a reality.*"

She looked at Hugh, and he realised she was awaiting a response.

'*I see, so, does this mean that the future is already written? Like the Weavers when they make their cloths?*'

'*No, the Weaver's business deals with the fate of the world. Seers deal with events on the road of life. They process what has been and attempt to see what will be. Think of it as a journey to a destination. There may be many routes which you can take, all with different outcomes along the way … outcomes which affect the end goal. It is our job to advise you of the best path to take, but the ultimate decision lies with the one walking the path.*'

'*So, what is it you can tell me?*'

'*What is it you would like to know? I can see you hold many questions within you, but you are the one who has to decide which to ask.*'

Hugh stood and thought for a moment, letting out a long sigh.

He did indeed have many questions each seemingly as important as the next. He simply needed to decide what to ask first.

'How are we to find the next book? We have no way of knowing where to look, other than the limited instructions from my father's letter and journal, and from what little Balinas has told us. Have you heard of Balinas?'

'Of course. He holds counsel with the seers regularly. I must consult the waters for the answers you seek.'

Dee made her way across to a fast-flowing stream and knelt at its bank. She then encouraged Hugh to do the same. The opposite bank looked foreboding, and Hugh had an ominous tingle inside. It was an eternity of darkness, and he thought he saw shadows moving, but then again, it could be his mind playing tricks. He saw a bridge spanning the waters, and a tingle of uncertainty shivered down his spine.

'Where does that lead?'

'Over.'

'Over? Into the sight?'

'Yes, but you will only ever cross that bridge once.'

'Oh, I see.'

'Come, sit with me.'

As he sat down next to Dee and gazed into the flowing water, he could see wisps of white tendrils flowing by. He was about to ask what they were, but she answered his unasked question.

'The spirits that dwell in these waters are powerful. They flow between the plane of the living and that of the sight. The waters cycle through the plane of the living, before returning here to be cleansed, then heading back down into the cycle once more. Its source lays within the Isle of Fey and is used to water the tree of life. We can talk to the spirits within these

waters and may receive a prediction of what may come to pass. Naturally, the ultimate journey is decided by the ones who are walking the path, but having knowledge of what may come to pass is always helpful.'

'So what does it say about the path I am on? Will we make it to the end and get the book?'

'The bigger picture is not mine to see, but let's look where your journey may end up if you continue not to change.'

Dee held out her hand for Hugh to take. He did, and she dipped her other hand into the flowing waters. The pull was instant. It was the most peculiar sensation, one of falling, but not wet like he expected. The sound of rushing filled his ears, as though he were falling through air, and his jacket flapped on his back. Hugh could see images around him, but it was difficult to make out what was going on. He caught sight of someone struggling in the water, which looked all too real. There were people in great pain, flashes of light and many bodies. It was an unsettling sight. He felt Dee's grip loosen, and their hands parted. Hugh was now in freefall, taking in numerous images. He was out of control and unable to stop it. Then, as quickly as it had all begun, everything stopped. He was suspended in what appeared to be an all-encompassing night sky. It was serene, and he felt at peace. Dee was coming towards him, floating like an ethereal body of light. She stopped next to him.

'Yours is a hard path to read, but some events are easier to see. From what has already been, I see your life is fractured, friendships strained, almost to breaking point. But I can see you are rebuilding the bonds needed to go forwards. You are trying to win back the affection of someone close to you. The time is coming for you to take a stand, fight your fears and do what is right. I see a test of strength, one which only you can decide to take, or not. You must pick correctly. If this does not happen, then the road ahead will not be a pleasant one. The books you seek will be found, that much

is clear, but by who I cannot say. There is much misery and pain in your reading, it's hard to pick out what is likely to happen. What you choose to do with this information is up to you, but choose you must, for it is your own journey, and let the fates decide your outcome.'

Hugh knew she was right.

'But how do I do that? I know that finding all the books is important, but I cannot force the future to bend to my will.'

'That is true. You may not be able to change the future, but you can change the choices you make along the way. Look inside yourself, and you will find the answers you are searching for. Sometimes it takes an act of bravery to change a situation. Only you will know when that time is, Hugh Geber. The only question is, are you ready to stand up and face the challenge? We must be heading back now, as your friends will wonder where we have disappeared to.'

With that, Hugh sensed another large pulling motion.

–POP–

They were back in the room, with the others. Barrington was looking expectantly at Dee.

"Right, so are we going to get started with all this then?" he asked.

"You have the answers that you came to seek," said Dee, sounding as mysterious as ever.

"Errrm, sorry? We've just sat down," said Barrington, looking at the rest of the party around the table. Emily looked at Hugh, and he knew she was searching inside of him. He opened up and let her in.

"I think we've missed a step," she said, "but Hugh has the answers that we need."

"That is correct," said Dee.

"I really don't understand what is going on," said Barrington.

"I shall leave you now, Hugh Geber," said Dee. "Think on what we have discussed, remember it and when the time comes, use it wisely."

With that, she stood up from the table, exiting back through the silks. A servant appeared behind them and requested they follow him out of the room, leaving Barrington to protest further.

"Listen, I will explain all to you when we find somewhere to sit down," said Hugh, cutting his friend off between mutterings. He turned back to the servant. "Can we go somewhere private?"

"Certainly, follow me."

With that, the servant was off down the stairs, with the rest of the group in tow. He led them through the door that Stanley used, and they were back in the room where they first talked. Once the servant had left, Hugh wasted no time in filling in the rest of the group on the events that occurred with Dee and how she took him off to the land between the planes.

"And all that happened in a blink of an eye?" asked Barrington.

"Apparently so," said Hugh. "I thought we had been a lot longer, but it really proves that time moves slower on the different planes. The question now is what are we going to do?"

"What do you mean?" said Emily.

"Well, if what Dee said is true and the books of lore are indeed going to be found, then we have to be the ones to find them."

"But isn't that what we're doing?"

"Yes, but the odds are stacked against us."

"I'm not sure it's as bad as that," said Emily. "Yes, Smithson has the upper hand, and he is probably already searching the area high and low, but we have something he doesn't have."

"What's that?"

"We have us, our friendships and support for each other, plus a network of allies willing to help us. He has a servant at best, and then paid help, who we can take a guess are having a rough time. We will find these books because we have to."

"Em's right. There's nae need being negative. Do that, and ye may as well let the other side win," said Heather. "Ye've to set that aside and get a move on with getting the lore books home to where they belong. After all, that was the other part of Dee's reading for Hugh. Did she not say that we have a chance of finding them?"

"Well, that's easier said than done," said Barrington. "We've no clue where to look or which direction to go in. We don't even have a map."

"Thas nae quite true," said Heather.

She reached deep into her pocket and pulled out what appeared to be a large folded up piece of paper. Once again, her bottomless pockets were living up to their name.

"What in the name of all things spritely is that?" said Barrington.

"It's a map, of course," she said. "Surely even ye can figure that one out."

Barrington flushed but said nothing as Heather opened up the map. It seemed to shimmer in the glow of the rune lights, and a wave of goosebumps passed through Hugh. He realised the map was laced with runes, which caused it to come alive. The features almost seemed to ride out of the parchment, with miniature mountains that looked like he could touch them. It was a map of the Isle of Fey, with the name glowing in an ancient scrawl at the top. In the waters, mythical beasts seemed to jump in and out of the seas surrounding the island. *The Forest of Fey* seemed to twinkle like fireflies on a warm summer's eve.

"Dad gave me this as I was leaving," said Heather. "He said it always came in handy with his trips as a guide. It's called the Mundi Dux. It can show ye the up-to-date view of the world in relation to where ye are. It also does *this* ..."

She drew out some runes in the air, which wove together. She cupped them in her hands and blew on them. They glowed with a warm light, and she cast them across the map. Hugh watched in awe, as the island they were on dissolved away, with the rest of the world now drawing itself into view. He also noticed the name at the top had changed, and it now read *Tellus*. He looked over the map, seeing the liminal line glowing like a formidable border, fencing in the many countries of the New World. Beyond that were the many countries of the Old World and place that he was now yearning to explore.

"I've seen this before," said Emily, looking at the map with reverence. "Hamish would get this out when I was a young girl and talk me through it. I haven't seen it since then, but there's something else that goes with it. I inherited it from my mother."

She reached into her pocket and pulled out a watch, similar to the one that Hugh had in his pocket. He felt in his pocket, and the watch was vibrating gently to itself.

"This is one of the Ever-Right collection. It will always show the correct time wherever you are in the world. But it also has other tricks."

Emily placed the watch onto the map, and it briefly glowed. They all watched, as the hands appeared to synchronise with the time zone where Emily had placed it. As she moved it across the map, the hands slowly adjusted according to the zone it was over. Heather was now reaching into her pocket, and she too pulled out a similar watch. Inside his own pocket, Hugh felt a warmth against his leg, and he pulled out the Tempus. The three of them looked at each other in awe.

"Humph! That's the end of my plan then," said Barrington, making them all jump.

"What's wrong with you?" asked Hugh.

"What's wrong with me? To think of all that time I wasted building my clock. It was going to change the way of seafaring for the better, give you an accurate time at sea, but once again, my plan has been foiled. It also appears that I'm left out of the club once more. I don't have one of those."

"But you do," said Emily.

"No, I don't. I've never set eyes on one of those."

"I beg to differ. Your father has one of these, and you will be the next owner of it. I'm sure he was planning to give it to you, he even said so in one of his many letters to you."

"Yes, well, I don't have them; they were mislaid. Besides, how do you know what was in those letters?"

"I know because I had to transcribe for him when his hands were sore. I can see there was little point in going to all that hard work."

She gave Barrington a hard stare, and he looked at the map.

"I think we're straying too far from the point," said Hugh. "We need to stop this infighting between ourselves, otherwise we risk a lot more than not getting this book. We need to know where to go and make plans to get out of here. At the rate this mobile home moves, it'll be next year before we get anywhere."

He stood looking at the rest of them with raised eyebrows, and Emily let out a sigh.

"Fine, let's look at the map again. Can you get this back to where we currently are?"

Heather nodded, reworking the runes to bring the map to the view of the island.

"So, have ye got any idea where we're to be heading for?" she asked.

"Well, if we look up *here*, there's Syreni Bay, and the *Book of Prophecy* definitely mentioned that. And here's Killinsfolk; it sits right on the bay. It must have something to do with the book. Maybe there's a dockyard or something? Or a safe house, where the book is kept?"

"Yes, perhaps they also stuck a sign above the house," Barrington said, spreading his hands theatrically. "Book of Lore Here!"

"If you have a better idea, then please, share it with the room. No? Then I think this is as good as any a place to start. I bet you anything Smithson's already there, and we can only hope that he hasn't found the book yet."

With no argument left to come back with at Hugh, Barrington finally stepped down. A search of the map told them they were already on the main road north. If they stayed on this route, it would take them most of the way to the top of the island, but the road was long and winding. Another route, marked out as a foot trail, led almost straight through the isle. They set to, planning out what they may need for the route up the country. Heather talked of a path around the outside of the forest that Hamish had informed her of. It would take them around the Forest of Fey, the only issue being that the road wasn't marked through the forest itself.

"Surely it's quicker to go straight through the forest. If time is not on our side, it has to be the only route," said Hugh.

"Aye, ye'd think, but Dad expressed extreme caution about going in there. He said to take one of the outer routes. Sybil also said not to take the route through the forest, as we would have nae protection."

"But that'll add an extra day to our journey. I'm sorry, but I think we must choose the quickest route. We cannot lose the book, which is why I think we should take the road through the forest."

He looked to Emily for some support, and she mulled the idea over.

"On this occasion, I think Hugh is right. We need to get to the books as soon as possible, and if that means taking the riskier route, then that is how it will have to be."

"But Dad and Sybil both said not to go there," said Heather. "I dinnae want to go against their word. It may be the shorter route, but we dinnae know what we'll face in there. At least on the open road we'll have less risk of obstacles."

"Yes, I understand that, but they are not here, looking at the situation first hand, and we are. Either way we are on foot, so the time can't be that much less. The longer we spend debating this, the larger advantage Smithson is getting. Barrington, what say you?"

He looked at Emily, mouth open, caught between the two logical thoughts in front of him.

Heather's eyes widened.

"Dinnae tell me you're actually considering this as an option?

We'll risk the entire mission if ye choose that route."

Barrington's head swung between Heather and Emily before he looked to Hugh for support, but he just shrugged back.

"Don't look at me for an answer, you know my position on this."

Barrington cleared his throat awkwardly.

"Well, this is, as you have to understand, a very difficult situation for me to decide on. However, I must come to a decision that is true to my own feelings. I know that the path looks longer by road, but we have been warned not to go through the forest. It seems silly not to take the advice of those who know the area. However, I do understand the urgency of the situation. But the fact still remains, it is better to turn up in one piece, than not at all. I say we take the road around the outside, and if we're lucky we can hitch a lift with a passer-by."

Emily huffed.

"Look, how's about this," said Hugh, in an attempt to find the middle ground. "If we take this path here from Meadow Down to the edge of the forest, we can assess the situation. If the path looks too dangerous or impassable, then we can take the road. Either way, we need to be moving faster than we are now. Agreed?"

With no one throwing up any other objections, Heather rolled up the map, and they left the room to find Stanley to update him on their plans.

Chapter 24

In a clearing off to the side of the road, the huge mass of the Weavers' mobile home had come to a grinding halt, settling next to a meadow full of flowers. The three-mile tailback of carts, which were too big to squeeze past whilst the vehicle was on the road, finally overtook, with the drivers jeering insults as they passed. The woodland locals had come out to see why it had chosen this spot to park up. As the crew lowered the house into position for a rest, they pulled down the steps to the veranda and some occupants alighted from the vehicle. To the locals, they seemed awfully large, and nobody this size really bothered to stop along this stretch of the road. As Hugh, Barrington, Emily and Heather stood back on terra firma, they didn't initially notice the interest currently being paid to them.

"This should be a'right for you to find the path north from here," said Stanley, stepping down from the veranda. "Follow this path down to the river and walk upstream. It'll cut the corner off this road, nothin' but switchbacks all the way along here."

"Thank you, Stanley," said Hugh. "We couldn't have got this far without your help."

"S'a'right as long as you is all safe, that's the main thing. Now you'd best be gettin' a move on. If you're quick, you should make it to the edge of the Forest of Fey before nightfall, only be careful. Lots of locals about who ain't used to seeing tall folk like yourselves."

"Errrm, alright," said Hugh, not really sure what he meant by 'tall folk'.

"You gots all the food and supplies I gave you?"

"Aye, I've got them packed away in me coat," said Heather, tapping her bottomless pocket.

"Right you are. I'll be seein' yous lot down the road then," said Stanley, giving the group a wink. "Good luck, and takes care, and leave the weavin' to me. I can't promise much, but I'll see what I can do."

With that, he made his way back up the steps and into the house. They stood back, as a horn sounded somewhere above them, and the mobile home rattled back into life. The ground around Hugh trembled as the steps lifted and the house rose, and it began its sluggish creep up the roads.

"Right, I think he said to head down this path here," he said. "Come on, we need to get a move on."

"Where do you think you're going?" said a gruff voice behind him, and he turned to look at Barrington.

"I just said that we need to take this path down to the river."

Barrington looked affronted, which annoyed Hugh.

"Listen, if you are going to be like this the whole trip, it's going to be a long walk."

"But *I* didn't say anything."

Hugh shook his head and turned to walk on.

"Bloody fool ain't listening," said another voice off to Hugh's right.

"Now hang on a minute, Hugh, there's no need for that sort of talk," said Barrington.

Hugh spun round on his heel.

"I didn't say anything. It's you who's muttering under his breath."

"I beg your pardon!"

"Will you two pack it in!" said Emily, cutting through the argument.

"Neither of you were speaking."

The pair looked at her, totally flummoxed.

"It's these fine people, down here," she said, and crouched.

"What, the flowers?" said Hugh, half confused, smirking.

"Oi! We ain't flowers!" said the flower to Emily's right.

And then Hugh realised it was a tiny person. Another white-petalled flower hovered over to join the first, and it was then that Hugh realised the meadow wasn't full of flowers, but tiny people, all clinging to various blades grass and plants. All of them had wings, and indeed, some of them had taken flight.

"Well, I never," said Barrington. "I've never seen anyone so small."

He bent down to take a closer look. The yellow flower top poked him in the nose with a small spear.

"Ow!"

"Watch it, big nose! We ain't small; you're the giants around here."

"I apologise for my friend's lack of tact. I'm Emily," she said, holding out her little finger.

"Nice to meet yer," said the grub-voiced, yellow-topped flower. "I'm Buttercup, and this 'ere is Daisy."

"Nice to meet yer, miss," said Daisy.

"A pleasure it is to meet you too," said Emily.

"So what brings you to Meadow Down?"

"We're only passing through. We need to get to the path through the trees over there, and head to the Deep Dale road."

"Cor, Blimey! That's a trek an' a half."

"But it's only a hundred yards over there, if that," said Hugh.

"Alright, big foot, who was askin' you? Sorry miss, you were sayin' you need to pass through to the Deep Dale road?"

"Yes, if that's alright with you?"

"Certainly, we can assist you through Meadow Down, but the road's a bit rough in places."

"Don't you mean the path?" asked Hugh.

"What is your problem?" said Daisy, fluttering up to meet Hugh's eyes. "You got a thing against small people have yer? Eh?"

Hugh pulled his head back to avoid the small fists attempting to make contact with his face.

"Alright Daisy, that's enough!" said Buttercup, who had come to pull his friend back. "What you doin', settin' him off like that for, eh?"

"But I didn't," Hugh said. "I only said—"

But Emily cut him off to avoid any more offence.

"What he *meant* to say was that would be lovely." Emily elbowed Hugh in the ribs.

He looked at her as though about to reply, but she shook her head, so he chose to keep quiet. Several of the flower folk had gathered around them now, all looking displeased. He didn't know why, but they were quite intimidating. His train of thought was broken by a loud sneeze from Barrington.

He was still crouching down, looking at the many flowers in front of him, and the blast of air cut a swathe through the mass of flora. Numerous cries of shock and pain came from the fallen fairies.

"Steady on, whatcha think you're doing?" said Buttercup, going to the aid of his friends.

"I didn't mean to do it," said Barrington, sounding sniffly. "It's because I'm allergic to the pollen."

"I'm beginning to think you don't like us. It's always the same with you big folk. No respect."

"It's not like that," said Barrington in protest.

"I think this is getting a wee bit out of hand," said Heather.

"I agree," said Emily, and she turned to Buttercup and Daisy. "If you're alright to show us the way, we'll be out of the meadow right away."

Buttercup dwelled on this for a moment before coming to a conclusion.

"Righto, this is what we're gonna do. I'll lead you through the meadow, and Daisy here will bring up the rear. We don't want these two oafs destroying anything else," he said, waving his thumb over his shoulder at Hugh and Barrington.

They were about to come back with a response, but Emily shot them a look, and they decided against it.

"This way if you please," said Buttercup.

The crowd parted in front of them as Buttercup led the way. Hugh avoided the mass of tiny eyes drilling into the side of his head, feeling guilty each time he heard the sobbing of an injured fairy. They followed Buttercup slowly through the meadow, as he worked up a fine bead of dew, attempting to fly as fast as his little wings would take him. Now and then, Hugh would get an unfriendly reminder that Daisy was still behind him, as a spear prodded into his bottom. For all intents and purposes, it looked like a standard meadow surrounded by trees, with the grass blowing in the gentle breeze in a mesmerising way. However, on closer inspection he saw small houses woven out of the grass. He was surprised to see that they had chimneys, and some had tiny wisps of smoke rising out of them.

With the sun on his face and birdsong filling the air, it seemed like an idyllic place to live. He could now hear running water and saw a stream up ahead with steppingstones to cross. Buttercup landed on a bench out of breath, and Daisy came to sit next to him, looking much the same.

"We don't fly all that often these days," said Buttercup. "The meadow used to be a lot bigger, and the community spread across it, so we could fly daily. In recent years, the woods have encroached on our lands. Damned elves trying to land grab, if you ask me. What you passed through was the last of our tribe, so it's just as easy to walk to your neighbour."

"So have you all but given up on flying?" asked Emily.

"We fly to defend or when the odd intrusions occur. This raging torrent marks the edge of our territory now," he said, thumbing towards the gentle stream. Hugh was about to say something, but Emily sensed this.

"*Don't!*"

"What? I wasn't going to say anything."

"Hrmmm, likely story."

"This is where we leave you," said Buttercup. "We don't cross the stream, far too dangerous for us to cross, especially when we're tired. Will you be alright crossing over by yourselves?"

"I think we'll be alright," said Emily, who couldn't resist a little smile.

"You may find it funny missy, but we lost two younglings just last week. Thought they could hack the jump, but their little wings weren't developed enough. Terrible tragedy."

"Terrible," said Daisy, wiping a tear from his eye.

"Where're you headed, anyway?"

"We're off to Killinsfolk and Syreni Bay at the north of the island," said Emily.

"Tha's a long way to go, must be a good ten miles that. Whatcha reckon, Daisy?"

"Yeah, at least, and that's if you take the route through the forest," he said, and he gave a little shiver.

"What exactly is wrong with the forest?" asked Hugh.

"What's wrong with it?" said Buttercup. "There's things in there that'll curl the buds on your chest, big foot."

Hugh scowled at him, but Buttercup seemed not to notice.

"You may not believe me, but most who enter never come out. If the Ferryman don't get you, the Wisps will. Whatever you do, don't cross the river till you reach the head. Only then can you pass safely."

"The Ferryman will take us over the river safely. That's his job, surely? He'd make a pretty poor ferryman if he couldn't manage that," said Barrington.

"Nay, ye never take a lift from the Ferryman," said Heather, who beat Daisy to the answer. Her voice quivered as she spoke, and her eyes widened. "He'll only take ye to the other side."

"But surely that's the idea?"

"I don't think you and Heather are on the same page here, Barrington," said Hugh. "I think she means he'll take you to the other side in a *figurative* sense, rather than a literal one."

"Aye, so if ye ever see a ferryman, never take his offer of a lift, or it might be the last one ye ever take."

"Exactly," said Buttercup. "So if you want to make it through the forest in one piece, keep your wits about you."

Heather was now looking at Emily and Hugh with raised eyebrows.

"Ye know, it's nae too late to change yer minds. We can still take the route around the outside and get there in one piece."

"There, on any normal day, I would have to agree with you, miss. However, that road's been out of action since the passing trolls took out the bridges along the route, and there are some big rivers, even for folk like you, trust me."

"But Sybil, I mean, the High Enchantress didnae mention anything about trolls destroying bridges," said Heather.

"Them lot in the palace ain't got a clue. It's always the same with those in power. As long as they're alright, who cares about the small people?"

"They dinnae strike me as uncaring people."

"Fact is, they delegate all the work to the districts, and the funds that go with it. Then the money ends up lining the elders' pockets. A pack of trolls taking out the bridges will be causing big headaches, cos they ain't got no money to fix 'em properly, but they can't ask for more money without revealing the truth."

"But why did the trolls do that in the first place?" asked Hugh.

They were on their way to join the Elf King in Morcarthia and caused mass destruction in their wake. These parts haven't seen violence like that since the dark days of the Great War. Best bet is to wait for them to get some temporary bridges set up. It's only a matter of a week or so."

"So that decides the route that we must take then," he said, with a tone of finality. "It saddens me to hear that, even here, you're affected by the troubles in the Old World."

"None of us is immune to such things. The fact we're here, having this conversation with each other, should be enough to prove that. It ain't gonna be an easy ride; that's for sure."

"Indeed, it won't, and I hope for all our sakes, we get out of this mess intact, which is another reminder that we really ought to be getting a move on."

"Right you are, big foot. I seem to have had the wrong impression of you, and I apologise," said Buttercup, holding out a hand to shake. "What's your name?"

"Hugh Geber," he said, "and thank you, Buttercup, apology accepted."

"Hugh Geber, eh? You are walking a well-trodden path, Mr Geber. Make sure you take care of your companions, and you lot take care of him."

"Ye speak as though ye know him?" said Heather.

"Course we know of him. His father was a regular and welcomed visitor to these parts. He would always do his best to help our kind and always spoke highly of you, I might add."

"My father spoke to you about me?"

"Certainly did, and it feels nice to return the favour. He was a troubled man, mind. I think he knew that his time on this plain was coming to an end. The last time we saw him, he was alone and said he had to see the ferryman."

These words sunk into Hugh ears like a steam hammer and seemed to reach the very core of his inner mind. So his father was gone then, but why was he still in the sight?

"I wouldn't let this news trouble you though," said Daisy. "He said he had a plan and — Ow! Whatcha kick me for?"

"He's got to figure it out himself," said Buttercup, "remember?"

"Figure what out? What did my father tell you?"

"It's not our place to say, only that you must figure out your own path. Anyway, we ought to get back before he reveals too much. Good luck, to all of you. You're gonna need it."

And before Hugh could interject anymore, the pair of flower fairies took to the sky again and headed back to the meadow, leaving Hugh lost for words.

Chapter 25

Out in the middle of Syreni Bay, a ship named the *Fey Flyer* had come to an all stop. The locals who had heard about the antics of the New Worlders, had gathered around the harbour wall, partially in interest, but mostly to grumble about the foreigners, who were disturbing the water dwelling creatures that lived in the marine blue waters. They looked on out across bay, some armed with binoculars and telescopes, those without relying on a running commentary from their neighbour. They were all waiting with bated breath, to see what would happen next. They did all agree on one thing – the out of towners were dabbling in things that ought not to be dabbled with.

There were a few gasps as a submersible was lifted off the deck and dropped unceremoniously into the bay, sending water up into the sky. Until this point, they had attempted to scupper all the plans being put in place, but to no avail. Now they watched as three people jumped onto the vessel and climbed inside. This would be a day to remember.

On the deck of the *Fey Flyer,* a debate had broken out over who should go down. Smithson was refusing point-blank to enter the tight compartment of the submersible named *Dragon of the Sea*.

"I don't wish to spend my time cooped up in that thing," he said.

"I'm more than comfortable up here."

"If *sir* wishes to find the items he's looking for, then I suggest he joins the crew under the waves," said Collins. "I'm getting tired of doing all these little jobs for you. It's above and beyond my duty."

"Then why don't you step aside and let the real men do the work? I can easily have you replaced, so don't you forget which side your bread is buttered."

"Oh, not this old line again. Do I need to remind you of the rules of conduct once more?"

"Sod the rules. Just get on with your job before I throw you overboard!"

Collins looked as though he were about to retort, but he thought better of it as Captain Johnson approached the pair.

"Is everything alright here, gentleman? Only I can hear your conversation from my cabin," he said. "Might I make so bold as to suggest that we get on with this little project?"

"Keep out of this," Smithson barked back, causing a few sharp intakes of breath from the surrounding crew.

"May I also remind you that, whilst you are on board this ship, you are under my jurisdiction. If you wish to carry on with this charade, then you will do as I say. Either get a move on, or I call my men back, and we head to shore."

"Fine," said Smithson, obviously holding back from what he wanted to say. "Collins, if you will, climb aboard so we can get moving."

He nudged him towards the gap in the rail, causing Collins to stumble and nearly fall overboard. Maso, who was already on the *Dragon of the Sea*, came to his aid and helped him down to where he was standing.

"Well?" said Collins, looking Smithson in the eye.

Water sloshed over where he was standing on the bobbing vessel, causing his feet to get soaked.

"I think I'll stay here where it's dry. I wouldn't want to get my feet wet."

And with that, he shut the gate on the side of the ship with a defiant slam. Collins reddened in the face.

"Get in there, boy," he said, pointing to the open hatch. "We shall pick this up when we surface."

"I'm sure we will," said Smithson. "Oh, and Collins …"

His servant stopped with one leg on the ladder to climb up and in. "Yes?"

"Don't come back empty-handed. I say, Captain Johnson, is that bottle of port still open in your cabin?"

Smithson turned and walked off with the captain.

Collins scowled once more as he climbed into the *Dragon of the Sea*, slamming the hatch shut and locking it tight. The vessel was cast off from the deck and disappeared under the waves in a frenzy of foam and bubbles. On deck, two crew members began pumping air whilst the rest worked to feed the umbilical line into the water.

Chapter 26

Hugh, Barrington, Emily and Heather had made it to the river. Though it wasn't fast flowing, it was still too much to cross on foot. With the words of Buttercup still ringing in their ears, they opted to take the path alongside the river. Although they hadn't reached the forest, they were still walking under the cooling canopy of trees. Dappled daylight shone through the branches, highlighting the path ahead. The conversation was light between the group of travellers, each lost in their own thoughts.

Hugh was enjoying taking in the new surroundings he found himself in. All around him he could hear unusual birdsong and caught glimpses of exotic, multicoloured creatures flying through the air. His thought was broken by the sight of a hooded man standing on a flat barge. Hugh slowed to a stop, and Emily bumped into him.

"What's wrong?" she asked.

"Look, it's the Ferryman," he said.

He didn't know why, but he had an uncontrolled urge to step towards him. It was as though he was being pulled by some unseen force. Everything around him went still, and a chill passed through his body. Emily's hand reached out into his and pulled him back, his chest tingling at her touch.

"Hugh, don't go towards him. Remember what Buttercup and Daisy said?"

"Hrmmm, oh yes, right," he said, coming out of the daydream.

He still continued towards the man on the barge.

Barrington was incredulous. "Hugh! Didn't you hear what Emily just said? Don't go near him."

"It's alright, I won't get too close, I just have a question to ask him." He knew he wouldn't like the answer, but he had to know.

"You wish to cross over?" said the Ferryman, his voice unusually quiet.

"Is it true?" asked Hugh. "Is this where people come to cross over?"

"Yes, that is true, though it's a one-way trip, mind. Here, let me help you aboard."

Hugh had to resist the urge to take the outstretched hand and felt Emily pulling him away.

"No, please," he said to her, "I need to ask him something."

"Come on, he's giving me the creeps."

"Just one more question," he said and turned back to the Ferryman. "Can you tell me … did you take him over?"

Emily step close to him. "Who are you talking about, Hugh?"

"I know of whom you speak," said the Ferryman, "and I did indeed take him over."

"Who?" asked Emily, more impatiently.

"He's talking about his dad," said Heather. "Ye cannae bring him back, Hugh. He's gone."

"But he saw us in the sight. There has to be a way, surely?"

"There's nae way back," said Heather, who was talking to Hugh but watching the Ferryman. "Come on, we've a job to do. Now's not yer time to cross over. We'll find the source soon enough and cross over there."

"Wise words she speaks," said the Ferryman. "Pass on my regards to your father, Heather."

"Aye, that I'll do." She held the man with a fiery gaze, as though there was a hidden conversation going on, then pulled Hugh and Emily away from the riverbank. "Come on yese two, we need to get a move on if we're to get to the forest."

"How does he know you and Hamish?" asked Barrington with fear in his voice.

"It's family stuff, and ye'll be best to keep yer nose out of it, if ye know what's good for ye."

"Alright, I was only asking," he replied, taken aback. "I don't want to lose you, that's all."

"Well, I'm staying here, so yiv nae need to worry." Then she marched off down the riverbank.

"Heather …? Heather!"

Barrington chased after her, leaving Hugh and Emily with the Ferryman. Hugh looked at him.

"Thank you. Your offer to cross was a tempting one, but my friends are right. We need to finish the job we're here to do. If I step out now, it will leave a lot more than friendship in the lurch."

"As you wish. I will always be here as a means to cross over, should you ever wish to use my service."

Hugh nodded as he and Emily backed further up the path before turning to head after Barrington and Heather. They had made a good distance, and by the time they had caught up, the path had risen upwards. Down below, Hugh could hear the river flowing by, and he chanced a look over the edge. His head spun, and he felt something block his fall, and bring him back onto the path. He looked down to see Emily's staff, which she had placed out in front of him to prevent him from falling.

"Let's *not* look over the edge," she said, now steadying Hugh. "We wouldn't want to lose you that way."

Hugh shuddered at the thought.

"Right," she said, "what's the plan? Shall we stop to eat?"

"That sounds like an excellent plan," said Barrington. "There's a clearing just up here that looks like the perfect spot."

They headed to where he was pointing.

Heather rummaged in her bottomless pockets and pulled out a seal pelt coat. She passed it to Barrington, who carefully placed it over a low-hanging branch. Eventually, she found what she was looking for – pulling out a picnic blanket.

"Ah, here we are," she said, laying it out on the ground. "Right who's carrying the bag of food?"

"I have it," said Hugh, relieved to take the weight off his back, which was damp from carrying the backpack. "I didn't realise you were still carrying that old coat around, Barrington. I doubt you'll be needing it any time soon."

"It's more than just an old coat, Hugh. This was an eighteenth birthday gift from my father, and it's come in handy over the years. It keeps me dry in wet situations."

"Yeah, even so," said Hugh, pointing to the sun which was beating down upon them.

"I'll keep it, if it's all the same," he said, patting it. Hugh was now laying out the spread from Stanley. "Ah good, now … what in the name of all things spritely?"

The cuisine they had been given was not what Hugh would call a picnic. He looked at the leg of uncooked meat he had just unwrapped, followed by the platter of eyeballs, which wobbled and rolled around the plate they were on. No wonder his backpack was so heavy. Emily was looking a tad green in the face.

"Ah, sheep's eyes," said Heather, "my favourite. I've nae had these for ages."

She picked one up and shoved it into her mouth. She bit down, and something gave an audible 'pop'.

"Aww, ye gotta try these, they're the best," she said with her mouth full, and a bit of eye jelly dribbled down her chin. "Oops, sorry!"

She slurped it back in. This was too much for Emily, who ran back to the edge of the path and heaved into the ravine.

It was as she turned away from the edge that it happened.

One moment she was there, wiping the residue off her face, the next she had disappeared, the ground beneath her feet crumbling away into the river below. Hugh didn't even stop to think. He was on his feet, ignoring the calls from Barrington who was wrestling with his coat. Without a second thought of the height or the danger it represented, Hugh took a running leap into the river.

As his feet left the ground, a wave of tension flowed through his body, as though it were preparing him for a landing on something solid, but it never came. It was at this point he realised what he had done and looked down. His emotions took over as he screamed, flailing his arms and legs like an out-of-control ballet dancer, all the way into the river's icy depths. He landed hard in the bottom of the fast-flowing river, the water eating into him like thousands of daggers. He heard a crack, followed by a searing amount of pain in his right ankle. A momentary feeling of faintness fell over him, and he was under the water. Lungs screaming for air, he pushed up on his good ankle, and broke the surface of the water once more. It was then that he saw her.

Emily's body was limp, caught between two rocks, the fast-flowing current pinning her there, and the water flowing over her head. Hugh fought against the river, and with outstretched arms, he clung onto one of the rocks next to Emily. His body was still moving downstream, nearly losing his grip as the weight of his body came to a sudden stop, almost pulling his arms out of their sockets. He thought his fingernails were going to rip off. With great effort, Hugh hauled himself towards Emily, water hitting him dead on in the face. He had to turn in the opposite direction to breathe, before attempting to get Emily's head out of the water. The pain in his ankle was excruciating.

As he struggled to pull her from the grip of the river, he was aware of something else joining them in the water. The mass of something huge came lumbering towards them. It looked to be half man, half … seal? Hugh couldn't believe what he was seeing as the creature bobbed its way up and down towards him. He was fascinated and petrified at the same time. Unable to see clearly, barely clinging onto life itself, Hugh grabbed Emily as best he could to protect her from the beast. But it was no good. Now blind with fear, Hugh struggled to fend it off. He had to protect Emily, but he was slipping into the darkness, and with one last gulp of watery air, he slipped away.

–POP–

He was cold and shivering in the semidarkness of the sight. He was carrying something heavy, and he looked down to see Emily's lifeless body, limp in his arms. He looked around to see if there was anyone to help, but all he could see were malevolent shadows moving around them. Their life-links were weak, and he knew they weren't in the sight full body.

'Help! Anyone?'

'Hugh, is that you?'

'Father, where are you? I can't see you.'

Something was now tugging at him, as though it were pulling at his soul. The shadows were closing in all around him, and some were reaching out to them, with others attacking their life-links. He knew he had to try to find the runes of protection, but to do so would mean letting go of Emily, and he refused to consider such an idea.

'Father, I need your help. I cannot protect myself and Emily. Our bodies are in the plane of the living, and our lifelines are being attacked.'

'Hang on in there, Hugh. Help is on the way. Stay strong.'

'Hurry, we can't hold on much longer!'

It was then that he felt a surge of warmth. At first he thought it was his father – maybe he had found them and was drawing on the runes of protection. But there was no sign of him. Then, from way down his life-link, he saw Aeolus making his way towards them, batting the malevolent beings away as he moved. But there was something else with him. A great white, winged mare, holding strong next to Aeolus. As they beat their path towards them, Hugh could feel his energy growing. The pair made their way to Hugh and Emily, with the unicorn coming to join them, and the winged horse forming a shield of protection around the pair.

'Aeolus? It sure is a relief to see you. We need to get out of here. Can you help?'

'We shall do what we can for you and Mistress Emily.'

'Alright, I need you to find Heather McDougall for me. Find her and bring her here.'

Although some of his strength had returned, he hadn't enough energy to get Emily back home safely.

'That I will do. I will leave you with Aife.'

Aeolus turned to face the winged mare.

'Aife, my love, after all this time, we meet again. But alas, I have a job to do, for my mistress needs help. Though it pains me to leave you so soon after reuniting with you, I will return. Look after mistress and Hugh. They are weak and will need help to return.'

'That I will do, Aeolus, my one true love. Now go quick, my master and Emily will not last long.'

Aeolus rubbed noses with Aife, then turned and batted away the shadows as he went down the life-links. Hugh was now left alone with Emily and Aife. He didn't know why, but the creature had a feeling of familiarity to him, as though he somehow knew her but couldn't place where from.

'That is because you have known me all your life. Though you were

not aware of it, I have always been here for you. My name is Aife, I'm an alicorn, who will always be there whenever you need me.'

'Why have I not seen you before?'

'It is because you weren't ready to see me until now. I am you, as you are me, and I will always stand beside you for all eternity.'

'Wow, well, I'm very pleased to meet you, Aife.'

'And I you, Hugh. This has been a long time coming, and it means we are about to face some difficult times. Ah, good, here comes Aeolus with some help.'

Sure enough, racing back up the life-links, Hugh saw Aeolus returning alongside two other balls of light. It transpired that he had found Heather and Barrington, who also had something accompanying him. It was a large seal, that appeared to be swimming around him in a protective manner.

When Heather reached them, her voice was full of concern.

'Ah, thank goodness for that, we thought we'd lost yese both. What's happened to Emily?'

'She's taken a beating, I'm afraid. We need to get her back, and I don't think I can hold on to her for much longer.'

Barrington came up next to him.

'Let her go, Hugh, we can take her from here.'

'No! I won't let go of her. I'm never letting go of her again.'

Aeolus and Aife came together once more in a protective manner around Hugh and Emily. Heather spoke.

'There's a way we can do this, but ye have to trust me, otherwise those two wilnae let yese go anywhere.'

Hugh nodded, and Heather put her fingers to her lips as if she were about to whistle, but a long, loud drone, quite unlike any noise Hugh had heard before, emanated from her mouth. Moments later, the sound of a cat being skinned with a blunt knife filled the sight, and alongside that, came the sound of beating wings. The cacophony of noise grew to a crescendo, and the mighty dragon known as Betsie came into view.

Standing atop of her, legs akimbo, kilt flapping in the non-existent breeze, with knees bending in time with the great beast's wings, was Hamish McDougall. His cheeks bellowed in and out as he played his bladder pipes, the noise unrelenting. As Betsie made it to the group, she let out a huge burst of fire, removing all danger from the area in one fell swoop.

Heather had to shout to be heard over the immense din.

'Everyone, climb on,'

Aeolus and Aife helped Hugh and Emily onto the back of the beast and stood strong together with them, refusing to break their protective bond. Heather, Barrington and his seal also climbed aboard. Heather hugged her father, and he winked at her, but did not stop playing his pipes. His eyes widened as he saw the sight of Hugh and Emily, and he changed his tune immediately. The beast was off, clearing a path as she went, following the trail of the life-links through the emptiness of the sight. With a feeling of being pulled through a keyhole backwards, and a

–POP–

the group landed back in the plane of the living. Hugh patted himself down, checking he really was back in reality. He then quickly turned his attention back to Emily and realised she was not awake. Aeolus and Aife were still standing close to them, and he sensed what to do next. Looking inside himself, he searched all the different runes, looking for the ones of healing that were used on him by his uncle just a few months before. He found them, called them forth, and drew them out in the air in front of him. He watched them weave together and cupped his hands around them before casting the ball of energy gently over Emily's body. He watched as they slowly sank in and begged for them to work. After what seemed like a lifetime, she rolled over and coughed out a lungful of water before rolling back and gasping.

It was only now, as the adrenaline began to ease off, did the full reality of the situation come back to Hugh, and he was reminded of his broken ankle. Searing hot pain shot up his leg, so much so, that he thought he might pass out. Aeolus and Aife came alongside him, Aeolus touching Aife's head with his horn. Momentarily distracted from the pain, Hugh watched as a horn began growing from Aife's head, right where Aeolus had touched it.

"You know what to do," said the unicorn to the alicorn. Aife knelt down, placing her newly grown horn on Hugh's ankle. Warmth spread up from the spot where she touched him, and he felt the pain ease. She stood back up, returning to nuzzling Aeolus.

"Here, take some of this, laddie," said Hamish, passing Hugh his flask.

The contents burned as he drank it, yet he felt invigorated, and he passed it to Emily, who drank between coughs. Somewhere in the background came the sound of a dying goat, as the bladder pipes slowly deflated on the floor. Hamish saw Hugh looking at them and laughed.

"What?" said Hugh.

"I told ye, ma music was magic," he said and patted Hugh firmly on the back.

"It's good to see you Hamish," said Hugh, standing awkwardly, giving the old man a hearty hug.

"Ye too, laddie. Ye too. I think me other daughter is looking for yer attention," he said, pointing to Emily.

Hugh looked back to Emily, who was now back on her feet.

"I thought I'd lost you," he said, embracing her. They stood forehead to forehead.

"Thank you, from the bottom of my heart. I see Aeolus has a new friend."

"Quite the opposite. It appears they have known each other for some time, but I think they may have lost each other for a while."

"I know the feeling," she said, now looking into his eyes. "You must have shown loyalty and courage for your spirit guide to show up. The fact they are linked speaks a thousand words."

She now spoke inside Hugh's head.

'I love you, Hugh Geber.'

'And I you, Emily Le Fey.'

He didn't care that they had fought. He knew that his heart would always belong to Emily, and hers to him. At that moment he knew they were as one.

A cough from behind them brought them back to reality.

"Not wanting to interrupt," said Barrington, who was dripping wet and holding his sodden coat. "We need to get a move on if we are going to set up camp."

Hugh looked towards the sun that was already setting behind the canopy of trees.

"Yes, I totally agree, but I also want an explanation as to what happened back there, and why are you so wet?"

Barrington flushed, but Heather stepped up before he could say anything.

"We'll get to that part soon. If yese two would be so kind as to light your firestones so we can all dry off, that'd be lovely."

"Oh yes," said Hugh, realising how cold he was. He and Emily lit their stones, and the group began to dry off and warm up. Hamish requested that all the spirit guides make their way back to the sight, as it would take a lot of explaining if anyone saw them – they would also need to rest up after such a big adventure. After bidding farewell to their respective animals and beasts, they made their way back to where they had left their belongings, deciding that it would be as good a place as any to set up camp for the night. They managed to light a fire and cook the food that was given to them, with only Heather and Hamish opting to eat the sheep's eyes.

Whilst they were preparing to eat the main course, the hooded figure of the Ferryman appeared down the track. Hamish was the only one to see him, and his eyes glinted with a glow not from the campfire. He momentarily stared, fixated with the man, before coming back to his senses and taking a swig from his flask. When he turned back, the figure was gone, along with Hamish's memory of him which had faded away with the drink.

Chapter 27

It was only after they had eaten that Hugh decided to broach the subject of what had happened at the river. There was a patch of memory he didn't have, namely, getting downstream to a place of safety and being taken out of the fast-moving current. There was also the lingering question of the beast he'd seen before he drifted into the sight.

"So, what was it then?" he asked.

All chatter and merriment died down around the campfire, and Hugh could have sworn his friend's cheeks had flushed.

"What?"

"What was it that was in the water with us? And why were you so wet?"

"It's alright," said Heather, taking Barrington's hand. "I think it's time they knew."

"Knew what?"

Barrington took in a deep breath and sighed.

"This is complicated and a little off the wall, so please hear me out and don't interrupt me. That old coat that you called it, isn't just any old coat."

"I know, you said it was a present from your father."

"Hugh, please. I need to say this without being interrupted every ten seconds, otherwise we'll be here all night."

Hugh chewed the inside of his mouth and swallowed but said nothing. Barrington nodded.

"Sorry, but this is a big thing for me to talk about. I haven't really got my head around it all myself yet. The coat is something everyone on my side of the family receives on their eighteenth birthday. I had an inkling of what it was, and what it meant for me, but I never really believed it, even when my father gave me the coat.

"It was on the night of the big storm that I used it for the first time. When I told you in Skellig-Krieg of all the events that happened that night, I omitted a few *minor* details. This coat gives me the ability to transform from being a human, into a selkie, that is part man, part seal. When I saw Emily drop off the edge into the river, I immediately went for my coat, but you beat me off the mark. Before I had time to stop you, it was too late, and you had jumped in after her. Very brave, I might add, if a tad foolish. Heather, of course, saw my transformation when I hit the water, and she is very accepting of the situation. Most women would probably run a mile."

"Ye know, I'm nae like most women. You could've told me before now, but I understand why ye didnae wanna tell me."

"Thank you, that means a lot."

"You could have told me too," said Hugh a little miffed. "I would have been accepting of the situation as well."

"But would you? Can you imagine how silly it would have sounded? For a long time I was ashamed of it, being linked so close to the Old World, when all around us was changing to a pro New World view. I couldn't take the risk. I put it to the back of my mind and hoped I would never have to use it again, though I held true to my word to my father and always kept the coat nearby. Today has proved to me how wrong my view was and how important is that I keep the tradition and old ways alive."

"Well, we're both grateful," said Emily. "Though I had my suspicions that you were a selkie."

"You did?"

"Of course, there were many questions raised after your accident, and I did my research. Eventually, that led me to your parents' door, and only after I gained their trust and proved my loyalty to the old ways, did your father entrust me with the Delphin family secret. I told you I knew the truth back in Skellig-Krieg, remember?"

"I remember, but I didn't conceive that you were referring to that. I only thought you were talking about the sinking in general."

"So, how did you get us out of the water?" asked Hugh. "I thought we were done for."

"That was easy for me, once I had my coat on, that is. I could scoop the pair of you up, then I rolled on my back with you both laying on my front. We floated downstream to where the current eased, and I could get to the bank. Heather was running alongside, and she helped to retrieve you from the water.

"It was shortly after we pulled you free and I took the coat off that the unicorn turned up. We followed it into the sight where we found you, and the rest you know from that point. I was surprised to see a seal by my side in the sight though, I'm not sure why it was there."

"Thas an easy one to explain," said Hamish. "If ye have ever heard some people say, 'someone was looking out for me that day,' what they dinnae realise is that *that someone* is their spirit guide. It's a bit like the feeling ye get when ye drift off to sleep, and ye think someone is in the room with ye. It's yer guide. They are always there when you need protection, and the transition over into sleep being one of them. It's seen as a time of weakness, and the best time for a malevolent being to try to get into yer body.

"Most will never get to see their guides, as they're blind to the ways of the sight. Those who gain access to higher plains are still nae guaranteed to see them. It takes a change within the person themselves, similar to a coming of age, for the guide to appear. The fact ye ran to Emily's aid in the river without considering the danger to yer own life, shows ye had chosen yer path, though I wouldnae recommend doing that too often. Yer family background isnae fully in line with the water beings. Jumping into waters without thinking is dangerous, especially to save others, as ye found out today. If yer body is in danger in the plane of the living, ye can still pass over. Spirit animals are there to learn from and to guide ye. They will assist where possible, but dinnae take them for granted. They're nae there for personal gain."

"Well, all I can say is thank you for your help, Barrington and Heather. We have a tremendous amount of gratitude for your help today," said Hugh, before turning to address Barrington directly. "I will always accept you for who you are, whether it be in human form or selkie. You are my best and most trusted friend and always have been. Your secret will always be safe with me, well with all of us, really. I think we can all agree that we've all found out more about each other today than we've ever known."

The rest of the group nodded.

"Thank you, everyone, that means more than you will ever know," said Barrington.

"So, without this getting too soppy," said Heather, "what's our next move going to be?"

"Well, we need to get through the Forest of Fey tomorrow," said Hugh, "if we are to get to Syreni Bay before Smithson finds the next book."

"Hang on there, laddie, ye say yer gonna walk through the Forest of Fey?" said Hamish.

"That's correct. It's the quickest way to get to the north of the island, and as we have to be there as soon as possible, we have no other choice."

"I gave instruction to Heather to nae let ye travel through there. It's too dangerous."

"We understand that, but given that Smithson is already ahead of us, and the bridges around the outside track are destroyed, we have little choice."

"Well if that's true what yer sayin', then it looks like ye'll be needing my assistance. Ye'll need yer wits about yese all when going through the Forest of Fey, and a guide that knows the way through. Even then we're nae guaranteed a safe passage."

"Are ye sure ye can stay, Dad? What about fixing the rune wing?"

"Thas important, I agree with ye on that, but we cannae re-enter the site fir a wee while. We'll all need to recharge after such an experience. Besides, the forest is full of beasts and creatures, all looking fir their next meal. Ye'll need an experienced guide, and I've walked that path many times over the years. I need to guarantee my daughters are both safe, nae to mention their respective partners. We're all family, and families stick together."

"Ach, I'm so glad yer staying, Dad," said Heather, giving him a hug.

"Aye, well if yer gonna get the book and the trident ye'll need ma help with that too."

"The trident?" asked Barrington.

"Aye, ye do know about it?"

"Nobody mentioned anything about a trident. I was under the impression that we were getting the book, then going home. It sounds like a lot more work than we were first expecting."

"Aye, well if ye want to use the book of lore, ye'll need to find the trident. The pair go hand in hand, and without it ye'll nae be able to work the powers held within its pages."

"But Balinas never mentioned anything about the trident," said Hugh.

"Aye, well he widnae have done. The trident only came into existence *after* the book was returned to its place of safety during the Great War. The story goes that it was created using some of the power of the book, meaning that on their own, neither object is of much use, but together they make one hell of a weapon. It's a big legend on the isle; most of the folk know about it. It caused great fear to the islanders, as they thought they could be killed at any moment. Luckily, without the book, it's useless."

"Oh, well that's good to hear," said Barrington. "What were they thinking when they made the damn thing? If the Elf King gets hold of that, he'll have a weapon of mass destruction."

"There yer in luck, laddie, because the trident has been lost for some twenty years or so."

"Lost? Well that's made the job ten times harder. How do we find an object that is lost?"

"Ma guess is as good as yers, but if we start with the book, we might find the trident."

"I say there's no need worrying about it now," said Emily. "It hasn't surfaced in the last twenty years, and I doubt it will reappear overnight. The important thing is still to find the book of lore, as that is what we are tasked to find. Get that to the chamber, and it will be safe, trident or not."

"Alright, if that's all good with yese all, then I might suggest we all get some shut-eye? We need to be on the road early tomorrow."

They all reluctantly agreed to put the subject to bed for the night. It wasn't long before the sound of conversation ebbed away, and the sound of snoring was added to the background noise of the river, backlit by the glowing embers of the dying fire.

Chapter 28

"Hamish … Hamish … HAMISH!"

The sound of the bladder pipes, which were punching through the morning air like an unwelcome house guest, died away like an over talkative parrot being run over by a steam car.

"Ah, morning, Hugh laddie. I see yer an early riser like me, eh?"

"No, it's that infernal racket that woke me!"

"Me too," came the muffled voice of Emily.

"Me three." Barrington, looked over at Heather still sound asleep. "It would appear daughter number two is more immune to the dreadful sounds."

"Watch what yer calling dreadful. I've already explained more than once that ma music's magic. Let's wake the lassie, shall we, and get the day started?"

With a large amount of grumbling from the rest of the camp, they all freshened up for the day ahead. Hamish had already got a fire going and was boiling up a pot of tea.

"Where on earth did you dig that out from?" asked Barrington.

"Bottomless sporran, laddie, one of Heather's little creations. It's one of the most useful things I carry, and it only looks like an ordinary pouch.

I dinnae know how I managed so long without it."

He poured some of the water into another pan, which was full of oats. Emily pulled her bag out from her tent and retrieved some vanilla pods.

"Here," she said, handing them to Hamish. "Put some of these in there. I can't stand the taste of raw porridge."

As they sat down to eat, the sun was breaking through, banishing the night away for the rest of the day. Hugh watched the shadow as it decreased on the hillside opposite them, and Hamish announced they had to be on the move if they were to win the day. They packed up camp and headed out along the track, with the sound of birdsong and flowing water for company. The air was fresh, but dry, and they could tell that it was going to be another warm day. Well, at least it was for those not about to enter the Forest of Fey.

Hugh sighted along the ominous-looking path which disappeared off into the darkness. It seemed the most uninviting place to be taking a walk. A cool breeze emanated from the wooded area, and though he couldn't see anything moving within the trees, he had the feeling that many pairs of eyes were looking back at them. He was beginning to question in his mind whether it was a good idea to consider entering the forest at all, when Hamish broke the silence.

"Right, listen up. Yese have all gotta pay close attention in there. It's real easy to get separated, so we must stick together, and for sprite's sake, dinnae interact with anything that appears friendly. The Forest of Fey is well known for its creatures of deception, so dinnae fall for any of its tricks, yese hear?"

They all nodded, whilst looking into the uninviting darkness.

"If I say run, we run, and if I tell ye all to get out of sight, well, ye know what to do. Just keep yer eyes peeled and call out anything suspicious. Alright, follow me," he said and marched off into the woods.

It was like stepping into the darkness of night. Hugh and Emily lit their firestones and had to use hole two for heat just to keep the chill off the group. Emily also had the advantage of lighting her staff – the turquoise orb only adding to the eerie light being given off by the firestones. Other than the sound of their feet on the path, there were no other sounds to be heard, not even the flowing waters of the river. Low hanging vines covered the path in places, calling to Hugh's mind the memories of the Vipera fronde in the greenhouses of Skellig-Krieg. How Hamish knew the way was beyond Hugh, but on he walked. He felt as though the trees themselves were watching them, and he thought he could hear something whispering, almost like the great wooden pillars were talking amongst themselves.

"Come along, Hugh," said Barrington from behind him, "stop daydreaming. We're going to lose the others if we don't keep pace."

"Can you hear that whispering?"

"What whispering? I think this place is getting to you, dear boy."

Something chuckled malevolently to Hugh's left.

"There," he said, pointing into the dense vegetation. "Did you hear that?"

"Hugh, there's nothing there. I think it's just your mind playing tricks, is all."

"Shhh, keep yer voices down, or ye'll give our location away," said Hamish, who had come to a stop. "Nobody move."

"What now?" said Barrington with a tone of frustration.

"Will ye shut up!"

Barrington muttered something inaudible, then looked to his left. Then yelled.

It all happened so fast Hugh didn't know what had occurred for a few moments. Barrington had leapt to one side in shock back towards the group huddled on the path, looked down and realized their peril, just as they were hoisted into the air in a massive net. They were now hanging from a branch, all squashed together.

"Did I not tell ye to be quiet? Now look at the mess yiv got us into!"

"I didn't do it on purpose," Barrington protested. "It was those things that made me jump."

They all looked down to see a small crowd had gathered below them, joyous with the day's catch swinging above their heads. They were small, ugly beings with pointy noses that seemed to take up the whole of their faces, and pointy ears that looked like they hadn't grown into them yet. Their dark eyes seemed soulless in the lights flickering from their torches, and they stood looking up at the group in the net, licking the pointy teeth that filled their mouths. Their clothing was camouflaged so well with the surrounding woods that Hugh found it hard to make out their bodies. They spoke a strange language which made it sound like they were constantly attempting to clear their throats. To his amazement, Hamish was talking back in the same language.

"What are they saying?" asked Hugh.

"The news isnae good. I think we're to be the main course in tonight's meal."

"Can't you arrange for our release? I don't fancy being made into a pie," said Barrington.

"If ye give me a chance to talk to them, then maybe I can, but yese all need to keep quiet. It's hard enough to figure out what they're saying, without yese lot blabbering over the top of them."

Another five minutes of throat clearing and phlegm spitting continued, before one of the goblins pulled out a machete.

"What the devil is that for?" asked Barrington.

"They've agreed to let us down," said Hamish.

"Ah, that is good news," said Barrington, as the machete–wielding goblin walked up to a tree and raised the weapon above his head.

The rest of the pack began chuckling, high pitched, as if they were up to no good.

"Hang on a minute, what's he …"

The goblin with the machete swung it back over his head and into the tree trunk, where it cut the rope holding up the net. They fell to the floor in a crumpled heap and were immediately set upon by the ravenous goblins.

"Oi, gerroff!" Hugh shouted at a goblin whose pointy teeth were menacing his arm. "I thought they were going to let us go?"

"Errrm, that's nae the case anymore. It would appear that we are to be bumped up to be the main course at an afternoon tea."

"Goblins have afternoon tea?"

"Aye, they do today!"

The ugly creatures fought amongst themselves for a minute or two, some wanting to eat the captives there and then, the rest wanting to take them back. Eventually, the net was gathered up, and they were rather unceremoniously dragged off into the undergrowth. Sticks and thorny branches dug into Hugh's side and scratched at his face, as they were pulled over the rough terrain.

"How far away do they live?" Barrington asked irritably, as he got whipped on the arm with a thorny bramble. "Ow!"

"I dinnae know, but we'd best start thinking of a plan to get out of here, and quickly. I dinnae want to make it to the dish of the day."

"Emily, have you got your staff on you?" asked Barrington. "You could use it to rustle something up to cut this net."

"No, I think I dropped it on the path back there," she said sounding panicked. "Ranny's going to kill me when he finds out I lost it."

"Thas nae gonna happen," said Hamish. "When we escape this, and we're gonna have to, we can head out along the path into here. We've left a sizeable gap to follow."

They finally made it out into a dimly lit clearing criss-crossed with walkways. Hugh looked up at the surrounding canopy, seeing walkways strung from tree to tree. Torches were set into holders around the area, and the flames cast flickering shadows, which danced around the clearing. They had attracted a large gathering of goblins, all of whom were looking at them with ravenous eyes. They were talking amongst themselves, all rasps and spits, and the crowd parted to reveal a goblin being brought through on a sedan chair decorated with the skeletons of birds and what appeared to be human skulls. It was set to rest in front of the captured guests, and the crowd fell silent. The door opened, and a rotund goblin dressed in what Hugh could only think of as goblin finery stepped out.

This goblin chief commanded the attention of the entire tribe. Speaking with a deep guttural voice, he addressed the group bundled in the catch net.

"So, you think you can wander into our lands and get away with it, do you?"

"Nae," said Hamish, "we were only passing through."

But the head goblin was in no mood for conversation.

"*Silence!* I gave you no permission to talk, and you shall hold your tongue. You think you can wander into our lands freely, without permission, with the arrogance that only man can possess. This cannot go unpunished. What do you have to say for yourselves?"

"Thank ye for letting me speak. We were only passing through and were unaware that yer territory had expanded out this far. The last time I passed through the forest, it was nowhere near the main track through."

"Times have changed, and the era of goblins shall reign strong once more. With the world distracted by the Elf King" —and at this he spat at the ground— "we shall have all the time to expand our lands and take the power first from the enchantress and then the world at large."

"Thas some grand plans ye have there. Tell me, have ye taken the entire forest yet?"

"No ... not yet ... but there's still plenty of time. We'll take the forest, then the entire Isle of Fey, you mark my words."

"Oh aye, we will do, but if ye cannae get out of the forest, how will ye take the rest of the isle? And if yer so fierce as all that why have ye nae killed us yet? A net won't stop an army."

"Hamish," Hugh said under his breath, "what are you doing? Don't goad them!"

"Dinnae worry lad, I know what I'm doing."

"Who are you talking to?" said the great goblin. "I won't take talking amongst yourselves."

"None of yer business. If yer nae gonna kill us now, get on with yer feast, and let us relax." He twisted in the net to turn his back on the goblin and did his best to put his hands behind his head.

The goblin was furious.

"You dare turn your back on the Goblin King? I'm talking to you … Fine, have it your way."

The Goblin King turned to the surrounding crowd and spoke to them in the native tongue, then got back into his chair and slammed the door shut. The crowd parted as he left, then dispersed, leaving the group alone in the clearing.

"Errrm, what did you just do?" asked Barrington. "Have you not just sent us all to our deaths?"

"On the contrary, laddie. I've just bought us time to escape."

"I don't quite see how? This net is so well made, it would impress the best fisherman. I doubt we will get out of it, no matter how hard we try."

"We've plenty of time, they'll be a good hour foraging for wood to build the fire."

"*Fire!*" said Hugh. "We don't have time to sit here and wait to get burned alive, Hamish."

"Aye, and I dinnae intend to. Speaking of fire, Emily, can you or Hugh reach for your stones? We could burn our way out of here."

"I'm hard pressed to move, let alone reach my firestone to activate it," said Emily. "My hands are stuck near my legs."

"Same here," said Hugh. "I can't believe we are stuck in this position."

"Has anyone got the time? We need to keep an eye on how long they are away for. Goblins are nothing if creatures of habit."

"I can't reach my watch," said Hugh from the bottom of the net.

"Oh, no! Mine's gone!" said Heather, awkwardly shuffling around in the scrum of people, putting a muddy boot into Hugh's face. "Oops, sorry Hugh. I must have dropped it when we were hoisted up on the path."

"Nae worries lass, we'll have to retrieve it on our way out of here when we get Emily's staff."

"Sorry?" said Barrington. "You wish to not only escape from here, but also retrieve an old pocket watch plus Emily's staff? How much time do you think we have?"

"Aye, that's correct, and it's not only some old pocket watch, it's an Ever-Right. It's part of the Tempus collection."

"The Tempus collection? Do you mean to say they're all linked?" said Emily.

"Aye, they are, so there's still a chance to escape from here. Yer mother had one and should've passed it onto ye."

"She did, hang on." With more shuffling, and yet another muddy boot in Hugh's face, Emily pulled her watch free. "Oh, stop complaining, Hugh. Here," she said.

The watch dropped down in front of Hugh's face. He looked up to see Emily's hand sticking out of the net, and she started to swing the watch back and forth like a pendulum. It got higher and higher until it swung full circle, landing in Hamish's outstretched hand.

"Excellent, just what we need." He opened it up and began twisting the bezel. Something buzzed in Hugh's tight pocket. "Nope, that appears to be somewhere dark," and he continued, turning the bezel. "Hang on … no, another dark place …"

"You might want to hurry up with whatever you're doing, Hamish," said Hugh. He was looking into the clearing and saw goblins returning with handfuls of wood. "It appears our friends are efficient at collecting kindling."

"Almost there, laddie."

"Well, you'd better make it quick, as I think the feast plans are in full swing."

Hugh was now looking at what appeared to be pointed, rusted, metal spikes that the goblins were wielding as they approached the group. Some also seemed to be carrying flaming torches. They appeared to have noticed Hamish playing with something and had picked up their pace.

"Hamish!"

The lead goblin had started running.

"Ah! Here we go, hold on …"

Hugh felt the end of a spike nick his leg, before another odd sensation took over. The sound of ticking filled his soul, and he thought for a moment his body had been pulled inside out. He was moving this way and that, being jarred roughly in circles. He attempted to look upwards, and saw what looked like a large, confused goblin peering through a window and tapping it, before a bright light flashed, and he was moving at speed. He was now being stretched in and out in time with the beating, which was so loud, he thought his head was going to explode. Then it felt as though the process was happening in reverse, and a moment later, he found himself back on the forest track.

He had no time to come to his senses, as someone had grabbed him by his collar. Suddenly, he was back on his feet being dragged along the rough terrain. Emily was retrieving her staff and Heather's watch. He watched in slow motion as the goblin that had taken Emily's Ever-Right appeared on the track. Emily blasted it with her staff, caught the watch mid-air, then turned to run. Spears were now coming out of the wooded area behind them, and Hugh was aware of voices shouting instructions at him.

"Come on, laddie," said Hamish. "Ye need to run!"

Hugh's head engaged with the rest of his body, and his legs moved underneath him. He turned and ran with the rest of the group, with Hamish by his side. They crashed through the undergrowth, not paying attention to the chaos following in their wake. All around them, he saw plants with odd flowers. He had to double take, as he could have sworn they were smiling at him. He could sense Aeolus and Aife now running alongside them – but then they disappeared. Hugh's heart sank. Their only protection had left them, for even they could sense the hopelessness of the situation. He was about admit defeat when their luck suddenly changed.

Arriving onto the track, now running alongside the group, were beautiful women clad in feather cloaks. Hugh couldn't understand what was happening, but he looked to his right and saw Hamish leap onto the back of one of the women. Instinct took over, and he, too, jumped onto the back of one of the women. The pace picked up, and he hoped the others had also caught their own rides. Everything on either side was now a blur, with all he could see being that in front of him. They were heading for a large lake, and he realised that if they didn't stop soon, they would end up in the water with nowhere to go. He was about to voice his concerns, but the woman he was on leapt into the air, landing in the water with an almighty splash. They were underwater, and he seemed attached to his ride, unable to detach. He was going to drown. He was sure of it.

Yet he was still breathing and felt himself bobbing up and down. Hugh opened his eyes to see that he was no longer on the back of the woman but riding gracefully on the back of a swan. He looked all around him, seeing the rest of the group looking just as elated, leaving the sound of angry goblins on the bank far behind them.

Chapter 29

Somewhere over Syreni Bay, a boat was hoisting the *Dragon of the Sea* out of the water. Seaweed covered its hull so thickly that the *Fey Flyer*'s crew were cutting it away so they could open the hatch. It was pitted with dents, and small stone spines. The occupants disembarked onto the deck of the *Fey Flyer*, all hot and dripping in sweat, having been cooped up underwater together for hours. There was currently a heated debate happening on deck, with some explorers refusing to go back down for further attempts.

"I'm telling you that you must go back down and search the area. I refuse to leave here empty-handed, and if that means we stay here all week, then so be it."

"I'm telling you, Mr Smithson," said Team Leader Squamae, "my men are tired, and given what we have just experienced down there, I can understand their reluctance to submerge again."

"Ah yes, remind me of what decorated your vessel again? Mermaids, wasn't it?"

"See, I told you he wouldn't believe you," said Collins from behind the pair. He bit into an apple with a loud crunch.

"Let me guess, you've had a hand in this mutiny, have you, Collins?"

"Me, sir? However could you suggest such a thing? I merely questioned whether it was a suitable idea to carry on in these conditions. I didn't tell the crew to return. They did that of their own accord. I doubt my words had anything to do with it. At my guess, it was the amount of water pouring in through the cracks and holes which changed their minds."

"There's no way she's even fit to return underwater," said Squamae, looking to the captain for support.

Captain Johnson looked at the pair as if summing up the best option for a bad situation, finally letting out a sigh.

"I'll grant you the permission to go again …"

At this, Smithson smiled smugly at Squamae, who went to protest, but the captain held up a hand to stop him.

"*However*, we must return to shore to change the submersibles over and get this one in for repairs. That will give my crew the time they need to rest before going down again. We will also require another payment, in cash, before we leave port, otherwise the deal is off."

"That's preposterous," said Smithson. "I have already paid you enough money for the job, and if we leave now, we risk going home empty-handed. I *still* don't see why you can't just send some divers down there for the thing."

He was looking at the overly weighted diving suit on the rack near the submersible with its brass helmet and lead boots.

The captain's patience was now at its end.

"As I've *already* told you, that suit is not appropriately rated for the depth required. As for the risk of going home empty-handed, you will either comply with my demands or there will be no *risk* about it. Empty-handed is what you will be. Is that clear?"

"Oooh, I think he has you there, sir," said Collins, taking another bite of his apple. Smithson turned and scowled at him before returning to the conversation.

"Well, it appears that my assistant's unwanted observations are true once more. Fine, we will …"

He paused and reached into his pocket, pulling out his watch.

"What's wrong now?" asked Collins, who was getting fed up with watching Smithson squirm. "Can't you just agree with the man, just for once, and not worry about the time?"

"For your information, I am not checking the time, *Collins*. I must be going mad, but I could swear this thing just vibrated in my pocket."

"That is ridiculous, unless …"

"Unless what?"

"Unless it's one of the Tempus collection," said Collins. "Where did you get it from?"

"I took it from my father. You know that. You were there."

"Oh yes, I remember now," he said, now looking at the watch with new eyes.

Smithson stepped back, returning the watch to his pocket before Collins could see anything more.

"If you two have quite finished lamenting over a sentimental object, we have work to do. I am still waiting for an answer, otherwise the deal is off."

"I am not lamenting anything," said Smithson. He huffed. "Fine, I'll pay you the damned money, now just get us back to port so we can stop wasting time."

Captain Johnson looked at him with raised eyebrows, tutted, then walked away, letting out a sigh and shaking his head. The communications officer came out of a door behind him, looking the deck up and down. When he saw Smithson, he made a beeline for him.

"Urgent message just in from the shore, Mr Smithson." He handed the note over and watched Smithson anxiously.

"What the devil?" said Smithson, as he unfolded the note in his hand.

Collins watched on with interest as Smithson's eyes scanned through the note. He began shaking with anger, and when he was done, he thrust the note into Collins's chest.

"I want this sorting as soon as we get back to shore. This time don't fail me."

He marched off down the deck, and went through a door, slamming it behind him. Collins looked down at the note and smiled.

GEBER MANAGED TO EVADE CUSTODY STOP WORD IS THEY ARE HEADED YOUR WAY STOP TRY HARDER STOP THEY MUST NOT GET THE BOOK STOP MUST BEAT THEM AT ALL COSTS STOP PORTIS-MONTIS ALLY END OF MESSAGE

"Tell me," said Collins, handing the note to his assistant and looking at the communications officer. "Do you have any connections on shore that know the lie of the land?"

"Errrm, I might have some for you, sir."

"Good, then take me to your post so that we can discuss this further. Come, Maso, we have work to do."

Chapter 30

Hugh had made it to the opposite side of the lake. They all watched in awe as the swans transformed back into the feather-cloaked women.

"Thank ye, lassies, we cuidna done it without ye," said Hamish.

"That's not a problem, Hamish of the Marsh. We are always willing to help close friends," said the lead swan maiden. "Take care of yourselves, for your journey is one of great importance."

"Is there anyone who doesn't know what we're up to?" said Barrington to nobody in particular.

"The universe foretells many things," said the maiden, "but it is up to each and every one of us to read it. If some choose to ignore it, then that is their loss, not ours. Now if you will excuse us, we have urgent business to take care of. You can always rely on our help. You only have to ask. Stay safe."

With that, the group of swan maidens dived back into the water, transforming once again into magnificent waterfowl.

"Well, that told me," said Barrington under his breath. "Are you alright, old bean?"

Everyone turned to look at Hugh, who had broken out into a cold sweat. He couldn't explain it, but his leg throbbed where it had been poked by the goblin. He lifted his trouser leg to reveal the spot where he had been caught – the area was red and inflamed, the blood vessels appeared angry and large.

"Do you know, I don't think I am," he said and passed out onto the floor.

Inside Hugh's mind, he felt as though his entire body was under attack. Pain coursed through his body, and strange visions were appearing all around him. His ears were filled with the sound of screaming as he watched and re-watched his mother falling off the cliff into the gorge. He fought the hands that were holding him back as he attempted to lunge after her. Then the visions changed, and he was outside the city of Skellig-Krieg. He was being chased by the city guards, and he was struggling to get away from them.

Hugh was back on his feet, with the rest of the group watching him in confusion.

"Where in all things spritely is he going now? Hugh, come back," Barrington shouted to him. "What's wrong with him?"

"It's poison from the goblins. They must have got him before we entered the Tempus network," said Hamish.

"You catch him, I'll look for an antidote," said Emily, falling back, her voice uneasy.

"We'll do our best … *no, Hugh*, not through there!"

Hugh was sure they were going to catch him – though there was some reluctance from his pursuers to follow him – and he could feel things whipping him in his face. He turned in time to see a great mass of snakes writhing in front of him. They struck out at him but could not reach his body as he recoiled. He was trapped between the guards on one side and the snakes on the other. He had no choice but to turn back, and he ran headlong into the awaiting group … who were no longer guards but menacing trolls and stood like an impenetrable wall. He could now see why they smelled so bad, as they looked to be wearing necklaces of rotten onions. But it was alright, as his firestone was there to protect him, floating in the air in front of his face. It seemed calming in the madness all around him.

"Get the firestone off his neck, before it chokes him," said Hamish, who was wrestling along with Barrington to keep Hugh from running off again. Heather leaned in quickly and snapped it off his neck, holding it up. Hugh stopped struggling, fixated on the triangle.

"Let's get back to Emily, hopefully she'll have an antidote for this," said Barrington, not loosening his restraint on Hugh.

Hugh was walking through a meadow, following the firestone. It was as if he had been here before as he passed over a stream and into a wooded area. Shadowy forms were swaying in his peripheral vision, as if encouraging him to move forward. He stumbled forwards and crashed out onto a path next to a river.

"What's he doing?" asked Heather.

"The poor laddie's hallucinating," said Hamish. "We may not have much time. I need my bladder pipes, where are they?"

"Nae Dad, ye cannae do it. Yer nae strong enough, and we need him!"

"I'm nae gonna guide him away. I wanna bring him back, but if it's his time, then there's little I can do."

"What do you mean? And why do you need to play those awful pipes?" said Barrington, who was looking from Hamish to Hugh.

"I cannae explain in detail, but just know I have another job much bigger than ye can comprehend, and ma music's magic. Let me guide him, Heather. Thas ma job. Emily, get a panacea, as quick as ye can."

"I'm doing my best," she said, running her fingers down a list of ingredients. She was writing as she went and passed the piece of paper to Barrington. "Here, find these, quick."

He looked at her, confused, and Heather took the list from him. "Give it here, I'll find them with ye," she said.

Hamish's cheeks puffed out, and the bladder pipes squawked into life, like a flock of lost geese trying to find each other.

Hugh was now standing next to a river. He looked at the boat with the ferryman, who stood with an outstretched hand. Something deep inside told him it would be a bad idea to take it, but the urge to do so was overwhelming.

'I thought I might see you soon, Hugh.'

'Do you think I should go with you?'

'Why, of course. It's not painful. I can assure you of that. It's as quick and simple as falling asleep.'

'I suppose it wouldn't hurt to try ...'

The sound of the bladder pipes drowned out the sound of the fast flowing river.

'Then again, I'm not so sure after all.'

'Don't pay attention to the music. He only wants you for himself.'

The ferryman reached out to Hugh and almost made contact, but the sound of flapping came from Hugh's right, followed by the horn of Aife, swooping in between the pair.

'No master, you must not do it. Listen to your heart; this is not the way.'

'Ah, hello Aife. Good to see you. So you think I shouldn't go?'

'No, master, stay away from the ferryman.'

The alicorn was promptly joined by Aeolus.

'Hugh, this is not the way.'

Aeolus turned and kicked the ferryman with his hind legs. Hugh watched the man windmill his bony hands then fall backwards into the river, which seemed to hiss and boil.

'Is it supposed to do that?'

Aife nudged him away from the edge.

'He'll be fine. He'll just be lost within the sight for a little while, that's all. Now look in your heart and find your way out of here.'

Hugh looked around, searching inside himself, trying to find the answer he so desperately needed. He looked down the bank towards the bridge and walked over to it.

'Could I go over here?'

Aeolus seemed to give him a hard look.

'You could, but is that really the way you want to take yet?'

'I would see my father once more.'

'Not if you take that path. What about those who you care about most, the ones fighting to keep you alive?'

'To keep me alive?'

'Yes, mistress is working hard right now. That is why I am here, to help get you back. Now listen to what is true in your heart and follow the music as a guide.'

Hugh looked at Aife and Aeolus, who seemed to look into his soul, and when he looked back, it was as if the entire universe itself opened up in front of him. He was floating in the massive expanse, free to go where he …

'Ow!'

… bumped into something and came back to the current reality in his mind. Aeolus and Aife were standing, crossed horns, preventing him for stepping onto the bridge.

Aife looked at him and touched her horn to his throat.

'Not this way, not now.'

He felt a tingling sensation, that flowed downwards into his stomach. The alicorn seemed to nod at him.

'That's it, now off you go.'

It was as if a large crook had hooked itself around his midriff and yanked him backwards. He was moving so fast that Aife and Aeolus shrank away at an alarming rate. The screeching sound of bladder pipes filled his ears, as though he were a part of the sack itself. He was swirling in circles and sensed himself being squeezed and stretched. His entire being was being vibrated to its core. Then everything went black.

He opened his eyes and took in a huge gasp of air. Three people were looking down on him, one holding a staff which was glowing, and another person stood to his right, deflating his cheeks in time with the bladder pipes, which wheezed away like a male goat who'd caught his jewels in the stable door.

"I cannot tell you how pleased I am to hear those things stop," he said, looking across at Hamish.

He looked up at Emily, who had dropped her staff to the floor and was now kneeling down next to him, wiping the hair out of his face.

"I thought I'd lost you again," she said.

"What, me? Never. My place is here, by you. Aeolus and Aife made sure of that."

"Aeolus and Aife?" said Barrington.

Hugh recounted everything that had happened whilst he was out for the count, and when he reached the part with the ferryman, Hamish let out a disgruntled noise. Hugh was too deep into recalling the story to question him on it. When he had finished, Barrington filled him in with the real-life events that had occurred in his absence of consciousness.

"So you had to chase me?" asked Hugh.

"We certainly did," said Barrington, "and you nearly ran into some of that Vipera fronde. Luckily for you, something made you see sense, and you ran back into our grasp. You're very strong for one so slight, I can assure you."

"Aye, ye are, but that'll be down to the poison. Yer body was fighting, that's for sure," said Hamish.

Hugh looked at him.

"The ferryman said something odd to me."

"Oh, aye, what's that then?"

"He said I was to go with him, and not with you, as you only wanted me for yourself. What do you think he meant by that?"

Unseen by the rest of the group, Heather glanced a look to her father, and he shook his head.

"The ferryman will always try to take people before their time. He likes to ferry people at their weakest points. It's ma job to guide people, like I've done fir countless years. He's probably referring to the fact I saved ye from drowning in the river, saving yer life, not fir the first time I might add. I wouldnae listen to him. He's a grumpy wee man with too much time on his hands."

"Well, he gives me the creeps," said Barrington. "There's something about him that isn't right."

"Aye, an' that's why yiv to stay away from him. It's a natural feeling to have around him, and one that ye should take heed of. As for that bridge, well let's just say it's a good thing ye didnae pass over it, laddie. That would have been a trip ye'd have never returned from." The words hung in the air, and he let out a large sigh. "I think it's time we got moving, if yer alright to move on, Hugh. It disna do well to dwell in the Forest of Fey."

Hugh nodded but said nothing. He was too busy trying to process what he had just been through. It scared him to think how close he had been to crossing over the bridge, and if Aife and Aeolus hadn't been there to stop him …

As they set off back down the track, Hugh couldn't help noticing that his limbs felt like dead weights. He felt as though he had done a lifetime of fighting in a wrestling ring. Whatever was on the tip of the spear that poked him certainly was potent stuff.

'It was,' said Emily's voice in his head, making him jump. *'Sorry for intruding, I just wanted to check in with you, make sure you are alright. I didn't think I would get you back this time.'*

'That's fine, I'm pleased you were there to save me. I don't think I could have made it back without you.'

'And Hamish.'

'Hamish?'

'Yes, it was his idea to go in and retrieve you. I doubt I could have managed to get you back here on my own. I'm glad you are safe.'

He sensed the firestone glowing on his chest and felt its healing power flow through him and an overwhelming urge to be close to Emily. She held out her hand, and he took it, a tingling feeling passing through his chest.

They were walking uphill now, by the light of Emily's staff, as the canopy became dense once more. It wasn't long before they had to call on the light of the firestones again, with the path becoming treacherous underfoot, as they scrambled over tree roots which were as thick as Hamish's legs. They were still following the river to their right, but it was now nothing more than a trickling dribble of water, before disappearing altogether. Hamish came to a stop as if deciding which direction was best to take.

"It's too quiet for my liking," he said, looking around warily. "We've to be careful, understand? Stay close and don't wander off the path."

He turned and looked at the group, who all nodded back, then his eyes widened with fear.

"Barrington, no!"

Everyone else turned to see what Hamish was talking about.

Barrington had parted from what remained of the path and was walking towards a glowing trail of lights. They seemed to be willing him towards them, and he walked with arms outstretched.

"This is the way," he said, almost dreamily. "I can sense that this is the way to go."

"Dinnae follow the lights, laddie, it's a … *Hugh?* Oh for sprites sake! Will yese two pack it in?"

Hugh was now caught by the trancelike lure of the lights and was being drawn towards them. There was a malevolent cackling coming from within the boggy area, but he couldn't resist the urge to follow the lights.

"I'm sure it's perfectly safe," said Hugh, looking vacant.

"It's nae safe. Ye dinnae realise where yer headed. I'm pleased yese two lassies … oh not yese as well?"

Emily and Heather were now caught by the lights, mesmerised by their beauty. Hamish jumped into action, pulling Emily and Heather away from the danger, just as they were about to enter the bog. Heather was able to step back with ease, but Emily found that her feet were starting to sink in. The ground beneath her feet gave a deep slurping noise as she pulled her feet out of the edge of the bog's grip. The three of them turned around, the power over Emily and Heather now broken.

"Hugh, Barrington, come back!" Emily shouted to the pair, which seemed to bring them around from the trance.

Hugh was already up to his ankles, but Barrington was sinking past his knees.

"Arrrgh! Help us!" said Barrington, panicking.

As he fought the pull of the bog, he seemed to sink faster.

"Quickly!"

An eerily squeaky, disembodied voice that seemed to cut through the dense air like a blade resonated deep within Hugh's core.

"You're too late, little human. You entered the bog of the will-o'-the-wisp, and now you shall pay with your lives!"

It let out an evil cackle.

"Help us!" said Hugh, looking to Emily.

He was also fighting a losing battle against the bog, now finding himself up to his knees. It was as though another force was pulling him downwards, taking him to his inevitable doom. He looked across to Barrington, seeing that he was up to his chest.

"Quickly!"

Emily looked to Heather, who looked equally worried and was rooting around in her bottomless pockets for something. Emily attempted to reach out to Hugh with her staff, but his fingers only just reached the tip before Emily nearly lost her balance. Hamish was there just in time to stop her from falling in. Heather had finished rummaging in her pockets but came out empty-handed.

"I cannae find the rope, it's a total mess in there." The pair looked at Hamish, who let out another sigh.

"I suppose it's down to me again," he said, pulling out his bladder pipes.

"No, not those awful things. I've heard of music to die by, but that's ridiculous," said Barrington, who was nearly at his neck.

He was holding his arms outstretched above his head.

"But ma music's magic."

"No! Get a branch or something. I don't wish to be screeched to death."

"Well, yese leave me with nae choice," he said, undoing his kilt. He whipped it off in one swift movement.

"Dad, what're ye doin'? Put 'em away, put 'em away! Nobody wants to see that," said Heather, looking away, flapping her hands.

"*Hamish!*" said Emily, also not knowing where to look, blushing.

"Egads," Barrington exclaimed, but the rest was muffled as his mouth sunk below the surface of the bog.

"Whatever it is you are doing, Hamish, hurry up," said Hugh with a grimace.

Hamish worked quickly. His eyes had a distinctive glow within them, as he was spinning and twisting the kilt over his head in one swift motion. His arm now appeared to be glowing. The light spread down to the kilt, and runes lit up the material. It appeared to stretch in front of their very eyes. He launched it out over the bog, keeping hold of one end. Barrington's eyes widened, and his hands grasped hold of the end of the kilt, which was pulled taught. Hugh also took a hold of the woollen rope.

"Hurry!" he said but was cut off by the voice of will-o'-the-wisp.

"'You're too late, for one of them is mine, and soon the other will be too.' Then it cackled once more."

"Oh, no ye dinnae," said Hamish in reply. "I think I'll have the final say in that."

He heaved on the kilt as Barrington's eyes disappeared into the murky depths. Hamish looked over to Emily and Heather.

"Well, dinnae jus' stand there, *help me!*"

Beads of sweat were trickling down his face, such was the effort that he was putting into the task in hand. Emily and Heather jumped to it at once and began pulling at the elongated kilt.

This seemed to make all the difference, and both Hugh and Barrington ceased their descent into the bog. Bubbles were now coming up from where Barrington's face was submerged, and when his head suddenly broke the surface, he took in a much-needed gasp of air. Hugh was also finding it easier to move, as he was pulled free from the tight grip of the bog's hold.

"What are you doing?" came the cry from the malevolent voice. "They're mine, I tell you, mine!"

For a moment, the group's efforts seemed to slow as the bog pulled against them. The group heaved harder still, and Hugh was free at last.

He made his way to the bank to join in with the others, and moments later, Barrington was freed. With so much force being exerted on him, he flew through the air, crashing into Hugh, Emily and Heather, who had landed in a pile on top of Hamish.

There was the briefest of pauses, long enough for Hamish to clear his throat and look down. The bank next to the bog was full of commotion as everyone attempted to get off Hamish as quick as possible.

"Thank ye," said Hamish, chuckling to himself as he picked up his kilt which had returned to its normal size. "Ye can all turn around now," he said, as he did up the last of his straps, and reattached his sporran.

"Did you really have to use that?" asked Barrington.

"Well, dinnae sound too grateful, will ye? If I cuidna use ma pipes, yese left me with nae option. At least I got yese out the bog!"

"Sorry, Hamish," said Hugh, attempting to keep the peace. "We're all very thankful that you were here to help us get out of the situation. Goodness only knows what would've happened if you hadn't been here."

He looked at Barrington, who refused to meet his eye, so Hugh kicked his ankle.

"Ow! Yes, sorry, Hamish. That was awfully rude of me. Thank you for saving us from the bog. We owe you a debt of gratitude for your help."

"I'll add it to the growing list."

"The only issue now is how to get rid of this stench and dirt from our clothes," said Hugh gesturing to himself and Barrington.

"That might be something that I can help with," said Emily reaching into her bag and pulling out a notebook that was full to bursting.

The rest of them looked on in interest as she riffled through the pages at speed, muttering to herself. Eventually, she slowed down until she settled on a page with her finger. She reached to the ground and picked up her staff, then looked back at the rest of the group, who were all looking on in amazement.

"What? You're not the only one to carry a notebook with you, Hugh.

I thought it might be prudent to make a few notes whilst studying the book of lore for magic."

"A few notes? It looks like you've transcribed the entire book," said Hugh, looking over her shoulder.

"No need to be rude. Now, stand back and let me work my magic."

Hugh and Barrington took a step back, and Emily planted her staff firmly on the ground whilst closing her eyes. The hairs on Hugh's neck and arms stood on end as he felt the energy grow around him. He watched as the end of the staff grew bright, then runes filled his vision. His entire body felt as though it were being bathed in warm water before the sensation ebbed away again. Emily opened her eyes and looked amazed.

"Wow, it actually worked this time!"

"Erm, not being funny," said Hugh, "but what exactly do you mean by *this time*?"

"Well, it's really nothing to worry about, really, just something I say, really."

"Really? Because I don't recall you saying that before?"

"Have I not …? Gosh, would you look at that," she said, pulling out her watch. "I think it's about time we cracked on with the day, don't you, Hamish?"

"Aye, I think yer right there, lassie. It's not too far to walk now."

"Good," she said and picked up the rest of her belongings and headed off around the bog.

"But that doesn't answer my question, Emily." Hugh called out after her. "*Emily?*"

Emily didn't appear to hear him. He chased after her, leaving Hamish chuckling to himself, and Barrington looked on confused.

"What was all that about?" he said, as he watched Hugh attempt to catch up with Emily, who had picked up quite a pace.

"Ah, I'm sure she was jus' messing with yese."

"Errrm?"

"Come on, they're gettin' away. We dinnae want to lose them." And with that, Hamish marched off after the pair, leaving Barrington to stand confused with Heather.

"Well, dinnae jus' stand there, let's get moving," she said and pecked him on the cheek, heading off after her father.

Realising that he would not get the answer he was looking for, Barrington picked up the rest of his belongings and ran to catch up with the group.

The rest of the walk seemed to take an age, with none of the group in a talkative mood. The track through the forest was proving hard going, and Heather produced a machete for Hamish to use on the thicker parts of the track. The smell of cut vegetation was filling the air, and the rhythmic sounds of Hamish swiping through the undergrowth was making Hugh feel quite drowsy. He was pleased when they finally reached a gloomy clearing and the call was made to stop and have lunch.

No sooner had they sat down and begun preparing their food, than they were disturbed by the sound of someone else entering the clearing. They were carrying a crossbow and wore a helmet with a visor.

"Halt, who goes there? Don't attempt to make a run for it, we have you surrounded," said the muffled voice from behind the helmet.

"Sorry, old chap, but you might want to lift the visor. We're struggling to hear you," said Barrington, not showing any inclination to move from the tree he was currently trying to snooze on. The man lifted his squeaky visor.

"Ah, a cheeky reprobate, I see! Well, let me tell you …"

Whatever it was, the armoured visitor was cut off with a loud '*CLANG*' as his visor snapped shut again. No matter how many times the armoured man tried to keep it up, it refused to stay in place. Eventually, he admitted defeat and held it open with a hand. He let out a sigh.

"As I was saying, what is your business in these parts?"

Hamish got to his feet.

"Look, laddie, we're headed to Killinsfolk and Syreni Bay on an important mission that has naething to do with ye," he said stepping forward.

"Halt right there, you scallywag! I don't want any funny business."

"I dinnae know what or who ye think we are," Hamish began.

And as he put his hands out in a non-confrontational manner, he accidentally caught the front of the man with the lightest of touches. The man stumbled back in an overly dramatic way, falling to the floor, with his visor slamming shut once more. The crossbow went off, the bolt disappearing into the canopy of the trees.

"You attacked me!" came the muffled voice.

"Eh? I cannae hear what yer sayin', laddie."

"You attacked me!" said the man, opening his visor, trying to get to his feet. He scrabbled around, attempting to reload another bolt.

"I did nae such a thing, laddie," said Hamish, looking confused.

The man dropped the crossbow, which misfired, sending a bolt into the tree next to Hamish's head.

"Are ye sure yer trained to use that thing, laddie?" he said, his patience wearing thin.

"Come on then. I'll have your arms off, I will! Talking to me like that. Nobody who's taken on Norman the Conqueror has ever lived to tell the tale!"

He had finally got his footing back and attempted to put his hands up in a fighting stance.

"Ye what, laddie?"

"What are you talking about," said Emily, getting to her feet and picking up her staff, which glanced Norman by accident, sending him to the floor once more.

"Playing dirty, eh? Two against one, eh? The sheer audacity of you. Just you wait until my comrades arrive. *Then* we'll see who's outnumbered!"

"What comrades?" said Hugh, getting to his feet. "I don't see anyone else here?"

"Get back! Get back, I tell you, or I'll bite your arms off. I may be outnumbered and on the ropes, but I'll fight till the bitter end, I tell you. Last man standing."

"Norman?"

A small group of nine men with walking staffs, lamps and backpacks had entered the clearing, looking puffed out and sweaty faced. They were all wearing leather waistcoats over smocks. On the back of each waistcoat was a badge showing them to be THE SYRENI BAY LAND AND SEA SEARCH AND RESCUE PARTY. They all wore hard hats to protect them from the harsh conditions they had to hack through. Each man had a bandolier, with numerous attachments. Some had machetes, and others carried ropes over their shoulders. The lead man had stepped forward and was already getting to his feet.

"Ah ha!" exclaimed Norman, now staggering to his feet. "Didn't I tell you they were coming? Now the many outnumber the few!"

"Oh, Norman. How many times do we have to do this? You are not a conqueror. We're a search and rescue party, not a defence battalion. And I told you not to wear this thing. Just because you have a helmet, it doesn't make you a knight. I wish you would stick to the standard uniform."

He poked the helmet, causing Norman to fall once more, the visor clanging shut again. The man tutted to himself and turned to address Hugh and the others.

"Must apologise for my friend's over-keenness to *defend his realm*. He sees all newcomers as a threat, and what with all the recent upheaval going on, he's taken things a bit far of late. As soon as we received the message that you were en route, he was out of the door quicker than a message travelling by firefly. We barely have time to put our boots on before he's out the door. He insists on wearing this damned helmet each time he's on duty."

He kicked the helmet, with Norman letting out a muffled and slightly disgruntled, "Ow!"

"Hang on a moment," said Hugh. "Who are you? And who sent you out here?"

"Ah, my apologies. Name's Harold, and the lads and I are part of the Syreni Bay search and rescue. From the point of the hill to the floor of the bay, we're ready to rescue, night and day."

"I see," said Hugh, warily backing away from the group. "And you knew we were here? How is that possible?"

"My apologies again, we don't wish to alarm you. We received a message from the High Palace in Androssan, informing us that we were to expect a party coming our way and to welcome them with open arms."

Hugh wondered if the last part was more for the benefit of Norman.

"When we realised the route you would have been taking, we knew that there was a high risk of you running into difficulty, and knowing how long it should normally take, we decided to come out and find you."

"Well, we're very grateful that you came to our aid," said Barrington. "Heaven knows how long it would have taken us to get out of this place."

Hamish cleared his throat, and Barrington glanced at him and loosened his collar.

"I mean to say, we have a fine guide here, and I'm sure we were merely hours away from reaching Syreni Bay." He looked quickly at the floor, as Harold lifted his lamp up into Hamish's face.

"Hamish? You're *the* Hamish McDougall? The person who mapped out the seven realms of the Old World single-handedly?"

"Aye, and what of it?"

"My Pa, Pip Nautilus, spoke tales of you all the time, of the adventures that he used to go on and the troubles you used to get into."

"Yer Pip's son? Well, there's nae wonder yer good at finding people, he's the best navigator in the area."

"Was …"

"Oh, I'm sorry to hear that, laddie. I knew that he had children, and he always spoke so fondly of ye. I wisnae aware of his passing, I'm sorry for yer loss. He was a great man."

Hamish drifted off, possibly into some distant memory, but Hugh thought he caught sight of a glow in the old man's eyes, before he realised it must have been the glow from the lamplight.

"It's no worry, he died doing what he loved doing the most, saving lives at sea. Ma's still about like, I'm sure she'd love to see you again."

"Mmm, I think she might see it differently, but I'd be up for that. But before we go anywhere, I was working on a wee broth for us all. Yer more than welcome ta join us if ye want?"

"Well, we can't refuse an invitation like that, can wc, lads? And we could do with a break from walking."

Hugh's gut was churning away, and he was unsure if it was the hunger or something *else* nagging at him.

"Hamish, a quick word if I may?" he said, pulling him away from everyone else.

"Aye, what's wrong, laddie?"

"Are you sure that we can trust these people? I mean to say that we don't really know them, and they found us here in the middle of the forest, which is not an easy task in itself, I must admit. They claim to know your friend Pip, but how do we know that's not a cover story?"

"Ah, young Hugh. Yer so much like yer father, more that ye'll ever know. He always questioned everything, and that's not surprising, given everything that happened with yer mother. I've known Pip for as long as I can remember, and he was the best man in the area for knowledge of these hills, the waters that surround it, and beyond."

"But that's my point. Anyone could claim to know him, especially if he was that well known. All I'm saying is that we need to be careful. After all, we're not the only ones who are out here seeking the book of lore."

"Ah laddie, I understand the caution, and I totally understand yer take on this situation, but trust me when I say, anyone who is the son of Pip Nautilus is a true friend of ours. We need all the help we can get if we're to get to those books before Smithson, or worse, the Elf King himself." He gave Hugh a good long stare, but said nothing else, leaving Hugh to sit with his answer.

"Alright, they're in, but let's not tell them everything, at least until we can prove their credibility. I'll pass a message to the others and let them know to do the same."

"Fine, but I still say that yer being overly cautious."

"Is everything alright, chaps?" said Barrington. "I'm running low on excuses as to why you are still over here."

"Aye, tis all fine. Hugh had a few things to discuss, but I think we can say we're clear for now," said Hamish, and he headed off to speak to Harold.

"What's going on?" said Barrington, giving Hugh a cautious eye. "I take it you are having the same suspicions I'm having?"

"You too, eh? Listen, I don't think we should reveal too much, at least not until we know we can trust these people." He looked over to where Hamish was now talking to the newcomers, and Harold smiled at Hugh, who smiled and waved back. "Definitely something suspicious going on here."

Barrington nodded.

They went to speak to Emily and Heather, both of whom agreed not to reveal too much, before rejoining the rest of the party for food and faux enjoyment.

Chapter 31

"Well?"

"Well, what?"

"Have you seen to it that the note I received has been dealt with?" said Smithson, irritably.

"Naturally," said Collins, "you don't think I would leave something like that to chance."

"I only enquire as our plans haven't been as smooth as they should have been of late. I would hate for Geber and his rogues to get away again."

"It's all in hand, don't you worry."

"Oh, but I do worry, Collins. I do. You don't realise how precarious the situation is. We need this book if we are to succeed in my plans."

"*Your* plans? I thought you were working on behalf of the New World and the Elf King?"

"Oh, do try to keep up, Collins. Things have progressed much further than the New World and your Elf King. No, no, I have greater plans, which I cannot reveal to anyone, let alone my servant. All I require of you is that you do your job as is required by your contract."

"I beg your pardon!" Collins was incredulous. "My *contract*? These *duties* fall well beyond what is expected of me and my contract. Don't think for one moment that I don't understand your reluctance to return to the university. One word for me would see the Collins family oust you from the position you so dearly cling onto. If it wasn't for this magical contract that sees me tied to your hip, I would have left months ago. Just you wait until we cross over the threshold of the university."

"Oh, I'm quaking in my boots. What will you do, get me *ousted,* then get your king to come and tell me off?"

"You really think you can defy the greatest king this world has ever seen? You must be truly out of your mind if you believe you will get away with this. He'll find out."

"Find out? Who's going to tell him, you? I rather doubt that the Elf King will believe the words of a mere servant. Why don't you stick to doing your job whilst I attempt to sort out the issues with this world? You never know, if you improve your track record, I may be inclined to up your job role."

"You are not seriously planning to do what I think you're planning to do."

"Welcome to the room at last, Collins. When I am finished, you and your assistant may find yourselves at the top of the tree, as long as you do all that I require."

Collins's eyes widened.

"Ah, finally," said Smithson. "I think I have got your attention at last. Now tell me, did you sort out the issue that I passed to you earlier?"

Collins said nothing, and handed over the note he was clutching. Smithson snatched it out of his hands, reading it eagerly, a smile forming across his face.

"My, my, Collins, it would seem that you have been busy. Dispatch your assistant as soon as we dock. I want eyes on them as soon as they are in town. With any luck, they'll lead us right to the honeypot."

Chapter 32

The walk down the hill out of the woods was a more straightforward affair, thanks to the path cleared by the search and rescue team on their way up. It was late afternoon by the time the now expanded group of explorers made their way into town. Rounds of applause greeted them as they approached Killinsfolk – it turned out the search and rescue team were revered for their bravery and willingness to put themselves in danger for others.

They entered the seaside town by way of a bridge that passed near a large reservoir diverted from a mountain stream. It was temporarily dammed off at the stream end with a wooden sluice gate attached to a cable, to prevent it from overflowing. The reservoir was almost full to the brim, and Hugh saw a series of pulleys and sluices attached to cogs, cables and a crank handle. Two of the sluices connected to channels disappeared into the pavement, whilst a larger one lined up with the road leading down to the sea.

Further on down the street, people were hard at work, sorting out the remnants of the day's catch and discarding parts unfit for sale. The curb stones were deep, and for good reason. All the fish guts and dead ends were thrown into the street, almost reaching the level of the pavements, and the smell was overwhelming. Hugh felt his stomach churn and feared he was about to see a return of their lunch broth.

A bell sounded, causing a flurry of action to break out. More rubbish, fish guts and bones flew out from shops and stalls, with some people even emptying large barrels, causing the pile to grow higher. Seabirds were circling and dropping into bold dives attracted by the easy pickings.

"Make sure you stay well back from the pavement edges," said Harold.

The rest of the search party had already heeded his advice, and the newcomers took a good step back.

A second bell rang out, and Hugh looked up the street, seeing someone opening the sluices at the top of the hill. An eerie gurgling sound followed, as water made its way into the system, and the pile of mush inched slowly downhill. Some piles collapsed onto the pavement edges, and as if by clockwork, the shop keepers lined the street with wooden shoving sticks, which looked like broom handles with a deep plank of wood attached to them. They used these to shunt the excess mess back into the river of fish guts. The shop keepers were followed up by their assistants, who swept up behind them. The river of guts made a sticky, slimy sound as it flowed by and picked up speed.

Hugh looked across at Barrington, Emily and Heather, who all looked as though they were good to hurl, too. Hamish stood watching, the scene having no effect on him whatsoever.

The river was now in full spate, with the last bits of rubbish exiting the shops into its downhill flow. Hugh could now see the water pouring out of gaps in the curb stones, helping to get the waste to where it needed to be. The flock of seabirds had followed the pile down the hill and were now fighting for supremacy somewhere over the harbour.

"So, does all that rubbish get dumped into the harbour then?" asked Barrington, looking horrified.

"Partially," said Harold, looking nonplussed by the thought. "Some of it is loaded back into the empty boats and used to attract more fish on the next trawl. There are plenty of people working down below to catch a majority of the throwback. What doesn't get collected is normally eaten by the seabirds, so there's not much left by the end."

"Oh, I see," said Barrington, not looking any better for knowing the truth. "Well, that explains the smell, at least."

"You get used to it when you live here. We certainly don't notice it. Right, shall we continue into town? I'm sure you have lots to sort out. What is it you are up to, anyway?"

"So you don't have any idea why we are here?" asked Hugh.

"Nah, we just got the message to come and find you. Nobody told us what you were up to. Is it something to do with the ships out in the bay?"

"What ships in the bay?" Hugh looked at Barrington with a worried look on his face.

"It's nothing to worry about. It's just some explorers that have been out searching the bay for something. They have submersibles and everything. We all think they are trying to look for relics out there, but we know if there was anything of value, it would have surfaced long before now."

"Has anyone spoken to the people on the boat?"

"Well, as a matter of fact, I've had the displeasure of meeting some of the people. I think his name was Robert Smithson; yes that's it, and he was very rude. Certainly not the kind of person I would want to be associated with, I must stress. What has all of this got to do with you, anyway?"

"We're here on official business," said Hugh. "I'm afraid we're not allowed to say what it is, only we need to know where we can get a boat with a trustworthy captain."

"If it's a trustworthy captain that you're looking for, then you need not look any further. I have a boat, *Me Old Duck III,* moored up down in the harbour, and if this is official business, then I am sure I can come up with a reasonable rate. The only thing I ask is that you tell me what the nature of the job is that I am to be undertaking. I don't wish to be embroiled in any funny business. I have a reputation to uphold."

"We wouldn't want to put you to any more trouble, especially as we have already taken up so much of your time already."

"Ah, it's not a bother," said Harold, batting the comment away with his hand. "Besides, I doubt you'll find anyone around here to help you. Most people are suspicious of outsiders, and given the state of the world at the moment, who could blame them? There's also the fact that the other chap has taken the only willing volunteers with him and insulted everyone else, so you have little choice, really."

"Hugh, a quick word in your ear if I may," said Barrington, pulling him, Emily and Heather to one side.

Harold was already lost in a conversation with Hamish, who had taken the chance to talk about his connections with the area. The four of them huddled together.

"I don't think that getting a boat with this chap is a good idea. I don't like the cut of his jib, and we don't even know his sailing credentials."

"I have to agree with you there," said Hugh. "He's asking too many questions if you ask me."

"I think ye should go a little easier on the poor man," said Heather, and everyone stopped to look at her. "What? I think we should take him up on his offer. After all, how long will it take us to locate a boat and get organised? Like he said, we have little choice in the matter, and we need all the help we can get right now."

"That's a valid point," said Emily. "I think we need to be moving as soon as we can. We don't know how far along Smithson is in finding the book."

Hugh considered this for a moment, before coming to a decision.

"I think we ought to give him a try."

Barrington went to protest, but Hugh put up a hand to stop him.

"Please don't. This is a hard enough decision, without adding more objections to the pile. Harold is the only link we have to the area, and I don't fancy dealing with any grumpy locals. Heather's right, we need all the help we can get, even if some of it is from an unknown source at this point. But how do we get around the issue of filling him in on what we are doing? I still don't think we should reveal all of our cards just yet."

"Mmm, that one is a tricky subject," said Barrington. They were joined again by Hamish, who had come to chivvy them along.

"Right folks. I believe that this fine fellow has offered yese a lift, so I think we ought not be rude and take him up on the offer. I've already filled him in with our plans, and what we're looking for, so I say we strike whilst the iron is hot."

The others looked back at him, agog.

"Now what have I done?"

"You told him our plans?" said Hugh in disbelief.

"Aye, and what of it?"

"And you specifically told him what we're up to?"

"Well, that would generally be considered the important part of telling him our plans. I didnae just talk about pressing flowers and the weather. Look, we're here to do a job, and I've already found out more information about our new friend. His father is indeed Pip, and he's shown me his pictures. He has a massive distrust for Smithson, and he wants to help wherever he can. We cannae refuse the offer, really."

"So it looks like it's a done deal then," said Hugh, trying but failing to hide his annoyance.

"Aye, so let's get on with it."

Hugh huffed.

"Fine, but I want it on record that I'm not comfortable with this situation.

Next time, speak to me first before you divulge any information."

"Alright, keep yer panties on. Yer sounding like yer father," he said, and turned quickly before Hugh could reply. "Harold, we're good to go, if ye could lead the way."

"Excellent news," he said, rubbing his hands together. He turned to address the rest of the rescue party. "Alright, you heard what they said.

We're on. A real adventure this time."

"Are you sure?" asked Norman. "Only, last time you said that, we ended up coming back empty-handed with a whacking great hole in the hull."

"Thank you, Norman. See you at the *Leaky Ship*, shall we say, twenty-hundred hours. That should be enough time to say farewell to your loved ones and get packed."

"Whoa there, hold on a minute," said Hugh, putting his hands out in front of him, to curb the man's enthusiasm. "This lot are coming too?"

"Of course. I can't sail without a crew!"

With the rest of the team dispersing down the narrow side streets, some of which were only one person wide, Hugh and the rest of the group had no choice but to follow Harold down the hill. Now that the road was clear, the area looked quite picturesque, that's if you blocked out the smell of rotting fish guts, which still hung heavy in the air.

Hugh had the nagging feeling that their presence wasn't welcome in the small fishing town, and he caught sight of people peering through windows, curtains twitching from hasty retreats by those not wanting to be seen snooping. It was as the road turned a corner that he nearly jumped out of his skin. He thought he caught sight of a face – one that he thought long departed from this world. But the hair, bright white and tied in a ponytail, didn't fit the picture.

"Are you alright, dear Hugh? You look as though you've seen a ghost."

"No … well … It's just that I thought I saw … but it can't have been. It almost looked like Collins, but then not like Collins. Does that make any sense to you?"

"Hugh, it makes perfect sense. We already know that Smithson is lingering in the area, so the fact that you might have seen Collins is quite logical. Wherever Smithson is, his pet is never far behind."

"Don't refer to Collins as his pet, please. It's not his fault he has to carry out all the duties Smithson asks of him."

"Sorry, I forgot you have a soft spot for the Collins family."

"It's not that I have a soft spot, it's just that I feel a bond between my family and theirs. Both have a long history associated with the university. What's bugging me is the fact the face didn't match the person?"

"That, too, has a simple answer. We're all tired, and given the experience that you've been through, I'm not surprised that your eyesight isn't up to scratch. What we need is a place to rest our feet. Harold, can you recommend anywhere to stop?"

"Well, I was going to suggest that you could all come back to my place. I'm sure Mavis won't mind rustling up some food for us all."

"Are ye sure? We dinnae want to put yese to any trouble. I was prepared to stop in a pub; I could do with a wee dram."

"Hamish is right, we wouldn't want to cause you more hassle," said Hugh, keen to get some distance between them and Harold.

"Don't you worry about it. Mavis loves to cook for guests."

Harold led everyone off down one of the tight side streets. They were jostling for space in a narrow street which would give Portis-Montis a run for its money. Hugh looked up at the narrow slit of the sky, turning red in the late afternoon sun. There was washing hanging in the tight space, and neighbours were busy greeting each other from opposing windows, so close that glasses of drink were being passed to and fro, and occasionally the odd neighbour would follow. As they passed under the windows, conversations paused to take in the latest out-of-towners to visit the area.

Harold stopped by a blue gate and pulled out a large, rusty key. With a bit of a wiggle, he squeezed it into the well-worn hole, and after a loud clunk, the gate opened into what turned out to be a surprisingly spacious courtyard. Hugh was happy to get off the street, where their brief pause had caused a considerable blockage in the narrow alleyway.

The courtyard featured a mosaic floor with a small fountain in the centre, its waters trickling gently in the background. Overhead was a washing line strung between two buildings, full of all manner of sheets and clothing. The walls were covered in jasmine, its white flowers looking like clouds, filling the air with their sweet smell.

"Mmm, jasmine," said Emily. "I do love this smell."

"It's a very relaxing space," said Hugh, in agreement.

"HAROLD! Is that you?"

A shrill voice cut through the air like a pressure wave from a bomb blast, which made everyone jump and wince in unison.

"Ah, that'll be Mavis. Bear with me whilst I update her on things." He sheepishly turned and headed to a set of stairs leading to the first floor. "Coming, dear," he said, leaving the rest to listen to the unravelling situation. It was safe to say Mavis was thoroughly unimpressed.

"What do you mean, 'we have guests dear?'"

"Please, keep your voice down."

"Don't you dare talk to me like that. I will not keep my voice down…"

"She certainly sounds like a welcoming kind of character," said Barrington.

"… it could be the High Enchantress herself, and my reaction would be the same."

"You know, you often sound like your mother at times like this …"

"Blimey," said Hugh, "the man's either got balls of steel, or he's totally stupid. Pulling out the mother-in-law card. I mean …" Hugh caught Emily's eye and looked to the sky, clearing his throat awkwardly.

"… bring my mother into this, Harold Nautilus, don't you bloody well dare. She'd be turning in her grave if she saw how you were behaving. I've told you time and time again, don't bring your work home. But do you listen? No!"

"But the money, dear, think of the money."

"I do, all the time. Whilst you and your friends go gallivanting off into the woods or in that beat-up boat of yours …"

"Ship, dear, ship. Remember, a boat can fit on a ship, but a ship cannot fit onto a boat. It's really quite simple to remember …"

"Man's got a bloody death wish," said Hamish.

"Shhh!" said Emily and Heather in unison, both craning their necks and flapping their arms.

"… Spending all day washing and ironing for you to piss it up the wall at any given moment. This cannot continue, Harold. You mark my words."

A long pause followed, in which nobody moved, neither in the courtyard, nor as it happened, in the alley outside. All were waiting for Harold's next move, knowing that it could make or break the current situation.

"So, errrm … about our visitors …"

There was a collective sigh not only in the courtyard but also in the alley outside, with the sound of many hands being slapped into foreheads. Everything that followed next happened at such a high speed that Hugh didn't have time to piece the order together.

An iron flew out of the open doorway and, from the sounds of it, narrowly missed Harold. Everyone in the courtyard below ducked out of the way as it landed in the fountain with a splash of bubbles and steam.

All manner of items then followed out the door, as normally befits a situation such as this. They included, but were not limited to, pillowcases, a frying pan, a bedsheet, someone's under garments, a bucket – including its contents of water and scrubbing brush – pegs, a kettle, Harold's bag, a chair, Harold's clothes, a shrieking cat, and finally Harold himself, who half stumbled, half fell down the stairs, landing at the bottom in a crumpled heap.

He had no sooner got to his feet, when Mavis herself appeared at the top of the stairs, rolling pin in hand, menacingly slapping it into her palm.

"But, Mavis, please … you're overreacting, dear."

"Ah for goodness sake, laddie," said Hamish as Harold ducked out of the way of the rolling pin. "Have ye nae learned when to shut yer trap?"

"Don't you 'dear' me, Harold! Get out of my sight."

Harold looked as though he were about to reply, then thought better of it. He quickly began scooping up his belongings, as Mavis turned her attention to the rest of the people in the courtyard.

"You lot can bugger off too!"

"Mrs Nautilus, I believe there may have been a misunderstanding of sorts," Barrington began in an attempt to woo the raging woman.

"There ain't no misunderstanding other than you lot thinking you're going to get fed. This ain't no free house. And you lot," she said, addressing the street at large. "Get on with your lives, you nosey—"

But whatever she said, it was cut off by her slamming the door shut behind her, as she returned into the house.

Everyone turned to Harold, who looked dishevelled, and he cleared his throat.

"Pub?"

Chapter 33

Smithson was sitting in a private booth at the *Leaky Ship Inn*, awaiting an update from Collins, who had just entered by the doors that separated the small room from the rest of the inn. He was being followed, as always, by his assistant, who was looking thoroughly chastised. Smithson was flabbergasted by the news he was currently hearing.

"What do you mean by 'he was seen'?"

"Well, generally, when someone says they were seen, that would suggest that somebody saw them."

"Thank you, Collins. Your tone is not welcome in this room. As for you, what do you have to say for yourself, boy?"

The abashed assistant stood with his head down, looking at his feet.

"I've already had words with him, and he assures me that this will not happen again."

"But that's not the point, is it, Collins?"

"And what point would that be, *sir?*"

"The point to which you are so oblivious is that we're not supposed to be here. This is supposed to be a quiet affair – get the book and get out. Now that Geber knows we are here, he will double his efforts to get there before we do. Honestly, talk about sending a boy to do a man's job."

"And you think we don't already stand out? We've had a ship moored out in the bay for the last two days. You've been drinking in here whenever we are on shore. We're hardly keeping a low profile."

"That's beside the point. Geber will now look out for us. We could have at least had a slim chance of getting away with it and following him to where the book is. Now we must rethink the entire mission. We can't just follow them as planned."

"You really think you're good at this, don't you?"

"What are you blithering on about now, Collins?"

"The point I'm trying to make is—"

"Shhh!"

"What now?"

"Be quiet man! Listen."

They both stopped to hear what Smithson had tuned into.

"… Nah, I'm sorry, Harold, the booth's in use right now. We can squeeze you into the corner, over there. So, this is Mr Geber, eh?…"

Smithson and Collins stared each other, wide-eyed, but neither could match the look of fear Collins's assistant had on his face.

"What are we going to do?" Smithson hissed.

Collins shrugged, not wanting to make a noise. The conversation was happening right on the other side of the doors to the room.

"… father's well known in these parts, Mr Geber."

"Please do, call me Hugh."

"And you're just as generous, I see."

"I think I'm getting déjà vu," said Barrington, and Emily chuckled. "All we need now, is for this chap to be related to Trevor and Eric, and we'll have gone full circle."

"Sorry, but did I hear you mention Trevor? Not the same Trevor that runs the Rangles in Skellig-Krieg?"

"Really?"

"Oh yes, he's my mother's cousin's uncle, ain't seen him for a while though …"

Smithson looked at Collins. It looked as though their conversation would have to wait for another time. He looked at the boy, and saw he had gone as pale as parchment, then followed a damp patch down to a growing pool down by his right foot. Smithson sank his head into his hands, wondering how he got himself into these situations.

"Is there anyone that Trevor isn't related to?" said Barrington as they took their seats.

"It would appear not, laddie, but then he descends from one of the older families of this world, so it's not surprising … ah, perfect, thank ye," said Hamish, taking a bottle of whisky from the innkeeper and topping up his flask.

"But I can't fathom out how they're related."

"Ye've to remember that a lot of the older families split up after the great war. Some chose to live within the Old World, whilst others, who may have sided with the wrong side during the war or had a vested interest in the New World, chose to stay put. But just because they chose to live within the different worlds, it disna mean they didnae want to keep in touch. There are lines of communication still open between both worlds, especially since the rules were relaxed slightly, though that's all changing again now."

"So that's how my father could travel so far," said Hugh.

"Aye, as far as we can tell, yer family had a lot of links with the Old World, and it was this that your father was researching before his untimely death."

"Yes, but he never found anything out," said Emily. "The trail stopped dead at the Great War, and there's no record of the Geber lineage before then."

"Aye, well again, there's a lot of families had to change their names for safety reasons. Some trusted families stayed behind to try and keep the old ways going, but naturally their Old World names would've given them away. Take the Collins family. They're made up of various families who came together to protect the Great Library. One condition of that was they had to adopt a new name, so the Collins family was born."

Hugh had a niggling feeling in the pit of his stomach at the mention of the Collins family. There was something not right with their encounter earlier, and even now, his gut was trying to tell him something. Emily put her hand on his.

"Are you alright?"

"Yeah, ignore me, I'm just having a moment."

'*You don't have to hold it in Hugh, you can trust us,*' she said in his head, making him jump.

"Sorry, not been in there for a while," she said. "It seems a tad chaotic, if you don't mind me saying?"

Hugh let out a sigh.

"Alright. Is anyone else not the slightest bit worried we saw a Collins earlier?"

"Don't you mean we saw Collins himself?" said Barrington. "We covered this one earlier, dear Hugh."

"Yes, I realise that, but have we considered that it *may* have been a different Collins? I mean, how do we know that the family hasn't been infiltrated?"

"That's a bit farfetched?"

"Is it though? Collins has been following me around for a while now. How do we know they haven't recruited more of them to help? I still feel like I'm being watched now, if I'm being totally honest with you all."

"You always feel as though you're being watched."

"Well, I think on this occasion I may be correct."

"Oh really, how so, my friend?"

"Because I just caught sight of Collins in that room there."

"*What?*" the others exclaimed in alarm.

"It's alright," said Hugh, seeming totally nonplussed.

"I thought I told you before. You must tell me if you think, or know, we're being followed," said Emily. "We need to get out of here!"

"No, I think we should stay."

"*Stay?* Have you completely left all sense and logic? We need to get out of here, and fast. We must get ahead of them and get to the book as soon as we can."

"Em, will ye calm down, lassie," said Hamish. "I think I can see the angle that young Hugh is coming from here."

"What angle? What are you talking about?"

"I'm talking about the fact that as long as we're in here, they're nae coming out of there. As long as they stay in there, they cannot do anything to get away."

"How can you be sure? They could burst out at any point and bring us down."

"But the point is, they hivnae done it yet. There's been ample time for them to come up with a plan, and they hivnae found one. There're more of us than there are of them, and our numbers are only growing."

"Then let's take them on," said Barrington.

"No, Barrington, nobody is to *take anyone on,*" said Hugh. "Look around you. The locals are already unsettled with our presence, and I doubt they will take a liking to a bar brawl. No, we are going to stay here, have a nice meal, and plan our next step. If we get this right, we can throw them off the scent and get to the book before they do."

"Since when did you become the sly devil?"

"I've had time to practise. It's about time we had a little luck on our side for once. Right," he said, clapping his hands together. "I'm in need of a decent meal and a drink. Innkeeper?"

"What are they doing now?" said Smithson. It had been a tense half hour.

"Well, they have just finished the starters, and it looks like they are moving onto the main course. They are still talking in hushed voices, and … yes, I think they're being joined by *more* people."

"*More people?* That's preposterous! They've only just arrived, how do *they* have connections? Can't you send your boy servant out to spy on them?" The colour drained from Maso's face, as he looked to Collins pleadingly.

"I would remind you not to use that tone with him, and no, I will not be sending him out to spy on them. Have you already forgotten that they know his face? If he were to stroll out there, as if all were normal, they would recognise him, and know that we are in here."

"Well, this is another fine mess you've got us into, Collins."

"*I've got us into?* This is a mess of your own making. You didn't need my help."

"When we get back to Portis-Montis, remind me to dig out your contract. It'll need some amendments."

"Will you two keep your voices down! You'll give us all away, and I for one cannot afford to get caught!"

Maso's voice took both Collins and Smithson by surprise. He stood there, his face beginning to flush, moving uneasily on the spot.

"If I can pull you away from this wonderful conversation, I think I may have an idea."

Smithson looked aghast.

"I beg your pardon? Collins, pull your servant to order, this instant!"

"To start off with, he is not my servant, but my apprentice," said Collins before turning to look at Maso. "As for you, I would think that I've taught you better than this! What do you have to say for yourself?"

"Sorry, sir."

"That's more like it. Now tell me, Maso, what is this plan you have?"

"Well, it involves *this*," he said, pulling out a small vial of sleeping draught.

Out in the bar, the group of new travellers were making themselves at home, soaking up the atmosphere of the *Leakey Ship*. It turned out Harold was a regular visitor, so much so that he had his own room upstairs. He claimed it was for the nights he arrived back late from his search and rescue job, but Hugh suspected his wife played a larger role in the reason. Though Hugh was putting on a brave face, deep down he was feeling more anxious by the minute. He knew Smithson was still stuck in the booth with no means of escape, and he saw the innkeeper making more regular visits there. He would also come out and speak to Harold, and then the pair would look across to Hugh, making him feel more uneasy.

'What's wrong?' said Emily, her voice ringing out inside his head. *'I can see you're not happy.'*

Hugh looked into her eyes and let her see what he was thinking. Emily looked across at Harold.

'Don't look over; you'll make it obvious.'

'No, I won't. Besides, Harold's too distracted at the moment.'

That was indeed the case. Harold had a young woman sitting on his lap, vying for his attention and winning. Hugh looked across at the rest of the group, attempting to get their attention.

"What is it, laddie?" said Hamish, leaning across.

Though he was necking the whisky, it seemed to have little effect on him. They all spoke in hushed tones.

"There's a lot of communication going on between the innkeeper, the booth and Harold. I still don't know if we can trust these people."

Hugh looked around the rest of the table, seeing the way the crew, which had joined the party, kit bags in hand, were necking back the jars of dark ale.

"For a crew who are about to go to sea, they don't seem very seaworthy."

"I agree," said Barrington. "The last time I put to sea with a load of drunkards, it didn't end well. I say we try to get out of here, make our own way."

"Nay, we cannae do that," said Heather. "We'll nae find a crew now, not at this short notice."

"I understand that, but there's only so much ale a pot plant can handle," said Barrington, nudging the plant behind him. It bobbed up and down gently in its pot. "And by the looks of it, the rest of you are running out of ideas to lose the liquid too, except you, Hamish. How do you manage it?"

"Years of practice, laddie," he said, patting his belly. "One day, ye'll be a fine specimen, just like me."

Before anyone else could reply, Harold looked over to them.

"What's wrong with you lot? Why the long faces and whispering?"

"Errrm, well …" said Hugh, stumbling to find the right words.

"Ha! The looks on all of your faces. Come along, another round for all."

Hugh looked at the rest of the group, who were all at a loss at for what to do. He saw the innkeeper preparing the drinks, and then he turned his back to them for the briefest of moments. Moments later, he was back facing the room now. Though it was rowdy in the *Leaky Ship*, the table of weary travellers were lost for conversation. The innkeeper brought the tray of drinks to the table, setting them down with a thump causing some spillage.

"Careful, Ron, we don't want to waste any of the good stuff," said Harold, winking at the innkeeper, who grunted and walked off, disappearing with another tray into the back room. Harold passed the drinks around keenly.

"Come along now, drink up, drink up, make sure you don't waste a drop."

Hugh looked around the table at the faces all staring back at him. He looked at the drink in his hand, then at Barrington, who gave the slightest of shrugs.

"Come along now, it's not poisoned."

"Why would you say that?" said Hugh, his voice now full of suspicion.

"Turn of phrase?" Hugh stared back, nonplussed. "Well, if you're not going to start, I will. Cheers lads!"

All the tankards came together in the middle of the table, and Hugh was splashed with ale. The search and rescue party necked the lot in three large gulps. Hugh watched, expecting there to be a reaction, but none came forth.

"What now?"

"Nothing … I just … well …"

"Get drinking then, we haven't got long."

"For what?"

"The tide, we always have the one for the road or the *sea* in this case."

"But the drinks, they're spiked," said Hugh, unable to hold back his words anymore.

"What? I don't understand what you mean?" said Harold, looking at his tankard I fear.

"But you've been plotting it all night. We've all seen it, you and Ron, if that's his real name."

Harold slapped a hand to his forehead.

"I see now. The game is up. Ron, would you come here please? Hugh has stumbled on our little plan."

"Keep your voice down, they'll hear us," said Hugh, looking over to the private booth.

"Wouldn't worry 'bout that," said Ron, walking up to the table.

"What's going on here?" Barrington demanded, slamming his hand on the table.

"It's alright, nothing to worry about," said Harold, getting to his feet. "I believe I should have been more open with you from the start, but I feared the more I spoke of it, the more risk there was of the plan going wrong. Where to start …? Well, I know you thought you saw Ron putting something inside the drinks, well that bit is true."

"What? What have you put in our drinks, you traitor!" said Barrington, getting to his feet. The rest of the search and rescue team were on theirs less than a second later.

"Will everyone just calm down, and remember that the enemy is in that room *there* not out here?"

"How can you say that, when you have just admitted your crime?"

"Because, Barrington, it wasn't your drinks that were tampered with."

"Come again?"

"Ron, here, came to me with a message, saying that the chaps in there wanted to spike your drinks, and make you fall asleep. No doubt they had plans of grandeur, wanted to escape, and get you arrested, or at least delayed in getting to the prize. They didn't plan on running into the loyalty of my friend and innkeeper here, who alerted me to their plan. With a few swift changes, we have been able to turn the situation on its head, and with the amount of sleeping draught they have had, we'll be far away before they wake up."

Hugh looked at Harold from a different perspective.

"So, if I have it right, they are now asleep, and we can trust you, after all?"

"That, my friend, is correct, but I fear we mustn't rest on our laurels. We need to make the most of our advantage before those fellows wake and realise their misfortune."

"You're not seriously suggesting that we leave now, after the fistful this lot have had?" said Barrington. "They're in no fit state to be in charge of a vessel."

"I think you are mistaking us for mere mortals, Barrington. This day has been spoken of for millennia – people coming on a quest. What my old man would have done to be here right now? He always thought it would be him to be in this position. It appears we need to be getting moving. We have little time to talk, and the more we stand here, the more time we give to those chaps to catch us up. Ladies and gentleman, if you will, your ship awaits."

He gestured to the open door, and Emily led the group out into the early morning air.

Harold finished giving some last instructions to Ron before joining everyone outside to head down to the harbour. Hugh had expected the streets to be deserted, but he found it quite the opposite. There were numerous groups of men flooding out of the alleyways, all carrying nets and ropes of various sizes over their shoulders. They were being waved off by their partners and wives, wishing them safe journeys, making sure they promised to return home safely. Everyone gave the newcomers a wide berth but said nothing as they joined the throng heading to the moored-up boats.

"You can see now why I wanted to get a move on," said Harold. "We are not the only ones wishing to leave the harbour this morning. It's a spring tide as well, so everyone wants to get out on the high tide and make the most of the day's catch. This way if you will. My ship is moored up away from the rest of the melee, but it will mean we're at the back of the queue to exit the harbour."

They walked further down the quayside, and the crowds thinned out along with the boats. Leaving the larger trawlers behind them, they were now amongst the smaller boats, which bobbed up and down on the early morning tide, gently bumping alongside each other. As he looked along the seemingly endless row of boats, Hugh watched the numerous lights swaying in time with the water, and he couldn't help but think that the scene looked quite picturesque.

The sun was just starting to tinge the sky with its early morning rays, and Hugh took in a deep yawn, now realising that they were missing out on a night's sleep. The air was full of the smell of fish and seaweed. They passed over a slipway, still slimy with residue from the previous day's effluent. Harold came to a stop next to a boat with two hulls and a net stretched between them.

"Ta–da!" he said throwing out his arms in the vessel's direction.

"Erm? Not wanting to sound rude, but is this it?" said Barrington, casting a critical eye over the twin hulls. "I can't see how, one, you'll even get that out onto open water, and two, how we will all fit on it?"

"It's all a matter of perspective. *Me Old Duck III* has been on many a mission."

"*Me Old Duck III*?" said Hugh, looking for a boat with that name on it.

"Yes, that's her name," said Harold, pointing to the side of the ship. Hugh could just about make out the *M*, *ld*, and *uck* along the side. The rest was either scratched off from many scuffs or underneath what looked to be many layers of silver tape. The crew were already boarding and seeming to defy the impossible, disappearing into the hulls. The boat dropped an inch or two with air bubbles making their way to the surface.

"Are you *sure* this thing is seaworthy? It looks like it has been through the wars," Barrington said, unable to hide the worried tone.

"Listen, I can assure you, this vessel is older than you or I put together. My father's, father's, father built the *Me Old Duck I*, and the *Me Old Duck II*. Then he created this mighty boat that you see before you."

Emily looked concerned.

"And Ducks I and II are … ?"

"Let's just say, you have to crack a few eggs to make an omelette."

"Right," she said, looking from the boat to Hugh. "So, who's going to be the first to step aboard?" Nobody moved. "Well, don't all volunteer at once."

"Ah, come on. It cannae be that bad," said Hamish, stepping forward.

"That's the spirit. Oh, almost forgot." Harold turned to a pile of buckets behind him and picked them up before turning back to Hamish. "Here you go, one bucket each, and take the hull to the right-hand side. It's great to have the extra hands."

"What are they for?" asked Heather.

"Again, just precaution. You wouldn't jump out of an Air-wing without a parachute. Now hurry up, will you? We'll never set off at this rate."

They all reluctantly shuffled forwards in the line, each taking a bucket from Harold as they passed. Hugh was last in line, and Harold patted him on the back reassuringly. He stepped off the quay and onto the boat – the waterline creeping ever closer to the level of the narrow deck, which was just wide enough for two people to pass each other. Hugh looked at the warm light coming up from the open hatch and followed Barrington down the steps. His friend had stopped halfway down and was popping his head up and down between the cabin and the outside.

"Well, I'll be …" he said in amazement.

"What?"

"Just you wait, dear Hugh; you're in for a surprise." Then he disappeared below deck.

Hugh followed his friend down, unsure of what to expect. As he stepped off the stairs, he had to stand agog, unable to comprehend what his eyes were seeing. He was currently standing in a wide cabin, with comfy seating, and what looked to be a small kitchen, and beyond that, there was a doorway with "sleeping quarters" written above it. One of the members of the search and rescue team – they were now the crew – had already got a pot of tea on the go. Hugh rubbed his hand along the wall as he moved through the boat, and his hair stood on end. Hamish had already made himself at home on one of the larger seats, and Hugh looked at him.

"Runes?" he said.

"Aye, laddie, 'tis amazing what can be achieved when ye put yer mind to it."

Barrington was busy examining a wooden wedge sticking out of the wall. He was rubbing his hand over it and looked about to take hold of it before Harold ran over to him.

"***Don't*** do that," he said, batting his hand away quickly. "It's … errrm, part of the structural integrity of the ship."

"Structural integrity?"

"Yeah, you know, helps keep us afloat, prevents there being a need for a *Me Old Duck IV*."

Leaving Barrington looking wide-eyed and appalled, Harold turned to everyone else. "Right, who's up for a cuppa?"

After a warming mug of tea, Harold guided them to the beds in the forward compartment. It would be a while before they exited the harbour, and Hugh didn't need telling twice. He climbed into the nearest available hammock, and within a matter of moments, he was asleep. His dreams involved being chased, and of Elgrid Collins stepping out of every alley in Syreni, blocking him at every twist and turn, then of all people … Thomas.

Thomas?

Hugh woke with a jolt, breathing fast. But the dream drifted away like a distant memory as he rolled over and fell back into restful sleep.

Chapter 34

Somewhere down a dark alley, they were coming round. Smithson sat up, pulling a melon rind from his face. His hand was warm, and he looked around in time to see a dog with its leg cocked, relieving itself on his arm. Smithson swore loudly at the animal, which had no intention of moving until the last drop was out. The dog snapped at Smithson, causing him to lurch back. His head was thumping as though caught in a vice, and his memory seemed patchy at best. How, where and why were they there? Geber and his cronies were in the bar and were about to take the potion to make them go to sleep. The innkeeper came through with drinks, and then all went dark …

"Damn you, Geber! Collins … Collins, wake up, damn you!" he said, throwing a rotten fish corpse at him.

"What? Who? Where are we?"

"That blithering idiot of an innkeeper put the vial into the wrong drinks. Now we are out here, sharing a bed with the local rodents whilst Geber and his posse of fools get a head start to the book."

Collins's apprentice was now coming round.

"This is all your fault!" Smithson said. "If you hadn't suggested using that damned potion, we wouldn't be in this mess."

"I ask again that you refrain from talking to him in that manner. If anyone is to chastise the boy, it shall be me, as *I* am head of the Collins family. I don't see that you can blame him for this. You were more than up for the idea last night. If anyone is to blame, it's that idiot innkeeper."

"Right, that's it!"

"Now where are you going?"

"To give that innkeeper a thorough going over."

"What, *you*? You're as strong as a blade of grass in hay season."

"I've won my share of fights, I'll have you know."

"Really? This isn't the school playground anymore. Need I remind you of the incident in Portis-Montis, the one where Delphin floored you. You have as much stamina as a swimming goat."

Smithson stared at Collins, realised he had been beaten and marched off.

"Where are you going now?"

"Have you forgotten your place in this world, *Collins?*"

"*Sorry,* where are you going now, *sir?*"

"I may not have the stamina to fight, but I can jolly well give that buffoon a piece of my mind."

He marched out of the alley and around the corner, out of sight, only to march past in the opposite direction a moment later, before reappearing back at the end again.

"Where is that bloody pub? Take me there."

Collins sighed, helped his apprentice up from the alley and began walking away from Smithson.

"Collins? I'm talking to you. I gave you a direct order. Don't you walk away from me!"

Collins stopped abruptly, causing his apprentice to walk into him. He let out a sigh, then turned to face Smithson.

"If, *sir,* would care to follow me in the right direction, I will take him there. Come, boy."

He turned and walked off towards the opposite end of the alley.

"Right, yes. Well, I always knew it was this way. I just needed to stretch my legs first, that's all."

"Indeed."

They walked the rest of the alley in silence, their feet squelching in the detritus of daily life that nobody wanted to deal with. They emerged into the bright daylight of the street and had to shield their eyes, as the sun was already well above the horizon. The locals steered clear of the trio, not wanting to get too close to the stench. Smithson caught sight of the sign swinging above the *Leakey Ship* and pushed passed Collins to get to the door first, only to find it locked shut. He pounded on the ornate window, causing it to rattle in its frame.

"Innkeeper, I know you're in there. Open up, this instant."

People were now stopping to watch the unfolding events with interest – though still keeping their distance. Collins stepped up to talk to Smithson, who tried to shoo him away to no avail.

"If I may be so polite as to suggest that we return to the ship and leave this poor man to his business? He doesn't appear to be in, or if he is, he is not willing to answer. I, for one, need to change out of these clothes and have a wash, as indeed do you, sir."

Smithson looked at Collins, chewing the inside of his mouth, then looked around at the gathering crowd. They all looked back in anticipation, waiting for the next instalment.

"Fine, let's get back to the ship."

There were a few audible sounds of moans at the entertainment being cut short.

"This isn't a circus. Get on with your lives …"

A tomato came from within the crowd, hitting Smithson square in the face. This was met with hysterics from the crowd. He wiped it away with angry distaste and stared wide eyed, nostrils flared, which only caused the raucous laughter to increase. Smithson took a step forward, only to find his way barred by Collins.

"The ship, sir, if you will."

He held out an arm towards the direction of the harbour.

"I'll remember this, just you mark my words," said Smithson to nobody in particular, more to the crowd at large. The laughing only increased as Smithson, Collins and Maso marched off back in the direction of the ship.

Chapter 35

Out in Syreni Bay, *Me Old Duck III* had cleared the harbour wall and was making good progress. Hugh was awake now and feeling the consequences of being at sea. His stomach churned with each wave as he sat in a chair, trying to focus on anything that wasn't moving. The problem being the boat had the character and trappings of a vessel its age.

All manner of objects hung from the ceiling and were moving in time with the swell of the waves. Hugh chose to look carefully at each object with the hope of distracting himself, even if only for a moment. Polished lamps, not unlike those in Barrington's shop, were swinging gently from the ceiling. They were not fuelled by oil but by small orbs working with runes. Between them were ropes and nets and a life ring tangled up in yet more netting.

There was flotsam and jetsam interweaved into the gaps, a chest, which appeared securely locked, a trident, a diver's suit, various old glass bottles found over the years, et cetera. All these items would normally be enough to overwhelm the senses, but somehow they made the boat feel very homely. Harold came down from the deck, bringing Hugh back to his senses.

"Morning all. I trust you've had yourselves a good sleep?"

"Oh yes," said Barrington. "There really isn't anything that compares to sleeping at sea. Tell me, what does the old girl run on, steam power?"

"No, we use orbs and runes this side of the liminal line. How you New Worlders – I believe that's how you view yourselves – can cope with all that smoke is beyond me."

"Aye, well, not all of us rely on all that dirty power," said Hamish, taking a swig from his hip flask.

"Naturally, I wouldn't include the great reader of runes in that group of people. Your inventions are well used this side of the liminal line, though nobody I know has a clue about where you live. You are very talented nonetheless."

Heather cleared her throat, and Hamish looked awkwardly back at Harold.

"But I thought everyone knew you lived on the — OW! What did you do that for?" said Barrington, looking at Heather.

"Ye know why."

"Aye, the family homestead is supposed to be a secret," said Hamish, looking less than impressed, "except to those who know of it. I also cannae take all the credit for the inventions. My daughter Heather, here, is most talented when it comes to that department. We cannae use them in the New World, as the technology would scare too many people."

"Yes, we hear the stories daily from those coming over the liminal line. Those poor persecuted people, such a narrow view on life those New Worlders have."

"Aye, well, there's a way to start putting those wrongs to right. That's the reason we're here, and the reason we need yer help."

"Go on."

"Hamish, is this a good idea?" said Hugh. "We've already said too much of the plan. Any more and we'll have to induct him.

"Induct me into what? I'm not the guy that enjoys joining cults, you know," said Harold, backing away slightly, "or whatever you New Worlders like to do."

"It's not like that," said Hugh, in an attempt to calm him down. "When you last saw my father, did he allude to what he might be up to?"

"Listen, all I know is that he was on a quest of sorts, and that if things were to go wrong – which clearly they did – then one day you too would darken my door. It also lines up with what Hamish said, but neither told me of the specific task in hand. I'm willing to help you, for a small fee, of course, but what you are up to is your business. Our job is to aid and rescue. As long as we don't get dragged into your troubles, we are happy."

"Then that suits me," said Hugh. "All you need to know is that we are looking for relics from the Old World, which must come back together in the right place and in the right hands. Sprites knows what'll happen if we don't complete the task, but you can bet the situation the New World is in now will be more dire if we get this wrong, and it risks dragging the Old World down with it."

"So, where would you like to go?"

"Well, we're not sure. If Smithson has already been looking out here in the bay and not found anything, then we can assume that he hasn't been looking in the right place. This may seem an odd question, but would you know the whereabouts of any merfolk?"

Harold looked as though he might throw up.

"Are you alright?"

Harold swallowed.

"Yes, yes, I'm fine … well, I'm not fine, but I'm fine, if that makes sense?" He cleared his throat.

"Are you sure?" asked Emily, now looking directly into Harold's eyes. "Because if there is something that you are not telling us, we have ways of finding out."

Harold licked his lips, and he refused to meet Emily's gaze. His eyes were darting all over the place, and he looked as though he was fighting the urge to run away.

"Oh, there's nowhere to run to, so I wouldn't even try it." Emily seemed to grow in stature, and Hugh recognised where it was going.

"Emily, that's enough," he said. "I'm sure he has a valid explanation for his reaction, don't you, Harold?"

"Blimey, you two are worse than me wife. You could give her a run for her money, I could tell you."

"Answer the question, Harold, or Emily, here, will carry on with her style of questioning. And this time, I won't step in."

Silence followed, with only the sound of water lapping on the boat for company. Harold looked from Hugh to Emily, then back to Hugh before his shoulders dropped.

"Alright, but you won't like the answer."

"Try us," said Emily, tilting her head.

"In answer to your question, yes, I know where the merfolk are."

"See, that wasn't so bad, was it?" said Hugh.

"Why do I feel like there's a 'but' about to come?" said Heather.

"But I cannot take you there," said Harold.

Barrington got to his feet.

"Hang on a minute. I thought we had an agreement. You said that anywhere we needed to go, you would take us, for a small fee. Don't renege on your deal now. We haven't the time to go back and forth to shore and find a new crew."

"Look, it's not as simple as that. If I could take you there, then I would, but I can't. I'm banned by the merfolk from setting foot *or anchor* near them."

"What did ye do to provoke that sort of reaction?" asked Hamish.

Harold remained tight-lipped, but his eyes gave him away, as they darted to the trident.

"Oh, ye didnae, did ye? Ye silly arse!"

"What? What did he do wrong?" said Hugh.

"He only went and took one of the most prized items from them," said Hamish, pulling the trident free from where it was lodged. "This trident belongs to the mer-people, and he stole it from them."

"Stole is such a harsh word to use. Discovered, found, even borrowed, all seem a much better way to describe it."

"It disnae matter what ye use to describe it, ye still took it without permission. No wonder they are angry with ye, laddie."

Harold looked to the floor in shame.

"Hang on," said Barrington. "Are you saying that trident is the one we're also looking for?"

"Aye, like I said before, it was thought to be lost, when in actual fact our wee friend here had it all the time."

"Well, I can see why you don't want to return back down there, old bean, though it was a foolish mistake on your part."

"It does, however," Hamish continued, "give us a ticket to grant an audience with the merfolk."

"It does?" said Harold, looking up from the floor.

"Aye, it does, and ye'll have to be the one to complete the transaction."

"I will?"

"Aye, yer gonna have to take this back to where ye got it from and furnish apologies for yer wrongdoing."

"But if I go back there, I'm a dead man! And who will look after the boat? I can't leave her without a captain."

"I can take care of that for ye, along with yer second in command, Guppy is it? These four will be coming with you, so ye'll have help if things go wrong."

"We will?" said Barrington.

"Aye, ye will. This may be the only chance ye get to retrieve what ye need. If it means looking after this wee fella too, then so be it. Right, we need to plan the next steps. It won't be long before Smithson is back on our heels."

Hugh looked at Hamish and thought about a counterargument, but he quickly realised that to fight would be futile. By the looks of things, Barrington and the others had come to the same conclusion. With no more arguments to be heard, the group sat around the table to begin planning in earnest. Harold informed them they were about half an hour away from their destination, and he could fill them in on how to get into the realm of the mer-people.

"What your friend Smithson hasn't realised is that you need *this* to get in." He pulled a clamshell out of his pocket, placing it on the table. "Without it, you'll be unable to gain access to Aquitania."

"First," said Hugh, "Smithson is not our friend. Second, what is that? Third, what is Aquitania?"

"This is a clam-key. It's the only way to gain access to the city under the waves, otherwise known as Aquitania. Without this, you'll find an unwelcome response if you make any attempt to gain entry to the place. Oh yes, and you have to be of underwater origin. Seeing as none of you fit into that category, I guess we can turn around and head home now."

"Now hold on a minute," said Barrington. "Who said none of us were descended from an underwater heritage?"

"Really? Don't tell me. You have a magic coat which allows you to change in to a selkie? Did one of the crew put you up to this, because I'll have to be having serious words with them. It's not something I like to brag about."

"Hang on, are you saying that you're a selkie too?"

"Yes, from my father's side. So this isn't a wind up?"

"No, but I too have kept my coat in the closet for a long time, until this trip, that is. Hang on, what is your name again?"

"Nautilus, but my mother was a Delphin. Why? What's yours?"

"Delphin. You don't suppose we're related somewhere down the line?"

"Well, my father did talk of some of the family staying within the liminal line and having to try and help keep the peace over there."

"So, technically, we could be cousins?"

"I guess so. Who would have thought it? Bring it on cuz." Harold stood up with his arms open wide, ready for a hug.

Barrington stood still. Harold dropped his arms.

"No? Too early?"

"If yese two are done playing happy families," said Heather, "can we get on with planning the next step?"

Harold sat back down again, and the group got into the finer details of the plan. They agreed with Hamish that he would stay aboard the boat whilst Harold guided the rest down to Aquitania. How they would get the book, they did not know.

"One question. How do you plan on getting us into the city itself?" said Emily.

"What do you mean?"

"Well, you and Barrington will fit in nicely down there, but we lack the flippers and fins."

"I'll be able to get you in there, don't you worry about it. I have friends in high places, and as long as you are with me, you'll all be alright."

"On that specific part of being alright," said Emily, not giving up, "how, exactly, are we three to breathe underwater?" She gestured to herself, Hugh and Heather. "I can hold my breath for a short time but not for the duration you're talking about."

"We have a diving suit," said Harold, gesturing to the cumbersome equipment hanging in the corner. "But it's not suitable for the depths we're going to."

"There is only one of those anyway, and there's three of us. I'll leave the maths to you. That also looks like it's seen better days."

"That's a vintage suit, I'll have you know."

"My point exactly."

"If yese two would stop yer bickering for a moment, I might have the solution that yer looking for," said Heather.

She rummaged in her bottomless pockets, with many items crashing around. Her arm was nearly in up to her armpit, when she finally stopped searching and pulled it back out. She was holding a wooden box, which had AL2 inscribed on the top. She opened the lid and spun the box around for the rest to look at. As Hugh looked at the open container, he saw a purple velvet pillow with what looked to be three mouth pieces attached to small pipes and an elongated oval. On the front of the oval appeared to be a set of three gills, gently filtering in and out.

"These are the Aqua Lung 2. They will help you breathe underwater and should have enough charge in there for what we need."

"Charge?" said Barrington.

"Aye, they have runes that activate when they are inserted into yer mouth. They use the power of the sight and the natural world.

Only issue is, they dinnae last forever. They need to recharge before we use them again, but we'll have more than enough time to use them and return to the surface."

"Wow, that truly is amazing. How do they work?" said Hugh in amazement.

"That's a family secret, but I can tell you that, when inserted it into the mouth, a bubble will form around you. That'll give you a protective layer, so you dinnae get wet. We'll still have free movement and be able to stay warm and dry."

"That answers the question, then," said Emily. "We'll be able to get the book, and then get out of there and away to Portis-Montis. Barrington, you will have to do the talking with Harold, as you will have the closest connection, and you're good at that sort of thing. Hugh … you just say nothing."

"What? Surely it would be good to have two of us at the negotiating table?"

"Fine, Heather, you can accompany Barrington, whilst Hugh and I keep quiet."

"Hang on, why can't I negotiate? What?"

Barrington was looking at Hugh with raised eyebrows.

"Need we remind you, dear Hugh, of the last time you negotiated for us? If you have forgotten, let me remind you. It was a painful experience, one which I need not repeat. If my style is likened to the painted ceiling in the great library, then yours would be closer to a child's drawing. You have all the right apparatus, you just lack the finesse and skill. You could also compare it to the time when—"

"Alright, I get the idea. I'll keep quiet."

Hugh looked away and sulked.

"It's not that we don't trust you, Hugh," said Emily, trying to reassure him. "It's that every time you try, it always seems to come out wrong. You get edgy, a bit like an overactive puppy ... this isn't helping, is it?"

Hugh shook his head. Emily gave in and put her arms around him.

"Right, well, it seems we have a plan, so I'll leave you folks to prepare whilst I let the chaps know what we're going to do."

"Are you sure that's a good plan, old chap?" asked Barrington.

"It's fine, I trust them, and I won't tell them everything, just what they need to know."

With that, he climbed the steps up to the deck, leaving the others to prepare for what was to come. Nobody was speaking, all were focussed on what they were about to do. Hugh didn't know why, but that feeling in the pit of his stomach was back again, and this time it wasn't down to sea sickness.

Chapter 36

Back across the bay, the *Fey Flyer* was leaving the empty harbour. The Elf King was sitting in his cabin, talking to his son Tavish about the upcoming plan.

"So, I'm pretty sure that fool Smithson has absolutely no idea that we are aboard. We must continue our covert operation and not be seen. Though we can shape shift, and you have listened to all I have taught you, we must still be careful. You are not as skilled in the art yet, and I fear you will not be able to hide your true identity. It will only take one false step for our plan to unravel. Have I made myself clear?"

Tavish looked at his father and nodded.

"Yes, Father, I understand. So how are we to do this?"

"We must wait until the time is right and keep our distance in the meantime. We can let the plundering oaf make all the mistakes then pick up all the pieces afterwards. If we play this game correctly, we will have all the books of power."

"What about the lore book of magic? I thought you said that would require too much effort to get."

"For now, yes, but I am getting all of my players, *our* players, into place, and when the time is right, we will strike. This is a game of patience, my boy. Those who can last the longest will get the largest reward, you mark my words. For now, blend in and keep your head low."

"What of the others, the ones out in the bay already looking for the book?"

"Well, that is also an interesting thing. If the oaf is correct, we can use them to our advantage and use them to find the book of lore with ease. I have already spoken to the chief of the merfolk and have paid him handsomely. By the time that group has realised they've walked into a trap, it'll be too late. Smithson can follow them and get the book, and we can snatch the book from under Smithson's nose."

"But I thought you said they were run by the council of elders?"

"That *was* the case, but times are changing. The one I spoke to has a following behind him and commands all the respect around the table. The fools down there don't even realise it yet, but he will be the true leader of the merfolk. He will be a great ally in the coming months, trust me."

"Father, what happens if Geber gets the book," asked Tavish. "Then we'll be two books down."

"I am sure of the plan, and you must be too. If we don't trust it, then we will fail in our task. Have faith, the books will be ours. I will not let you down, my son."

"Yes, Father."

"Good, now away with you. We must prepare for the next stage. If all goes well, we should have the book by sundown."

Chapter 37

Back on *Me Old Duck III,* six people were lined up on deck whilst two selkies were in the water.

"Are you sure these will work?" asked Hugh.

"Aye, it'll be fine," said Heather, "and Dad will be up here monitoring everything else with Guppy."

"Alright, so how's best to do this? Do we put the AL2 in our mouths first, then jump in, or the other way around?"

"Place it in your mouth, as ye jump into the water. Ye should have time to get it in before ye hit the water."

"And if we don't?"

"Then ye'll get wet. Right, jump in on the count of three. One … two … *three*!"

They all jumped off the edge of the boat. With a helpful kick from Hamish, Hugh found himself heading down to the deep blue water, which seemed to be approaching at an alarming rate. He was aware of Emily muttering something under her breath, and the pace of the world seemed to slow. The watch in his pocket was vibrating so much that he feared it would fall out.

The speed of their descent had turned to a crawl, and Hugh found himself able to think with a clear head. He slowly moved his hand towards his face, opening his mouth, ready to receive the respirator. The water was edging closer, and he was mere inches away when it happened.

A film enveloped him, protecting his body from all the elements, and it joined up at his feet just before they hit the water. Everything sped back up to normal time as Hugh plunged into the bay, surrounded by frothing bubbles. Though his hearing was muffled by the protective shield surrounding him, he could hear the water bubbles heading to the surface above, gurgling as they ascended. He expected to feel the cold of the water any moment, but it didn't come. It seemed the protection given by the AL2 extended to temperature as well. He went to speak but realised the respirator was preventing him from doing so, so he had to use the power of the sight, communicating directly into everyone's heads.

'*Well, this is a new experience,*' he said, moving his arms and legs.

He looked at his hands, seeing the protective covering gripping around his skin. As he bobbed up and down in blue abyss, he opened and closed his fingers, the covering filling the space with a thin membrane, making it look as though he had webbed fingers. The same happened when he opened his legs, but this time it looked like a large flipper. He looked around at the others, who were all experiencing the same phenomenon. He tried to swim through the water, finding that he could move with ease. Barrington came alongside him, sculling on his back.

'*See, it's not so bad, this underwater malarkey, eh?*'

'*It's quite fun. I could do this all day,*' said Hugh, swimming around his friend. Dappled light was making its way through the water, casting a blue rippling effect across the group surrounding him.

'*Glad yese are all having fun, but ye do get to swim all day whilst ye look fir the book,*' said Hamish, his voice coming as a surprise to everyone.

'*Well, ye are broadcasting to the whole group, so I widnae be that surprised. Now get in, yiv little time.*'

'*Sorry, Hamish. So, where do we go now?*' said Hugh, looking at the rest of the group.

Everyone turned to look at Harold, who jumped into action.

'*Ah, yes, apologies. We need to be heading this way,*' he said, swimming off towards a forest of kelp. '*Follow me, if you will.*'

The others set off after him, trying their best not to lose him in the dense foliage. As he swam, Hugh had to duck and weave through the fronds, which was hard work. They kept trying to wrap around his arms and flipper leg, as if they were trying to prevent anyone from going further down. At one point Hugh became totally entangled, and Barrington had to help free him. He noticed that the kelp wasn't bothering Barrington at all; in fact, it seemed to part before him.

'*Why is it not affecting you, like it is me?*' he asked.

'*Probably because I'm allowed to be here. You forget that this is my ancestral home, so whatever this is will recognise me as one of their own.*'

'*This is the first line of defence for Aquitania, the great city of the merfolk, my people,*' said Harold.

'*It doesn't seem much of a deterrent,*' said Emily, pulling herself free from an over friendly piece of kelp.

'*Well, this is where you are lucky that Barrington and I are here. If you were attempting to gain entry on your own, there would be razor sharp rocks being fired at you at this point. What you can't see are the water blasters set within the fronds. They fire the pointy rock splinters that stick into you. They're shaped like those pikes they use in Androssan. Most unpleasant. That's the point where the majority of people turn around.*'

'*The majority of people? Ye meant to say people get through the rocks?*' said Heather.

'*Indeed, there are those whose need to see the place is just too great.*'

'*What happened to them?*' she asked. '*I've nae heard stories of this place before, and I'm sure Dad would've told me if there had been.*'

'*Of course you haven't heard any stories, and that's because those who have made it past this stage, never live to tell the tale.*'

'*What? Ye mean to say that they were killed?*'

'*Goodness me, no. We aren't heathens. No, they normally get thrown into "The Pots" and left to die. It's our version of prison. Either they eventually run out of air, or they die from starvation.*'

'*I dinnae ken how that is better to tell ye the truth.*'

'*No? Well, I suppose not. Still the point is we're not an aggressive race unless provoked.*'

'*And what would provoke them?*' asked Hugh.

'*Many things, but they especially dislike their property being taken. That is one of the big no-no's.*'

'*Why am I getting the feeling like this is not the best of plans?*' he said, looking at the trident tucked under Harold's flipper.

'*It's too late to turn around now.*'

'*Why?*'

'*Because they already know we are here.*'

The forest of kelp opened up, and they were swimming towards an underwater wall. A set of massive gates barred a large hole which disappeared off into a black abyss. Above it read EASTERN PORTAL.

A line of guards were posted at the front of the defence. They wore lobster armour and carried smaller tridents, similar to the one Harold was carrying.

'Well, look who seems to have crawled out of the rock he's been hiding under. What happened? She finally kicked you out?' said the head guard, gracefully guiding over to Harold.

'Hello, Kai, long time no see, eh?'

'You have some nerve coming back to these gates, Harold Nautilus. You shamed our family, the day you not only took a drylander wife, but then had the audacity to steal our prized trident.'

'I thought your father was dead?' said Barrington.

'He is, this is my brother, Kai.'

'Our father died because of you and your reckless ways, Harold. Our father was the head of the Selkies and representers our kind at the table of the great Mer Council. He used to have the knowledge of the top world and guided those drylanders whose lives depended on his knowledge. He even spent all those years training you up, showing you the way of our family trade, only for you to betray us. Oh, and I'll take that, thank you very much.'

He took the trident from under his brother's arm.

'Kai, you know it wasn't like that. I was merely ... errr, borrowing it and had every intention of bringing it back. It just had to be at the right time. The fact I'm here with it now should be enough proof of that.'

'Piffle. You knew what you were doing the day you left here, and by looking at your unwelcome guests here, they have a different view of the situation.'

Harold looked at Hugh then to everyone else, realising his world was unravelling. They were all wearing a look of confusion.

'I may not have been totally truthful with you chaps, but you have to believe me when I say I had every intention of bringing the trident back. And I'm sorry about not being honest with you about my father.'

Hugh didn't know what to think.

'I knew there was something about you," he said, *"but I thought I'd give you the benefit of the doubt. The fact you lied about your father's death is just wrong. I lost my father nearly two years ago, and I may never see him in person ever again, yet here you are gaining our trust through deception, playing on our emotions to get us to follow you. Can we trust anything you've said?'*

'It's really not like that,' Harold said in protest. *'I had no intention of misleading you, honest. Had I known that we would have to be coming here, then maybe I would have passed the job on. But I had already said yes, and I knew that nobody else would take you on, so what was I supposed to do?'*

'Be honest with us from the start?'

'Oh yeah, like that would work. I'm sure you would have dropped me at the first opportunity.'

'Perhaps, but then again perhaps not. We are very forgiving within our little group. We all have secrets we've held onto and subsequently had dragged out into the open, yet we still all support each other. Sometimes you just have to trust those you're with.'

Hugh looked at Barrington as he said this, and his friend nodded his agreement. He then turned back to Harold. Bubbles were coming out of his respirator at a higher rate compared to everyone else.

'Hugh, try not to get too worked up,' said Heather. *'Ye'll end up using more of the energy in yer AL2.'*

'*Fine, I'll do my best, but you can understand why I am upset.*' He turned back to Harold. '*Were you yelling the truth when you said that you could get us in here?*'

'*You promised what?*' roared Kai. '*Is it not bad enough that you have disgraced us all, only to promise drylanders access to our great city? Well, this is where you'll be able to keep your end of the bargain.*'

'*What do you mean, dearest brother?*'

'*Don't dearest brother me! Guards, arrest all these urchins. We'll see what the Mer Council has to say about this!*'

'*Now hang on a minute,*' said Barrington. '*Let's not be hasty about this. I'm sure there is an arrangement that we can come to, and we can all go about our business.*'

'*And who, may I ask, are you?*'

'*My name is Barrington Delphin, son of Mariteus and Constantine Delphin.*' He waited for his words to sink in, but no reaction came. '*Does that ring any bells?*'

Kai looked Barrington up and down, and Hugh thought he might have won him over.

'*None whatsoever. Guards, arrest these people and selkies and throw them in the lobster pots. A couple of hours wet turkey should see them fit, then we can interrogate them further. The Mer Council will need a full assessment before they come in front of them.*'

The guards swam in front of Kai with menacing looks on their faces. Hugh swallowed hard as he looked into the closest one's eyes, realising what was coming this way.

'*This is going to hurt, isn't it?*'

'*Yeah, but it will hurt more if you try to resist.*'

And with that, he felt the now familiar feeling of something blowing down on top of his neck, and his world went dark once more.

Hugh came round in unfamiliar surroundings, and he was unsure if everything had been a dream. He seemed to feel dry, which was a good thing, but when he went to pat himself, he realised his sense of touch was numbed. He dared to open his eyes, and saw that the dream, or nightmare rather, was all too real. His hands were bound with seaweed – so tight that he thought the circulation might be cut off from the rest of his body – and lashed to a rusted metal pole. He looked around at the others. Emily and Heather floated eerily in the water, anchored by their seaweed bonds. They too were coming around from being knocked out.

'Can someone please tell me how and why we keep finding ourselves in this situation?' he said.

'I don't know, but it is becoming very tiresome, old bean,' said Barrington, attempting to stretch his bound limbs. *'The question now is, how do we get out of this one?'*

'Aye, and more importantly, how much time do we have left?' said Heather.

'What do you mean?'

'Well, these respirators will run out of power eventually, and I dinnae want to go through what happens after that.'

'What do you mean, run out? I thought you built these to last?' said Hugh, unable to hide his panic.

'Aye, I did, but they still have to have time to recharge. It's like when you enter the sight for too long. Ye need to recharge before ye enter again. The more ye use it, the more energy it sucks out of ye, and the longer ye

need to recharge. It's one of the basic rules of runes. Thas why dad has opted to stay on with us. To get back, or use Betsie, would be too much of a risk. He could end up being stuck in the in between, neither in this world, nor in the sight.'

'So, are you saying that we are running the risk of drowning down here?'

'In a word, yes. We have to find out how to get out of here soon, otherwise we'll end up as shark bait. I know it's hard, but ye must try not to panic.'

'Well, that's easier said than done. I don't fancy being shark bait or drowning. Would that information not have been useful before we set off?'

'I didnae know at the time that this buffoon widnae be able to get us entry into the city; otherwise I would've suggested something different.'

'I think you'll find I was coerced here against my will!' said Harold. 'Anyway, If Barrington and I don't reach a selkie pipe soon, we will be facing the same fate as you.'

'What do you mean by that? What's a selkie pipe?' asked Hugh.

'Barrington and I can last around two hours before we run out of usable oxygen. There is a system of pipes feeding air down from the surface, which allow us selkies to stay down here for longer periods.'

'Would that information have been more helpful during the planning sessions?' asked Barrington.

'I didn't envisage being down here for this amount of time either. I thought the job was going to be easier than this. Besides, I thought you might be a little more grateful. I did get you into the city, did I not?'

'Excuse me?' said Emily.

'*For what, my dear?*'

'*No, excuse me, meaning what on earth are you talking about?*'

'*I'm saying that you wanted access to the city, and you are now in the city.*

So I think I have kept up my end of the bargain,' he said. "*Now you need to keep yours.*'

'*You are kidding? I hardly think you can call this getting into the city. We have no access beyond this cell that we're in, and we are bound up so tight that we cannot move our hands.*'

'*Plus, you have to help us find the book,*' Hugh added.

'*I don't think you lot realise what sort of trouble you're in,*' said Harold. '*One doesn't just walk up to the book of lore and take it out like it's a lending library. It's the most guarded book in the city. I can hardly see a bunch of drylanders, such as yourselves, walking up and taking it. When the book arrived back here nearly three hundred years ago, everyone agreed it should never leave again. After all, it was sent here because your lot couldn't look after it.*

'*As for getting out of the cells of Aquitania, well, that is a completely unattainable dream. If you don't believe me, ask that pile of bones down there.*' He pointed to the remains of a dive suit, which had been reduced to tatters and bones. '*You're as likely to get out of here as you are to start a fire, and I don't need to tell you how impossible that is.*'

'*That's it,*' said Hugh.

'*That's what?*'

'*A fire. We can use our firestones to burn through these cuffs.*' He attempted to get his chest close enough to his hands but found the task quite impossible.

'*I've told you, there's no point trying to escape. You're bound tight. There's no shaking off these knots.*'

'*I'm not trying to get free, just get to my firestone, but it's out of reach. Emily, can you reach yours?*'

Hugh looked over to see Emily was already trying to get to hers, but she found herself in the same position as Hugh.

'*Sorry, it's no good. We'll have to look for a different option.*'

'*If you just give me a hand, I might have a solution,*' said Barrington, wriggling around.

'*You haven't got a firestone, Barrington, I don't see what you have that can help us?*' said Hugh.

'*Ah ha, but that, dearest Hugh, is where you are wrong. I may not possess a firestone, but I happen to have one of these.*' He began wriggling around, in a way that looked as though he were in discomfort, before something appeared under his flipper. He craned his neck around and pulled out a pipe, which he held between his lips.

'*Barrington, I hardly think that this is the time to have a smoke of your pipe. Besides, I think it is very hard to use under water.*'

'*On the contrary, old bean, this is the perfect time for a smoke.*' He moved the pipe around awkwardly to the corner of his mouth. '*This is a phoenix pipe, and one of the outstanding features of this particular piece of smoking paraphernalia is that it stays lit in all conditions, even when totally submerged. I've waited all of my pipe-smoking life for one of these, and I was lucky enough to gain one from our glass-eyed captain.*' He leaned over and began puffing away vigorously, placing the end on his restraints. They popped off immediately, and fell slowly to the depths, still smouldering. He continued across the group until they all were freed from the seaweed bindings.

'*Ye did it,*' said Heather, as she swam up to him, putting her arms around his sleek neck.

'*I don't wish to hurry you, but we need to get out of here sooner rather than later,*' said Harold. '*It won't be long before the next cell checks come round, and if we're discovered like this, we'll be done for.*'

'*Aye, and I doubt we have long to get the book and escape from here, before the AL2s run out of power.*'

'*How long do you think we have?*' asked Emily.

'*Well, it depends on how long we were out for. The warning signs will be if ye start to feel damp. That means that the runes are wearing off. Ye'll also feel the mouthpiece vibrate, at which point ye only have about ten minutes max.*'

'*Oh good,*' said Hugh. '*Shall we get a move on, then? How do we get out of this, Harold?*'

As Hugh looked around, he could see that they were trapped in what looked to be a huge lobster pot, though it had no obvious exits. Harold began gliding around the edge of the pot, looking for something in particular, though Hugh couldn't make out anything discernible. Harold came to a stop next to a nobbled bit of the wall.

'*Here. If you can burn through these points, the door will drop out and we'll be able to escape.*' He gestured to certain points along the wall, going up from the floor, and around in an arch.

As Hugh drew up close with the others, he saw that there was indeed a double layer, marking out an entrance. Barrington began puffing away, making slow work of the job. Smokey bubbles rose upwards, and Hugh feared they might give them away.

'*Well? Don't all offer to help?*' Barrington said, looking across at Hugh and Emily.

'*Ah, sorry,*' said the pair in unison. They went to reach for their firestones, only to realise the protective bubbles keeping them safe, also prevented them from accessing the items they so desperately needed. Hugh looked to Heather for help.

'*Is there any way we can get around this?*'

'*I'm afraid not. If ye break the runes, then ye'll lose all the protection they give ye. Again, I didnae foresee this as being a scenario that we would come across.*'

'*Sorry, Barrington, but it's on you,*' said Hugh.

They watched with anxiety as he moved from joint to joint, slowly unravelling the bindings around the door. They had to stop on more than one occasion, as they worried someone was swimming in their direction. It turned out to be a jelly fish or a lonely turtle, passing through the reef overhead. Eventually, Barrington succeeded in breaking through the barrier.

'*Well done, old boy,*' said Hugh.

'*Don't count your starfish yet,*' said Harold. '*We still have to get the book and get you lot out of here, and gauging by the water pooling at your feet, I don't think we have much time.*'

Hugh looked down, seeing a small amount of water, which sloshed around as he moved.

'*No time to lose, then. Where do we go?*'

Harold led them down what appeared to be a coral corridor, with numerous lobster pot cells running off it. The inhabitants looked on, wondering how they'd got out and why they wouldn't spring them as well. As much as the group tried to hush them down, the louder the inmates appeared to become. It wasn't long before they saw the shadow of a guard swimming down towards the corridor. Harold ushered everyone into a darker corner in an attempt to hide their location.

The guard was carrying a lamp, lit by phosphorescent algae. They waited in silence, as the guard made his way down the cells, ignoring the rants of the occupants, and stunning them with an electric eel, silencing them one by one. Hugh sank further back into the wall, his breathing increasing with his fear, the AL2 bubbling furiously. A tentacle wrapped itself around his arm, pulling him tight against the bars of a cell.

'Please, you don't understand. We mean you no harm, but we need to be out of here.'

'Don't we all, sonny,' said a raspy slimy voice. *'Don't we all?'*

Hugh dared not look around for fear of what he might see.

'Please, don't do this. Maybe we can come to some sort of arrangement, maybe we could set you free?'

The guard was a matter of feet away from them. He was dealing with a tricky customer, who was refusing to be stunned by the eel, jumping out of the way and taunting the guard.

'Oh, I don't think so, do you? We both know that the moment you escape, I'll be nothing more than a vague memory, a story to tell the fish spawn about. 'Ere, Conch, I got a present for you!'

It all happened so quickly, the guard didn't have time to react. He turned to look in the direction of the group, who all jumped him, much to the enjoyment of those who were not yet stunned. They disarmed him in the blink of an eye, the eel happy to be free of its captor, swimming off in the opposite direction. Hugh was left unable to help, still pinned as he was to the bars of the cell behind him.

'Looks like I'm going to have to finish this off by myself,' said the occupant, sending chills down Hugh's spine.

Feeling more tentacles wrap themselves around Hugh, it was all he could to try to get anyone's attention. He thought for sure that bones were going to break at any moment, and that his eyes were going to pop out of their sockets.

Then, from out of nowhere, a searing heat passed through Hugh and into the tentacles holding onto him. An intense, high-pitched scream filled the cells, and all momentarily stopped what they were doing.

Hugh was released instantly, and the thing that had been holding him seemed banished to the back of its gloomy pot. Hugh looked down, panting, to see his firestone illuminated under his shirt, and then looked up to see Emily coming towards him.

'I think you'll find that's my man you had a hold of there.' She held out a hand for Hugh, who was filled with a feeling of relief, pride and a warm glow inside. *'No time for that now, we need to get out of here before he comes round and raises the alarm.'* She pointed to the unconscious guard floating limp in the water.

The rest of the prisoners were coming back to their senses and had found their voices once more. Hugh looked once again to Harold.

'Where to now, Captain?

The words seemed to fill the old selkie with pride, and he puffed out his chest.

'Follow me.'

He led them down to the end of the passage and through a doorway. They spiralled up through the reef, the colours glinting by the light of more phosphorescent algae lamps. They came out into an underwater courtyard, its floor covered in mussel shells. Harold motioned Barrington over to a bubbling pipe sticking out of the wall. They both took it in turns the breathe in more air, whilst the others kept watch.

Once the pair had recharged their lungs with oxygen, Harold led the group out through a small gate. The guards on duty, who looked as though they hadn't seen action for a long time, were dozing at their post. The escapees neutralised them with ease as they made their way out onto the busy street. At first Hugh thought it looked like any other reef, swaying about in the late afternoon currents, but as he looked closely, he saw it was teeming with life.

'*Wow! This is amazing,*' he said, looking around in awe.

'*I know,*' said Harold. '*I forget how beautiful the old home is sometimes.*'

'*It's so light. How do you manage it?*'

'*Don't let it deceive you. We are protected by a large rune dome, which not only boosts the light from the world above but also helps protect us from the drylanders. Water can flow through, but objects cannot. I wouldn't advise trying to swim through it either.*'

'*Why not?*'

'*Let's just say you would be turned into bait for more than one shark. It's similar to a razor-sharp mesh, only you can't see it until it's too late. It also has a cloaking element, meaning anyone looking down from above will only see a barren seabed. Anyway, that's enough chit chat for now; we need to get a move on.*'

Hugh watched him swim gracefully off into the reef and was distracted once again by what he saw. Shoals of fish were navigating organised routes through the reef, with signs pointing off for different exit portals. There were billboards advertising the way to the superhighway streams, the high speed currents that would whisk their occupants to faraway places.

The reef itself was dotted with dwellings. Here and there were lights in shop windows, which were filled with all sorts of fine items, from polished pearl necklaces and clam bags, which floated around merfolk mannequins, to a shop called *Tridents' R' Us — for all your trident needs.* Further along there was a shop that went by the name of *Trawl Guard,* selling numerous ways to protect your home from the dangers above. Another was *Gillgads — your local independent gill cleaning service.* He was brought back to his senses by a large trout, roughly pushing past him, whose path he had drifted into on the underwater current.

'*Ay, watch where you're gawking, bozo! I'm swimmin' here!*'

'*Sorry, I didn't mean to,*' Hugh started, but the fish was already long gone.

He turned and bumped into a prawn hiding in a lobster shell. It was carrying a sign around its neck which read, *The end of the reef is nigh.* The prawn with the sign took a long look at Hugh and began bellowing at him.

'*Behold! The drylanders swim among us! The day of reckoning has come! Repent your sins or be forever tied in with your fate!*'

Other fish were stopping to look at the disruption to daily life, making Hugh feel uncomfortable.

'*Will you be quiet?*'

'*Listen to the way he tries to silence my voice. He will bring fiery balls of death and destruction. Repent your sins, I tell you, before we are all destroyed!*'

Hugh looked desperately around for an exit route and noticed the others were already swimming their way down the reef, so he rushed to catch up with them, leaving the mad crustacean to his ranting. He had to work his flipper hard to catch up with them.

'*There you are! We were just wondering where you had got to,*' said Emily, looking at the crowd gathering up the reef. The prawn was now pointing in their direction.

'*I hope you're not drawing too much attention to yourself,*' she said.

'*No, no, just a rambling nutter, that's all.*'

Harold came back to see what the issue was.

'*Come along, you two, we must stick close to the shadows. If we are seen out here in the open, they'll take us all back into the lobster pots. It's not like most of us can blend in here, you are all in way out of your depth.*'

'*Fine, then stop getting your flippers in a twist, and get us out of here.*'

Harold turned and shot Emily a raised eyebrow, as much as a selkie can do such a thing, before swimming off in the opposite direction. He was now leading them upwards, along a part of the reef that looked grander than its surroundings. They spiralled upwards once more, moving from shadow to shadow, hiding from guards who were moving in the opposite direction overhead. It was becoming obvious to all that their escape hadn't gone unnoticed. Hugh was becoming more uneasy by the minute, not only because of the increased security, but also because of the damp feeling he was getting all over his body. It was also becoming harder to swim as the runes wore off.

'*Where are you taking us?*'

'*Upwards to the high plateau of the Mer Council.*'

'*What? Isn't that a tad dangerous? Surely it's well guarded?*'

'*Normally, yes, but given that most of them have passed us going into town, I think we'll be alright. It would appear that even they think it a ludicrous idea for us to gain entry to the most important place on the reef. I dare say they will be checking the tunnel out of the reef, as they'll be thinking you're trying to head for safety.*'

They continued upwards until the reef levelled and thinned out, revealing a large hollowed out coral structure, with a purpose-built stone arch. Up here the currents were more erratic, and Hugh had to fight being pulled off course. He could feel himself starting to rise and feared being caught up in the rune dome.

'*Hugh, where are you going?*' said Emily.

'*I'm struggling to keep a steady path,*' he said reaching out to her outstretched hand. She pulled him back down, and they fought to catch up with the others.

Harold's suspicions about the guards heading out to look for them turned out to be correct, as there wasn't a soul in sight. They entered the deserted area unheeded and saw the prize they were after. At the end of a long table, wrapped up and placed on a plinth, was a book. It seemed to glow, illuminating the surrounding waters. Next to it was the trident, the same one that was on Harold's boat. This was too easy.

'Well, here we are. The journey's end,' said Harold.

'For you maybe, but we have to get this back home yet,' said Emily.

'I still don't understand how you think you can get this out of here, and all the way back to where you're going without being caught. There are others who seek this book, you know? Oh yes, I'm fully aware of how sought after this book is. It was my and my father's job to protect the whereabouts of this relic and stop those such as yourselves from getting to it.'

'So why let us get this far?' said Hugh.

'It was aways written that this day would come. My brother would never have it, but my father always spoke of a group of travellers who would come and retrieved the Lore Book of Water. He said it would be their job to take it back to where it could be kept safe. Most believe that place is here, but seeing the attempts others have made, even in recent days, has made me realise that its days of safety here are numbered. But I need to know that you are the ones who will truly look after it and guarantee its safety until it's home.'

'How are we to prove that to you, other than by our word?'

'Father always said the one who would come would bear a mark, the same as is on his right flipper. Before I brought shame upon the family, he tattooed the mark on me in case it was I who discovered the chosen people.

You'll have to forgive me, for I laced the tea on the boat with a light draught, one to put you asleep long enough to carry out my checks.

All but one have the mark, which is enough for me to let you three take the book,' he said, gesturing to Hugh, Barrington and Heather. *'That is, as long as you promise not to reveal the secrets within to anyone without the mark.'* He now made a look towards Emily.

'Why can't I look at the book?' said Emily in protest.

'Because you do not bear the mark.'

'But it's foolish to have it so blatantly about yourself like that!'

'I don't make the rules, only abide by them … most of the time.'

'This is ridiculous. I have access to a book of lore, you know? The Lore Book of Earth, and I've read its pages.'

'Emily, just calm down. We can sort this out,' said Hugh.

'Don't you tell me to calm down, Hugh Geber!'

'Will the pair of yese just pack it in!' said Heather, and she turned back to Harold. *'If we promise to keep the book safe, and not let those without the mark see or read the book, then will ye let us take it away with us today?'*

'Yes, that is correct.'

'Alright, then we promise to not let anyone see this who does not bear the mark.'

'That's good enough for me.'

Emily stormed off, and Hugh went after her.

'The only other issue,' Harold said, *'is I need to pass the knowledge on officially, in order for the exchange to happen.'*

'And how would ye go about doing that?'

'It has to be done with one who has the way of water within them.' He looked towards Barrington. *'It has to be you.'*

'Me?'

'Yes you. Once I pass over the knowledge, it will be your responsibility to get the book to safety, do you understand?'

'We've nae time for this. I'm starting to feel less than dry here, which means time is running out.'

'I need Barrington's word on this, or there's no book.' He looked Barrington in the eye.

'Yes, I agree to the terms.'

'Good, then we can proceed. Once you have the knowledge, you can proceed with the book and the trident to the tunnel, which is due east from here.'

'Due east? How do we know which way that is?'

'Swim back along the path we took to get here, then the route past the lobster pots and keep going straight on. Stick to the darker parts of the reef. The key thing is not to be seen, and don't try leaving by going directly upwards! The elders will know of the book's movement from the moment we touch it. Now come to me and stand right flipper to right flipper.'

Barrington followed the instructions, and was about to touch Harold, when a voice called out to them.

'Hold it right there, or these two get it.'

Harold, Barrington and Heather turned around. Three guards were wrestling with Hugh and Emily, but the pair were unable to shake them off, thrashing like fish on the end of a line. They finally gave in their fight, bobbing up and down. Kai swam between the pair, placing a flipper behind each respirator, ready to knock them out at any moment.

Chapter 38

Everyone bobbed up and down for what seemed like an eternity to Hugh. He and Emily fought with the fear that they could drown at any moment, and it was hard to tell if he was sweating, or wet from the failing runes, which were depleting by the minute. He looked across to Emily, whose eyes were as wide as his, and then back to Barrington, who appeared to have frozen in time. Why weren't they moving quicker? He didn't know, but if someone didn't do something soon, they would drown either way.

'*So, what is it to be?*' said Kai, who showed no intention of changing his position on the respirators. '*Well, brother?*'

'*It doesn't have to be like this, Kai.*'

'*Oh, I think you and I both know that it does. You shamed this family once already, and I cannot allow it to happen again.*'

'*If you knew the truth … the reasons why I took the trident and why it must leave with these people today, you might have a different view on the situation.*'

'*Don't trick me with some petty sob story. I'm not willing to listen. Guards, arrest these people and take them back to the cells.*'

'*No, don't listen to him,*' Harold said to the advancing guards, who stopped in their tracks, looking from one brother to the other. '*You need to know the truth before you make your minds up whether to arrest us.*'

The guards, whose lives had been pretty uneventful during the past few decades, considered this last statement. Who were they to stand in the way of a good story?

'*I can see that I have your undivided attention. All those years ago, when you all banished me from Aquitania, you spread the story that I stole the trident which stands next to the book of lore. You even went as far as to send people to search the drylanders' world, asking many, too many, questions. You sparked an urban legend of the trident, which has caused some of their kind to start looking down here for it and in the Forest of Fey. We've conducted many a rescue of the fools who have gone out in search of it and then got themselves into trouble.*

'*As for the rumours about me, well some say I took it out of greed to make a quick profit, but as you can see, I did not sell it. Why do you think I held onto it for all those years? It was because I didn't steal it. It was the intention of my father that I take it away from here in order to keep it safe until the right time.*'

'*Don't listen to him. He's lying like he always does. Arrest him now!*'

Still the guards didn't move.

'*Father was well aware of the power the book and trident represented. But he was on his own when he voted against the idea of the trident's creation. The others on the council were blinded by the power they would have, instead of looking at the bigger picture. Father knew that someday, someone would come to retrieve the relics and take them back to where they belong, for the book, at least, had a home before it came here. He also knew that others would likely come in search of the items. But the book is of no use without the trident, which is why he knew they had to be separated at all cost. Sadly, I fear your involvement, Kai, will have caused some people to join the dots, and realise the power of the trident and the book of lore. Sending me away with the trident wasn't an easy choice for father or me. For him, it was the loss of pride; for me, losing my family and banishment. But I knew the bigger picture and what was at stake if both objects were to fall into the wrong hands.'*

'You cannot seriously expect us to believe this? Why didn't you come clean before now, live the life you could have had, if you were honest? No, I think this is another ruse to take the book for yourself. That's the real reason for coming back, isn't it, dear brother? I cannot and will not let this happen.'

'Kai, you're not seeing the bigger picture. You have to believe me when I say that I don't wish for this to be the way, but the truth is it had to be, for that is how it's written. I want to keep this within the family, and if that has to be a cousin, so be it. We must think of the greater good, and I have to do this for that to happen.'

He turned around and slapped flippers with Barrington. A flash of light filled Hugh's eyes, quickly followed by a feeling of extreme damp. In one swift move, Kai had removed his and Emily's respirators, causing his mouth extreme pain as the seal was broken. It was all he could do to not take a deep breath in. His vision went blurry, and his eyes stung, as the cold salt water slammed into his face. He couldn't see what was happening, other than blocks of colour moving about. Someone bumped into him, and he was floating out towards the stone archway, where the currents beyond would surely take him up to the rune net and his certain death. Then, out of nowhere, he felt someone tugging him back in the opposite direction and something was roughly placed into his mouth. He sensed the protective bubble forming around him, the water being squeezed out as it formed. His sight was restored though his eyes still watered from the invasion from the ocean.

He looked around to see Heather helping Emily, who was also getting her bubble restored. Then he saw Harold fighting with Kai. The guards were too stunned, watching the battle unfold in front of them to watch anything else. Barrington was already making his way to the plinth to get the book and trident. Kai had his flipper curled around his own trident and was advancing on Harold.

'*Kai, you need not do this. You don't understand the reasons it must leave, and I doubt you ever will.*'

'*You speak to me as if I were a simpleton, dear brother, but do you not think that our father also entrusted me with information? I knew of his plan to separate the items, and what it would do to the family name. Unimaginable shame would be cast upon us for decades to come, and I was supposed to just sit there and let it happen? No, I think not. Then he chose you over me. That's what hurt the most. His distrust in me was enough to make me realise he had gone too far. That is why I had to do something about it. I couldn't let the pair of you get away with it, so that is why I had to remove him from the picture.*

'*Yes, Harold, I was the one that killed our father. It was easy enough to cover it up as a suicide, with the shame he was going through in the Mer Council. I then took his place at the table. I knew you would return one day, and I had to be ready. The book cannot leave here, and I intend to keep the power for myself. I've been planning this for too long for you to ruin it now. I have great plans for this reef, one where I intend to call the shots. Plans are already in place, and I am leader in all but name.*'

'*I knew you were low, but I didn't think you could ever stoop to such levels, Kai. Father had his suspicions that this may happen. Yes, he spoke to me about it. You could have played a role in this, been on the right side of history, but alas, you have chosen your colours.*'

'*The right side of history? I think you're the delusional one here, brother. The elves let the books go once; who's to say they won't do it again?*'

'*We have to trust in this group here. They are the only hope. You are more than aware that others are after the book and trident. The council cannot keep them safe forever. It's written that this day would come, and it has finally arrived. I will do right by our father's honour, and I will fight for it to the death!*'

'*So be it!*' said Kai.

Some guards swam forward.

'*Kai Nautilus, we believe it is our duty to take you into our custody, as is our duty and oath to protect the Mer Council,*' said the most senior guard.

'*No! Stay back!*'

Kai swiped his trident around, slashing him across the neck. Blood spewed out into the water like an inky cloud. One of the other guards swam to his aid, whilst the other attempted to disarm Kai. Once again, Kai swiped out, narrowly missing him. He pulled back, wary of being injured himself.

'*Just as I thought. You may be part of the guard, but you are as battle-ready as a turtle. Now stay back, this is between me and him.*'

Kai advanced on Harold, but the latter was quicker and slapped a flipper across his brother's cheek. Kai let out an angry roar, advancing on Harold with such force, that he pinned him to the sea floor. Sand and debris was being kicked up into the water as Harold moved his body, writhing all over, trying to get out of his brother's grip. But it had been many years since he lived under the waves, and his strength wasn't as it once was. Kai went to swing the trident round, and Harold used this distraction to push his brother off.

He turned to spin around and face Kai once more, but his brother drove the trident into his tail, removing a large portion of it. More blood filled the already murky water. Harold let out a howl of pain, which rang out across the reef. He turned in time to see Kai plunge the trident into his chest. All went still, as Harold looked in disbelief from Kai to the trident and then back to his brother.

'I was always going to win this battle, brother. How apt that the trident that killed our father is also the one to finish you too! Say hello to the old man for me.'

He twisted the trident further into Harold's chest, and his brother went limp.

'No!' said Hugh, who went to run towards Harold. But the free guard stopped him, wrapping Hugh in his flippers.

'No, drylander, he will kill you too!'

Hugh looked over at the others, who were still looking over behind Harold and Kai.

'What are you all looking at? Surely you can see the truth in all this?' said Kai. *'It doesn't matter now. I can manage without you. I want my book ... Oh!'*

He stared down, following the cloud of blood to see a trident sticking out of his own chest, then up into the eyes of Barrington, who looked back at him with a tilted head. He twisted and pulled it out, and Kai sunk to the floor, still wearing an expression of surprise. The guard holding Hugh, released his flippers.

'Barrington? What have you done?' said Hugh.

'What I had to do. It was all in the knowledge passed to me by Harold. No time to explain now. We have to get out of here.'

'But how?'

'We follow the plan that Harold laid out for us.'

'What plan? Barrington, what's going on?'

'Hugh, there is no time to explain. We have to get out of here, NOW!'

He didn't stop to fight with Hugh anymore. He turned and headed through the arch, leaving the others to follow in his wake, the remaining guards too engaged in saving their comrade to notice.

'How are we supposed to get out of here?' said Emily. *'Half the city guard are looking for us, and those guards will have alerted the rest to what's going on.'*

'I think they'll have a little more on their minds,' said Heather, pointing off into the distance.

They all came to a stop to look at what Heather had seen. A plume of smoke was bubbling up through the water, defying all physics, and flames were licking out of the windows of the jail building they were in. It was baffling to see such a sight under water.

'But how?' asked Hugh. Emily looked at the scene, then slapped a hand to her forehead.

'Barrington, did you extinguish all the smouldering ash from the phoenix pipe?'

'Erm, come to think of it, I may have been a bit hasty to get out of the cell.'

'Right, then what we are witnessing here is the result of a phoenix fire. It'll be quite impossible to put out, unless they know the right incantation to use.'

'And is that something you know?' asked Hugh.

'Yes, but we haven't time to stop and hand it over, without being caught.'

'But what of all those who were in the cells?'

'*I think they should be alright.*' She pointed to a small crowd of people who were under guard outside the jail.

'*That's not good to see.*'

'*What, you wish they were in there?*'

'*No, I'm glad they're out, but it will make walking past very difficult, as they all know our faces.*'

'*Good point, dear Hugh,*' said Barrington, '*but it is a risk that we have to take. We'll have to hide within the crowds and hope nobody raises any alarm.*'

'*Mmm, seems a little impossible to me.*'

'*Unless you have any other plans, may I suggest you keep your opinion to yourself.*'

'*Alright, keep your fins on. I was only making a comment. What's got you on edge?*'

'*Hugh, in the last ten minutes, I have had to take on an enormous task, a burden that I wasn't expecting. Not only that, I saw Harold killed close up, moments after being told it was going to happen, then had to kill his brother, a thing that will haunt me until my dying day. So if I seem a little tetchy, then I can only apologise. Now, can we please make moves to get out of here before we end up in more trouble than we are already in?*'

Barrington headed off towards the commotion with Heather, leaving Hugh red-faced and unable to reply. Emily came alongside him, and he sensed her warmth.

'*He doesn't mean to be short with you.*'

'*I know, but I did also witness the same as he did, albeit from a little further away.*'

'I think you have to see it from his perspective. There's more going on here than meets the eye. Come on, let's keep up with them. We don't want to get split up.'

Hugh nodded, and the pair headed off after the others. The scene down the road was one of utter chaos and commotion, not only because fires were an uncommon sight, but also because nobody had a clue how to put it out. The group of escapees had to keep their heads down and hope that nobody saw or recognised them, but as the crowd was too busy gawping at the fire, the task was significantly easier than it might otherwise have been. The guards were trying their best to control the crowd, a task that was becoming more difficult as the fire inexorably grew and spread. It had now jumped to the reef on either side with fish fleeing for their lives. Hugh was glad for the extra distraction, for it would give them more cover to make good their escape. He was so distracted by the raging inferno, he'd lost track of where he was swimming and bumped into a prawn.

'Oh no, not you!'

'Behold, the end is upon us!'

A prawn on the other side of Hugh turned in recognition.

'Dave? Is that you? I thought you had ambitions to be a lobster?'

'Yes, Christian, it is I, Dave. I wanted to be a lobster, but no more! The Almighty Cod has spoken to me, and I'm a prawn again, Christian! As was written in the almighty scriptures "And the drylanders shall enter the city, an unstoppable fury shall be released on the reef, and the Almighty Cod shall send one of his own, and he shall be recognised by his trident and a book of lore to control all those of an aquatic nature, and he shall save us all!" And behold, here is the one who carries the trident and book!'

Word spread through the crowd faster than the fire itself. They ceased their shouting and hysteria, and turned to look at Barrington, who looked back awkwardly. They all dropped to the ground in reverence.

'*Oh mighty one, save us from this hell that hath been unleashed on our humble city!*

This was backed up with other cries and pleas of help. Barrington cleared his thoughts.

'*Listen, I really think you have the wrong person here. I mean, it's not like I can just put out the fire…*'

On his words, the trident glowed brightly, and a spark of light shot out of the end, towards the fire. It grew to cover the area that was ablaze, extinguishing it in one fell swoop. The crowd gasped, and some people even fainted.

'*He has saved us all! Almighty one, how are we to rebuild our lives, from this great destruction?*'

Barrington looked from the trident, then to the crowd.

'*I don't know how to rebuild the reef.*'

Again, the trident glowed, and after a flash of light, the reef began growing, an exact copy of what was there before.

'*See how he works his miracles!*'

'*Errrm, it was the trident, honestly. I don't know how it happened.*'

'*Listen to how humbled he is. May we all learn from you, and walk in your steps, oh great one. Let us make him an offering. See how the drylanders have taken him hostage. Let us kill the drylanders in his honour!*'

'*Now hang on a minute,*' said Hugh as fish began tugging at his depleting runes. '*Barrington, call them off quickly!*'

'*Listen here … errrm … I decree that the drylanders … Oh this is ridiculous,*' he said, as the crowds began regrouping, and heading towards him. He swung the trident round to keep the crowds at bay. '*May I be as so polite to suggest that you all swim as fast as you can!*'

The group didn't need telling twice, as they made a dash towards the open mouth of the tunnel. Hugh was finding it tough going and realised that his mouthpiece was vibrating.

'Are any of your mouth pieces vibrating?'

'Aye, so we'd best hurry up. We've around ten minutes left!'

'What do you mean by 'around ten minutes?' You have tested these, haven't you?'

'Aye, but not under a stressful situation such as this. Let's just get to the tunnel.'

They swam for all they were worth, water beginning to seep in through all areas. Behind them, Barrington was bringing up the rear and being followed by the crowd, all eager to get their hands on the drylanders. As they reached the end of the tunnel, Hugh called back to Barrington.

'Can't you use that thing to stop them?'

'I've already said, I don't know how this thing works. It's not like I can ask it to blow up the tunnel …'

–KaBOOM–

The force of the explosion hurled the group out of the tunnel like a cork flying out of a bottle. Barrington's massive body ploughed into the rest of the group, hurtling them through the forest of kelp, cutting a great swathe through the centre. They tumbled out the other side, ears ringing and heads spinning.

'That's one way to do it,' said Hugh, though he was finding it hard to concentrate. The mouthpiece was vibrating so hard, he thought his teeth were going to fall out. *'What's happening?'*

'I told ye, we've literally minutes left to get to the surface. Kick as hard as ye can!'

Hugh kicked and kicked with all of his might. But as hard as he tried, he wasn't going anywhere. He soon realised that his clothes were weighing him down, and that the protective bubble was fast evaporating from around him. He saw the others heading for the surface, but he was sinking.

–POP–

'Oh, not this again.'

It looked as though, for all the training that he had, some habits were difficult to shake off. He had fallen into the sight again, but this time he was finding it hard to stay still. He realised he was not in full body and scrambled to find the right runes to protect himself. His life-link looked weak, and it kept coming in and out of view. He realised he was slowly rotating, as if he were still in water.

'Hugh? Hugh, is that you?'

'Father?'

'Yes, it's me. Where are you?'

'I'm here in the sight. Where are you?'

'I can see that, but where is your body?'

'In Syreni Bay, I think?'

'Wait, are you underwater?'

Concern was filling his voice.

'Yes. Why?'

'Please tell me you are above it and not below the waterline.'

'Below it. Why?'

'If you are in the water and you cannot breathe, then you are in grave danger!'

'What do you mean?'

He coughed.

'What I'm saying is, if you are underwater, it doesn't make a difference if you are in the sight. If your body is underwater on the plane of reality, then you can still drown.'

'What ... Wha ...'

Hugh knew the words that he wanted to say, but he found his mouth was filling with water. He coughed, and mouthfuls dribbled down his front. He tried to breathe but found that his breaths were restricted. He was drowning, and there was nothing he could do to stop it. Slowly but surely, his world drifted into a peaceful darkness.

Chapter 39

Emily and Heather surfaced, gasping for air next to *Me Old Duck III*. Barrington bobbed up next to them and looked up to Hamish, Guppy and the rest of the crew. They were all applauding their success in the mission.

"We got it, well them," said Barrington.

He passed the book and the trident up to Hamish, who took them with a look of concern. Barrington took off his coat, and transformed back into human form so he could climb up the ladder hanging from the side of the boat. As the crew were welcoming Barrington back onto the boat, Guppy came up to him.

"Where's Harold?"

"Ah, there we have some bad news to report."

The joviality stopped in an instant on Barrington's words.

"Not Harold," said Guppy, his eyes tearing up.

"I'm afraid so, but he passed me a message. He wanted you to take over as the head of the Syreni Bay Search and Rescue Party."

"I'm honoured to take the reins," said Guppy, wiping a stray tear from his eye.

Behind them, Hamish was busy talking to Emily and Heather.

"Where's Hugh? Ye didnae have to trade him for these did ye?"

He gave an uneasy chuckle but stopped when he saw the look on Emily's face. "He's nae still down there, is he?"

"He's not with you?"

"Well … nae, otherwise I widnae be asking yese."

"What's going on?" said Barrington, who had left the crew to mourn the loss of their captain.

"It's Hugh," said Hamish. "He's nae made it back yet."

Barrington looked around in the waters in alarm, then to the ladder. "*What?*"

"He's nae here laddie!" Hamish looked into the water, and his eyes had the faintest glow in them. "He's passing over …"

"What? Hamish, no! He can't be! We have to help him …" said Emily, who was starting to shiver in the water.

"You two, get out before you freeze to death." said Barrington, fighting to get his coat back on. "I'm going back down now. I'll bring him back."

Emily was repeatedly put the respirator into her mouth, wanting a bubble to form, but none came.

"Why won't this thing work?"

"Because it needs charging," said Heather, climbing the ladder. "Ye know that."

"Don't you have a spare?"

"Aye but we used it. I built three altogether. Two were for me and Dad to use, with the one spare being the back-up. They're a complex bit of kit to make, I didnae get to make any more. I'm sorry, Emily, but we're all out. Now please get out of the water. We don't want to lose anyone else."

Barrington almost had his coat back on and was preparing to dive in at the right point.

"It's too late, Barrington. Dad said he's already passing over, there's nothing we can do for him now."

"Nae, lassie, there's a way, but I'll have to go in and retrieve him."

"Dad, ye cannae risk it. Yer nae strong enough."

"What are you talking about?" said Emily, now climbing out of the water. She was shivering violently, and a crew member wrapped her in a blanket. "You can't go down there, we've used the respirators."

"Nae lassie, 'tisnae what we're talking about. I'm gonna go into the sight and fetch young Hugh myself."

"But Dad!"

A great splash washed over her face. Barrington was back in the water once more, preparing to dive down and retrieve Hugh's body.

"I can do this, Heather," Hamish said. "I have to. Without Hugh, this'll all be fir nothing. I will come back to ye, lassie. I promise."

"Nae Dad, I willnae let ye. I cannae lose ye …" Tears were falling down her face.

"I have to, and that's the end of it, do ye hear?" He turned to Barrington. "Ye go down, retrieve the body, do ye hear? Dinnae go being brave, trying to revive him underwater, ye hear me? Yiv to bring him back here and wait for my return."

Barrington nodded and dived under the waves once more. Hamish tuned back to his daughters.

"No funny business. No entering the sight till I return, ye hear, and under nae circumstances are ye to try to revive him. If he wakes at the wrong moment, he'll be stuck in the between. Heather, me pipes and the seventh level chanter, if ye will."

"Hang on," said Emily, "you're not seriously thinking about breaking the lore of the sight, are you?"

"Ye bet yer life on it, I am. I'll get yer Hugh back, dinnae ye worry, Em."

"But Hamish, if it goes wrong, we'll lose both of you."

"Leave it to me. I've guided many lost souls in my time, and I hivnae lost one yet. What's the point in having my talents if I cannae use them? Heather, if ye will."

He held out his hand, and Heather pulled out the bladder pipes and then a large chanter, seemingly oversized for the instrument.

"What is that?" Emily asked.

"It's the seventh level chanter, the deepest and most magical of ma chanters," said Hamish. "If I'm to save Hugh, I'll need to cross right over to the other side. It's the only way, but it's somewhere I've nae been fir many years."

"But Dad, ye know what this means?"

"Aye, I'm fully aware, but it's time. They'll be ready, all of them will be."

"What are you two talking about?"

"It's the other side to ma job, Emily. I'm naw just a guide on this side of the plane but also a guide in the sight. Sadly, I've been avoiding it since I lost Heather's mother. I dare say there's a large queue waiting to cross over."

"But does that mean my mother is waiting too?"

"Aye, so if ye dinnae mind, I've a wee jobbie to be doing."

He screwed the chanter into the pipe bag, inflated his cheeks, and the pipes came to life. Hamish inflated his cheeks to the size of two large balloons, and the sound of a seagull being mangled in a propeller filled the air. The noise was deep and sounded unlike any music he had played up until now. In a swirl of light and noise, Hamish stepped off the boat and into nothingness, disappearing with the faintest of pops.

Somewhere deep within the sight, Hugh had finished regurgitating water and was feeling pretty sorry for himself. Of all the ways he could have left the land of the living, he would not have thought it would be drowning that got him. He had always considered himself a respectful person around water, but it appeared the odds were not in his favour on this occasion. He had failed at the single most important task of his life, and he could only hope that the others would continue on in his name.

He had lost contact with his father and was now back in the meadow next to the stream. Aife was there, along with Aeolus, both with tears sparkling down their cheeks. Hugh looked at Aife.

'*So you have heard, then?*'

'*Yes, master, we have heard, but I cannot bear to part from my beloved Aeolus again.*'

'*I'm sorry I couldn't do a better job for you both. It seems I have made a mess of things here too. Is there not a way you can stay here together?*'

Aeolus threw his head.

'*No, for this is the way of the sight. We shall all be reunited again one day, of that I am sure. All living things must come to an end and pass over into the next world. We will all feel the grief of loss, but do not fear it, for it is important to help heal the broken heart.*'

Hugh was now also shedding a tear.

'*What is the point of grief? It only makes us upset and angry. I know I'm certainly upset for the life I could have lived. I've only just got back on speaking terms with Emily.*'

'*That is where you are wrong, Hugh. It is not anger that you feel, deep down, it's love. Grief is love with nowhere to go, but if we channel that love into something positive, then only good can come of it. To remain negative for too long is to do wrong to those you care about most. It is natural to feel upset, but do not let that hold you back in your next life. Let your energy be positive, and may it light up the sky for us all to see. Goodbye, Hugh Geber.*'

Aeolus rubbed noses with Aife one last time, before turning away, and disappearing into the mists of the sight.

Hugh's shoulders fell.

'*So this is it then. Are you ready for one last journey?*'

'*Not really, master.*'

Hugh rubbed Aife's neck, and they made their way towards the river. There, they faced a choice. They could either cross the bridge that was unmanned or take the ferry. The ferryman held out a bony hand, and Hugh now saw he had the addition of a scythe, which glinted in the soft light.

'*Come with me. It's less painful this way, one swipe through your lifeline and you're off to your new life.*'

Hugh looked back over his fading life-link. He was unsure if he should trust the ferryman.

'*Where would you take me?*'

'*On, of course, and my way is a lot quicker, less paperwork.*'

'*Paperwork?*'

'*Yes, if you take the bridge, there are forms to fill, explanations to give, all very tedious. Not to mention that you may get lost, and then where would you be? Lost in the in between, with no guide to help.*'

'*The in between? What's that?*'

'*Oh, just a vast place of nothingness, between here and the sight. You have to feed off the souls of the living that enter unprotected until you are found and dealt with. It's all very tedious, and you run the risk of being forgotten and fading into nothing.*'

'*Being forgotten?*'

'*Why, yes. Whilst you are remembered, there is always hope. Think of it as still living, but in a dead kind of way. You would never be able to return, mind, just live eternity with your own thoughts and possibly have the odd chat with old friends if you bump into them. If you come with me, I can remove all that uncertainty, take you to a place where nothing will matter.*'

Aife pulled at Hugh's sleeve.

'*Master, I don't like him. He fills me with uncertainty.*'

'*I know, Aife, but the alternative doesn't sound much better. What if we get lost, or worse, forgotten?*'

'*And you think you won't get forgotten this way? Aeolus always spoke of another who used to guard that bridge and guide them to the right place. He would never leave a soul behind.*'

'*But he's not there now, so they can't be that good, can they? This way seems a lot easier.*'

'*Sometimes the easiest path is not the best to take. You only get to do this once, Hugh.*'

The use of his name seemed to bring him back to his senses. He looked at the outstretched arm that only moments ago looked so tempting. His own hand was already stretching out the meet with the bony fingertip, but he stopped, less than an inch from touching. Music was filling the air, a music that was drawing him away from the ferryman.

'*No, ignore your Alicorn and that blasted music. It is my voice you should be listening to. Come to me.*'

He raised his scythe, as if preparing to let it drop.

Hugh was torn, being drawn in from one side, yet being pulled away by the ever-growing sound of music. It sounded familiar, but more tuneful than he had ever heard it. He could say it was a magical sound, as the connection between himself and the ferryman finally broke away. He turned to see an amazing sight. Hamish was walking towards him, with many people following him. He walked up to, then past, Hugh. The queue seemed never-ending, as the souls of the dead kept flowing by. They were picking up speed now as Hamish took his place by the bridge. His eyes were aglow with energy, as they whizzed by and over the footpath across the river. It seemed an age for the back of the queue to come through. Hugh looked at the ferryman, who looked livid – well, as livid as a skeletal person hiding under a hood could look.

'*Dang you, Hamish! You disappear for an eternity then waltz back in here and take all my trade as if all were normal. I shall register a complaint to the head office about this!*'

Hugh stepped up to his friend, choosing to pay little attention to the ferryman.

'*So, this is what you walked away from?*'

Hamish nodded.

'*And you work between here and up top?*'

Hamish nodded again, this time a tear falling down his face.

'*But I don't understand why you left it so long to return …*'

Hugh broke off as two women approached him. One he recognised straight away as Emily's mother, and the other looked familiar, but he could not place. It was only when she let down a mane of flowing auburn hair that he realised who this was. Hamish stopped playing the bladder pipes to address the newcomers.

'*Ladies. I see ye've met.*'

Jasmin was Emily's mother.

'*Yes, I know we said we'd have to move on, but I thought you may have let the bed go cold first.*'

She looked at him with raised eyebrows, and he shuffled uneasily on the spot.

'*Not to worry now. That's in the past. So, does this mean it's time for us to finally go over the bridge? You've done a great job avoiding the area all this time.*'

She turned to Hugh.

'*Ah, hello, Hugh. Lovely to see you again. Sorry about the circumstances.*'

'*Hi, are you telling me you didn't pass over then?*'

'*No, we chose not to reach the final destination until we had a proper guide to take us over. It took some time for you to return, Hamish. Agnes has been waiting years for your return.*'

'*Aye, well, I didnae want to face up to the fact I'd have to take yese over. It was a thought too painful for me, ye know, the final goodbye.*'

Agnes thumbed over her shoulder at Hugh.

'*Ye got here quick enough for him. Nae offence, me dear.*'

But before Hugh could answer, Hamish cleared his throat.

'*Aye, well, he's nae actually due to pass over today.*'

'*He's not?*'

'*I'm not?*'

'*Nae laddie, there's been a clerical error, nothing that cannae be sorted out, I'm sure. Let's get over to processing, and I'll explain all en route.*'

He bellowed his cheeks out once more and began playing a different tune to the one he played before, then he started heading over the bridge. Confused, but drawn to the music, the others followed him into the bleakness of the in between.

Meanwhile, back on the boat, very little time had passed. Emily and Heather were sitting beneath blankets provided by the ship's crew. Neither of them had spoken a word since Hamish stepped off into the sight, and they sat there shivering. Bubbles began breaking the surface of the bay, shortly followed by Barrington surfacing once more, carrying the limp body of Hugh. The crew aboard the *Duck III* jumped into action. They hooked Hugh from the water, dragging his lifeless form onto the deck. Emily jumped across to Hugh, throwing her blanket into the water as she did so, where it landed on Barrington.

"Emily!" he said, his voice muffled by the material, but Emily paid him no heed.

"Hugh … *Hugh …?* Why is he not breathing? *HUGH!*"

She pounded him on the chest and tried to shake him, but there was no use, he was dead. Barrington was out of the water and drying off once again.

"Emily, I'm sorry … but … I fear he's …"

He couldn't finish the words that he wanted to say, as they were caught in his throat.

"Don't you dare, Barrington Delphin. Don't you bloody well dare! Hamish said he could bring him back. Why is he not back yet?"

The pair looked to Heather, who stared back in a daze.

"I dinnae know where he is, but he said he'd be back, and I believe him. We have to believe he can do it, but he looks so …"

She looked down into Hugh's pale face, and his lips were tinged with blue.

"Damn it, Hugh, wake up! Where the bloody hell is Hamish?"

A large queue was forming at the main gate counter of the seventh level Clerical Office for Registration & Dispatches. Those in the growing line were getting annoyed at the newcomers who had pushed their way to the front, claiming it was a matter of life or death, though what that had to do with things was beyond those waiting. As far as they could see, the inevitable had happened, and most were finally glad to be moving on. Things were being delayed, once again, by the man in the kilt who'd summoned them here, and he was deep in conversation with those charged with checking people through the gate.

The woman in charge appeared stern. She a large, purple, roll-permed hairstyle and wore thick-rimmed glasses, which were as pointed as the nose they sat upon. Her hair was tied into a tight bun, which seemed to pull her face back. She and all the workers within the space behind her wore white lab coats. Behind her, teams of people were rushing around, bringing stacks of long-empty hour glasses on trolleys, ready for processing.

'Listen, Margaret, I know it's not the usual thing to bring them back the other way. All I'm asking for is a little favour, thas all.'

'A little favour? Hamish McDougall, you've a nerve coming down here asking for favours. You neglected your duties for far too long. Then you turn up with all this lot.'

The woman, Margaret, gestured to the growing line behind him.

'And you expect me to do you a favour? I think not. It's going to take eons to unravel this mess, and the weavers are not happy with you. I can tell you that. You've altered the weft, and they frown down on things like that."

She stood with her arms folded, an unfaltering gaze behind her glasses.

'Aye, but I was doing a job on behalf of the Weavers, ye know that.'

'Yes, two of them, by the looks of it.'

Margaret looked at Jasmin and Agnes with raised eyebrows, and then all three looked back at Hamish, who loosened his collar.

'I may have got a tad distracted on the job ...'

Hugh winced.

'Oh, we were only mere distractions now, were we?'

The pair now had their hands on their hips. Hamish seemed to shrink under their hardened gaze.

'I didnae mean it like that, ladies, honestly.'

'Really? Then perhaps you'd care to enlighten us on what you did mean?'

Jasmin seemed to grow in stature, and Hugh could see where Emily got her skills from.

'*Please, can we not just talk about this in a civilised manner?*'

Jasmin and Agnes broke out into laughter.

'*See, Agnes, I told you I could still make him squirm, even after all these years. Oh Hamish, you just make it too easy.*'

Hamish turned a deeper shade of red and cleared his throat.

'*So, anyway, Margaret, can we look past this situation, and come to an agreement on this little issue? Only time is pushing on, ye know, and if I dinnae get Hugh's energy back soon, his husk'll be nay good. If we get Hugh out of here, we'll nae cause you any more bother.*'

No sooner had the words finished coming out Hamish's mouth, than two trolleys collided, causing several timers to smash on to the floor. Everyone stopped dead and looked out down the line. Hugh made out numerous outlines of souls evaporating into nothingness. The entire line now turned to look at Hamish, who let out a little uncharacteristic whimper, then turned back to Margaret.

'*Great, that's more lost to the other side. You realise how much paperwork you've caused us? That ferryboat man all those New Worlders believe in, with his big scythe — he's made a big impact on your numbers, you know? And it's not something the powers like.*'

'*Margaret, ye know I would never intentionally leave ma duties, not if I didnae have good reason to.*'

Hamish winked at her, and Hugh noticed a little glint in the man's eye, and Margaret's hardened shell melted away. She let out a large sigh.

'*Fine, as it's you, Hamish, I will overlook this clerical error.*'

Hamish let out a sigh of relief.

'*However, I want regular reports on the assignment, and these two have to pass over today, plus you have to keep on top of all of your duties from now on. Have I made myself clear?*'

Hamish looked from Margaret to Jasmin and Agnes, and a tear rolled down his cheek.

'*But I'm nae ready to let em go yet.*'

'*Hamish, I need something to work with here. I can't just let him go. If we let people return willy nilly, it'll cause all manner of problems. If I can show that I traded him fair and square, then that will appease those in the top office.*'

Agnes reached out to him.

'*It's alright, Hamish. We've been ready to pass over for some time now, and we have each other fir company.*'

'*But I dinnae want to lose ye, either of yese.*'

Jasmin gave him a sweet, reassuring smile.

'*It's fine, really. Besides, we'll only be on the other side, and as long as our memory lives on, then we'll always be alive.*'

Hamish pulled out a handkerchief, blowing his nose into it loudly.

'*Aye, I know, but it's just hard to let go, ye know.*'

'*We understand, but you're needed elsewhere. Now get a move on. Our daughters need your help.*'

'*Aye, yer right as always. Right, young Hugh, it's time we got ye back to where ye need to be.*'

'*And where do you think you are going?*'

Margaret. Hamish stopped mid turn.

'*What now?*'

'*You have to sign the release forms, of course.*'

'*Ah, silly me. Well, if ye bring the form out, then we can be on our way.*'

'*Certainly. Brian, can you bring the 35B release forms please?*'

Brian nodded and pulled two large binders off the shelf and brought them over to the counter.

'Will it take long to find?'

'No, we'll just start in binder one, page one, and go from there.'

She opened up the binder and placed it in front of Hugh. The writing was minuscule, and he could hardly read it.

'Just sign at the bottom, please.'

She handed him a quill.

'Then I can go?'

'Yes, once you have all thirteen hundred forms and declarations filled out, you are free to return to your body.'

'Thirteen hundred?'

'There's a lot of work to bring back the dead, you know. Page one, at the bottom, if you will, Mr Geber.'

Chapter 40

The Fey Flyer was leaving the harbour, heading out into Syreni Bay with a very anxious Smithson on board. It was safe to say that the crew were less than sympathetic to the events of the night before.

It angered Smithson that not only had his confiding in Captain Johnson been leaked, but now the entire ship's company appeared to be up to speed with what happened, causing great hilarity. The captain insisted that he had nothing to do with the crew finding out, but Smithson wasn't so sure. He was now in his cabin, sipping a cup of tea and awaiting news of Geber and his posse. The box from Dallum sat on the desk in front of him, and he was trying to open it, when a knock at the door disturbed his train of thought.

"Enter." The door opened to reveal Collins and his assistant. "Oh, how wonderful! The dauntless duo returns with news, or perhaps some more sleeping draught. We could do with a nap."

"Someone got up out of the wrong side of the rubbish heap this morning," said Collins.

Maso's laughter was cut short when Smithson glared at him. Collins surveyed the cabin and his eyes fell upon the desk.

"Oh dear, have you still not opened that thing yet?"

"All in good time, Collins. Meanwhile you have other matters to attend to. Geber has a head start on us. For all we know, he may even have the book by now." He wheeled on Maso. "And I suggest you stop your sniggering and tell me something positive, or given the mood I'm in, I may just throw you overboard."

"Well, you can drop that attitude. The boy is mine to chastise not yours, and it'll pay you to remember that fact down the line," said Collins.

"Whatever," said Smithson, waving the comment away.

Collins stood patiently waiting for a proper response from the man.

"Oh, please don't tell me you wish for me to apologise to the boy …? Fine, have your way. I apologise for how I have spoken to you, *Maso*, and I will watch my tone in the future."

"Mmm. You speak the words, but the tone's nowhere near … well never mind, we can't have everything. I suppose you would like the news, would you?"

"Please get on with it. I have a terrible headache, and I wish to lie down before we take on Geber again. I can't wait to see the look on that swine's face when he sees us turn up."

"We have located the vessel that Geber left port in this morning. They've dropped anchor five miles due west from our position."

"Good, at least there is some good news to come out of this."

"However, there are two other vessels in the area, and we all look to be heading towards the same coordinates."

Smithson sprayed tea out across Collins.

"Charming," said Collins, wiping tea from his eye.

"What do you mean, there are two other ships heading in the same direction? We need to get there as soon as we can. I must see the captain immediately."

"Never fear. I have already spoken to the man. We are sailing into the wind, which is holding us back. The other ships are approaching from the opposite direction, so we can only hope that we get there in time."

Smithson slammed his fist into the desk, making the box jump.

"We haven't got time to live in hope! We need action, and we need it now. Therefore, I should be the one talking to the captain, not you."

"I think you'll find I have a good grasp of the situation, thank you very much. The captain has asked us not to disturb him any further, as he has to negotiate the local waters, which are riddled with hidden rocks. We are also on the outgoing tide, making it more imperative that we leave him to his job. Now why don't you get some rest, sir? You look as though you need some. I need to change because of my recent shower of tea. Come, Maso."

Smithson sat, mouthing like a goldfish as the pair left the room, closing the door firmly behind them. How was it that he was on the back foot, he who was taking orders from his servant. Unable to comprehend this new train of thought, he shook the idea away and retired to his bed. He would need all of his energy, what with the upcoming events, and to attempt to retake the high ground with Collins. As he rolled over under the covers, another thought popped into his head. Why was he now calling his apprentice *Maso*? With too much to think about, and sleep a matter of moments away, he closed his eyes and drifted off.

Up on the bridge of the *Fey Flyer,* the captain received a message from the telegraph officer, which read:

EN ROUTE TO ENGAGE WITH THE ME OLD DUCK III STOP THANK YOU FOR INTELLIGENCE STOP DELAY SMITHSON STOP WE WILL DEAL WITH ME OLD DUCK III STOP

Chapter 41

Hugh dropped the quill, now finished signing the many documents. His hand ached and was covered in ink. The quill appeared to have an endless supply of the stuff, and occasionally it oozed out a bit too much, causing Margaret to tut and wipe it away with a cloth, leaving no mark on the paper whatsoever. Margaret closed the files and passed them back to the awaiting team.

'Bring me Hugh Geber's hourglass. You'll find it in the Jabir collection, under the New World branch.'

'Jabir collection?'

'Yes, Mr Geber, the Jabir collection. All New-World names will have an old family name line. We keep them together for filing purposes. It makes them easier to link up in the afterlife. Ah, thank you.'

She took the hourglass being passed to her, and Hugh saw his own name etched into it.

'Forgive me, this may feel a little odd.'

She unscrewed the wooden top, which hissed as it opened. Hugh felt a wave of dizziness flow through him, as though his internal pressure had evaporated. He watched Margaret pick up a jar of sand, marked life, and she began pouring it into the top of Hugh's timer. He could hear the hissing between his ears, as the grains flowed into the top of the jar, and she filled it right to the top. She tamped the sand down, before filling up the remaining space.

'You look surprised? You wish me to be less generous with the sand of life when filling up your timer? Not everybody gets a second chance, so we ought to fill it good and proper, unless you don't wish me to do so?'

'No, please. I'm only taken back by your generosity, I mean no offence. Thank you.'

'You're most welcome. It's rarely we get them going the other way, so I may as well make a good job of it.'

She screwed the lid back on, and the sands flowed once more, with Hugh feeling more normal with each passing grain.

'Well? What are you sitting around here for? Haven't you got a world to save?'

Back on board the *Duck III,* Emily was still lying across Hugh's chest, sobbing – the rest of the crew, Barrington and Heather standing around in mournful respect for the death of Hugh. Ten minutes had passed, with no sign if life. They were all so caught up in the emotions of it all, that nobody realised Hugh had opened his eyes. It took a moment for the entirety of Hugh to return to himself, and only then did he realise he needed to breathe. With an almighty heave, his lungs began ridding themselves of the last of the salty water, and he took in great gasps of air.

"Arrrgh!"

The surrounding deck erupted in pandemonium. The crew thought his body was being possessed by a demon, scrabbling to get away from him as fast as possible. Emily let out a huge shriek, whilst Heather and

Barrington gasped. Hugh lay blinking, unsure of what was happening around him.

"What's going on?"

"But you're alive? You were dead. But now you're alive!" was all that Emily could say.

"Yes, am I not supposed to be? I filled out enough paperwork to be here."

"What happened?" said Barrington into his ear, as he had come down to embrace his friend. "You were dead, dear Hugh, dead I tell you! Dead!" He planted a huge kiss onto his cheek, before letting go. "This is a miracle from the sprites, it has to be."

"Errrm, nae laddie, I think ye'll find it was I who found wee Hugh here and brought him back to the living. Girls, I have a message from yer mas. They say to look after yer old man, and to keep fighting fir as long as it takes."

"Yiv seen mam?" said Heather, who had run over to embrace her father.

"Aye, and Jasmin too, Emily."

"You saw her? How was she? How did you see her?"

"It's a long tale, one that is too big to tell right now. Now if ye don't mind— what in the hell's bells! Look out!"

Everyone turned to see what he was looking at and saw the bow of a large ship coming alongside. Everyone hit the deck, with some of the crew falling backwards into the net between the twin hulls. Hugh read the name of the ship now roughly coming alongside, buffeting *Me Old Duck III* out of the way, and couldn't believe what he was seeing. The SS *Orthina II* came to a steady halt, and her crew harpooned lines onto the deck with a lot less care than when they encountered *A Ship With No Name*. A gangplank slammed onto the deck, followed by the one known as Number Two and the rest of his boarding party. The crew of *Me Old Duck III* attempted to resist, but it was no use. Outnumbered three to one, they fell limp in their captors' arms.

"Men, arrest the crew of *Me Old Duck III*, take them aboard and throw them in the brig whilst I deal with these scallywags." Number Two turned to Hugh and the others. "Alright, where is the book and trident?"

"What do you mean?"

"Don't play dumb with me, you Ranthinian scum!" He spat into the water.

"Now, now, Number Two, there's no need to play rough with our friends here."

Number Two banged his feet together and saluted the captain aboard.

"At ease, Number Two, at ease." Geoffrey Cavendish stepped off the gangplank and walked up to Barrington. "Alright, where is it, then? I take it Captain Nautilus has it?" he said looking around for the captain.

"Nautilus is dead," said Barrington.

"Oh that's a shame," said Cavendish dismissively. "Well if you hand over the book and the trident, I take it you did find the trident, then we can be on our merry way."

"Cavendish? Why, it's me, Barrington, and Hugh, Emily and Heather. This here is Hamish. We only saw you last week, man. What's the matter with you?"

"What? Oh, I haven't forgotten who you are, though I am rather surprised to see you here. I would have thought my request to have you locked up would have been taken more seriously, I must say."

"Your request to have us locked up? What are you talking about?"

"I'm talking about the plan to get you all out of the way. You should still be locked in the cell and the key thrown away."

"Out of the way?"

"Oh, do try to keep up, dear boy," he said, patting Barrington on the head. "If you keep repeating everything I say, we'll be here all day.

When we heard a ship had come from Portis-Montis, I assumed they were the ones who were after the book. After all, they sailed carrying all the correct papers and documents required for such a trip. The plan was simple. Follow them, let them find the goods on our behalf, then steal the book and trident once they returned to the surface. There was only one issue with our plan.

"We were preparing to set off to follow in their wake, then we saw your ship coming in. As soon as I saw your friend, Mr Geber, I knew exactly what you were here for, as his father wanted the same thing. We dissuaded him from looking for the book though he was a hard one to put off. The scent of a possible book of lore in Morcarthia was too alluring for him not to go. There was no way that I would let him get hold of the book I've been searching for these last few years, and now we have it, or will do when you hand them over to me. Perhaps we can get the rest of the books as well?"

"How do *you* know about the books?" asked Hugh.

"My dear boy, legends of the books go back centuries. I knew that if I were to get my hands on the lore book of water, then I would be the one to command the power of the oceans and waters around the world. Too good an opportunity to miss really, so I got a password to jump the line and faked our disappearance, giving us the perfect way to be free and find the book. When we arrived here and started to ask questions, the locals were more than forthcoming, filling us in on the legend of the trident as well. It was all too good to be true.

"I bumped into a few hiccups along the way, which includes Number Two. Picked him and his men up in El Salatore a couple of islands along. Turns out they were looking for the book too, so I employed their service in return for a share in the winnings, as it were." He winked at Barrington, who stared back open-mouthed. "I thought the other chaps managed to get here first, but it appears you have beaten us all to it. Very clever, I must say. How did you manage to get hold of it?

I heard it's nigh on impossible to get past the security down there. Oh well, that doesn't matter now. If you'd just like to hand over the goods, and we'll be on our way."

He stood smiling at Barrington, as if it were a perfectly normal request.

"You double-crossing bastard! I thought we were friends?"

"Now now, there's no need to be like that, old bean. After all, I have been most polite and amenable until now. We can still be friends," he said, holding out a hand for Barrington to shake.

Barrington did not hold out his.

"No? Your choice then." He turned and headed back to the gang plank. "Number Two, if you could just find the book and the trident, tie this lot up, and scuttle the boat. Oh, make sure to split them up, use the sight-proof rope. There's a good chap."

He continued up the gangplank whilst Number Two and his men surrounded Hugh and everyone else. Barrington fought the most, especially when he saw a crew member from the *Orthina II* step up from below deck with the book and trident. He eagerly followed the captain up the gangplank.

"You'll never get away with this, Cavendish. You mark my words!"

Cavendish paused and turned to look down at Barrington, chuckling to himself.

"Won't I? I think you'll find I already have. Farewell, Barrington Delphin." He turned and continued his journey up the gangplank, humming a pleasant tune to himself.

They attempted to struggle, but Number Two and his men were strong. They wrestled Emily and Heather below deck, and tied Hugh, Barrington, and Hamish to the deck rail. They were all too weak from their previous experience to do much else, but to sit there and accept their fate. Number Two was the last to head back to the ship.

"Never you worry, Ranthinian scum"—he spat once again—"the book is in the right hands now."

He climbed aboard the *Orthina II,* and the gangplank was raised. Then with a long blast of the ship's horn, they released the lines. The ship moved away, leaving them stranded in the middle of the bay.

"Well, isn't this just perfect," said Barrington. "Not only have I lost the book and trident entrusted to me, but we are now tied up on a sinking boat."

"But *are* we sinking?" asked Hugh.

"Well, Cavendish said to scuttle the boat, so I presume they've done something to make it sink."

"We don't appear to be dropping downwards though?"

The crew of the *Orthina II* threw two objects from the back of the ship, landing in the water as it steamed away from the *Me Old Duck III.* Barrington tutted to himself.

"We'd never throw rubbish into the ocean like that in my day. Not environmentally conscious of them."

Two dull thunks rattled through the hull, followed by air bubbles coming to the surface.

"Rubbish? They look more like underwater mines to me," said Hugh.

"Aye, just enough to puncture the ship to give us a nice slow send off," said Hamish.

"It's not all that bad," said Hugh, listening to what sounded like water gurgling in somewhere down below.

"Hugh, we're tied up on a sinking boat, out in the middle of a bay, with nobody within miles of us, other than the boat that tried to sink us. How could things possibly be worse?"

"Alright, no need to be negative. After all, you ought to look on the bright side, they could have killed us outright. I was only trying to lighten the mood a little. Besides, there's that boat over there."

"What boat?"

"The one that seems to be heading our way."

"So there is … HEY! HELP! HELP!"

"I dinnae think they can hear ye from here, laddie," said Hamish. "Though it looks as though they're slowing, so we may be in luck."

The ship was indeed heading their way, and they watched as it approached and came alongside the slowly tipping boat. Someone came out and leaned out over the side. It was Smithson, and he looked as though all his luck had come at once.

"Well, would you look who it is? Are you not supposed to be finding something of importance to save your job, Geber? I don't think you've the time to be sitting around."

"For goodness sake, man, as you can see, we are not just sitting around here," said Barrington, not hiding his frustration.

"Delphin, is that you? This is a turnup for the books, eh? And who's this? Not Hamish McDougall of all people? My, your standards have dropped, running amok with wanted criminals, tut tut indeed."

"Fir yer information, laddie, I'm not a criminal, just a believer in all things that are true in this world. Yer father would be ashamed of the man yiv become."

"*Don't* bring my father into this. He got what he deserved, and about time too. Bringing the family name to shame, hanging around with that worthless alchemist who was a coward at best."

"My father wasn't worthless nor a coward!" said Hugh.

"No? Then why did he abandon my father in his time of need? Why did he run off, leaving my father to be shot? Got to love these New World inventions."

He pulled a gun from his pocket, waving it at Hugh, who shook his head in disbelief.

"Oh, you may not believe me, Geber, but I speak the truth. He ran away like a little sissy, who daren't even look me in the eye before I shot my father."

"You did *what*? How could you do such a thing?"

"Quite easy, really. You just pull the trigger and they're gone. Trust me, I would have got your father too, had he not run off. I've had enough of this. Where's the book?"

"What book?"

"Don't play dumb with me. I'm after the same book that you are after, so tell me where it is."

"Sorry, but we're a little tied up any the moment. If you come down here and help us, then maybe we can help you."

"I don't think so, Geber. I can only deduce from your current situation that you are now not in possession of it?"

"Bravo, Smithy, you're so clever. As usual, you're about ten steps behind everyone else. The book is no longer with us, so you're out of luck again."

"If you haven't got the book, then who has?"

"They do," said Barrington, nodding over to the ship steaming off out of the bay.

"Damn and blast it!" Smithson hit the rail with his fist. "Well, there's no time to lose then." He turned to walk off.

"Errrm, aren't ye forgetting something, laddie?"

"No, I don't think so …? Oh, you want me to be the hero and rescue you? Not today. I think this will be the fitting end for the lot of you. Goodbye, Geber, Delphin and McDougall."

"You can't just leave us here!" said Hugh. "We'll die, and that'll be on your conscience for the rest of your life!"

"No, as a matter of fact, I can live with it. This frees me up to go after the books of power and removes you from the picture, once and for all. Don't worry, I'll tell all the media at home how I tried valiantly to save your lives but was too late and had to watch you sink below the waves." He pulled out his handkerchief and mimed wiping away fake tears.

"But Emily and Heather are below decks, surely you can't let *them* die?"

"Meh. Neither here nor there, really. Emily had her chance to join me, but she chose you instead. Her loss. Right, must be going, lots to do, books to get. Ah, good Captain Johnson, it appears we have a ship to catch up with."

The captain looked at the group tied up on the *Me Old Duck III*, then back to Smithson with raised eyebrows.

"That is correct. We do have a boat to catch up with, then we can deal with our other situation."

"What other situation?"

"You," said Captain Johnson. He looked back to the group tied up on the *Me Old Duck III*. "Oh, I have a message from Captain Cavendish. He wishes you all the best, and no hard feelings."

He turned and walked off, ignoring the barrage of questions being fired at him by Smithson. Minutes later, the ship was on the move, sloshing water over the decks of the sinking boat. Hugh looked around for any solution to their predicament, but he found none.

"Poor Emily and Heather, all alone down there. If we had a way of getting out of here, we could save them and jump ship," said Barrington.

"Remind me never to come sailing with you again. You seem to be earning yourself a reputation for sinking," said Hugh. "But yes, I hate to think of what the ladies are going through below decks. They must be scared out of their minds."

"Why dinnae ye ask them?" said Hamish, nodding over to a hatch, which had just hissed open. Emily and Heather were already clambering out, as the rate of the sinking increased tenfold.

"Are you not out yet?" said Emily. She pulled out a knife and made her way over to Hugh, Barrington and Hamish, who were now waist deep in the water. She sliced through the thick strands with ease, and just in time. The boat was pitching at such an angle that they found it hard to stay on the deck.

"Oh no! All of our things are in the cabin!" said Hugh.

"It's alright, we've sorted that out already, but we've no time to worry. We need to get off this boat before we all go down with it." She didn't need to tell them twice, as the boat had already made their minds up for them. It tipped upright, sending them all into the water.

"Quick, Barrington, put this on," said Heather, pulling out his jacket from her pocket and passing it to him.

He struggled to kick water, and take the heavy object from her, and disappeared under the water. When he came back up, he was transformed once again into a selkie.

"Now get us out of here, will ye?"

"Everyone grab hold," he said.

As soon as they had done so, he was off, pulling them away fast from the sinking boat. Hugh looked over his shoulder to see the last of the stern disappear under the waves, leaving them well and truly stranded.

"What now? Can you get us back to the shore?"

"No need," said Barrington, changing direction and heading towards a ship.

"Barrington, how do you know if we can trust them?"

"Because it's Shackleton."

They were out from the protection of the bay now, and the water was cold and choppy. As Hugh looked out over the swell, he saw the *A Ship With No Name* making its way to their position. It didn't take long for the two groups to meet, though the ship was moving at such a pace, it overshot. Barrington turned to chase after the ship, when Hugh saw a large net being lowered into the water.

Barrington gave one last push, pulling the group clear out of the water and into the net. He released the group, but still had forward momentum, causing him to land headfirst into the side of the ship and slide back into the water. Hamish leant back over the side of the net, as fast as lighting, and caught hold of Barrington by the scruff of the neck.

With help from the rest of the group, he hauled Barrington over into the net, before they were hoisted into the ship by the crew. They landed on the deck in a crumpled heap, under the watchful gaze of Captain Shackleton, who ran over to the group.

"Bustin' barnacles, are ye all alright?" he said, checking them all over and passing over numerous blankets.

Hugh noticed him blow over each one as he handed them out, and they glowed with a dull lustre but gave off a surprising amount of warmth.

"Thank you."

"Ach, 'tis alright lad. I'm glad we found ye. We realised ye were in trouble when we was split up, and I've some bad news for you."

"Not *more* bad news."

"Sorry, but I has to tell you this, and it's a hard one to believe. Someone's already looking for the books, a chap called Smithson, but not only that, it's Cavendish. He's a wrong'un!"

Hugh went to reply, but was too exhausted, and he slumped backwards onto the deck, staring vacantly at the sky.

Chapter 42

The Elf King sat in his cabin, digesting the news that Tavish had just shared. The entire room was shaking with the speed the ship was now travelling at. He was frustrated and disappointed that his plans had again been thwarted. They were so close to getting the book, a mere gnat's whisker from holding one of the books of lore.

"And you are sure that this Cavendish has the book and trident?"

"Yes, Father. According to the captain. I listened in to his conversation with Mr Smithson. To be fair, I'm surprised you didn't hear it down here."

The Elf King sat and stroked his goatee. There had to be a way around this.

"Honestly, talk about following a fool into battle. We're going to have to change the way we do things, starting with mopping up this mess. We must get that book."

"But the captain says we're going full pelt, and they are still getting away."

"Then I think this calls for a little intervention, don't you?"

"Intervention?"

"Yes, Tavish. Can you not think of a way that we could catch the boat in question?"

"I don't understand, Father? How can we make the ship go faster if it is already travelling at full speed?"

"Let me enlighten you. It's time to up your training and open your mind to the world of magic."

"You know such things?"

"Dear boy, there are many things that I know, and one day you shall know them too. Now come, we need to get access to the ship's engines. With a bit of tinkering from me, this ship will move like a hot knife through butter."

Chapter 43

Hugh was recovering aboard *A Ship With No Name* with everyone else. It had taken some time to revive Barrington. The ship's surgeon had used a range of his finest smelling salts, a tonic which seemed to bubble and smoke as he poured it into Barrington's mouth and finally, a shamanic chant, but none of them seemed to rouse him. It was only when Shackleton walked into the room and slapped him round the face that he woke up with a start. Barrington grabbed the man by the collar and caused his glass eye to come out and roll around the room in time with the swell. It took a few minutes to calm the scene down enough to get Barrington to release him.

"Sometimes it's the oldest ways that work the best," said Shackleton, chuckling. He put his glass eye in his mouth to clean it then popped it back into the empty socket.

"What happened?" said Barrington, still groggy from the experience.

Heather had her arms around him tightly and was refusing to let go.

"Other than ye saving our lives," she said, "well, we've been picked up by Monty, and now we're in hot pursuit of Smithson, who is in hot pursuit of Cavendish, who has the book."

Barrington groaned.

"And the trident as well – yes, please don't remind me."

"It's nae all that bad. We're in safe company now, and we'll make damned sure we get everything back as it should be."

"So, how did ye end up in the drink," asked Shackleton, drawing up a chair, "and what happened in our absence?" He gestured to the rest of the group to join him, and they all chose a place to rest.

Hugh thought he was tired enough to fall asleep, but he set to filling in Captain Shackleton with all that had happened since they were split up in Androssan. Shackleton sat looking grave he listened to all Hugh had to tell him – slowly drinking his way through a bottle of rum which he passed around the group. All were past the point of caring for manners and glad for a drink, though Hamish stuck to his whisky.

"… and that's when you came alongside us and pulled us out of the water," said Hugh, "for which we're eternally grateful, of course."

"I'm sure you'd do the same if it were me in that situation. I can't get over the way the captain of the other ship left yer like that. Ye also say Smithson killed his dad? Did I hear yer right? Man sounds like a lunatic to me."

"Yes," said Hugh, swilling a mouthful of rum, which warmed his chest as it went down. "I would say the same, but I really don't know the man anymore." He shook his head in dismay. "What on earth could have turned a man into such a beast that he would even consider doing such a thing?"

"I don't know," said Emily, putting a comforting arm around him. "But I wouldn't place too much weight on what he said."

"What do you mean? Do you think he didn't do it? He seemed pretty gleeful about it."

"Oh no, I certainly believe that he's possible of carrying out such a heinous task. I'm talking about what he said about your father. He wasn't a coward, Hugh, and you mustn't doubt it. Life through Smithson's eyes is distorted, and the truth will always shine through. It always does."

"I guess, but it was the way he talked about the whole thing. The man showed little to no remorse."

"Ach, he was the same when he was a kid though," said Hamish.

"He was broken long before this, and maybe one day we'll find out why or how … and maybe we won't. Emily's right. Don't doubt Frederick. He was a good man. We need to set all this aside for now and come up with a plan for the next step."

"The next step?"

"Aye, unless ye've all forgotten, there's a book sailing away that we need to retrieve."

Hugh let out a sigh.

"You're right," he said. "We need to figure all this out, but if they are that far ahead, we'll need more information than we currently have. I can't see us catching those boats, and we haven't the manpower to take on all those people."

"Are you saying we give in?" said Barrington. "I was entrusted with those relics, and I let them get away. I'll never forgive myself until the day I die."

"We're goin' as fast as this ship'll move," said Monty. "We're on their tail, an' that's all we can manage right now. I don't think we should be giving up the chase though."

"I'm not saying that we don't go after them," said Hugh. "We just need more information on the situation before we go getting into more trouble. We need some sort of advantage."

"And where do we find that? It's not like it's just written in a book somewhere."

"Ah, but it is, Barrington." Hugh let his words hang in the air long enough for Barrington to catch up with what he was talking about.

"The Book of Prophecy!"

With a plan in place, there was nothing more they could do but nurse their wounds and get some rest. The night was drawing in, and the smell of a fine meal was making its way through the ship from the kitchen below decks.

It was the best meal Hugh had eaten in a long time, and he was thoroughly stuffed by the end. With heavy eyes, they decided it was time to turn in for the night, hoping the boat they were chasing would have to slow, giving them a chance to redeem their losses.

It was a moonless sky. Somewhere ahead, under the cover of darkness, a submersible came alongside the starboard side of the SS *Orthina II*. A rope ladder was thrown over the side of the ship, and the boarding party wasted no time in killing most of the ship's crew. The night watch wasn't expecting an attack and was silenced with ease. The captain slept through the entire attack, such was the stealth of the killers. Geoffrey Cavendish became aware that something was amiss when a knife was drawn across his throat.

The prizes were found in the captain's arms. A book and a trident, which they duly relieved him of. They found a group of prisoners in the hold, which they set free on one of the ship's life rafts, before setting the ship on its last course for a nearby coastline and setting a fire for good measure. They disembarked back onto their submersible, sinking silently once more below the waves, leaving the SS *Orthina II* to her fate.

Meanwhile, just as the raiders were making good their escape from the starboard side, the *Fey Flyer* was pulling up alongside the port side of the *Orthina II*. As the party of sailors jumped aboard the ship, it soon became apparent that all was not well. Back in the captain's cabin of the *Fey Flyer*, a heated discussion was taking place.

"What do you mean they are all dead?" said Smithson.

"Well, given the fact the captain's throat is slit," said Captain Johnson, "and the rest of the crew have fallen to the same fate, it would suggest they are no longer on the plane of the living."

"Don't talk to me with that Old World mumbo jumbo."

"Fine. They are deceased. They are no more. The captain has set sail for the fjords of the afterlife. Ergo, they are dead. Does that make it any clearer?"

"Well, well, well. That does put you in a sticky situation, doesn't it? Tell me, Johnson, what were you going to do with us once we caught up with Cavendish? Throw us to the sharks?"

"What? No, we were going to head back to Androssan to the awaiting team there. Cavendish wanted the book for himself, but we were being paid to double-cross him *and* you. Your fate would have been the cells of Androssan before a trial. Without the book, we cannot return. I fear our lives may be in danger."

"Double-cross me? You're as pathetic as Geber and his merry band. At least that is one issue we need not worry about anymore. If it's money you are interested in, then that is something we can deal with. It appears you cannot return to Androssan, and we are in need of a lift home."

Their conversation was cut short by the sound of alarm bells ringing and red lights flashing. A member of the ship's watch burst through the door, out of breath.

"What is the matter?"

"Rocks sir, dead ahead."

"Have all the boarding party returned?"

"Yessir!"

"Then bloody well turn this ship around," Johnson barked his orders.

The crew of *A Ship With No Name* chased the *Fey Flyer* into the darkness, losing sight of her completely. When they saw the ship's hull upending in the distance, backlit by a fireball and disappearing from sight, Shackleton called the ship to action stations. Hugh and the others joined the captain on deck.

"What is it? What's wrong?" asked Barrington.

"It be the *Fey Flyer* we think," said Monty.

"Egads, that looks awful. We have to go and look for survivors."

"You think there'll be any?" asked Hugh.

"We must at least look."

They raced to the site to see if there were any survivors. Whilst making their way to the scene of devastation, they happened upon the crew of the *Me Old Duck III*. Once onboard, they were able to relay what had happened. It soon became clear that it wasn't the *Fey Flyer* which had foundered but the *Orthina II*. They also reported watching the silhouette of the ship disappearing without them, with another ship pulled up alongside.

"That has to be the *Fey Flyer,*" said Hugh. "But who was the mystery group that saved you?"

"We don't know," said Guppy. "They all had balaclavas on. They just dropped us into the sea and left. Perhaps Captain Harold sent a message before he left port. You said, Mr Barrington sir, that he foresaw his own future, perhaps he knew we'd need rescuing."

"It is a possibility. But for now we must head for the site of the wrecked ship. It is our duty to search for anyone in the wreckage. There might be someone out there who needs our help."

The thought of another hostile boat in the area made the ship's crew uneasy, but they had to check for survivors. Shackleton kept the *A Ship With No Name* to one side of the burning wreckage, hoping to hide their outline in the darker areas. It was soon clear that nobody had survived the incident. Barrington was still keen to search the waters.

"We need to keep searching, Hugh. I owe it to the lives of these poor sailors."

"Barrington, I understand your need to look for survivors, but we have been here for hours. The sun is starting to rise, and we need to move from here or risk being caught by Smithson."

"Do you think that's what they said when the *SS Portis-Montis* sank? No, I doubt that very much."

"But this isn't the same Barrington. Look, I know you still hold a lot of guilt from that night, and if things looked more promising, we might be willing to stay longer. It's not your fault these sailors died, the same as the *SS Portis-Montis*. Both were being led by deranged captains, with no care for anyone's life but their own. I'm pretty sure the crew who lost their lives on that horrid night have finally passed over, so you need not worry any more. Now please, can we get out of here?"

Downhearted, with nothing else left to do, Barrington made his way out of the water. The crew had made a makeshift wreath out of some old rope, which was thrown overboard as they turned and headed back to Portis-Montis.

The journey back was a less eventful trip. The jump across the Demon's Gap and the Liminal Line was as hair-raising as before. Any magical effects it had on the passengers of the *A Ship With No Name* during the outward leg of their journey seemed to have been reversed. This meant Captain Shackleton's eyesight had resumed its normal service, much to his annoyance. The Minch gave them clear passage back through the Sea of Lost Souls without Hugh having to come up with any more rhymes, and it gave everyone time to rest up and plan for the next step.

Hugh, Barrington and Emily would make their way through the tunnel back to the university whilst Hamish and Heather stayed aboard *A Ship With No Name* with Shackleton and carried on up the coast. They needed to return home to check up on Betsie and finish repairing the rune flyer. Hugh tossed and turned each night, getting little sleep. He knew the closer they sailed to home, the closer the time would come to confess to Balinas that the book of lore for water was lost forever. He pictured the disappointment he expected to see on the elf's face, to the point where he felt sick.

They were now on their last day aboard ship, and Hugh was feeling even more edgy about their return to Portis-Montis. He was on deck trying to get some fresh air when his ears were greeted by a familiar sound, which at the same time seemed impossible. He thought he had heard a donkey bird, but they were nowhere near land. Barrington ran onto the deck.

"What's that? Is it not bad enough that they destroyed my clock, but now they mock me with the sounds of it?"

"I don't think it's the crew mocking you Barrington. It appears to be coming from the galley."

Emily and Heather were now on deck, along with some of the ship's crew. They were all looking to Barrington for an answer, who just shrugged, as he was not to blame. Monty Shackleton stumbled through the door to the galley, to greet the awaiting crowd on deck. Steam from the galley billowed out around him, making his entrance more mysterious.

"I see ye have heard the call of the donkey bird. Yer ears be not deceiving yer. Follow me."

He turned and walked into the doorframe, causing his eye to pop out and roll back into the galley, and Hugh heard it bounce down the stairs to below deck. Shackleton swore loudly and staggered back into the darkness. Hugh followed everyone else, as they pursued the captain into the gloom.

Hugh had not ventured down into this part of the ship as yet. As his senses adjusted to the unfamiliar space around him, he was taken back by what he saw. It was hot, humid and unlike any kitchen he had seen before. There were pots and pans bubbling away, all swinging on their levelling gimbal stoves, allowing food to be cooked in even the roughest of seas. The smell of a promising lunch made Hugh's mouth water.

Aside from the usual paraphernalia for cooking, the room also seemed to be doubling up as a workshop. The smell of food mixed with that of grease and metal workings. Spatulas were lined up next to wrenches, all swinging in neat order upon the wall. Many different gadgets were at various stages of creation, and there were plenty more completed.

One in particular was a whisk-o-matic, according to its nameplate, which was busy whirring away to itself, mixing up a batter.

But the most obvious thing in the room was Barrington's clock, which had been rebuilt and repurposed within the room. Tinker, the ship's cook, was putting the final touches onto the magnificent machine, which now appeared to have gained an oven. Tinker himself was deep within the machine, and on the arrival of his new audience, extracted himself. He was dripping in sweat, with the light reflecting off his bald head, and he had a magnifying monocle strapped to one eye. In one hand he had a pair of needle point pliers. in the other, a small pick.

"It's alright Tink, we ain't meaning to disturb ye," said Shackleton.

Tinker nodded and headed back into the guts of the clock.

"That's my clock," said Barrington in amazement.

"Aye, 'tis. Tink here asked if he could make use of the parts, and seein' as they were in me way, I agreed. He's made some improvements to it."

"I can see. I take it he knows it runs half an hour out?"

"It *did* run half an hour out. He's fixed it now. It works with that cookin' thing in the middle. He said it does something to do with timing the food? Anyway, he reckons it'll save him hours in the kitchen. He discovered these little helpers, like, which give him all sorts of help around the kitchen. I tell yer, the food's never tasted so good."

Tinker extracted himself from the machine once more and grunted at Shackleton.

"No offence, Tink," said Shackleton.

Tinker grunted his reply and returned to retuning the clock.

Hugh looked around the room and saw many of the mini Collinses working away, helping Tinker with his daily list of cooking chores. Shackleton led them all back into the fresh air, which seemed a lot cooler after the sweltering conditions of Tink's kitchen.

It was the early hours of the morning when the *A Ship With No Name* followed the Portis-Montis fishing fleet into dock. Being a regular visitor to the harbour, the port authorities gave permission for the ship to berth at its usual moorings. Hugh hid with the others whilst the harbour night watch checked the boat over. Hugh listened to the jovial banter that was taking place, which made him feel at ease. Monty Shackleton took to his mission like a true professional, not giving any hints about where they had been these past few weeks. After completing the arrival documentation, the ship and her crew were left to go about their business.

"Yer be alright to come out now," said Shackleton, as he lifted the trapdoor in the deck. "It appears there's a change in the watch patterns, as there are loads of the city guard all over the harbour."

Hugh's chest fluttered with anxiety as they climbed up onto the deck. He looked out across the quayside, seeing guards posted at each of the exits. He surveyed the rest of the harbour, seeing if there was another way around the security, but he couldn't see anything.

"I don't know how we're going to get through that lot?" he said, downhearted.

"S'alright," said Shackleton, bringing out an armful of rough-spun burlap cloaks.

They appeared to have a whole ecosystem of their own, and Barrington tapped the pile with his foot. Hugh wasn't sure, but he thought he heard it grumble back in response. Barrington looked appalled.

"What are they for?" he said, wrinkling his nose.

"They is for puttin' on, of course. Then you can leave the ship as one of me crew. They'll all be heading off in a bit, as they're due a bit of shore time."

"I wouldn't get dressed in anything that's been near those filthy things, let alone the filthy things themselves. They smell horrendous."

"Suit yerself, but I can guarantee that if you try going past those guards as you are now, you'll be arrested and locked away for life. The one they call Ablator-Sedes is ruling things with a tight fist, and she ain't gonna take lightly to you lot strolling up."

The group looked at the festering pile of rags on the floor in front of them and realised they had little choice in the matter. As Hugh bent down to pick up one of the cloaks, he wretched at the overpowering smell. He shook off the small critters that was infesting it then held his breath as he pulled the item over his head, making sure to keep all orifices shut. He felt as though his skin was crawling, and it wasn't because of the rough nature of the material. A shiver went down his spine at the idea, and he quickly put it out of his mind. Trying not to breathe through his nose, he bid farewell to Hamish and Heather – they were now keeping their distance – and promised to be in touch through usual channels to let them know they were back safely.

They left the ship down the bouncy gangway and were back on solid ground once more. Hugh still felt as though he was swaying in time to phantom waves. They followed the ship's crew, with Shackleton leading the party. As they approached the gates, the crew surrounded Hugh and the others to blend them in.

"Who's this lot then?" said the guards dealing with Shackleton.

"Me crew, of course. Feel free to take a closer look at them," he said to the gatepost next to the guard. Guppy leaned in to point him in the right direction.

Hugh's entire body went rigid with fear. Why would Shackleton invite them to do such a thing? They were as good as caught. He saw Barrington and Emily were also standing like statues.

"I'll have to warn you, we ain't seen anything close to a washing facility for some time, so they may be a tad pongy, if you catch me drift."

Hugh prayed the guard wouldn't be too long cottoning on, as he was becoming overpowered by the smell. Luckily, the guard had also got a good whiff and clapped a hand over his mouth and nose.

"It's alright Captain Shackleton, sir, you be moving along now. Make sure to get this lot washed soon, though. They smell like they're in desperate need of a cleanse."

The guard waved them through, and Hugh let out a sigh of relief, which was the wrong thing to do. The smell hit him full on, causing a return of the little breakfast he had managed to eat, right onto the foot of the guard.

"Thas a surprise," said Shackleton. "Must be the city air, not as fresh as the sea breeze we're accustomed to."

"Captain Shackleton, please follow Sergeant Wiseman here."

He gestured to the man on his right. "He will take your crew to the inspection hall for assessment."

"But I assure ye, we're clean. Well, once ye get past the stench that is."

"Take them away, Wisemen."

"Follow me please," said Sergeant Wiseman. "Oh, and before you get any ideas about running off, we have guards stationed all across the dock. We know what your sort are like." He marched off, leaving them no choice but to follow.

"How do we get out of this?" said Hugh in a low voice.

"I don't know, but we'd best think of something quickly, otherwise we're done for," said Barrington.

The crew remained huddled around Hugh and the others, until they reached a building with a sign on it that read ARRIVALS HEALTH INSPECTION HALL. Hugh looked to the others, only to find them looking back with the same fearful expression. They were ordered to stand in single file, which they reluctantly did. A guard was sorting the line out, ordering members of the crew to remove head coverings. He eventually made it to Hugh, Barrington and Emily, grimacing at the smell emanating from the three of them and took a step back.

"Alright, hoods down," he said in a gruff voice. Nobody moved. "I said hoods down."

"Don't want to," said Barrington, in a deeper voice than usual.

"I don't give diddly squat what you want to do, sonny; either remove your hoods, or the guards will do it for you."

He called three guards over, and they came and stood next to him. Nobody moved. Hugh was aware that the crowds milling around them had come to a standstill, all looking at the newcomers with interest, wondering what they would do next.

"And what's this?" said the guard, now looking at Emily's staff with interest.

"Nuffin for you to be lookin' at mister," said Emily, in a voice totally unrecognisable as her own.

"I beg your pardon? I don't think you're in a position to tell me what I can and cannot do. I'll take a look at that, if you don't mind."

Everything happened in a flash. The guard went to grab the staff but let out a yelp, and stumbled backwards, landing on the floor and holding his hand. Hugh could see the guard's palm was smoking, with the smell of singed flesh now filling the air. The guard looked as though he was about to speak, but Hugh got there first.

"*Run!*" he yelled.

Chaos broke out, as the three of them made a break for it. The crew of the *A Ship With No Name* also took this as their cue to charge at the waiting guards. Hugh, Barrington and Emily managed to wriggle free from the guards, none of whom were too keen on touching their filthy burlap coverings. The crowds who had gathered to watch fell back, partly to avoid the stench, but mainly to not get caught up in the fracas.

"*This way!*" Hugh shouted, heading for the nearest alley, trying not to breathe in the overwhelming smell, which was beginning to burn his throat. He clocked the sign for the Alley of Iniquity as they ran past, but it was too late to change their minds now.

The city guard had regrouped, and were now hot on their heels, pushing through the crowd. Now running down the alley, Hugh made to run towards the tea rooms of Mme Domina-Noctis, but scantily clad women were leaning out from the balcony, urging them to keep running.

And for good reason.

More guards appeared in the doorway, half dressed and attempting to pull their trousers up around their waists. Facing this, and with the sound of the oncoming guards bringing up the rear, Hugh looked down the alley ahead of them. He grabbed Barrington and Emily and began dragging the pair with him.

"Hugh, what are you doing?"

"Going to the one place where they won't follow."

"We can't go down here. We'll never make it out alive!"

"And you want to face the other option?" he said, nodding back to the feet pounding towards them. "Come on!"

And so they ran to a place where only the most underhanded and cut-throat of the city's residents would dare to go – and even then only some would ever come out again. They ran, that is, directly into the notorious Den of Thieves.

Chapter 44

The Den of Thieves was in one of the oldest parts of Portis-Montis. A run-down, ramshackle part of town, it was a place that most townsfolk would do anything to avoid. Instead of flattening the area and rebuilding from scratch, the city planners cut a deal with the inhabitants of the area so that they could remain in the Den, as long as they didn't cause any trouble to the rest of the city and resolved any disputes amongst themselves. And so the city grew up around, and sometimes over, the squalid area.

Where roads had to pass through it at higher elevations, stone bridges were constructed to help people avoid the displeasure of walking through the area. Where these cut through, shafts of light shone through to the normally dark and dingy streets and alleys below. It would also give those on the bridge a chance to peer down into another world, though most chose not to linger for fear of bridge trolls that might come and steal their possessions.

The Den of Thieves was the kind of place where your pet cat could easily hold you to ransom for your life savings, armed with nothing but a tin opener. That is unless said cat hadn't already made it to the dinner table as the previous Sunday's roast, which is where the common local phrase *"Rob to eat and eat to rob"* came from.

The three people who were now venturing into this unexplored territory were doing so with a heightened awareness that at least one of them ran the risk of not coming out again. They appeared to be eager to get undressed as they threw their burlap coverings to the floor and began patting themselves down vigorously. None of them noticed the burlaps scurry off to a corner, into the darkness.

As Hugh walked down the dank alleyway, the smell of sulphur filled his nasal cavity. On a normal day, this would repel him, but given what they had just removed, it was a welcome change. He realised it was coming from the flickering streetlights, which gave a dim, yellowish glow to the scene. The city's coal gas network had been tapped into. However, no one from the company dared to accuse – or even question – anyone about it.

Another common phrase was "you point a finger, you might just lose it."

The trio walked past the Gambling Pig, one of the many local haunts of the Den. Though it was the middle of the night, a bar brawl was in full swing. A body crashed out of a window, landing in the mud in front of Hugh, who jumped out of the way at the last moment. A man appeared at the window. He had a blackened eye, a split lip and was missing numerous teeth. He glared at Hugh.

"Wot you lookin' at?"

Hugh let out a whimper in response.

"Leave it, Vince," said a bouncer, standing outside the door.

"Sorry, boss," said Vince, before rejoining the fight.

"You lot. You're too late for this brawl. Either come back at three or wait till next week," said the bouncer, pointing to a sign.

BAR BRAWL

GAMBLING PIG VS THE SPECULATIVE COCK

FURST BRAWL 2 AM

SECUND BRAWL 3AM

LATECOMERS NOT ADMITTED.

The group politely declined and hurried on. The ground squelched underfoot as they walked along, but nobody dared to wonder what it was they were walking on or in. Hugh sensed many pairs of eyes watching them as they braved the unknown. There was not a soul to be seen except for the odd vagrant, one of whom scared the living daylights out of Hugh. She had approached from the shadows, smiling with whatever teeth remained in her filthy mouth.

"Pound of flesh for the poor, sir?" she said in a husky, gummy voice, spraying Hugh with bits of spit.

All he could do was whimper again as she cackled loudly at him, walking off muttering to herself.

"What do we do now?" he said to the others, who looked just as out of place as he did.

"I don't know, dear Hugh," said Barrington, giving him a reassuring pat on the shoulder. "The best we can currently hope for is that we make it through the night in one piece."

Emily nodded.

"I agree, though how we get out of here is anyone's guess. Our way back is blocked by the city guard, and no doubt they will have secured the rest of the alleys and streets as well. They just have to wait until we walk out of here ... *if* we walk out of here."

She stopped walking, looking further down the alley. A light was approaching them, swaying in its holder as the owner slipped and slid their way towards them.

"Who's that?" said Hugh, as they all began taking steps back in retreat.

"I don't know, but I don't think we're going to like the answer," said Barrington.

He had instinctively moved in front of the others with his arms out to the side.

"Listen," said Hugh, "we don't know who you are or what you want with us, but we mean you no harm – Arrrgh!"

She had snuck up on him.

"Pound of flesh, just a little nibble, perhaps an earlobe or a little pinkie?"

"Get back, you old hag!" said Hugh, trying to push her away, but she appeared to be quite sturdy for one who looked so frail. She picked a beetle out of Hugh's hair, and put it into her mouth, crunching down on it.

"No need to be rude," she said, licking a stray leg off her lip. "Tastes nice."

She smiled back at him malevolently.

"Barrington, a little help here!"

But Barrington was watching the approaching figure, whose pace had now picked up, the lamp moving fervently as they moved.

"Get back, I tell you, keep your distance! I'm ex-navy trained, and I'm not afraid to use it."

"Ooo, big man," called another voice, and a man jumped out of the shadows, swapping a knife from hand to hand. "Did you train for this, eh, navy boy? Something tells me from your quiver, that you ain't expectin' this."

He lashed out at Barrington, who narrowly ducked out of the way, the blade nicking his cheek.

"Ooo, first blood of the night! Lucky me!"

Behind Barrington, Emily was fighting off another stranger, who had jumped on her from behind. He was trying to reach her staff, which had dropped to the floor, and Hugh was still fighting his own battle.

"Arrrgh, geroff!" he said, as the old woman attempted to sink her gummy mouth into his shoulder. As Emily threw her attacker to the ground, she spun and pulled Hugh away, and a few of the old woman's remaining teeth dropped to the ground.

"Ere, I was savin' them! That'll cost yer," she said, spitting blood as she spoke. "Davin, get 'em, this one stole my teeth."

"No, I didn't," Hugh said in protest.

The one who stepped out onto the alley was called Davin the Destroyer, and he was as big as he was wide. He towered over Hugh, who had to crane his neck to look up into the man's face, the yellow light glittering off his head. He wore a bloodstained apron and was wiping the remnants of his last victim off his hands with a dirty rag.

Hugh gulped.

"You … insult … Ma! You … steal … teeff?"

"He's the one," she said, her raspy voice choking on the blood. "Destroy him, Davin. Protect yer ma!"

"No, Davin, don't destroy the nice man," said Hugh, who braced for impact.

Davin lifted him off his feet, his ham-sized fist closing easily around Hugh's turkey-width neck. But then he stopped, leaving Hugh dangling mid-air, choking. Davin was looking past him at something behind him. The newcomer with the lamp had arrived, causing the whole scene to pause in some sort of obscure tableau.

"Leave, em!"

The one attacking Barrington tutted.

"Oh, but I was just gettin' started. Let me finish him."

"Nah, boss wants him and those two."

"Well, if that's the case, don't let me stand in the way of the overlord of this humble area."

The man gave up his attack and shuffled back into the shadows from which he came, taking his other friend with him.

"Davin. Drop."

Hugh, whose face was now the colour of a late summer raspberry, dropped to the alley floor, gasping for air.

"Leave us," said the newcomer.

The old lady and her son dared not disobey the order, and they, too, withdrew back to where they had come from. The newcomer turned without saying a word and walked back in the direction he had come. Hugh, Barrington and Emily followed without being told. More eyes watched as they ventured deeper into the Den, all sound seemingly deadened by the close surroundings, apart from the occasional drip of water or a faint scuffle that announced another soul departing from the world. Nobody approached the group, but everybody watched, unseen. There were shadowy movements behind sooted-out glass, backlit by flickering lamps. Somewhere in the distance, a blood-curdling scream pierced the night, making the group jump, and the man with the lamp chuckled silently to himself. Hugh dared to look up, seeing a brief glimpse of the world above as they walked under one of the many bridges. They came to a stop outside a door, and the man rapped on it.

A hatch snapped open.

"Who is it?"

"Me. Lep, yer fool. Open the door. I've got the goods."

"Oh."

The hatch snapped shut, and the sound of several locks unlocking was heard. The door creaked open, casting a golden light out across the alleyway. They all walked into the unknown. The doorman wore black trousers, a white shirt and braces. His attempt at a bow tie was lopsided at best, and his arms hung down at his sides, making him look like an oversized ape. He thumbed over his shoulder.

"They're out the back." He spoke slowly, emphasising the ends of the words, his fat bottom lip hanging down.

"Thank you, Rech."

Rech slammed the door shut behind them, re-locking everything once more, whilst Lep guided the group through into another room. It was dimly lit with cigar smoke filling the air. The only light was from a lamp which hung low over a green felt-topped table, currently playing host to a game of poker. An old man sat in the corner in a rocking chair, smoking a pipe, oblivious to everything that was happening around him. This was obviously a high-ranking room in the heart of the Den of Thieves. Hugh looked around the table at the unruly group of men. All had scars and tattoos, except for one, and he stood out from the rest with his smart uniform.

"Art?" said Barrington in confusion. "What's going on? Why are you here with these … uh *gentlemen*?"

"Ah, good, I'm glad they found you. I must say, you're very brave entering the Den of Thieves without an escort."

"Sorry? What's going on? What are you doing here?"

"It's alright, Barrington. Please, draw up a seat." He gestured to some empty chairs behind him.

Barrington looked at his friend as though he didn't know him.

"Barrington, this will all be a lot easier if you just do as I ask."

The rest of the table looked at the trio with an unfaltering gaze.

"Well?"

Hugh broke the tension by walking over to one of the chairs and dragging it slowly across the floor with a plaintive scrape. Barrington looked at him in disbelief, but Hugh just shrugged. Emily let out a sigh and followed Hugh's lead, pulling a chair up next to him. This left Barrington standing on his own. he finally capitulated under the pressure to conform.

"Gentlemen," said Art, "may I introduce Hugh Geber, Barrington Delphin and Emily Le Fey. They are all good friends of mine, and I trust you will spread the word that they aren't to be harmed in any way."

The group around the table nodded in agreement, with a few grunts here and there. Hugh noticed that although they all had cards in their hands, not an eye was on them.

"Good, then please can we adjourn this meeting for a later date? We have some things to discuss."

One by one, those around the table stood and departed, leaving Hugh and the others alone with Art and the old man in the corner.

"Art? What the hell?" said Barrington, looking at his friend and shaking his head.

"Listen, I know this doesn't look good, but I can assure you this isn't what it looks like."

"Really? Because to me it looks like you're the one in charge around here, and a man I knew wouldn't be seen dead with folk like these."

"Now hang on a minute. They may be a little rough around the edges, but they're decent people once you get to know them."

"Decent people? Art, one of them tried to have a nibble on Hugh, before getting her offspring to hold him by the neck, and another had his friend attack Emily whilst leaving his mark on me," he said, pointing at his cheek.

"Alright, well look at it from their point of view. You wandered in unannounced and uninvited. To be fair to the locals, you were lucky to get as far as you did without being killed."

"Well, that is good to know!"

"It is! Now listen to me. We have little time. This place has always run itself on the basis that we don't touch them, and they don't touch us. All that changed when Ablator-Sedes decided to shake things up. Believe it or not, the head of the city guard has aways worked hand in hand with the head of the Den of Thieves to keep law and order within the city."

"Oh really? That's funny because, from where I'm standing, it looks as though you *are* the head honcho around here."

"Don't be unrealistic. I could never hold that position, and I would never take it away from Maude."

"Maude?"

At that moment, the door opened, and Maude stepped into the room.

"Oh, thank goodness, my loves! I thought you'd be in a right pickle, especially being scared off by them guards."

"I thought Art said the guards worked with the Den of Thieves," said Hugh, looking confused.

"They do, well did, until Ablator-Sedes marched in there with her folks and took over the joint."

"You have to remember that times are changing fast," said Art. "Some of the lads have fought against it, of course, but there are some who seem to welcome it with open arms. Ablator–Sedes has made it her mission to try to rout certain inhabitants from the Den of Thieves and gain control of the whole city. She wishes to see an end of the old ways and has sent those unwilling to toe the line in here to do the dirty work. That's why she brought in all the extra manpower from those loyal to the New World. Once they realised they had missed the boat with you, they moved onto the Den of Thieves."

"So are we for or against the Den of Thieves?" said Emily.

"It's not as easy as that. There will always be an underhand element – no offence Maude …"

"None taken, luv."

"… and so no matter how hard Ablator–Sedes tries, there will always be the issue of how to live in harmony with each other."

"Does that not mean that crimes are never dealt with?"

"Oh no, they are dealt with, but anything that happens within the Den of Thieves, stays within the Den of Thieves. It is split into thirteen chapters, with each one respecting the next chapter up. They have their own court, trading system and currency. As the city guard, we take care of things in the city at large. It means that we have to be quick if we want to catch thieves around the city. If they come in here, we have no powers, and those from our side who enter the area without prior permission, rarely come out, or at least, not in one piece. It's one of the few things Maude and I disagree on."

"That's right," said Maude, "and I ain't gonna discuss it now, so don't go changing the situation. You need our help, and don't you forget it."

"I don't understand," said Emily. "Why do you need the Den of Thieves to help you?"

"*That* is a matter best left between myself and Maude for the time being," said Art. "The important thing now is that we need to get you all back to the university. Maude, are we totally surrounded?"

"Yes, but they daren't step a foot closer for fear of their lives. I overheard one of their lot sayin' that you'll either be flushed out or dismembered and sent out in pieces. Either way, it's a win for them."

Hugh shuddered at the thought.

"We can't sit here and wait for eternity," he said. "We need to get the book back from Smithson."

"Wait, so Smithson has the book?"

"Long story," said Barrington. "We can tell you that we had the book, lost it to Geoffrey Cavendish, then he lost it to Smithson."

"Sorry, is that Captain Geoffrey Cavendish, the one that went down with the *Orthina II*? I thought he was dead?"

"So did I, and I wouldn't have believed it if we hadn't seen him with our own eyes. They were seeking the book too and were lurking in the Old World."

"This web is getting more tangled by the second. No wonder nobody found the wreckage of that old ship. But we must focus now on getting you out of here. Though how we do it, I do not know."

"Can't we just use those on our side within the guards to get us out of here?" said Hugh.

"I'm afraid not," said Art. "All those who are on our side are in hiding in here with us. There's several us, I can tell you, but that's not the issue right now. Maude, did you have word from Balinas?"

"Yes, the tunnel's out of order," said Maude. "They've sent a guard of honour to the university atrium, in case *this lot* make a reappearance. He said to initiate the clockwork plan. He is all ready to meet you and lock the gate behind you. We just need the key to open the gate."

"There's no other way? Are we sure that system still works?"

"It's the last one we have left."

"What's the clockwork plan?" said Hugh.

"Balinas left you with one of the Tempus watches, correct?" said Art.

Hugh nodded and pulled the watch out of his pocket.

"We used Emily's watch in the Isle of Fey, so we know that one still works."

"Good, then with any luck your watch should also be in working order. It is the key to get you into the university. There is one in the room of time which Balinas set to line up with this particular watch. He will be waiting there for you."

"But he told me that *that* one was deactivated, to prevent anyone from entering the university."

"It is, unless Balinas unlocks it at his end, and you activate it with the key. Hidden within your watch is a set of runes that, when activated, will open the link to the watch in the room of time. He couldn't tell you in case you were caught. If someone discovered the Tempus and found out the link it held, it could bring down the university from the inside. Once that key has been used, it won't be able to be opened again, so if we get this wrong, we'll be left in a bit of a pickle."

"Meaning?"

"Meaning, if you don't all get out before he closes the gate, you could be stuck within the system forever. He also said they have not used this watch in a little while, so it may be a little ... clunky. He assures me you will know what to do, and Balinas will re-set the system after you are safely back."

"I will?"

"Yes, did he not leave you with instructions on how to use it?"

"No, he said I would figure it out, but I've been a little tied up of late."

"Well then," said Art, "there's no time like the present, is there? If you used Emily's watch, this will work the same way."

"But Hamish set that sequence going. What if it goes wrong?"

"Let's not dwell on the negative. We need to get a move on, he's been waiting for your arrival. I will return your watch to you in due course. Oh, he gave me this note."

Art reached into his pocket, and pulled out a letter sealed with wax, handing it over to Hugh, who looked from the letter to Barrington and Emily. He turned it over in his hand, seeing a message written on the other side.

Link arms and open.

"What is that supposed to mean?" he said.

"Beats me," said Barrington.

Hugh put the watch down on the table and cracked open the seal on the letter. Everything happened at once. Golden runes flowed from out of the letter, and swirled around in the air over the table, illuminating the room around them. They swarmed around Hugh, then began flowing towards the watch. It popped open, and the runes descended into the watch itself, taking Hugh with them. Barrington and Emily caught on just in time, grabbing Hugh by the ankles. He felt their weight pulling down on him as they too were sucked into the watch. He looked back in time to see the magnified image of Art and Maude looking into the watch face, then the cover closing in slow motion. The noise was horrendous, much louder than their previous experience of clockwork travel. They were jarred this way and that as they made their way through the system. Hugh felt like he was being pounded by the mechanism and could feel Barrington and Emily loosening their grip on him.

"*HOLD ON!*" he shouted in fear of losing them within the mechanism.

Light now poured in ahead of him, and he looked into the magnified smiling face of Balinas, seeing him place his eye right up to the face. Everything lit up in front of them, and Hugh began stretching out once more.

"Ow!"

They were lying in a heap on the floor of the room of time. Balinas had a hand over one eye, and was already sealing the master clock, making it impossible to for anyone else to follow. He turned to face the trio, wiping his now red and watery eye and blinking away the pain.

"Well that worked then," he said, helping Hugh up off the floor.

"Why did you put your face so close?"

"I was looking for your arrival, of course, though a little warning would have been nice. I heard you shouting, and I thought one of you might have let go."

"We nearly did," said Barrington, not looking impressed. "A little more instruction would have been helpful."

"I thought you would have figured out all the features by now, three great minds such as yours."

"Balinas, we've been imprisoned, held captive, nearly poisoned, and drowned. At what stage were we to figure out how this thing worked?"

"Please tell me you have the book?" They all looked at Balinas, mouthing like goldfish, unable to speak. "Oh dear me, this is not good news at all. I would have thought you would have given the task better attention. Come, we must consult the *Book of Prophecy* at once."

Without answering their look of frustration, Balinas swept from the room, leaving the rest of the group to catch up. The platform seemed to take an age to lower down. When they reached the Great Library, they were greeted with a scene of commotion. A small group of people had made it through the door, and Hugh feared it was the city guard. It wasn't the guard. To his shock he was standing face to face with Number Two, and a large group of his men.

"What are you doing here?" Both men shouted at once.

"I asked first!" they said again.

"Will both of you shut up!" said Balinas. "Who the devil are you, and what do you mean by pushing your way into my Library?"

"My name is Number two."

"Number two?" said Balinas.

"Yes, Number Two. I came from a very humble background, and my parents were very simple people. I am Number two, my older brother is Number One and my sister Number Three." Gestured to two of the people in his party, who leaned out and waved back.

"Oh, I see."

"We are the Bibliothecarii Populi of the Silver Dusk, and you sent our brethren out from this very room to retrieve the books of lore some two hundred years ago. We have returned with relics to place back into the room we do not speak of, so they may be reunited with their sisters, which we also do not know about."

He looked across at Balinas, giving him a wink, before looking at Hugh and the others through narrowed eyes.

"Goodness me, I thought all you chaps were dead."

"No, we are the last of our brethren, and we do not speak of our fellow cousins who failed you. What are these Ranthinian scum doing here?" He spat on the floor.

"Do you mind, you are in a place of knowledge and reverence." Number Two hung his head in shame.

"I apologise, oh great master."

"Hang on? My father told me about you. You're the brethren, the Silver Dusk Librarians of the People?" said Hugh. "Yes, that's right! Legend has it you were dispatched on a very important task. So that's what it was."

"Don't insult me, you Ranthinian scum. He stopped mid-way through spitting, after a curt look from Balinas and sucked it back in. "We are the Bibliothecarii Populi, the People's Library of the Silver Dusk not the Silver Dusk Librarians of the People. They failed in their mission. It appears we failed in one of ours." He wrinkled his nose up at Barrington.

"Am I to understand that your paths have crossed before? How exciting, I hope you assisted each other, common goal and all that?"

Number Two looked from Balinas to Hugh, Barrington and Emily. The realisation hit him.

"You mean to say … that you were … ah …"

Balinas listened on, as Hugh explained the events of the previous week. He looked appalled and upset at the actions of the People's Library of the Silver Dusk, distressed to hear how they treated Hugh and the others. When Hugh finished explaining, Balinas turned to Number Two.

"The mission I sent your predecessors on was to be one of peace, of great respect. Yet all I am sensing is that you abused the rights and privileges granted to your mission. Retrieve and protect the book so it is not lost."

"I think we were working at crossed purposes. We were always told to retrieve and protect the book at all costs." The rest of the party nodded in agreement.

"Oh dear me. It seems your forefathers altered the mission for their own liking, but never mind, at least she's safe here, and I see you have the trident as well, very good."

"So, what is our mission now, oh great one?"

"Well, it appears that we have a need for a guard at the library door. I'm sure we can find suitable accommodation for you, and we'll be able to pay handsomely for the role."

"We shall take the role with honour."

"Good. Now why don't make yourselves at home within the library, I have some business to take care of with these three."

Balinas turned to guide Hugh, Barrington and Emily to the room of prophecy, taking the well-trodden path down the steps to the hidden room. Adelia was there, busy tidying up the space. It was completely different to the space that they had left. The cobwebs and dust had gone, and the shelves sorted, the books giving off a dull lustre in the warm light.

"Someone's been busy," said Barrington, looking around the room.

"Yes, I put Adelia to work as my assistant. She's done a wonderful job at cleaning the old place up, and she's been sorting out the books for me."

"Thank you, Balinas," she said. As she walked up to Hugh, he could feel Emily's eyes drilling into the back of his head. Hugh knew what he had to say but didn't know how to go about telling her. His face, however, gave the game away, and she stopped dead in her tracks, realising that things had changed, and not in her favour.

"Oh, right, so it's to be like that, is it?" Though she was speaking to Hugh, she looked directly at Emily. Hugh found himself in the middle of a stare off, which he feared would only take one spark to flare.

The situation was broken, not by Hugh, or a fight, but by the sound of someone making their way down the stairs into the chamber.

Hugh and Barrington were about to get something to knock the newcomer out with when Balinas stopped them.

"No, wait." He looked to the stairwell in confusion. "This person seems laboured, listen."

They all did so, listening to the uneven sound of footsteps, as though the stranger was finding it hard to move. They were panting and groaning in pain, and the steps stopped as the person lost their footing. The group winced as they heard the person slam against the wall as they fell and come rolling round the corner at such speed, that everyone had to jump out of the way. It was a man. He was emaciated and smelled as though he had been on the run for a while. Emily looked at Hugh and tentatively walked up to the crumpled heap and rolled him over. She yelped out in shock, jumping into Hugh, wrapping her arms around him, sobbing into his chest. Hugh saw what had caused her so much distress, and his world went into a spin.

There, on the floor, was the lifeless body of Hugh's uncle, Alfred Geber.

Acknowledgements

Hello again, and thank you for taking the time to read this section. As we reach the end of another book, I would like to take the time to thank a few people. The first on my list is Warren Layberry, who once again has done a sterling job with the editing of this book. Next is Lynn Godson, The Digital Wordsmith, who has gone through the manuscript (some parts more than once) during the proofread. Both Warren and Lynn play a crucial part in bringing this story to life, not only through their skills as an editor and proofreader, but also through the many conversations we have had throughout the process, both about the book and about life in general.

On that note, I would also like to thank Rob, Ben and Andy. These three have kept me going with numerous cups of coffee whilst chewing the fat and keeping me sane along the way. I would also like to pay homage to the Monty Python crew, who have inspired me throughout my life and will continue to do so going forward.

Next up is my family. Once again I thank them for all their love and support over the last few years, including accepting the many weekends where I disappear off to the markets. I love you all very much.

Finally, I would like to say thank you to you, the reader. It goes without saying that without your continued investment in the books, none of this could be possible. I have met many of you over the last few months, all keen to get your hands on this book, and yes I have already started the next book, *Aura, book four in The Lore of Tellus series*. With any luck that will be out next year. If you haven't done so already, you can follow me on social media and via my mailing list. The links for them can be found in the back of this book.

Now I must go back to writing Aura, where I've left a character dangling in mid air, and his arm will be aching.

FIRESTONE
E A Purle

READER VIEWS
FIVE STAR REVIEW

Previous books in the series

Book One, Lore of Tellus

On the world of Tellus there are two ways of doing things: the Old Way and the New Way. In the city of Portis-Montis, these two ways and their worlds collide.

Hugh Geber is the alchemist at the University of Science and Progression. In a world where everyone follows the family career, he has found himself the last in line to carry the torch.

When a meeting with Chancellor Robert James Smithson leaves him with an impossible deadline and a mysterious package, Hugh is left with no choice but to try and save the family name along with his job. Fate, however, is not on his side, and his world is turned upside-down.

Now Hugh must not only fight for his place within the university, but also find out what lies behind the mysterious package before time runs out.

Review on next page

Firestone: (Lore of Tellus, Book One)
E. A. Purle Alicorn Books (2021) ISBN 91802270566
Reviewed by Tammy Ruggles for Reader Views (12/2021)

Talk about a YA steampunk lover's dream! What happens when the old way meets the new way? Tellus is a world where the old and the new clash on a daily basis, and main character, Hugh Geber, is the alchemist at the heart of the story.

At the University of Science and Progression, Hugh feels obligated to follow in his family's footsteps, but Chancellor Smithson throws a wrench into his plans by handing Hugh a challenging deadline and a strange package. Hugh now has to attempt to salvage his family name and his position, but it is a near-impossible task. His life is thrust into a whirlwind, which sets the stage for an amazing journey of suspense, conflict, drama, and steampunk.

Purle sets up this drama with intriguing, well-developed characters that you want to follow throughout the story. In fact, you get so immersed in their lives that you care about every single thing that happens to them. Add the mystery of the package, and the old-versus-new mentality, and you have a compelling story on your hands. Hugh is fighting for more than his job. He's battling for something bigger—his family name, his integrity, and tradition, but time is the enemy. How can he keep one world in the old, and one in the new? It comes down to pure survival.

This author has created a world in which you can easily become absorbed. Each scene opens up new possibilities, exploration, and descriptions which pique the senses and imagination. I love the author's use of vivid imagery and creative engineering. The unexpected events add spice to the story, and you really don't know what lies around the corner. The alchemy aspect is intriguing, of course, and the characters are easy to like—especially Hugh, as a heavy burden rests on his shoulders. I love the contrast of the old and the new, and there are parts of the book that will stay with you even after you've finished the tale.

There is a sweet quirkiness to some of the story that I enjoy, which adds a lot of personality to a book that's already overflowing with it, and so much more. "Firestone" could very well be the next "must-read" YA steampunk/fantasy series.

ORBIS

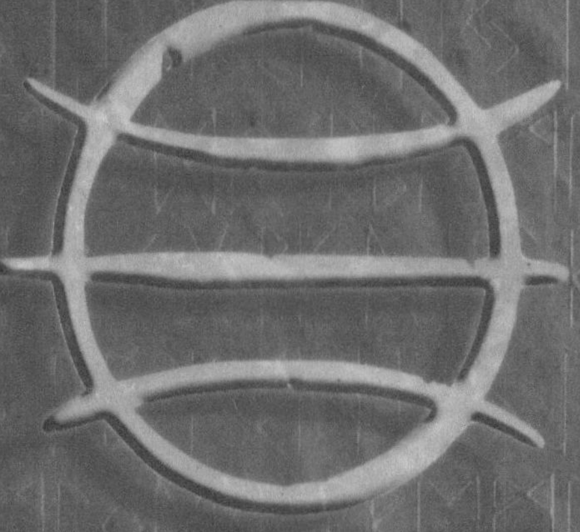

E A Purle

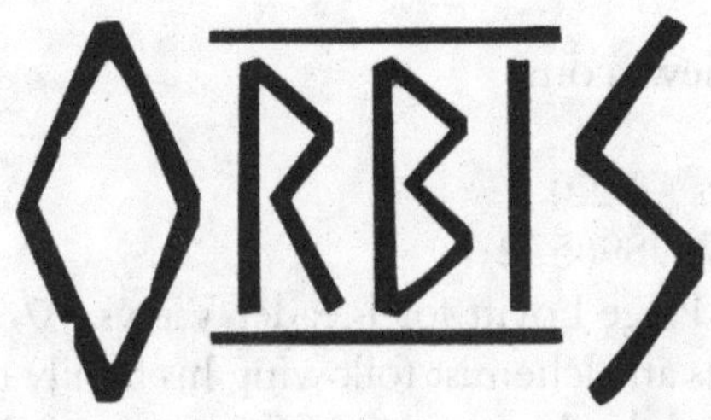

Book Two, Lore of Tellus

Hugh Geber has found himself at a dead end. Robert J Smithson is hot on their heels, and the Elf King is on the move once more. The book he and Barrington are desperate to find is missing, with a mysterious note in its place. Left with no other choice, they have to head home to Portis-Montis empty handed, knowing they are not the only ones seeking the book.

Hugh wants to bury his problems, but when he opens a letter from his presumed-deceased father, his decision to ignore his troubles comes back to bite him. A meeting with Balinas Collins in the university library adds to his woes, causing Hugh and Barrington to follow the path being laid in front of them.

Now they must continue searching for the missing book, but also try to carry out a task Balinas has set them, all whilst trying to evade the long arm of the law. Will they find the book first? Or will Smithson beat them to it? Will the Elf King regain his seat, and the power he so desperately yearns for? Only time will tell, but that time is running out. Fast!

Orbis
www.readerviews.com
E A Purle
Alicorn Books (2022)
ISBN: 978-1739896522
Reviewed by Paige Lovitt for Reader Views (07/22)

Hugh Geber is an alchemist following his family tradition of doing research in a lab at the University of Science and Progression. Until recently, this position has always been well respected and well-funded. Things have changed because there is now a clash between the Old Way and the New Way. Hugh follows the Old Way, in which magic is respected. Unfortunately, Robert Smithson, who is the Chancellor of the college, follows the New Way. Smithson declares war on the Old Way and is determined to ruin Hugh and his reputation.

"Orbis," the second book in the Lore of Tellus series, picks up after Hugh's lab is mysteriously destroyed in an explosion. Hugh sets out on a mission to discover what happened to his father and seeks out a book of lore on Alchemy so that he can earn back his reputation. Along the way, he discovers that there are four books of lore that need to be found, safely hidden away in a secret, magically protected place in the university library. Hugh is joined by his close friend Barrington and two women who share a special connection with each other. They use Steampunk technology and lots of magic to thwart their enemies, one of whom is a powerful Elf King. Romance is blossoming among these friends. Hugh also discovers that he has some powerful magical gifts, which he must learn how to control, or he will be destroyed.

I must start out by saying that I loved everything about this tale! The main characters are complex and compelling. It is fun to watch them evolve through this series. The supporting cast is also great. Most are quirky and fun. The villains are truly nefarious and upset the balance with their wicked ways. There are also lots of magical creatures involved, including a hungry kraken!

The colorful settings are vividly described with lots of Steampunk machines. While steampunk technology aids the characters, it is not perfect, especially in the wrong hands, and often has serious issues, which adds to the fun. While the author catches you up on what happened in the first book in the series, I feel it is best to read both books in order so that you will have a greater understanding of the characters and their relationships. "Orbis" immediately picks up where "Firestone," the first book in the series, ends.

Young adults and older ones, such as myself, who are fans of fantasy, will love getting their hands on books by this author, especially this one. I cannot wait to read the forthcoming book in this series! A highly recommended well done tale.

AURA

E A Purle

Coming soon

Book Four, Lore of Tellus

Hugh, Barrington, and Emily are in a race against time. With the untimely discovery of Hugh's uncle, Alfred lying lifelessly on the floor, they find themselves facing a world on the brink of tearing itself apart. Now hiding in the University of Science and Progression, the trio must embark on a daring quest to find the three parts of the book of lore for air and broker a deal with the current holders before their notorious foes, the Elf King and Smithson, catch up with them.

See below for the different ways to keep up to date
with E A Purle

You can subscribe to the
mailing list here:
http://eepurl.com/hol2A5

 @ EAPurle 

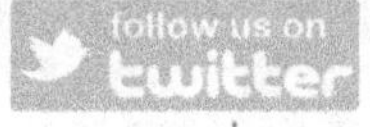 @ EAPurle 

 @ EAPurle 
EAPURLE

 @ EAPurle